REAGAN ARTHUR BOOKS

LITTLE, BROWN

LARGE PRINT

Summerland

A Novel

Elin Hilderbrand

A REAGAN ARTHUR BOOK

LITTLE, BROWN AND COMPANY

LARGE PRINT EDITION

Reagan Arthur Books / Little, Brown and Company
Hachette Book Group
237 Park Avenue, New York, NY 10017
hachettebookgroup.com

First Edition: June 2012

Reagan Arthur Books is an imprint of Little, Brown and Company, a division of Hachette Book Group, Inc. The Reagan Arthur Books name and logo are trademarks of Hachette Book Group, Inc.

The publisher is not responsible for websites (or their content) that are not owned by the publisher.

The Hachette Speakers Bureau provides a wide range of authors for speaking events. To find out more, go to hachettespeakersbureau.com or call (866) 376-6591.

Library of Congress Cataloging-in-Publication Data
Hilderbrand, Elin.
    Summerland : a novel / Elin Hilderbrand. — 1st ed.
       p. cm.
    ISBN 978-0-316-09983-7 (hc) / 978-0-316-20810-9 (large print) / 978-0-316-21891-7 (Can. ed)
    1. High school graduates — Fiction.   2. Summer — Fiction.
3. Accidents — Fiction.   4. Family secrets — Fiction.
5. Loss (Psychology) — Fiction.   I. Title.
    PS3558.I384355S865 2012
    813'.54 — dc23   2012004929

10   9   8   7   6   5   4   3   2   1

RRD-C

Printed in the United States of America

For my darling friend Manda Popovich Riggs.
No one stronger, no one smarter,
no one cooler, no one kinder.

PART ONE

June/July

NANTUCKET

Nantucket: the name of the island brought to mind rolling surf, cobblestone streets, the brick mansions of whaling captains, a battered Jeep Wrangler with a surfboard strapped to the roll bars. It brought to mind cocktail parties on undulating green lawns, investment bankers wearing faded red slacks and dock shoes without socks, a towheaded little girl holding a grape popsicle that dripped down the front of her seersucker dress. Nantucket: it was the land of wealth and privilege, a summer playground for those with a certain prep-school, old-money, I-used-to-row-with-him-on-the-Charles type of pedigree.

So few outsiders (and by "outsiders," we meant everyone from the casual day-tripper from West Bridgewater to Monica "Muffy" Duncombe-Cabot, who had been summering on the island since she was in utero in 1948) understood that Nantucket was a real place, populated by real people. Like any-where else, it was home to doctors and taxi drivers and a police chief and plumbers and dishwashers and insurance agents. It was home to mechanics and physical therapists and schoolteachers and bartend-ers. They were the real Nantucket: the ministers and the garbage collectors and the housewives and the members of the crew that filled in the potholes on Surfside Road.

Nantucket High School had a senior class of seventy-seven students graduating on June 16. This turned out to be one of the first balmy days of the year—warm enough to sit on the football field and wish that you, like Garrick Murray's grandmother, had worn a wide-brimmed straw hat.

Up on the podium stood Penelope Alistair. Although she was only a junior, Penny had been asked to sing the National Anthem. Hers was the voice of Nantucket, her tone so pure and ethereal that she didn't need any accompaniment. We mouthed the words along with her, but no one dared to sing out loud because no one wanted to hear any other voice than Penny's.

When Penny finished singing, there was a beat of thrumming silence, and then we all cheered. The seniors, sitting in neat rows on a makeshift stage behind the podium, whooped until the tassels on their caps shimmied.

Penny sat down in the audience between her twin brother, Hobson Alistair, and her mother, Zoe. Two chairs away sat Penny's boyfriend, Jake Randolph, who had attended the ceremony with his father, Jordan Randolph, publisher of the *Nantucket Standard*.

Patrick Loom, valedictorian of the senior class, took the podium, and some of us felt tears prick our eyes. Who among us didn't remember Patrick Loom in his Boy Scout uniform, collecting money in a mayonnaise jar for the victims of Hurricane Katrina? These were our kids, Nantucket's kids. This graduation, like other graduations, was part of our collective experience, our collective success.

Twenty-three of the seventy-seven graduating seniors had written a college essay entitled "What It's Like Growing Up on an Island Thirty Miles Out to Sea." These were kids who had been born at the Cottage Hospital; they had sand running through their veins. They were on intimate terms with Nor'easters and fog. They knew that north was marked by the Congregationalists, and south by the Unitarians. They lived in gray-shingled houses with white trim. They could distinguish bay scallops (small) from sea scallops (big). They had learned to drive on roads with no traffic lights, no off-ramps or on-ramps, no exits. They were safe from ax murderers and abductors and rapists and car thieves, as well as the more insidious evils of fast food and Walmart and adult bookstores and pawnshops and shooting ranges.

Some of us worried about sending these kids out into the wider world. Most of the seniors would go to college—Boston University or Holy Cross or, in Patrick Loom's case, Georgetown—but some would take a year off and ski in Stowe, and still others would remain on Nantucket and get jobs, living lives not so different from those of their parents. We worried that the celebration surrounding graduation weekend would lead our seniors to drink too much, have unprotected sex, experiment with drugs, or fight with their parents because they were eighteen, goddammit, and they could do what they wanted. We worried they would wake up on Monday morning believing that the best years of their lives were behind them. The electric buzz they had felt the last four autumns during the first Friday-night football game under the lights, when they ran out onto the field or led the crowd in cheering— those moments were gone forever. Next September the Nantucket Whalers would play again, the weather would be brisk again, the air would smell like grilled hot dogs again, but there would be a new guard, and the seniors who were, as we watched now, walking across the stage for their diplomas, would be old news.

Alumni.

High school was over.

There was a bittersweet element to June 16, graduation day, and as we walked off the field at the end of the ceremony, some of us said we would never forget this one in particular, either because the weather had been so spectacular or because Patrick Loom's speech had been so poignant.

It was true that we would always remember graduation that year, but not for these reasons. We would remember graduation that year because it was that night, the night of June 16, that Penelope Alistair was killed.

What? the world cried out in disbelief. The world wanted the Nantucket that resided in its imagination: the one with the icy gin and tonic resting on the porch railing, the sails billowing in the wind, the ripe tomatoes nestled in the back of the farm truck. The world did not want to picture a seventeen-year-old girl dead, but the world needed to know what we knew: Nantucket was a real place.

Where tragic things sometimes happened.

JAKE

Everything looked different from the air. There, below him, was Nantucket Island, the only home he'd ever known. There were Long Pond and the Miacomet Golf Course and the patchwork acres of Bartlett's Farm. There was the bowed white stretch of the South Shore. Already cars were lining up on the beach. Jake had spent every summer Sunday of his entire life on that very beach with his parents and the Alistairs and the Castles. They had body-surfed and played touch football; they had hidden in the dunes. They had constructed forts out of boogie boards and beach towels in the back of Mr. Castle's pickup truck. Jake recalled the smell of charcoal, the marinated steak, the ears of corn dripping with herbed butter. There was always a bonfire with marshmallows, and fireworks that Mr. Castle bought when he was away on business.

Jake felt his father's hand on his shoulder, a cupping, a squeeze. This happened four or five times an hour now, his father's touching him for no reason other than to reassure himself that his son was still there.

Jake picked out Hummock Pond Road, like a fortune teller reading a palm. It was a life line without life, a love line without love. The road ran due south from town. Seen from the air, it was just a path cut through the pine forest. The cars traveling it looked like toys.

Jake pressed his forehead against the vibrating window. The plane floated over Madaket and Eel Point. Nantucket was receding. No! Jake thought. He felt tears sting his eyes. He was losing Nantucket. Tuckernuck was below them now, then Muskegut, its shores crowded with seals. Then the Yankee-blue water of Nantucket Sound. If only he could jump out, land safely, swim back. So many terrible things had happened in the past four weeks, and one of those things was what his parents had deemed to be the solution: they were running away from home.

JORDAN

The phone had rung in the middle of the night. Nobody, and especially not the parent of a teenager with his own car, wanted to be woken up by that sound. But Jordan was the publisher of the island's newspaper, the *Nantucket Standard,* and so the phone rang in the middle of the night in the Randolph household more often than it did in other households. People called with news, or what they thought was news.

Zoe had been known to call in the middle of the night as well, but that was always Jordan's cell phone, and he'd taken to shutting it off when he went to bed to avoid unnecessary drama. Anything Zoe wanted to say to him at two in the morning would sound better at eight o'clock, once he was safely in the car and driving to the paper.

It was a Saturday night, or technically Sunday morning. It was eighteen minutes past one. Jordan had a pretty good handle on what was happening around the island at any hour of any day. At one o'clock in the morning on a Sunday in mid-June, the crowd would be spilling from the Chicken Box onto Dave Street. There would be a string of taxicabs waiting there, and a police cruiser. Downtown, there would be clusters of people on the sidewalk outside the Boarding House and the Pearl; there would be the inevitable woman who attempted to cross the cobblestone street in four-inch stilettos. An older, more sedate clientele would roll out of the Club Car once the piano player finished "Sweet Caroline."

Jordan had been at the Club Car with Zoe a few years earlier, on the night they experienced what they now referred to as "the moment." The moment when they both knew. They knew then, but they did not act. They didn't act until more than a year later, on Martha's Vineyard.

The phone, the phone. Jordan was awake. His mind was instantly alert, but it took him a few seconds to get his body to move.

He swung his legs to the floor. Ava was sleeping in Ernie's nursery with her earplugs in and the white-noise machine going, and the door locked and the shades pulled. And the magic elixir of her nightly Ambien silencing her demons. She would be completely dependent on him to rescue her in the event of a fire.

Fire? he thought.

And then he remembered: graduation.

He raced to the phone. The caller ID read *Town of Nantucket*. Which meant the police, or the hospital, or the school.

"Hello?" Jordan said. He tried to sound alive, awake, in control.

"Dad?"

That was the only word Jake was able to say. What followed was blubbering, but Jordan was buffered by the knowledge that Jake was alive, he could talk, he had remembered the phone number for the house.

A policeman came on the line. Jordan knew

many of the officers but not all of them, and especially not the summer hires.

"Mr. Randolph?" the officer, his voice unfamiliar, said. "Sir?"

ZOE

She had flaws, yes she did. What would be the worst? There was the obvious thing, but she would set that aside for a moment. She would travel back to before her love affair with Jordan Randolph. What had been her faults before? She was selfish, self-absorbed, self-centered—but really, wasn't everyone? She occasionally—but only occasionally—had put her own happiness before the happiness of the twins. There was the time she had left Hobby and Penny with the Castles and flown to Cabo San Lucas for a week. She had convinced herself, and Al and Lynne Castle, that she was suffering from Seasonal Affective Disorder. She had *lied* to Lynne and claimed that an off-island doctor, the mythical "Dr. Jones," had actually "diagnosed" her with SAD and "prescribed" the trip to Cabo. The lie had been unnecessary; Lynne said she understood, and Zoe deserved a week away, and it would be no trouble at all for her to take care of the twins. Lynne didn't know how Zoe did it, raising the two of them on her own.

The trip to Cabo had been a onetime thing. (It shimmered in Zoe's memory: the chaise longue by the edge of the infinity pool, the scallop ceviche and mango daiquiris, and the twenty-seven-year-old desk clerk whom she had easily seduced and slept with five out of the seven nights.) Had she felt any guilt about leaving her children that week? If she had, she couldn't remember it. And yet in that moment when they both rushed into her arms, shrieking with happiness at her return, she swore she would never leave them again. And she had kept her word.

There *had,* however, been nights when Zoe opened a bottle of good white Burgundy and watched six episodes of *The Sopranos* in one sitting while the children ate cereal for dinner and put themselves to bed. There had been other times when Zoe lost her temper with the twins for no reason other than that they were two complex creatures and she occasionally found herself at a loss as to how to deal with them. Zoe had squandered most of the inheritance from her parents on a beachfront cottage, an impractical choice for raising a family. She never exercised, and she was addicted to caffeine. She had uttered the sentence "My husband is dead" to gain sympathy from certain individuals. (The police officer who pulled her over for going ninety miles an hour on Route 3 was one example.)

She had so many flaws.

Zoe liked to think these were, for the most part, hidden, though she understood that among islanders she was considered to be not only a free spirit but a loose cannon. She felt that her parenting was constantly being judged because she was too lax, too lenient. She had been leaving the twins at home by themselves since they were eight years old. When they turned nine, she allowed them to ride their bikes into town. There had been an isolated incident when Hobby rode all the way to Main Street without a helmet. The police chief, Ed Kapenash, had called Zoe at work and told her that by law, he should give her a ticket for allowing her son to ride a bike without a helmet. Zoe replied that she didn't *allow* the kids to ride without helmets; since she was at work, she hadn't been home to see Hobby leave the house without one on. As soon as those words were out of her mouth, she knew how bad they sounded. She thought, Ed Kapenash is going to call Child Protective Services and have the kids taken from me. I am not competent to raise them by myself, after all. Ed Kapenash had sighed and said, "Please tell your children they are never again to ride their bikes without wearing helmets."

Zoe had left work right that instant. She was all set to punish Hobby, even spank him if necessary, until he told her that his old helmet was too small. Upon investigation, Zoe discovered he was right; there wasn't a helmet in the house that fit him. He was growing so quickly.

Zoe was sure that the story of Hobby's not wearing a helmet would spread, and that the citizens of Nantucket would have their suspicions confirmed: she was negligent. Not a helmet in the house that fit the boy! As if that weren't bad enough, Zoe drove an orange 1969 Karmann Ghia, which she'd bought while she was in culinary school. Although people always honked or waved when Zoe passed, she was sure they were all secretly wondering why she drove two kids around in a car without airbags.

She didn't buy organic milk.

She was flexible with bedtime and lax about movie ratings.

She allowed the twins to pick their own outfits, which had once resulted in Hobby's wearing his Little League All-Star jersey five days in a row. It also once led to Penny's wearing her nightgown to school over a pair of leggings.

But really, how could anyone criticize Zoe's parenting? She had fabulous, talented kids! The marquis students of the junior class: Hobson and Penelope Alistair.

Let's start with Hobson, known all his life as Hobby, born five minutes before Penny. He was the reincarnation of his father, also named Hobson Alistair. Hobson senior had been the incredibly tall and commanding man of Zoe's dreams, a man as big as a tree. Zoe had met him when she was a twenty-one-year-old student at the Culinary Institute of America, in Poughkeepsie. Hobson senior was only six years older than Zoe, but he was already an instructor at the CIA. He taught a class called Meats and was a master butcher; he could take apart a cow or a pig with a cleaver and a boning knife and make it look as elegant as a ballet.

Hobby was big like his father, and graceful and meticulous like his father. Hobby was shaping up to be the best athlete Nantucket Island had seen in forty years. He became the quarterback of the varsity football team as a sophomore; the Whalers had gone 11 and 2 last season and had, most important, beaten Martha's Vineyard. Hobby also played basketball for the varsity team; he'd been the top scorer since his freshman year. And he played baseball — ace pitcher, home-run king. Watching him, Zoe almost felt embarrassed, as though his prowess were something shameful. He was *so much better* than anyone else on his own or any opposing team that he commanded everyone's attention. Zoe always felt like apologizing to the other parents, though

Hobby was a good sport. He passed the ball, he cheered for his teammates, and he never claimed more than his share of the glory.

Zoe would overhear the other mothers say things like, "I guess the father was a giant."

"Are they divorced?"

"No, he died, I think."

Hobby wanted to be an architect when he grew up. This pleased Zoe. Hobby could be an architect and still live on Nantucket. She was afraid, most of all, of her kids' leaving the island and never coming back.

"But you can't force them to stay," Jordan would tell her. "You know that, right?"

Zoe was certain she would lose Penny. Penny was a gorgeous creature with long, straight black hair and blue eyes and a perfect little nose sprinkled with pale freckles. She had tripped around the house in Zoe's high heels at age three, had gotten into Zoe's makeup at age four, and had asked to have her ears pierced at age five. And then, one day when Penny was eight years old, Zoe went to pick up the twins after school, and Mrs. Yurick, the music teacher, was standing out in front with her hand on Penny's back, waiting for Zoe.

Zoe thought, What? Trouble? Neither of her kids ever misbehaved, so the trouble had to be with Zoe herself. But she wasn't even late for pickup that day (though she had been late in the past, but never by more than ten minutes—not bad for a working mother). Zoe knew she wasn't going to win any parenting awards, but she packed healthy lunches for the kids, and when it was cold, she always made sure they each had a hat and gloves. Okay, true, sometimes only one glove.

"Is everything okay?" Zoe asked Mrs. Yurick.

"Your daughter...," Mrs. Yurick said, and here she put her hand to her bosom, as if she were too overcome with emotion to continue.

What Mrs. Yurick was trying to say was that she had discovered Penelope's singing voice. A voice as sweet and pure and strong and clear as any Mrs. Yurick had heard.

"You have to do something about this," Mrs. Yurick said.

Do something? Zoe thought. Like what? But she knew what Mrs. Yurick meant. She, Zoe, the mother of the child with the exceptional singing voice, had to take steps to develop it, to squeeze out every ounce of its potential. Already, Zoe had clocked countless hours at the ball field and the Boys & Girls Club watching Hobby play baseball, football, and basketball. Now she would have to do the same for Penelope's singing.

And to her credit, Zoe had done it. It hadn't been easy, or cheap. There had been a voice coach off-island once a week and entire weekends spent with a renowned singing instructor in Boston. Both the voice coach and the singing instructor were wowed by Penny's talent. She had such range, such maturity. At twelve, she sounded like a woman of twenty-five. She sang "The Star-Spangled Banner" with the Boston Pops the summer following ninth grade. She got the lead in every school musical; she had solos in every madrigal concert.

She was a nightingale.

Zoe wasn't sure where it came from; she herself could barely carry a tune. Hobson senior had liked music (the Clash, the Sex Pistols), but in their short time together, Zoe couldn't remember his singing anything but "Should I Stay or Should I Go?" once, at a chefs' after-hours party.

If Zoe was to be very honest with herself, she would have to admit she wasn't sure that Penelope's voice was an unadulterated blessing. At times, Penny seemed almost burdened by it. Her voice had to be cared for like some exotic pet—a macaw, maybe, or a rare breed of chinchilla. Penny wouldn't eat spicy food or drink coffee; she wrapped her throat in a warm, damp cloth at night as she lay in bed and listened to Judy Collins sing "Send In the Clowns" over and over again. She couldn't stand smoke of any kind; every winter she begged Zoe to get rid of the woodstove.

It was during the year that Penny turned thirteen, which was also the year that she started her period, which was also the year that Ava and Jordan's baby died, that Zoe heard her sobbing in her bedroom one night. Zoe knocked, and when Penny didn't answer, she walked right in. She found Penny sitting on the floor of her closet, hugging herself and rocking in a way that made Zoe think that this sobbing was a ritual that she had missed many times before. Zoe had to pull Penny from the closet and drag her to the bed before demanding a reason for her tears.

"What is it?" Zoe asked. "What's wrong?"

Penny said that she felt like there was less love in the world for her than for other people. Because she had no father.

Whoa: that answer had leveled her. Hobson senior had died of a heart attack when Zoe was seven months pregnant with the twins. Zoe had given birth to them alone; she had raised them out of infancy alone. She had hunted for a job as a private chef, and an opportunity on Nantucket had fallen into her lap. She had moved to the island, she had bought the cottage, she had put the kids in day care, and she had worked for the Allencast family on upper Main Street. The Allencasts paid her a generous salary that included health insurance and an IRA, they gave her flexible hours, and they introduced her to people who provided her with side jobs. Zoe suddenly had a role on the island: she was an elite personal chef, as well as the mother of two exceptional kids. There were certainly times when Zoe felt like she was doing nothing right, but there were also times when she felt like she was doing *something* right.

But watching Penny sob and hiccup and fight for breath that night because she had no father made Zoe feel certain she had done nothing right. Nothing in thirteen years.

She said, "I love you twice as much as any other mother loves her child." She had grabbed Penny around the shoulders and kissed her fiercely in the part of her hair. "Goddammit, you know that, Penny." She had feared the kids would grow up with an empty space in them. She had worried it would be Hobby who would suffer, but Hobby had always had men in his life — coach after coach, and the admiring fathers of his friends. Jordan was like a father to him, as was Al Castle. But it wasn't Hobby Zoe had to worry about; it was Penny.

Zoe tightened her grip on her daughter and noticed how Penny seemed to slip through her grasp, like a handful of butter. Zoe had done all she could, but she couldn't be two people at once.

Zoe took Penny to see a psychologist. It was one more thing for Zoe to fit into her already bursting schedule, one more thing for her to pay for, but it had to be done. The psychologist, a kind, plain woman named Marcy, met with Penny alone half a dozen times before finally talking with Zoe.

"She's a terrific kid," Marcy said.

"Thank you," Zoe said. She smiled, waiting for more. Marcy smiled back, bobbing her head.

"That's it?" Zoe asked.

"Well...," Marcy said. She held her palms out, as if trying to show Zoe something — a baby chick or a milkweed pod — that Zoe couldn't see. "Penelope has a heart made from the finest bone china. Just be aware."

A heart made from the finest bone china? Zoe thought. That had been one of the rare times when she had craved a partner, a spouse, a husband, someone to turn to and ask, "Can you believe this crap?"

That was the end of Marcy the psychologist. "Just be aware": ha! Zoe was aware of that and a lot more. She would take care of her daughter herself.

Zoe had heard warnings from other mothers since Penny was a little girl: "She's cute now, but just you wait!" Something sinister lurked on the horizon; it would roll in like bad weather. Adolescence. But Zoe and Penny had remained close. They were *best friends*. As a parenting strategy, this was neither popular nor fashionable, but Zoe didn't care. She loved her intimacy with her daughter.

There were nights when Penny climbed into Zoe's bed and the two of them slept next to each other, sharing a pillow like orphaned sisters. Zoe continually told both the twins, "You can tell me anything." There would be no judgment, nothing to fear. She loved them unconditionally. *"You can tell me anything."*

And right up until the day she died, Penny had told Zoe everything, or what Zoe had assumed was everything.

JAKE

They flew to Boston, then boarded a shuttle bus that would take them to the international terminal. Jake's father kept doing the shoulder thing. He didn't touch Jake's mother at all, not even accidentally, but that wasn't unusual. Jake's mind was spinning and flashing like a police light. *Escape! Get back home!* He was ten months away from his eighteenth birthday.

The dirt on Penny's grave was as moist and black as chocolate cake. Grass would grow over it, but Jake couldn't decide if that would make things better or worse.

Terminal E. Boston to LAX, LAX to Sydney. After that interminable trip, another six-hour flight to Perth. They were traveling to the other side of the world.

Their gate was filled with jolly Australians. Was there such a thing as a national temperament? Jake wondered. Or were there Australians out there somewhere who *weren't* open and friendly and affable? Jake's mother perked up as soon as she heard the accent. It was as if she had been transported into an episode of *Home and Away,* the Australian soap opera that she watched incessantly on the bootlegged DVDs sent to her by her sister May. She swung her hair around gracefully and said, "I'm going for a coffee. You want?"

"No, thank you," Jake's father whispered.

Jake shook his head.

His mother gave him a genuine smile, an event that was so rare it actually spooked him. She was the unhappiest person Jake knew, though she hadn't always been that way. Before Jake's infant brother, Ernie, had died, Ava had been normal and momlike, maybe a little annoying, maybe a little uptight and preoccupied with giving Jake a sibling. But there were pictures of Ava in the red photo album where she was making silly faces and kissing baby Jake and Jake's father. There were pictures of her before Jake was born where she was deeply tanned and wearing a bikini, her golden-brown hair braided down her back. There were pictures of her surfing and kayaking and one of her leaping in midair, getting ready to pummel a volleyball. Jake used to stare at these pictures. That was the woman he wanted to claim as his mother. But since Ernie had died in his crib at eight weeks old, Ava had become jagged and shrill half the time, and mute and despondent the other half. Anger and bitterness—which were really sadness and deep, deep grief, his father said—lived inside her like a monster. Jake's father pleaded with Jake to try and forgive her for the way she sometimes acted. But it was too much to ask, Jake thought. Jake had grown calluses over his nerve endings where his mother was concerned.

Ernie had a tombstone in the cemetery, just as Penny now did. Jake's mother tended the plot at Ernie's grave; she bought bouquets of supermarket flowers every week. When Ava was home, she sequestered herself in the room where Ernie had— for no good or explicable reason—stopped breathing. Ava either watched episodes of *Home and Away* or reread passages of her favorite book, which was, shockingly, not an Australian classic but rather that most American of novels, *Moby-Dick,* because her father had read it to her when she was a child. Ernie's grave, the soap opera, *Moby-Dick:* these comprised 90 percent of the life of Ava Randolph. It was the other 10 percent, her interactions with the outside world, that glinted like shards of broken glass on the side of the road. There was her anger, which could take anyone's eye out like an errant arrow. And there was her venom, which she seemed to save solely for Jake's father.

Ava was present for the important stuff at school, such as Jake's induction into the National Honor Society and the final night of the musical. This past year, the musical had been *Grease,* with Jake playing Danny and Penny playing Sandy. His mother had taken a shower and brushed out her hair. She had put on makeup and perfume. She had entered the auditorium with her head held high and her eyes defiant, his father trailing three steps behind her like a loyal servant. Jake had peered at them from behind the heavy stage curtain. He could hear the audience murmuring: Ava Randolph was out. Sightings of her were as rare as comets, and everyone knew why, so everyone kept a respectful distance—except Lynne Castle, his mother's only stalwart friend. Lynne plopped herself down next to Ava and kissed the side of her face as though nothing were amiss, as though Ava weren't capable of lashing out even at her, or of standing up and walking out of the auditorium for no reason at all.

Ava had seemed to enjoy the musical. She had

clapped at the end, and when Jake and Penny took their final bows, she had joined in the standing ovation.

The only person who sought out Ava Randolph's company was Penny. Some afternoons, after Jake had stayed late at school working on *Veritas*, the student newspaper, or at a Student Council meeting, he would come home to find Penny in his mother's room, lying across the foot of her bed, the two of them watching *Home and Away*, Ava dutifully explaining the intricacies of the plot lines. Jake would be lying if he said this hadn't worried him.

He'd said to Penny, "You don't have to hang out with my mother, you know."

And Penny had said, "Oh, I know. But I like her."

Like her? Jake loved his mother—she was his *mother*, after all—but even he didn't *like* her. He was afraid of her. On her best days, she was like a ghost that lived in the house with his father and him, occasionally haunting the dinner table and eating a few bites of whatever they were having. (They ate a lot of pizza and Thai takeout.) Ava floated around the house—mostly in the predawn hours—dealing with the cut flowers for Ernie's grave. She slept alone in Ernie's nursery.

Jake didn't think his parents ever had sex. They didn't touch; they barely even spoke, though there were nights when Jake would be awakened by the sound of the two of them screaming at each other.

HIS MOTHER: I want out of here, Jordan!

HIS FATHER: You're free to go, Ava, you know that.

HIS MOTHER: I want to go for good, and I'm not going without Jake. Or you.

HIS FATHER: My family has owned and run the paper since 1870, Ava. Six generations of Randolphs. It's my birthright, and guess what else? I love it. You knew this when you married me. You knew my life had to be here.

HIS MOTHER: My life doesn't matter. My life has never mattered.

HIS FATHER: If you want to go, go. For God's sake, just go. Go by yourself, stay as long as you want! You used to have no problem doing that.

HIS MOTHER: But everything is different now. Isn't it?

HIS FATHER: [No response.]

HIS MOTHER: Isn't it?

HIS FATHER: Yes.

HIS MOTHER: Ernie is dead! Say it! I want to
hear you say it, Jordan!

HIS FATHER: Ernie is dead.

Now, in Terminal E, Ava reappeared with her steaming latte and her sesame bagel. Jake checked with his father to see if Jordan found this behavior as remarkable as he did, but Jordan was staring into the middle distance, thinking about something, and Jake knew not to interrupt him. Used to be that he'd be thinking up headlines or lead-ins, or maybe trying to figure out how to justify raising ad rates or how to fire the sports writer, or where to find a new sports writer from among such a limited pool of candidates. Or he'd be pondering the death of newspapers in general. But what would he be thinking about now? He was thinking backward and not forward. Jake could tell by the glazed look in his eyes.

Ava blew across her latte and picked a tiny piece off her bagel and popped it into her mouth. Jordan had told Jake that Ava didn't eat much because after Ernie died, it was one of the many things she had stopped taking pleasure in.

Now, however, she seemed to be savoring her snack. Sip of latte, bite of bagel. She even opened a tiny container of cream cheese and dragged the bagel through it.

Jake was as angry as he'd ever been in his life. His heart was a trash fire. We are leaving Nantucket because of you! he thought. He wanted to splash Ava's latte in her face. He wanted to choke her with her bagel. But the moment passed, followed by an immense ocean of self-pity.

They were leaving Nantucket because of *him*.

DEMETER

They took her to the hospital even though there was nothing wrong with her. Nothing wrong with her except that she couldn't stop shivering. Penny was dead. The car had gone up over the embankment at Cisco Beach, where the drop was…eight feet? ten feet? The car had seemed to fly at first, they had been going wicked fast, but Demeter was loving it, it was a carnival ride, scary and thrilling, right up until the very end, right up until she realized that Penny wasn't slowing down, Penny was on some kind of rampage, and they were going to crash.

There were police at the hospital. Demeter was confused. Doctors, nurses, police — but where were her parents? Maybe they hadn't come, though surely someone had called them. Demeter's fake Louis Vuitton bag had been in the car, and her license was in her wallet, and—sickening thought—there was a nearly empty fifth of Jim Beam in the bag, too. Demeter had drunk some of it in her bedroom alone while the rest of those guys went to the graduation party at Patrick Loom's house. Demeter hadn't been invited to Patrick Loom's party—or rather, she *had* been invited, but only through her parents, who got asked to everything because her father was a selectman. She hadn't been invited in earnest, on her own merit. She never was.

So she had drunk some of the Jim Beam in her bedroom, and then she'd locked the door and climbed out her window. She'd scooted on her butt down the sloping roof to just above the garage, where she was able to leap to soft grass. Her parents would never have believed Demeter capable of doing this, because she was overweight and the least coordinated human being alive. She would never be able to execute her escape in reverse, because how would she climb the drainpipe to the roof? *Someone* could—Hobby could, Jake could, possibly even Penny could—but not Demeter. She was too heavy. She would rip the drainpipe right off the side of the house. She would wait until her parents were home from their evening out—they had no less than four graduation parties to attend—and when she was sure they were asleep, she would walk right back in the house, and pop the lock on her bedroom door with a pin.

Demeter was being largely ignored at the hospital. There was a flurry of urgent-sounding business swirling around her like a tornado. She heard the letters *D.O.A.,* and she knew that that must be Penny. Penny had been dead on arrival. Demeter knew this, and she knew she was supposed to feel something, but she didn't feel anything. The room was warm, but Demeter couldn't stop shivering.

She heard the incoming helicopter. Medflight. Someone was being flown off-island. Someone was really hurt. Was it Penny? Penny was D.O.A. Did they fly dead people to Boston? Certainly not. So it must be someone else: Jake or Hobby. The Castles' house was on the flight path of the air ambulance, and every time Demeter's mother, Lynne, heard it incoming, she would genuflect and say, "God bless the patient. God bless the mother of the patient." In this way, Demeter had learned that it was even worse to be the mother of the hurt person that it was to be the hurt person herself.

A nurse approached Demeter and lifted up her chin. Demeter was convulsing into the pillow she held against her chest.

"I think she's in shock," the nurse said aloud to herself.

Shock? Probably certainly correct. When the Jeep smashed into the sand, there had been an impact like the apocalypse, a world-ending smash. A horrible shattering noise, an acrid smell. And then the Jeep had tipped over, and Demeter had gotten that roller coaster feeling in her stomach. She had tucked her head to her chest. One hand had gripped the door handle, one hand had pressed against the seat in front of her, the seat where Jake was sitting. The Jeep tilted to the left, and Demeter might have crushed Hobby with her oppressive weight, but she was literally dangling from the harness that was her seat belt.

At that moment she had seen the unnatural angle of Penny's head.

All of a sudden, everything that had happened in those seconds became unthinkable. Demeter's mind shut off. Dark screen. Was this shock?

To the nurse, Demeter whispered, "Are my parents here?"

The nurse wasn't familiar to Demeter. She said, "Yes. But I can't let them see you just yet. We have to examine you. And you have to talk to the police."

They had the bottle of Jim Beam, for sure.

She said, "Did someone get flown to Boston? Someone from the car?"

The nurse was taking her pulse. She looked levelly at Demeter. "Yes."

"Who was it?"

"I can't tell you that."

"Is it bad?" Demeter asked.

"Yes," the nurse said. "It's bad."

The nurse took her blood pressure, checked her eyes, her ears, her nose, her throat. Asked her to stand up, asked her to move her limbs, her digits. Asked her to say the alphabet backward, asked her her home address, her date of birth, and the date of Valentine's Day.

"February fourteenth," Demeter said. "Not a favorite."

The nurse gave a dry laugh. "Does anything hurt?"

"Not really," Demeter said, though there was something in her mind like a coin at the bottom of a well. Something shiny that she wanted to pick up but couldn't quite grasp. She closed her eyes and tried to concentrate. Then she realized that the shiny thing was Penny, but Penny was D.O.A. Dead. Demeter leaned forward and vomited all over the floor.

The nurse jumped out of the way, but she wasn't quite fast enough; she got splattered. Her turquoise scrubs, her nice white sneakers. Demeter vomited again. All that Jim Beam and the bag of cheese puffs that she'd eaten by big, guilty handfuls in her room, but not too guilty because cheese puffs were mostly air.

The nurse made a noise of disgust, which she then tried to cover up with gestures of concern and practical care. She reached for a shallow dish and called for someone to clean up Demeter's mess.

The nurse asked, "Have you been drinking tonight?"

Demeter gagged and spit in the shallow bowl. Should she lie and say no, or should she tell the truth? The truth didn't always help. This was a lesson Demeter had learned that very night: some truths should never see the light of day.

"Yes," Demeter whispered.

The nurse patted her on the back. She said, "The Chief is coming in to talk to you. Okay?"

Oh God, no, Demeter thought. Not okay. The Chief and her father were friends; they were in Rotary together. They passed the basket in church together. Demeter had known the Chief since she was little. She didn't want to talk to the Chief.

She thought they would move her to another room, a square white room with a simple wooden table, like an interrogation room on TV. She thought they would transport her in a cruiser to the beautiful, brand-new, bajillion-dollar police facility on Fairgrounds Road. Demeter's father had, thanks to his political clout, made it possible for that police station to get funded and built. Would the Chief take that into account when he was questioning her?

Oh God, the Jim Beam.

Oh God, the walk with Penny into the dunes at Steps Beach. What had Demeter *done?* It was true that Demeter had hated Penny a little, but she had loved her, too. A lot of love and a little hate, and maybe the hate was inexcusable, but Demeter dared the world to find a girl more worthy of hateful envy than Penelope Alistair—for her singing alone, her beauty alone, her relationship with Jake Randolph alone. They had all been friends since Montessori: Demeter, Penelope, Hobby, and Jake, sitting in a circle singing songs about magic pennies and grandfather clocks. They had painted in the art room, they had learned the names of the continents, they had sliced their own cucumbers at snack time. Penny and Demeter had sat together at lunch each day and talked about the things that four-year-olds talked about. Who remembered what those things were? They had played chase on the playground. Keep-away with the boys.

Penny was D.O.A.

The Chief walked into the ward. Demeter almost didn't recognize him; he was in street clothes. A pair of jeans, a gray hooded sweatshirt that said NANTUCKET WHALERS across the front in navy letters. He pulled a chair to the side of the bed where Demeter was sitting.

"Demeter," he said.

She nodded.

He put his face in his hands, and when he looked up, Demeter could see that he was close to tears.

He said, "Penelope Alistair is dead."

Demeter pursed her lips and nodded. She wanted to tell the Chief that she knew this already and explain that her brain wasn't allowing her an emotional response. Because she was probably certainly in shock.

"Hobson Alistair is in a coma. And he has sixteen broken bones. He's been flown to Boston."

Demeter gagged and spit in the bowl. Her body was in rejection mode. She made some ungodly retching noises. The Chief cast his eyes down.

"I have you, and I have the Randolph kid. It was Jake Randolph's Jeep, but he wasn't driving?"

"No, sir."

"Penelope was driving?"

"Yes, sir."

"Had she been drinking? You can tell me the truth. We're going to do a tox report."

"No," Demeter said. "Penny wasn't drinking. She doesn't…" Demeter blinked. "She doesn't drink at all, ever. Didn't, I mean."

"But the rest of you were drinking," the Chief said. Somehow he made Demeter's fake Louis Vuitton bag materialize, and he pulled out the nearly empty fifth of Jim Beam. "This. Where did you get this?"

Oh God. Lodged in Demeter's mind was a boulder she couldn't budge. The truth was that she had stolen the bottle from the Kingsley house, on a night when she had been babysitting for Barrett, Lyle, and Charlie Kingsley. Demeter had been the Kingsleys' babysitter for five years. The Kingsley parents went out a lot, and they paid Demeter well, and Mrs. Kingsley was always amazed and relieved to find that she was available. ("Because I have no life," Demeter wanted to confess.) Mrs. Kingsley kept her pantry stocked with potato chips and Doritos and Triscuits and white cheddar popcorn and cheese-filled pretzels and Italian rosemary crackers; Mr. Kingsley called it the 7-Eleven. The fridge was always packed with dips and smoked sausages and hunks of cheese and leftover containers of potato salad or fettuccine Alfredo. The bottom drawer was filled with Cokes and ginger ale, grape soda, root beer. And every single time that Demeter had babysat for her over the past five years, Mrs. Kingsley had opened her arms as wide as they would go and said, "Help yourself to whatever you want."

This had been a rare form of torture, especially after the kids were in bed and Demeter was faced with empty hours of homework or independent reading or the two hundred channels of the Kingsleys' satellite TV. Demeter's cell phone lay charging on the Kingsleys' granite countertop, but no one ever texted, and no one ever called. That wasn't strictly true: at least once a night, Demeter's mother, Lynne, would text her to ask how things were "coming along." Demeter never responded to these messages; she found receiving texts from her mother humiliating. Now and then Demeter sent a text out to Penny, but that was a shot in the dark. Demeter would write something general and innocuous like, what u doin? And on occasion, Penny would text back, hanging with J. Or, sometimes, hanging with A, who was Ava, Jake's mother. To Demeter, Ava Randolph was a tragic figure along the lines of Mr. Rochester's crazy wife locked in the attic in *Jane Eyre*. But to Penny, she was more like Sylvia Plath or Virginia Woolf: brilliant, artistic, bipolar, possibly suicidal.

"Is Mrs. Randolph okay?" Demeter had asked her mother once.

" 'Okay'?" Lynne Castle said.

"I mean, I know she's still really sad about the baby," Demeter said. The baby had died when Demeter and Jake and Penny and Hobby were in seventh grade. "But what does she do? Like, with her life, what does she *do?*"

"That's an interesting question," Lynne Castle said. This was the kind of answer that made Demeter want to scream. Her parents were all about validation. What Demeter wanted was the truth.

"Tell me, Mom," Demeter said.

"She's just..." Lynne held her hands out, as if checking for rain. "Well, it seems to me that Ava is lost."

Lost? Demeter was alarmed to learn that a person could make a career out of being *lost*. She worried that this might someday be *her* career.

"Did someone sell it to you?" the Chief asked. He held the bottle in two hands. "Someone on-island?"

Demeter was startled. Her thoughts had digressed so dramatically that she had forgotten she was under this line of questioning.

"No," she said, honestly.

"Someone off-island?" the Chief asked. He sounded relieved, and she couldn't blame him. He didn't want to have to shut down a local business for selling liquor to minors. Demeter knew she should just tell him she had bought the Jim Beam off-island. "Off-island" was the whole rest of the world, an infinite bigness filled with people and places and things. It was impossible to police "off-island," because where would you start?

Did Demeter want to lie? No, she did not. Her alternative was to admit that she'd stolen the Jim Beam from the Kingsleys, but to explain that it hadn't felt like stealing because Mrs. Kingsley always said, "Help yourself to whatever you want." And so last week, on a particularly fragrant spring night, the night of the Nantucket High School awards ceremony, which Demeter wasn't attending because she hadn't been selected to receive any awards, she had helped herself to the bottle of Jim Beam. And what she wouldn't be able to tell Chief Kapenash was how happy and liberated taking the bottle had made her feel. It was secret and contraband; it was a bandage to have ready for a time in the future that might be even worse than that night. It was numbness in a bottle, oblivion in liquid form. Demeter knew this because she had already systematically run through every drop of alcohol in her parents' house. Al and Lynne Castle weren't drinkers — not a beer at a ball game, not a glass of wine at book club. At dinner Al had water and Lynne drank a glass of milk, like a child. That they even kept any alcohol in the house stunned Demeter. She had stumbled across the stash by accident one night when her parents were out and she was ransacking the kitchen looking for chocolate. In the never-opened cabinet above the refrigerator, she discovered a bottle of vodka, a bottle of gin, a bottle of dark rum, a bottle of scotch, a bottle of vermouth, and a bottle of Kahlua. All of the bottles were opened, with an inch or so missing from each. They had been bought for some party years earlier and hadn't been touched or thought of since.

Demeter had drunk it all. The Kahlua with a little milk was her favorite. She drank the vodka with fresh-squeezed O.J. She mixed the gin with the vermouth—a martini! She replaced the missing vodka with water, the Dewar's with iced tea. Would her parents ever discover her treachery? No, Demeter was certain they wouldn't. Lynne Castle had forgotten that the bottles existed; even when company was over, they were never pulled out. By the time Al or Lynne happened upon these bottles, Demeter would be safely out of the house. At college, or beyond.

"Off-island," Demeter said. She willed herself not to flash the Chief shifty eyes.

He was scribbling on a pad. "And you're certain Penelope wasn't drinking?"

"She was not drinking."

"What about the boys?"

Demeter needed water. Her mouth was coated with a film of vomit. She asked the Chief if she could have some.

"Uhhhh...." He glanced around and caught the attention of the short Hispanic man who'd had the good fortune to clean up Demeter's Jim Beam–and-cheese-puff vomit. *"Agua? Por favor?"*

The man nodded. He reappeared a second later with a small blue cup of tepid water. Demeter was so grateful, she nearly cried. She sipped the water, though she wanted to gulp it.

"So, I was asking..."

Yes, Demeter knew what he was asking: he was asking her to rat out the boys. The truth was, both Jake and Hobby had taken swigs off the bottle. And then the four of them had gone to a bonfire on Steps Beach. It was just a general graduation party, there were lots of seniors there—refugees from earlier, legitimate parties—but there were juniors in attendance as well, and some sophomores. The party had livened up when Demeter arrived with Hobby and Jake and Penny. Everyone on earth loved those other three, and Demeter was lucky enough to be with them because she had texted Penny and said that she had a bottle, and not only that—she wasn't sure that one bottle of Jim Beam would offer enough allure—but there was something BIG and IMPORTANT that she needed to tell Penny. Something ginormous.

There had been a keg at the bonfire, sitting in a trash can filled with ice. There was a line for the keg, but somehow Demeter found herself in charge of the tap. She was a good pour, someone said. Not too much foam. She filled a hundred plastic cups at least. How many of those had been Hobby's or Jake's? Two or three apiece, maybe? And Demeter herself had had three or four beers, though after all the hard stuff she'd drunk at home alone, beer had very little effect on her. For her, drinking it was like drinking juice.

"We were at a bonfire on Steps Beach," Demeter said. "We were drinking beer."

"Hobson and Jake were drinking beer?"

"Yes."

"And then what happened?" the Chief asked.

Demeter drank her water down. She needed a hundred more cups just like that, but preferably colder.

"After that?" Demeter said. She wouldn't talk about after that. She couldn't. Besides, she was getting confused. Had the party she was talking about taken place that very night? Because it seemed like days ago. Last week. And was Penny really dead? She couldn't be dead if only hours before she had been talking to Demeter in the dunes. And was Hobby really on a helicopter, in a coma? Sixteen broken bones? Demeter had been in love with Hobby when she was younger. She had berated herself for how unoriginal this was, for everyone on

Nantucket was in love with Hobby Alistair—every girl, every mother, every father. Eventually Demeter had grown out of it and moved on to being in love with Patrick Loom, then Anders Peashway, then Jake Randolph, but Jake only because Penny loved him, and Demeter wanted to be like Penny.

Demeter let her face fall in fake disappointment-in-herself. "After that, I can't remember."

"You don't remember getting into the car?" the Chief asked.

Demeter gnawed on her lower lip. She had tried out for *Grease* this past winter—she'd desperately wanted to play Rizzo—but she'd gotten only a part in the chorus, so she'd quit, much to her parents' dismay. What Mr. Nelson and Mrs. Yurick hadn't realized during the auditions was that Demeter was an excellent actress.

"I remember getting in the car," she said. "I sat in the backseat, on the right. Hobby was in the backseat on the left. Jake was in the front passenger seat, and Penny was driving."

"Penny was driving even though it was Jake's car?"

"She was the only one who hadn't been drinking," Demeter said.

Even so, Jake had tried to take the keys. He'd held Penny's wrist and tried to pry open her fingers, but she had swung her arms at his face as if to hit him, and he'd backed off. Penny had been in full freak-out mode. That was exactly what Demeter had thought at the time: She's freaking out. Freaking freaking.

Hobby had said, with his unflappable calm, "Jeez, Pen, pull yourself together."

"Please," Jake had said. "Please let me drive."

Penny had screamed. No words, just a scream.

Demeter had felt her stomach do funny things. She was certain Penny was going to spill the beans, even though Demeter had made her promise. Had made her swear.

"And Penny drove out to Cisco Beach," Demeter said. "And she was going really fast." Even while they were still on the road, the car was shuddering. Jake was pleading with Penny to slow down, while Hobby was leaning forward, trying to see the speedometer. He seemed most interested in finding out how fast the Jeep could go. Demeter was in a drunken daze, a dreamlike state in which she wasn't sure if what seemed to be happening was really happening. She was, however, wearing her seat belt. And Jake was wearing his. That, she thought, was the result of good parenting. The twins were unbuckled because that was the kind of house they'd been raised in—an unbuckled household. Zoe laid down no rules. "Listen," Zoe had said recently to Lynne Castle. "Raising them without hard-and-fast rules has worked. Look how wonderfully they're turning out."

D.O.A.

Coma.

"And then we crashed," Demeter said.

ZOE

She had seen Jordan at the hospital. He was in the waiting room with the Castles. Ava wasn't there. The fact that Ava wasn't there was a relief, but not for the usual reason. If Ava wasn't there, Zoe thought, then things mustn't be that bad.

The police had called Zoe and told her that there had been an accident and that she should come to the hospital right away. When she arrived and saw the expression on Lynne Castle's face, she knew. It was death or near-death, but she didn't know which child. She had read *Sophie's Choice* along with everybody else, and along with everybody else she had thought, No, I wouldn't be able to pick. If they made me choose, I'd tell them to put a bullet in my head. I'd rather die than choose one over the other. Dr. Field came out. Zoe had known Dr. Field for fifteen years. He had sewed up her forefinger after a particularly bad accident with her Santoku knife. He had treated her kids for strep throat and pink-eye and something like fifty-two earaches between them. He had been the one to pop Hobby's dislocated shoulder back into place, right there on the thirty-five-yard line of the Whalers' field. He had been the one to show up at the Randolphs' house when Ernie Randolph died of SIDS. He was the island's doctor, on-call something like 350 days a year. Zoe felt proud to be his patient. She brought him a jar of homemade mustard and a bag of her from-scratch soft pretzels every Christmas.

She had never seen him look at anyone the way he was looking at her now. Tenderly, and with fear.

"Zoe," he said. "I need you to sit down."

"Tell me," she said. Her voice was froggy. The call had woken her up. "Just fucking tell me."

"Penelope," he said.

"Is dead."

"Yes," he said.

It was Penny, she thought.

"And Hobson has been flown to Boston. He's in a coma. And he has sixteen broken bones."

Zoe swooned. The room melted, and she thought, I'm going down. She thought, Put a bullet in my head.

"Patsy!" Dr. Field called out. He had Zoe by both arms, he was holding her, but she was done, gone, checking out. There was no life for her without those two. She had made her own way and found a modicum of personal happiness, but there was no life left to her without the twins.

Patsy, the nurse, helped carry Zoe to the chairs.

"Get her water and an Ativan," Dr. Field said.

"No," Zoe said. She wanted a bullet, yes, but not drugs. She wouldn't be weak like that. She opened her eyes and focused on the white of Dr. Field's coat.

He said, "Hobby is alive. He's on his way to Mass General. You have to get to Boston."

"Okay," she said. She was strong enough to open her eyes, but not strong enough to stand, and certainly not strong enough to get herself to Boston. "Can I ask? What happened?"

"There was a car accident," Dr. Field said. His voice was floating over her head. "Penelope was driving. Hobson was in the backseat."

"Whose car? Jake's car? The Jeep?"

"Yes. Jake Randolph was in the car, as was Demeter Castle."

"Are they dead?" Zoe asked, though she knew the answer.

"No," Dr. Field said. "They're fine. Cuts and bruises. A bad case of shock."

Cuts and bruises. A bad case of shock. Not dead. Not in a coma. Zoe wished she were the kind of person who could be happy that other people's children were alive and unharmed while her two children were dead and nearly dead—but she wasn't.

"Mr. Randolph has offered to make sure you get to Boston safely," Dr. Field said. "And the Castles have offered to help as well."

Zoe pivoted her head and saw the three of them sitting in chairs. Jordan sat on the edge of his seat, staring at her, and Al and Lynne were huddled together. Lynne was crying, and Al—steady, solid Al—was rubbing her back. The Castles and their smug togetherness, their unassailable bond, made Zoe want to scream. She had—admit it!—used their marriage as a fortress. They were her closest friends, and Zoe had ridden on the coattails of their outstanding citizenship.

Al was a selectman, he owned the local car dealership, he knew everybody, and Lynne, no slouch herself, owned a title-search and permitting business that she ran from home so she could always be around to tend to the fire. They had two sons away at college—Mark at Duke, Billy at Lehigh—and they had Demeter, who was, like Penny and Hobby, in eleventh grade. Demeter was something of a sore spot.

But she was still alive.

I don't have a daughter, Zoe thought. Anymore.

But no, this was impossible.

Zoe let out a high-pitched noise, a keening, a sound she had never made before in her life. Dr. Field was standing before her; she was staring at his belt buckle. He was an intelligent man, a distinguished man, and she needed him to fix this. When Hobby had taken that hit from the monstrous inside linebacker on the Blue Hills team and was lying on the field writhing in pain, Ted Field had jogged out and, with his magic hands, popped his shoulder back into place.

Zoe looked up at him. She was shaking, and this awful noise was escaping from her. Fix this! she thought. She had once carried Penny into the Emergency Room at two in the morning. Penny had been four years old, and she had vomited in her bed. When Zoe touched her forehead, she felt as if it nearly scorched her hand. She hunted around awhile in the bathroom for a functioning thermometer — this was the kind of object she never seemed to have at the ready — then she gave up. The child was on fire; she needed a doctor. It had been hard as a single mother. She'd had to carry Penny out to the car, then go back inside and wake up Hobby and take him, too. (She had considered calling Lynne Castle and asking her to come over and watch Hobby, but back then, Zoe was determined to handle everything herself.) Penny's cheeks had been bright pink, her hair damp around her face, but when Zoe had carried her into this very room so many years earlier, Ted Field had met them at the door and taken Penny into his arms. He had taken her temperature—104.5—and gotten some Tylenol into her. He'd discovered the problem: a raging double ear infection.

But he couldn't fix this. Penny was dead.

"Do you want to see her?" he asked.

Zoe wailed. The mere question was hideous. Did she want to see her dead daughter? It was a decision from a nightmare. This would be followed by other unholy decisions, such as whether to bury her daughter or cremate her.

"No," Zoe said. No: seeing Penelope dead would only do her further damage. Maybe that was the wrong decision; maybe another mother, a better mother, someone like Lynne Castle, would've been strong enough to look upon the body of her dead child, but Zoe couldn't do it. *I love you twice as much as any other mother loves her child,* she thought. *And therefore I cannot stand to see you dead.*

Penny. Her dark hair and rosy cheeks and the spray of freckles across her nose. Zoe wasn't religious, but every year the Catholics asked Penny to sing "Ave Maria" at their Christmas Eve service, and every year Zoe went to listen. Hearing her daughter sing that beautiful song made Zoe feel as close as she ever had to God.

The Castles had come over to her. They had been her friends for fifteen years, but Zoe could see that they didn't know how to proceed in this situation. They stood in front of her.

Lynne said, "Oh, Zoe."

Zoe nodded.

"It's too much," Lynne said.

Too much *what?* Zoe wondered.

Al said, "Can we take you to Boston? There's a flight leaving at five-thirty. I'll have a car waiting in Hyannis. We'll go with you."

Zoe stared. Al was as bland-looking as a person could get, which was why people liked him so much. He had brown hair and a bit of a paunch; he wore slacks and tie clips. He embodied some kind of American ideal: the local businessman, the selectman, the affable, reliable type. Nothing hidden or surprising. He seemed a little milquetoast, but he had a way of getting things done. He would put Zoe on the flight, he would have a car waiting for her at the airport, he would be Zoe's substitute husband now, on the worst night of her life, just as he'd been her substitute husband a hundred times before: scheduling her oil changes and her car inspections, checking her tire pressure before she drove out onto the beach, sending someone over to seal up her ocean-facing windows in the winter, calling the people at Yates Gas when they neglected to fill her tanks and her heat went off, giving her free tickets to the Boys & Girls Club clambake because he bought twenty-five for his employees and always had extras.

Al and Lynne Castle were her closest friends. But how to explain it? A chasm was opening between her and them now, expanding with every passing minute. Their daughter was alive, and Zoe's daughter was dead. She couldn't bear to be in their presence.

"I need to go alone," Zoe whispered.

"You can't go alone, Zoe. Don't be ridiculous." This came from Jordan. Jordan was looming above her now, but where had he been five minutes ago when Dr. Field delivered the blow? He should have been holding her, steeling her. Jordan Randolph was her substitute husband in all the ways that Al Castle was not. Jordan sent her flowers, he put suntan lotion on her back, he made love to her every Tuesday and Thursday morning while the kids were at school. He washed her hair in the outdoor shower afterward. He kissed her fingertips, he ate the food she made for him. They'd spent exactly six nights together: two nights in New York City, two nights in Boston, one night on Martha's Vineyard, and one night at the crummy Radisson in Hyannis. Those had been the six best nights of Zoe's life.

She loved him so much. He was *that man* for her. The one who made everything matter.

His dark, curly hair was matted. The lenses of his glasses were smudged. How many times had she lifted Jordan's glasses from his face, breathed on them, and wiped them off on her own shirttail?

He said to the Castles, "I'll take Zoe to Boston."

Zoe got to her feet. She slapped Jordan across the face, as hard as she could. Lynne Castle gasped. Jordan's glasses were askew. He set them straight again. He said nothing.

JORDAN

His father had cheated. Rory Randolph had conducted a classic martini-and-high-heels affair with the arts editor from the *Boston Globe;* for months he had kept a suite at the Eliot Hotel. There was a long-standing dalliance with a socialite from Philadelphia named Lulu Granville, who summered on Monomoy Road. Rory seduced one of his copyeditors; rumors flew that he had gotten her pregnant, then paid for her to have an abortion. Who knew if that was true? What *was* true was that the copyeditor had quit the newspaper after a tearful scene behind the closed door of Rory's office, on the night of a *deadline*. And then there was the nineteen-year-old journalism student who worked on the classifieds desk. She later went to law school and filed a retroactive sexual harassment suit that Rory had to spend ten thousand dollars to make go away. Those were the women Jordan knew about.

In his day, Rory Randolph had been the most powerful man on Nantucket. He was handsome and charming, he drank good scotch, he smoked a pack of Newports a day, he had a Purple Heart from Korea, he'd gone to Yale on the G.I. Bill, and he didn't care what people said. He was convinced of his own superiority. His family owned the newspaper and always had. He was the island's voice.

Jordan had grown up despising his father. He hated the cheating and the lying, the stink of cigarette smoke, and the taste of whisky. He hated that his mother threw away the hotel receipts with a sigh. She and Jordan never talked about the other women, though she knew that he knew, and he knew that she knew that he knew.

She cooked the roasts, she poured the scotch. She said to her son once, apropos of seemingly nothing, "I take the bad with the good."

*   *   *

Jordan took pleasure in doing things differently. He went to Tabor instead of Choate and Bennington instead of Yale, he smoked marijuana instead of cigarettes, he drank wine instead of whisky, he was a Democrat instead of a Republican, he was humble and self-effacing instead of pompous and self-congratulatory.

What was Jordan like with women? Well, like his father, he'd never had a problem there. He wore his hair over his collar, he wore rimless glasses, he wore faded jeans and flip-flops. He taught himself to play the guitar. There were always women. But Jordan wasn't interested in a wife, wasn't interested in a *family*—people he would inevitably let down. After watching his father for all those years, he decided it would be better for him to stay free and not owe anybody else a thing.

Then, one summer, there was Ava.

The best thing about Nantucket was that its allure drew people from all over the world. Jordan had grown up spending his summers with wealthy children from Manhattan, Boston, Washington, London, Paris, and Singapore. But he had never met anyone as bewitching as Ava Price.

She worked as a waitress at the Rope Walk. The first time Jordan saw her, she was wearing her uniform: Nantucket-red miniskirt, white T-shirt, white sneakers. She was bending over a table, clearing plates piled high with lobster carcasses. Her honey-blond hair was in one long braid down her back; she had a pencil tucked behind her ear. But what had gotten him was her accent. What American didn't love a British accent? Which in Ava's case was actually not British but Australian. Jordan didn't learn this until later, though, when he saw her at the beach, playing volleyball in her string bikini. It was a Saturday, a day he took off from the paper, and he was at the beach with a bottle of wine and a book of Robert Bly poems. He placed himself advantageously. The volleyball landed on or near his towel no less than half a dozen times, and each time Ava came to fetch it with increasingly amused apologies.

She said, "Perhaps you should move your towel."

He said, "Why would I want to do that?"

That was Ava Before: a twenty-three-year-old goddess from Perth, Australia, who had come to Nantucket for the summer because her father had read *Moby-Dick* out loud to her and her five siblings. It had taken them three years to finish it, she said. But as a result of that reading, Nantucket was the one place in the world she'd always wanted to visit.

Thank you, Herman Melville, Jordan thought when she told him that.

Ava Before was refreshing. She was intelligent and outspoken, she was a socialist in a good-natured Australian way, and she was an environmentalist before it was popular. She bought a secondhand ten-speed bike and rode everywhere with her straw bag tied to the back. She was a fierce volleyball player and a fearless swimmer—she had learned to swim when she was eighteen months old and happily took on waves Jordan wouldn't even consider. She agreed to go on a date with Jordan, but she didn't want anything serious, she said, because to her the idea of falling in love was about as attractive as the notion of having a piece of chewing gum stuck in her hair.

"Right," Jordan said. "Good," Jordan said. "I don't want anything serious either," Jordan said. "That's the last thing I want."

He took her to dinner at the Club Car, and to impress her he ordered the caviar, which was accompanied by a bottle of vodka encased in a block of ice. It cost seventy-five dollars, but it was worth every penny to watch Ava throw back shots of vodka and then grin at Jordan wickedly across the table. And then to have her, later, on top of him in the sand, kissing him, tasting of caviar. He took to picking her up on the nights when she didn't have to work and driving her out to Madaket to watch the sun set. They drank wine, they opened clams and oysters she brought from the raw bar at work, they talked. Her life, his life. They had almost nothing in common. He had been raised extravagantly on a tiny island, she had been raised frugally on a giant island. He hated his father and pitied his mother; Ava adored her father and feared her mother. He liked poetry and short stories; she read big, sweeping novels like *Moby-Dick* and *The Fountainhead*. He was an only child; she came from a brood of six, with two sisters and three brothers. His experience growing up had been lonely and sheltered: hers had been rollicking and egalitarian. He had never been in love; she had been, once, with a man named Roger Polly, who was fifteen years older than she, a relationship that had ended badly.

Jordan was working full-time at the newspaper, as second in command under his father. Jordan hated everything about Rory Randolph, but he couldn't bring himself to hate the paper. He had been bred to it. His father was itching to retire and buy a fishing boat in Islamorada. Jordan wanted his father to retire. There was no conflict where the paper was concerned; the handover was going to be seamless. Another year at the most, and then Jordan would be in charge. Did this impress Ava? He had thought it might, but she simply said she felt sorry for him because he was chained to this tiny island.

He took umbrage. "I'm not chained," he said. Ava stuck around until Columbus Day. Then the Rope Walk closed, and it became too cold to spend the day at the beach, and Ava announced that she was going home.

By that point, she and Jordan were spending every night together in the garage apartment that Jordan was renting on Rugged Road. He had gotten used to sleeping with Ava's long hair across his face; he had gotten used to her penchant for playing Crowded House while she took a shower. Jordan was reading *The Fountainhead* at her insistence. But now, when he finished, she would be gone. There would be no one for him to talk about it with. So what was the point? She packed up the things she'd been keeping at Jordan's apartment, and he threw the book across the room. Their eyes locked. She frowned at him.

Now, twenty-one years later, he thought, What if I'd just let her go?

Ava returned to Perth and got a job waitressing at one of the seafood restaurants in Fremantle. She was saving up money to buy a boat, she said. She wanted to sail to Rottnest Island on the weekends.

Jordan wrote her letters proclaiming his love, even though he knew it might be received badly. He called her on Sundays, when the rates were cheaper though still expensive.

He said, "I want you to come back."

She said, "Why don't you come here?"

He had no response to this. She laughed. "You can't. Can you?"

He thought again now, What if I'd just let her go?

Jordan had taken a week's vacation in the middle of March and traversed the globe to Perth, Australia. When he finally arrived, grungy and sleepless, at the cramped but charming bungalow on a tree-lined street on the banks of the Swan River—the childhood home of his beloved—Ava seemed more amused by his presence than overjoyed. She held him by the arm and introduced him to her siblings and her parents as though he were a curiosity at a traveling sideshow: "This is Jordan! He's American!" It soon became clear to Jordan that none of the members of Ava's family had ever heard his name mentioned before.

Ava's father, Dr. Price, gave the impression of being a thoughtful man. He was nearly seventy; heavily bearded, he smelled like pipe smoke and seemed always to be carrying the Book of Common Prayer. Ava's mother, whom everyone, including her own children, called Dearie, was an imposing, full-bosomed field marshal of a woman, with copper-colored hair pulled back so severely into a bun that it seemed to stretch her mouth into a grim, unsmiling line. Jordan didn't like to think ungenerously of anyone, but there was no way around it: the woman was imperious and terrifying. She sniffed at Jordan in greeting. She crossed her arms over her mountainous chest and said to Ava, "I guess he'll want a shower, then?"

Jordan said, "Hello, Mrs. Price. It's nice to meet you." He handed her the jar of Nantucket beachplum preserves that he'd painstakingly transported—wrapped up in his softest T-shirt—ten thousand miles. Dearie squinted at the label and, plainly presuming that the contents were poisonous, set it on the kitchen counter behind her. When Jordan, freshly showered and shaved, checked a little while later, the jar was gone. He suspected she'd thrown it away.

Jordan cornered Dr. Price on the second afternoon to ask for Ava's hand in marriage. Dr. Price seemed confused, or possibly frightened, by the words Jordan was uttering. Jordan *was* making himself clear, right? (He was so woefully jet-lagged that the words sounded jumbled to his own ears.) "I want to marry your daughter. I want to live with her in America. I'd like your blessing to do so, sir."

Dr. Price clutched the Book of Common Prayer to his chest, and Jordan felt like some kind of demonic presence that the man was trying to fend off.

Dr. Price said, "Oh, well, I don't know about that, son. You'll have to ask her yourself."

A couple of days later, Jordan chartered a sailboat with the last of his remaining money and proposed to Ava on the bow. He didn't have a ring to give her, but he hoped that wouldn't matter. If she said yes, he would buy a ring. He wanted to marry her. Would she marry him?

"*Marry* you?" Ava said. She looked as confused as her father, and perhaps a little bit horrified. "Are you *moving* here?"

No, he said. No, he wasn't moving here. He wanted her to come live with him on Nantucket.

"I don't get it," she said. "You mean, leave Australia?"

Jordan had made the journey home shortly thereafter, sleep-deprived and brutally heartbroken. For three months, he licked his wounds. Ava was right, he'd realized that during his seventy-two-hour Australian odyssey: he *was* chained to the island. So, he would embrace it. He would love the island, he would marry the island.

And then in June—on the eleventh, to be exact (he would never forget the date)—Ava came walking into the newspaper office. Jordan was sitting on the edge of his desk, eating an apple and talking to his layout manager, Marnie, about the size and placement of the Bartlett's Farm ad. He looked up, and Ava stood there, grinning.

She said, "I thought I might find you here."

Jordan reached out and touched Jake's shoulder in the Sydney airport as they hurried down the corridor for the Qantas flight to Perth, which would take them even farther away from Nantucket than they were already. Jake didn't turn around; he was as immune to Jordan's touch now as Ava was. Jordan wanted to catch his son's eye to make sure that Jake understood: they had left.

"For a year," Jordan had told Marnie, who was now his managing editor. "I'll be back next summer." "For a year," Jordan had told Ava. "I will give you one year." "For a year," Jordan had told Jake. "Just a year."

"My senior year," Jake had replied.

"Correct." Jordan couldn't figure out why Jake wasn't grateful. After what had happened, getting through his senior year on Nantucket would have been a daily torture. Everything would remind him. The water fountain where he'd met Penny after her French class would remind him. Trying out for the school musical would remind him.

Going to football games, organizing the car wash for the senior class, picking a theme song for the prom, opening his locker, hearing kids talk as they passed, confronting the sympathy in his teachers' voices: all of these things would remind him. "It's an island," Jordan had said. "We're contained. We're like ball bearings in a bowl."

"We're running away," Jake said. "I'd rather just stay and face it."

That was because he was young, Jordan thought. And either brave or stupid.

"I'll turn eighteen in May," Jake said. "So I can come back then."

Jordan had nodded. To fight Jake at this point would be fruitless. Jordan was thinking like a typical parent: the change would be good for his son. Jake needed to see another place, breathe different air, walk on different beaches, hear different points of view. They were getting away, not running away.

"I can't stand to be where she's not," Jake had said.

Jordan had closed his eyes and let that sentiment pierce him.

"She's dead, Jake," he'd said. "She's not on Nantucket."

JAKE

He had been to Australia before with his mother on three separate occasions, but that was before Ernie died, and the last time they'd come, which was the only time Jake could really remember, he was nine years old and they'd stayed with his grandparents in Applecross. Now he and his parents would be living in a rented bungalow in Fremantle, the port city twelve miles south of Perth. His mother loved Fremantle; she called it Freo. It was a magical place, she said. Like Nantucket, she said.

Whether she was being ironic or mean, Jake couldn't tell.

Out the car window, he spied streets of one-story limestone bungalows with brickwork around the windows, deep front porches covered by aluminum bullnose awnings with lush green plants hanging from them. Rocking chairs, a curled-up orange cat, bicycles, surfboards.

There was a bong sitting on the top of someone's front wall. His mother must have seen it too, because she laughed.

"I forgot what this place is like," she said.

Jake glanced at his father. Was his father finding Ava's apparent transformation as amazing as he was? It incensed Jake because it made it seem like his father had been right, or at least partially so.

"If we leave, things will be better for you," Jordan had said. "And they'll be better for your mother."

"Not better for me," Jake had responded. Then, meanly, he'd added, "And Mom is beyond help."

But here she was, laughing.

Jordan stopped the car in front of a house. The car was a beat-up Holden Ute; Jordan's father had bought it from the rental place. He'd bought it rather than rented it because this wasn't a vacation: they were *moving* here. The steering wheel was on the wrong side, everybody drove on the wrong side and parked on the wrong side, tight left, wide right—it made Jake dizzy just to watch. Twice during the drive, he'd been sure they were going to crash; his muscles and tendons had tightened like steel cables. One of the benefits of moving to Australia: he would never, ever drive here.

He was overtired, punchy, ridiculously sad. He wanted Penny. He loved her to distraction, had loved her since preschool, when he'd picked daisies for her on the playground and drawn a crayoned heart and left it in her cubby. They had been dating since ninth grade and having sex since the start of their junior year, and most of the time Jake had felt like nothing could separate them, though more and more often he had begun to suspect that Penny nurtured an interior life that he couldn't access. She was a complicated and serious person — that was good. She had more soul than the other girls in their school. But she harbored demons — that was bad. Her father had died before she was born, and so, in Penny's words, it was like there was half of herself that she didn't recognize and couldn't understand. She had shadows to dodge, but so did Jake, because his baby brother had died. "You just have to focus on the here-and-now," he had told Penny. Jake had a list of personal goals: he wanted to follow in Patrick Loom's footsteps and be valedictorian, he wanted to be president of the senior class, president of the school chapter of the National Honor Society, and editor of *Veritas,* and he wanted the lead role in the musical again. And he also wanted to be elected Homecoming King if Hobby didn't get chosen. There was a lot of pressure for Jake to succeed on multiple fronts; expectations were high.

Expectations were high for Penny, too. She had *serious* talent, talent that was too big for Nantucket. She didn't like opera, but she could sing on Broadway, or off-Broadway, or she could travel with the cast of *Mamma Mia* or *The Lion King.* She was that good. She would go to college at Juilliard or Curtis or Peabody in Baltimore, and someone would discover her, and she would be whisked away from him. But Penny didn't worry about things like that; increasingly her mind seemed to be elsewhere, on another plane, in another stratum. Her voice, she believed, was an accidental gift. "It's like it has nothing to do with me," she said. "With who I am inside."

His parents got out of the car. His father pulled their bags from the back.

Jake wanted Penny. He wanted to be standing on the ground where she was buried. His brother, Ernie, had been buried in the same cemetery, his body contained in a coffin the size of a shoebox. How could his mother stand to be half a world away from Ernie? Jake would have thought this impossible — but here she was, headed up the walkway to the house, making happy, breathy sounds.

There was a green front lawn, divided into two squares by the stone walk. There were two limestone walls divided by a set of three steps leading to the front porch. At the base of each of the walls was a water garden growing tall white flowers on stalks.

"Look how green everything is," Ava said. "This is winter."

Yes, Jordan remembered this from his previous visits. The winter was lush and green; the summer was hot and dry, leaving the grass brittle and brown. Right now, in early July, the heart of winter, the sun was out, and the temperature was about 70 degrees Fahrenheit. It might even be colder on Nantucket, where it was summer.

The porch had a long bench swing made of teak.

"Handsome," his mother said, touching it. If she sat on it, Jake was certain he would weep. How could she be returning to life when Penelope was dead?

There was a screen door, and beyond that, the house was open. There was no one here to meet them, though his mother had five siblings living nearby and he, Jordan, had twenty-six cousins. But his father had promised that for the first few weeks, it would be just the three of them getting used to things. Jake was grateful for that. In September he would enroll at the American School, but he would have to attend class only three days a week. The other two days would be dedicated to independent study.

The house smelled like eucalyptus. The floors were made of polished wood the color of Coca-Cola, but the rest of the house was finished in old wood pocked with nail holes and knots. The doors were mismatched, as if they had been salvaged from other houses. Jake moved tentatively forward. A doorway to his right revealed a bedroom with a stone fireplace, and on the left was the master, with its own attached sunroom and bathroom. Farther down the hallway was another door that opened up into the common space, a living room with wooden beams, a bigger stone fireplace, and a couple of comfortable-looking leather couches. Up one step was the kitchen, which had a red brick floor and a huge old stove with a blackened griddle. Next to the stove were a deep enamel sink and an old-fashioned refrigerator, white with rounded corners and a chrome pull handle. There were two sixteen-paned windows that faced the backyard, and in front of the windows a massive oak table with six chairs. A cast iron chandelier hung over the table. Jake liked the kitchen, then hated himself for liking it. His mother had stopped cooking after Ernie died, and she barely ate, and so what was the point of this warm, wonderful room? Maybe she was going to start cooking again, maybe the three of them would sit around the oak table and eat together as a family. The mere thought made Jake livid. But why? He had wanted that for so long, ever since that painful morning four years earlier when he'd been awoken by his mother's screaming.

"Mom?" Jake had called out. But she hadn't heard him.

Afterward, Jake and his father had gradually adjusted to the way things were, to the disturbing mystery of a human being that Ava had become. Dinnertime was all about eating from pizza boxes and takeout cartons whenever they got a free minute—more often separately than together. But *now*, now that Penny was dead and they had moved halfway across the world, *now* Ava was going to become the Barefoot Contessa?

The three of them stepped, single file, out the back door and into the garden. The yard was enclosed on either side by waist-high limestone walls with a spiked wrought iron fence above. The garden was a rectangle bordered by beige pebbles. Inside the pebbles was grass, inside the grass was a bed of red and orange flowers, and inside the bed was a circular limestone fountain. There was a bench in the grass where his mother, in her former state, would have sat and stared at the shooting plume of water all afternoon.

Jake felt his father's hand on his shoulder. Jake was going to start biting in a minute.

"And here's the best part," his father said.

There was a shed at the back of the property. But not a shed—a guesthouse. Jordan opened the door and stepped inside. One square bedroom with a sink and, behind a curtain enclosure, a toilet. There were two eyebrow windows high over the bed, two small tables flanking the bed, a bureau, a desk.

"Cool," Jake said.

"It's yours," Jordan said.

"What?"

"This space is yours. For you. Your mother and I thought you'd appreciate the privacy."

Jake made what Penny used to call his *face*. Well, forgive him, but he was exhausted, and what the fuck was going on here, exactly? This space was *his?* Again, it was all he'd ever wanted: his own space, away from the sad bullshit of his parents. And they were giving it to him now, when it no longer mattered. What he wouldn't have given for his own space on Nantucket when Penny was alive! As it was, they'd been forced to hang out in Jake's room, which shared a wall with Ernie's nursery. They'd never had sex in Jake's bedroom because Ava was always in the nursery watching her stupid goddamned TV show, or reading aloud passages from Melville. They'd had sex in Jake's Jeep (he couldn't think about that ever again) and on the beach and in the bleachers next to the football field at school and, many times, in the Alistairs' house while Zoe was at work.

This place where he would now be living was a bribe from his parents. But it was a useless treasure.

Ava wandered back into the house. Jake turned to his father. "So will you and Mom be sharing a room again, then?" he asked. "Or will you have separate bedrooms?"

Jordan stuffed one hand into his pants pocket and rubbed at his eyes with his other hand. It was an awkward question, Jake realized that, but he wanted to know how things were going to be. "We're going to try sharing a room," Jordan said. "The master bedroom."

"It's been a while," Jake said.

"That it has," his father said.

NANTUCKET

We followed Hobby Alistair's condition the same way we tracked the paths of hurricanes in September: hour by hour. There were updates at 11:00 a.m., 2:00 p.m., and 6:00 p.m. These updates were provided by an email chain that originated with Lynne Castle. Lynne Castle was the point person, which made sense; we all knew she was Zoe Alistair's closest friend. What we didn't know was that Zoe found herself unable to speak to Lynne, and so instead she gave the information to Al Castle, who then passed it along to his wife. We had heard that there had been some sort of scene—a fight? an incident?— between Zoe Alistair and Jordan Randolph at the hospital, but nobody knew exactly what had happened. Al and Lynne didn't say, and Dr. Field didn't say; the only eyewitness who had let anything slip was Patsy Ernst, the E.R. nurse on duty that night, and she had been vague in her description. "Emotions were running high," she said. To one person she said, "They had a fight." To someone else she said, "There was an incident."

We could see how Zoe Alistair might hold the Randolphs to blame, at least initially. It was Jake Randolph's car, after all.

Day 1: Hobby was in a coma, and the doctors didn't know if he would come out of it. He had sixteen broken bones, all on his left side, including a broken femur, broken pelvis, three broken ribs, broken ulna and radius, and broken clavicle. There were fathers across the island who sighed deeply at this news. They would never speak the reason for their private despair, but they didn't need to because we knew what they were thinking: Hobby Alistair would never play ball again. The greatest athlete the island had seen in decades, a boy Nantucket could call its own, who was destined for football at Notre Dame or basketball at Duke, or who might instead be drafted by the Pawtucket Red Sox right out of high school, had been shattered. Because his biological father was dead, any one of these men might claim him. They shared this right; he had played with their sons in their backyards. He had cracked the Glovers' powder-room window with a line drive. He had gone with Butch Farrow and Butch's son Colin to his first Patriots game. Anders

Peashway's father, Lars, had driven both boys to and from basketball camp in Springfield every June.

Hobby had bestowed a greatness on the island, a grace.

He would never play again, the fathers thought.

The mothers thought the same thing Zoe Alistair thought. Two words: *Wake up.*

Day 2: No change.

Day 3: No change. Al Castle reported that Zoe was refusing to eat. She wouldn't leave the hospital, even though Al had booked her a room at the Liberty Hotel next door. She slept across the chairs in the hallway outside Hobby's room. One of the nurses had brought her a pillow and a blanket.

Day 4: The junior class, which was now the senior class, organized a candlelight vigil. Normally any collective action by the junior class would have been spearheaded by Jake Randolph, but Jake wasn't part of this. Neither was Demeter Castle (though Demeter tended to run along the margin of things anyway). The general understanding was that Jake Randolph and Demeter Castle were both too intimately involved in what had happened to take part in the vigil. And so the vigil was led by other members of the junior class: Claire Buckley, who had gone to the prom with Hobby but who could not rightly claim to be his girlfriend, Annabel Wright, captain of the cheerleading squad, and

Winnie Potts, who had played Rizzo in the musical *Grease*. These three girls wore flowing white dresses and handed out white taper candles and long-stemmed white roses (Mr. Potts was a florist in town). A group gathered at dusk in a circle on the newly mowed football field. At first it was just the core group of girls and their siblings and their parents and their friends, but then the crowd grew. Several employees from Marine Home Center — where Hobby worked every summer hauling lumber — showed up, as did many of Hobby's teammates and parents of teammates and a handful of oldtimers who came to the games just to see Hobby play. The staff of Al Castle's car dealership came, as did the waitresses from the Downyflake, who served the football team weekly spaghetti dinners, and the volunteers from the Boys & Girls Club, where Hobby had honed his athletic skills as a kid, and the pilots who had flown Hobby and his teammates to their games off-island, and Hobby's teachers, and every member of the Board of Directors of the Nantucket Chamber of Commerce, and a group of nurses from the hospital, including Patsy Ernst. Dr. Field attended, as did the high school principal, Dr. Major, and the superintendent and several policemen, including Chief Kapenash. These people we expected. The people we didn't expect were the summer residents, newly arrived on island, who came to show their support because this, they suspected, was the real Nantucket. The summer people stood around the perimeter, nervously checking their Panerai watches and searching through their lightship baskets for a Kleenex. They weren't sure they were welcome at this ceremony, but Claire and Annabel and Winnie gave each of them a candle and a rose anyway. Strength in numbers.

Winnie Potts spoke first. Her voice was strong and clear. She asked us to pray—first for the departed soul of Penelope Alistair, and second for the safe return to consciousness of Hobson Alistair. The mothers all prayed for Zoe Alistair—we had been too harsh on her in the past, we realized— and then the Reverend Grinnell of the Unitarian Church materialized out of nowhere with a cordless microphone. He led us in a resonant, if rambling, beseechment to the Higher Power. We wondered, of course, if the Alistairs had attended the Unitarian Church. No one remembered their ever doing so. The only church the Alistairs had set foot inside, once a year, was the Catholic one, on Christmas Eve, though we knew the Alistairs weren't Catholic. We had a sneaking suspicion that the Alistair twins hadn't been baptized at all—which alarmed some of us more than others—but if this was the case, then the Unitarians were certainly the safest bet. Their religion seemed like a wide basket that would carry even the least pious souls among us to safety.

We all said "Amen."

Dr. Field, who was as spiritual a man as any of us, started the flame. He passed it to Chief Kapenash, who passed it to Claire and Annabel and Winnie, who each passed it along, and in this way the flame spread in concentric circles all the way to the slightly abashed summer residents hugging the outer border. Soon the football field was ablaze with golden light, and Winnie Potts started singing "Amazing Grace," and the girls were weeping because who could sing this song—or any other song—without thinking first of Penny? Even so, the vigil was a success. We could imagine Hobby's suspended consciousness hovering above the Earth, gazing down at the many-petaled flower of fire blossoming there on his beloved field, and deciding to come back down and join us.

Day 5: The vigil was a romantic notion. It had been held more for us, it seemed, than for Hobby. There was no change in his condition.

Of note was that it was Thursday, which meant the *Nantucket Standard* came out, just as it did every week. We rushed to the Hub to get our copies, wondering who had written the article and whose quotes had been used and how the matter would be spun, considering that the accident had involved the son of the publisher of the paper. We were stunned to find no mention at all of the accident or of Penny's death, except for a dry three-sentence blurb in the police blotter stating that at 12:53 a.m. Sunday, there had been a fatal one-car accident on Hummock Pond Road, which was still under investigation.

That's *it?* we thought. Nothing *else?*

Some people were outraged. Nantucket had only one newspaper. Didn't it owe its citizens a report of what had happened? But other people understood. No one really knew what had happened. Mrs. Yurick, the elementary school music teacher, felt that Penelope Alistair's life should have been eulogized. Her picture should have been splashed across the front page. Some people thought that Jordan Randolph was trying to sweep the whole matter under the rug because Penelope had been driving his son's car. Others suspected that Zoe Alistair had asked Jordan not to run a story at all — and could anyone blame Jordan if that was in fact true? There was talk that he was waiting to see if Hobson Alistair would recover before he published anything.

"There will be a story eventually," someone said. "Next week or the week after. We just have to wait."

Day 6: Al Castle checked out of the Liberty Hotel in Boston, where he had been staying in order to keep an eye on Zoe Alistair from a respectful distance. There was still no change in Hobby's condition, and Al was needed at home. Lynne was having a hard time with Demeter. She was acting strangely. The Randolph boy had apparently been calling five or six times a day, but Demeter refused to speak with him. And when he rode over on his bike, she locked herself in her bedroom and refused to see him. There was something he wanted to talk to her about, but she didn't seem interested.

Day 7: Claire Buckley and her mother, Rasha Buckley, took Al Castle's place in Boston. Rasha Buckley knew Zoe Alistair only slightly. She said to some of us, "Surely there are other people closer to the Alistair family, whose presence there would offer more comfort?" But no one else stepped forward, and Claire was desperate to go. She approached Zoe Alistair in the waiting room, with Rasha trailing ten feet behind her. Rasha and Zoe had had nice conversations half a dozen times over the years; they'd seen each other that spring, on prom night. Zoe had gone over to the Buckleys' house, where the kids were gathering for pictures. Hobby was wearing a tux jacket and a bow tie with a pair of madras Bermuda shorts and flip-flops. He was dazzling. Claire wore a white lace sheath and hot-pink satin heels to match the plaid of Hobby's shorts.

Rasha and Zoe had stood shoulder to shoulder, beaming at their children, taking pictures with their iPhones. Hobby had brought Claire a bouquet of white roses and calla lilies instead of a corsage.

"They look like they're getting married," Zoe had said.

"Don't they?" Rasha asked. She had smiled wistfully. Because what mother wouldn't want her daughter to marry Hobby Alistair?

Rasha's first report from the hospital was that Zoe seemed to be disappearing. She was thin, pale, and trembling. Her dark hair, always so stylishly cut and tipped with reddish highlights, was matted; she didn't smell that great. She wore gray sweatpants and a gray Nantucket Whalers T-shirt that belonged to Hobby.

Rasha learned that there had been no change in Hobby's condition.

But at that moment Rasha decided there would be one change, at least: Zoe was going to eat something. Rasha knew that the woman was a chef, that she appreciated good food, and that after a week of sustaining herself on nothing but crackers from the vending machine, she must be hungry. Rasha walked up Cambridge Street to Whole Foods and got one container of chilled summer squash soup and another of Asian chicken salad. She got freshly made hummus and Burrata cheese and bruschetta topping and a whole grain baguette and a pint of fresh raspberries and some bars of dark chocolate. She returned to the hospital with these riches, but by that point both Zoe and Claire were in the room with Hobby. Touching him, talking to him. Rasha herself was able to peek into the room and see Hobby, his left side bandaged like a mummy, his majestic form in repose as if he were a fallen king.

Zoe smoothed the hair off of her son's face.

Rasha had heard people say less-than-generous things about Zoe Alistair, but at that moment she saw nothing in her but strength and grace.

Day 8: We began to wonder about a funeral for Penny. Her body was at the Lewis Funeral Home on Union Street. Zoe had decided on a burial instead of cremation. But when?

Zoe ate half of the summer squash soup and ten raspberries. This was her first meal since the accident, and it was significant enough news to make the email chain.

Day 9: At ten o'clock at night, phones rang across the island. Annabel Wright, the cheerleading captain, whose family lived out in Sconset, had gotten permission to ring the bells of the Sconset Chapel.

Hobby Alistair had opened his eyes! He had regained consciousness!

ZOE

You would have to be a mother to understand. But how many mothers really could? There were some, Zoe knew this. There were mothers in the world who had sick children, sometimes more than one. There were mothers in the world with sons or daughters in Afghanistan or other war zones, sometimes more than one child. One killed in action, one still fighting.

That was Zoe.

Penny was dead, but Zoe had done some mental yoga and put that information aside for now so that she could focus on Hobby. Ever since the day the twins were born, this had been her modus operandi. Set one down, pick the other one up and nurse her. Give one a bath, put the other one on the soft bathroom rug and let him cry. Help one with her homework, let the other one sit and complain. Watch one play basketball, ask the other to sit in the stands and cheer. Zoe was one woman facing two sets of needs. Splitting her attention had never worked. The kids knew this: either they had her or they didn't.

For nine days she had given Hobby all of herself. A gatekeeper wielding a long, sharp machete lived in her mind: no other thoughts but of Hobby.

85

Zoe talked to the doctors. She talked, tersely, to Al Castle: "No change," she said. "No change." "Penny will be buried, not cremated." "No change." "Tell Jordan not to run a story—nothing, not one word." "No change."

Only a mother could be so single-minded. She went back over every second of his life. Everything! Holding him for the first time—just him alone, while the doctors were still pulling out Penny. His eyes squeezed shut, his tiny fist jammed in his mouth. They were twins, but he was technically her firstborn. He had made her a mother. In the first moment of holding him she had felt that magnificent rush of love, powerful and terrifying.

Hobby smiling for the first time, Hobby eating peaches from a jar, roly-poly Hobby, too chubby to pull himself up. His sister was already cruising around the room by holding on to the furniture. He would watch her and start to cry. Zoe had captured it on film. There had been one rare night a few months earlier when both Hobby and Penny were both home for dinner, and Zoe made shrimp and grits, their favorite, and after dinner she pulled out the old videos from when they were babies: Hobby sitting on the floor like a potted plant, bawling his eyes out, and Penny toddling circles around him.

Zoe had tousled Hobby's hair—sandy like his

father's, not dark like hers and Penny's—and said, "Oh, but did you catch up to her later!"

Hobby had mastered the art of skipping stones by the time he was four years old. He was always running and jumping, climbing things—trees, cars, bookshelves. Zoe signed him up for swimming lessons at the community pool. Other mothers gossiped or read books while their kids swam, but she rested her chin on the aluminum railing of the balcony and watched Hobby. Zoe could go on forever about the games. His first year playing football at the Boys & Girls Club, the coach had put him in at quarterback. He had quick hands, one of the fathers said, and quick feet. He was a head taller than everyone else on the team. On the basketball court, he shot 75 percent from the free-throw line. He hit his first home run at age ten. Zoe remembered jumping up and down in her chef's clogs, making a racket against the metal bleachers. Hobby later retrieved the ball out of right field and gave it to her. When Hobby was ten, his mother was his only girl.

There were private things about Hobby, too. For a stretch of months, he'd been afraid of the dark. This was Zoe's fault. She'd had the Castles and the Randolphs over for dinner one night, and they'd gotten onto the topic of the Columbine shootings. Hobby was still lingering around the dinner table, hoping that one of the adults would pass him an unfinished dessert. And, too, he liked adult conversation more than other kids did. He observed the adult world, then tried to process it so that it made sense to him. Zoe should have banished him from the table that night or put an abrupt end to the discussion, but she had had three or four glasses of Cabernet, and she liked to prove to other people that her kids could thrive in a house where they weren't constantly sheltered from the harsh realities of the world. And so she had let the conversation go on around him. About the two gunmen—boys hooked on violent video games—who had killed twelve of their classmates and a teacher and then themselves.

That night, Hobby had climbed into bed with her. He was crying. He couldn't stop thinking about those kids shooting other kids. Killing them.

"I'm sorry," Zoe had said. Here was her liberal parenting coming back to bite her in the ass. "I shouldn't have let you hear that."

He came in night after night for months, for a year.

"What happens when we die?" he asked her once.

Zoe could remember wanting to say something encouraging about Heaven, a place up above where you could sit on a puffy white cloud and watch what was happening on Earth. Where certain angels, maybe, even had the power to make the Red Sox win. But instead, she gave him the only truth she had: "I don't know. No one knows."

"Well, where is our father?" he asked.

"Honey," she said, "I don't know."

Hobby pouring milk on his cereal, Hobby lacing up his cleats, Hobby smiling at the girls lined up on the other side of the backstop as he approached the batter's box and did his own version of genuflecting—touching the end of his bat to each corner of the plate, Father, Son, Holy Spirit.

She should have taken them to church, Zoe thought. She should have given them something to believe in.

She refused to think about Jordan. This was difficult because Jordan had infiltrated all their lives and for two years had been as important to Zoe as oxygen. Jordan had talked to Hobby about colleges. Hobby could go anywhere he liked on a full scholarship, he said. Jordan kept telling Zoe, "You've got to stay on top of this. You want him to go to a great school."

"I want him to be happy," Zoe said. "He could be happy at UMass."

"One of thousands," Jordan said.

"Maybe after this island, he'd like that."

Jordan counseled Hobby about it. Jordan researched various architecture departments—their faculties, their degree requirements. Hobby liked the idea of going to a good college. Stanford, Georgetown, Harvard.

Jordan and Hobby talked about other things as well, including politics and music. Jordan downloaded songs that Hobby suggested—by Eminem, Arcade Fire, Spoon—and Hobby downloaded songs that Jordan suggested, by Neil Young and Joe Cocker, the Who, the Pretenders.

Jordan said to Zoe, "I want to ask him about girls, but I'm afraid."

"Why girls?" Zoe said.

"I'd like to talk to him about love."

Zoe could remember thinking, And what, Jordan Randolph, would you tell my son about love? There were times when Jordan's surrogate fathering bugged the shit out of her.

She said, "I'll be the one to talk to him about love, thank you very much."

She'd had a chance to do just that one day when she was driving him home from baseball practice. Penny had gotten her driver's license, but Hobby had been in the middle of basketball season and had been too busy. He seemed content to let Zoe or Penny chauffeur him around.

Hobby was in the passenger seat of Zoe's bright-orange Karmann Ghia in his usual slumped repose, his head back against the headrest, his long legs stretched out as far as they could go, which wasn't very far. He was wearing a sweaty T-shirt; his glove was in his lap.

Zoe asked, "Have you ever been in love, Hob?"

He'd breathed out a laugh and looked out the window. "Mom."

"Just curious." It wasn't a ridiculous question, was it? Hobby had girls calling and texting him day and night; even girls who had graduated from Nantucket High and were now in college texted him. Did any one in particular affect him, or were they all the same? He had asked Claire Buckley to the prom. Claire was bright and vivacious, a go-getter, an athlete in her own right, field hockey and basketball. She was pretty enough, though every time Zoe saw her she was ponytailed and perspiring, biting down on her mouthguard as if getting ready to kill somebody. "What about Claire?"

"Claire's cool," Hobby said.

Zoe nodded. That was correct: Claire was cool, and for Hobby, cool would trump beautiful or sexy. For now.

"But you don't love her?" she prodded.

"*Love* her?" he said. "You mean, like the way Penny loves Jake? No. No, I don't."

Zoe had shrunk away from the topic at that point. In their house, the standard by which all other love should be measured was Penny's love for Jake. Which was completely separate from Zoe's love for Jordan, but which mirrored it nonetheless.

What Zoe did *not* want Hobby to ask was, "Have *you* ever been in love, Mom?"

Hobby tying his necktie (Jordan had taught him how), Hobby sitting with Zoe up front at graduation, watching Penny sing the National Anthem. Hobby loosening his tie at Patrick Loom's party (but not taking it off completely, good kid). Hobby stealthily pouring a Heineken into a blue plastic Solo cup. (So a good kid but not a perfect kid. Zoe had turned a blind eye because he didn't drive, and baseball season was over.) Hobby kissing his mother good-bye before he left the party. He'd kissed her on the cheek, trying not to let her smell the beer on his breath, but she'd grabbed his face. He was a full foot taller than she was, but he was still her child. She said, "Where are you going?"

"Another party," he said. "At the beach."

"You're going with...?"

"Pen and Jake."

"Jake's driving?"

"Uh-huh."

"Be careful, please. Be smart."

"Yes, dear," Hobby said.

Zoe had enjoyed a sinful pride: everyone else at Patrick Loom's party was watching them talk. "This gorgeous creature is my son!" she felt like shouting. "Eat your hearts out."

She pushed him away. "Go," she said. "Have fun."

He pivoted away and yanked at his tie. She was about to remind him to thank the Looms for having him when he turned around.

"Hey, Mom?"

She raised her eyebrows.

"I talked to Patrick about Georgetown. He's going to let me visit and stay with him in his dorm so I can see what it's like."

"Great," Zoe said. As her son loped away, her mind turned to darker worries. Hobby would visit Patrick Loom in Washington, Hobby would possibly go to college in D.C., or Palo Alto, or Durham, North Carolina. She could barely stand the thought: she was going to lose him.

At the hospital, there were times when Zoe was allowed in the room with Hobby and times when she wasn't. When she was in with him, she touched his face and squeezed his good hand and talked about the past—stories he'd heard, stories he hadn't. He was still in a coma.

After who knows how many days, Al Castle left, and Claire Buckley and her mother, Rasha, showed up to take his place. Zoe saw them enter the hospital waiting room, and though she recognized them, she couldn't come up with their names. All of the facts of her life had blended into a gray soup. The girl and her mother approached Zoe, and she thought, Hobby's friend? Or Penny's? The girl looked as bereft as Zoe felt, her hair lank and greasy and pulled into a limp ponytail. She had a spray of acne on her chin; her eyes were swollen, as though she'd been in a prizefight. The mother looked slightly more pulled together, if sheepish, as though she had no idea what to say to Zoe. Of course she had no idea what to say. There was nothing *to* say.

"Zoe?" the woman said. "I'm Rasha Buckley? This is my daughter, Claire?"

Zoe stood up, mortified. It was Claire Buckley, Hobby's prom date, the girl whom he was not in love with but who he thought was cool. Claire Buckley must be in love with Hobby, however, because, well, just look at her.

Zoe embraced Claire Buckley. and Claire dissolved into tears, and it felt strange to Zoe to be the one offering comfort.

Claire whispered, "He has to wake up. He just has to."

Zoe held Claire tightly. There was something

beatific in Claire at that moment, Zoe thought, something holy. Claire had an aura about her, a good energy. Zoe was glad Al Castle had gone home to Nantucket. She was glad Claire had come in his place.

Claire and her mother stayed at the hospital each day from 10:00 a.m. until 5:00 p.m. Rasha brought Zoe food that looked so appetizing, Zoe couldn't resist it. Rasha brought her a fluffier pillow and a softer fleece blanket but didn't suggest that she leave the chairs. She didn't suggest that Zoe change out of Hobby's Whalers T-shirt, either. She understood that Zoe was keeping vigil and that being uncomfortable and unclean was part of it.

As grateful as Zoe was for the sensitive Buckley presence, she was relieved that in the evenings, when she went in to sit with Hobby, it was just the two of them alone.

On the ninth night, she decided to talk to Hobby about his father's death. Zoe had always meant to tell the twins when they were old enough to handle it, but then when they were old enough to handle it, she'd thought, Why burden them?

She should have told Penny on one of those nights when her daughter had crawled into her bed. Because now she'd lost her chance.

She wouldn't lose her chance with Hobby. He was unconscious, but the neurosurgeon was a spiritual man in addition to being a hyperintelligent wizard genius, and he had told her that he thought talking to coma patients helped them. It gave them a place to hook their consciousness. Something like 75 percent of coma patients who regained consciousness did so while being talked to, he said.

Hobson senior had been Zoe's professor; this the kids knew. What they didn't know, and might not appreciate, was how Zoe had fallen in love with him over the course of the semester, how she had anticipated Meats class with a thumping heart. She was mesmerized by the way he handled his knives and cleavers, she was smitten with his British accent, she was wowed by his physical size. She tried to figure out if he was married: he wore no ring, but many chefs chose not to wear rings. He seemed fond of Zoe, he lingered at her station, he occasionally touched her back. She played it cool, though she was hardly the only student hopelessly in love with him. Around campus he was known as either the Meatmeister, by the many fans of his bratwurst, or the Prime Minister of Meat, by the girls who swooned at his accent. There were female students who shamelessly flaunted their affections. A girl named Susannah brought him a hot latte before every class; another, named Kay, once sliced her thumb to the tendon — maybe an accident, maybe a cry for his attention.

Zoe saw Hobson out one night at Georgie O's, drinking a pitcher of beer with some other men. It was the first time she'd seen him out of his whites; he was wearing jeans and a Clash T-shirt. Zoe waved, he beckoned her over, she stopped to talk. He was with two other professors, both older, one of them the hard-ass chef from Lyon, Jean-Marc Volange, who taught Basic Skills I. Zoe knew not to linger. She moved to the bar. A while later, the bartender put a glass of good white Burgundy in front of her and told her it was from the professors. Zoe was afraid to turn around. She savored the wine; she suspected it was the Montrachet, which famously went for thirty dollars a glass. Hobson came over and put his hand lightly on her back, the way he did in class. She felt her face heat up. She said, "Thank you for the wine. You shouldn't have."

He said, "You're right, I shouldn't have. It's very bad form. But I couldn't resist."

"It's the Montrachet?" she said.

"I thought you should taste the best."

The night had ended with their passionately kissing against the side of his car.

He said, "In three weeks, the semester is over. We should wait."

Zoe agreed: "We should wait."

But he called her the next morning, and by the weekend they were inseparable.

Even to this day, Zoe could not believe how lucky she had been to be the one who won the heart of Hobson Alistair over other girls like Susannah and Kay. He was magnificent, a prince, a god, a rock star.

How many times had Zoe looked upon her children and thought, You will never know how kind and luminous and talented and dynamic your father was. I can tell you and tell you, but you'll never know.

"When your father died," Zoe said to Hobby now, "I was pregnant with you and Penny."

The pregnancy had been an accident. Faulty diaphragm. At the same time that Zoe was graduating from the CIA, at the same time that she was trying to decide if she should accept the sous chef job at Alison's on Dominick, the hottest restaurant in SoHo, she was also feeling dizzy and lightheaded and nauseated. Then she missed her period, and she thought, Oh God, no. She and Hobson were madly, stupidly in love. The love was so new, it hadn't lost any of its sheen. But it was all about Sunday mornings in bed, playing Billie Holiday and drinking champagne. It was about making each other dinner, trying to outcook each other. It was about playing darts at Georgie O's until two in the morning, then skinny-dipping in the Hudson, Zoe and Hobson floating on their backs naked, holding hands. It was about reading each other passages from M. F. K. Fisher. It was about planning trips to Berkeley to eat at Chez Panisse and Chicago to visit Charlie Trotter's. Their relationship was only about the immediate future. It was not about a baby.

And yet when she told Hobson she was pregnant, he was dazzled. He picked her up and swung her around. He said, "I'm going to marry you." Zoe opened her mouth to protest, and he said, "I'm going to marry you, woman."

Zoe and Hobson got married. His very proper British parents came, Zoe's very proper Connecticut parents came, a Justice of the Peace married them in their chefs' whites, then Zoe changed into a sundress and Hobson changed into a double-breasted navy blazer and they all had lunch at the Boathouse in Central Park, and everyone got drunk except Zoe.

Labor Day weekend, they learned it was twins. Everyone was excited. Who didn't love the news of twins? Zoe thought, My God, not one but two. At times in the middle of the night she felt as if she were being buried alive.

She managed to make it through the holidays. Hobson was teaching his Meats class, and he did the butchering not only for all of the Institute's classes but also for the five CIA restaurants as well as a few restaurants in greater Poughkeepsie and Rhinebeck. This brought in extra money. Zoe and Hobson attended the twinkling holiday parties on campus and a few more down in the city. Zoe wore the only dress she could still fit into, a stretchy black number with tiny silver rhinestones all over it. People cooed over her; they asked to touch her prodigious midsection. "You look like you're going to pop," they said. "Any day now, I'll bet," they said.

Zoe said, "I still have ten more weeks to go. I'm having twins." She sneaked glasses of wine and eggnog. The twins were encroaching on her internal organs, and Zoe found it impossible to eat a thing without suffering from debilitating heartburn.

Christmas passed, New Year's passed, January set in. It snowed a foot. Hobson and Zoe were living in a faculty apartment. It was nothing special: the countertops in the kitchen were Formica, and the cabinets were plastic laminate, and the bathroom had a molded fiberglass shower stall instead of a tub. Neither Hobson nor Zoe, in her pregnant state, fit in the shower stall properly. Zoe had to shower with the glass door open, and water flooded the bathroom floor. Hobson came home from work splattered with blood. He smelled like pig intestine and head cheese and chicken feet. The mere thought of the flesh and organs that he'd come in contact with over the course of the day made Zoe vomit.

Zoe became convinced that Hobson was romancing someone else, a Susannah or a Kay. She confronted him, screaming and crying, one night when he'd been out late after work. He'd been at the gym, he said, and then stopped at Georgie O's for a burger. That was it, he promised. That was all he was guilty of.

Zoe could not be consoled. She had been carrying two babies for seven months. Technically, she said, she'd been pregnant for fourteen months.

Hobson had the next day off from work. Sunday. He was taking Zoe down to the city, he said. They would ride the train in; they would do whatever they wanted, eat whatever they wanted, buy whatever they wanted. He gathered Zoe up into his arms and bent over to kiss the top of her head. The good thing about Hobson was that he was so big, he made Zoe feel small even when she was enormous.

"Let's forget you're pregnant," he said. "Tomorrow it will be just you and me."

"And that was what we did," Zoe said to Hobby in the dark of his hospital room. "We caught the morning train, we got two cups of gourmet coffee, we bought the Sunday *New York Times* and read it on the way in." They'd taken two double seats facing each other, seats for them and their coffee and the paper. "And then when we reached the city, we took a taxi to the Morgan Library." It was less than ten blocks from the station, Zoe had wanted to walk—why waste the money?—but Hobson had insisted on a cab.

"I thought we were going to forget I was pregnant," Zoe said.

Hobson said, "It's not you, it's me. I'm short of breath."

Zoe said, "Too much coffee, Meatmeister."

"The Morgan Library was a wonder," Zoe told her son. Neither she nor Hobson had been there before. They went to see the Richard Avedon photos of famous chefs—Julia Child, Marco Pierre White, Jacques Pepin, Georges Perrier, Paul Bocuse. But they were amazed, too, by the Gutenberg Bible and the other treasures of the permanent collection. They wandered the hushed rooms, feeling smart and cultured the way one nearly always did in a museum in the city and almost never did in a chilly white test kitchen in Poughkeepsie. "We ate lunch at the café there, at a table overlooking the courtyard. It had just started to snow."

Zoe looked at her broken, bandaged, comatose son, and she thought about the carrot-ginger soup and the toasted Gruyère sandwiches and Hobson's big hand over hers and the fat snowflakes falling onto the boxwood hedge.

"In the afternoon, we took a cab to Greenwich Village. There was a doo-wop group on the corner, five black guys, they sounded professional, your father was quite taken with them. He gave them ten dollars. Your dad bought a funny hat with earflaps, lined with fur. Then he wanted to go and find this one particular cheese store. It took us a while, but it was worth the hunt, because this place was a cheese mecca. They had all the stinky, runny cheeses you couldn't get anywhere else in the United States—the blues from England, the aged cheddars, the fresh goat cheeses and sheep's-milk cheeses from these tiny farms in the Midwest. We tasted and tasted. They had salamis hanging from the ceiling in loops and these wonderful olive oils. God, we went crazy in there. Your dad loved it."

They had spent a fortune, but they didn't care. Later in the week, they decided, they would invite their friends Pat and Dmitri over to try the cheeses and drink some wine. The thought of this had cheered Zoe as she stepped out into the street. She would have a small glass of wine and eat with her friends.

They went to see a French movie at the Angelika Film Center. They ate truffled popcorn and drank fizzy Italian water. The movie was all right; Hobson didn't mind subtitles, but Zoe had taken six years of French and found herself distracted by the effort to translate. Then she became distracted by the fact that Hobson's breathing sounded labored. He was sucking air in and forcing air out. He kept shaking out his left hand.

Zoe asked, "Are you okay?"

He said in his poshest British accent, "Yes, my darling, I'm fine."

Zoe said to Hobby now, "I wish we'd left the movie and gone to the hospital. If we'd gone then, they might have saved him. But that would have required foresight that I didn't have. I was concerned but not alarmed. If I had suggested the hospital, your father would have laughed at me. He would have said, 'What the hell for?' Your father was the healthiest person I knew."

When the movie was over, they took a cab back to Grand Central, with Hobson's new hat and their bag of excellent cheeses. They decided to have dinner at the Oyster Bar. Hobson ordered a glass of champagne, and Zoe took a few discreet sips, and between the two of them, they polished off three dozen oysters.

"It was divine," Zoe said. "So few things in my life have tasted better than the cold champagne and those oysters—fresh, sweet, creamy, with the tangy mignonette." Hobson had made jokes about how strong his libido would be once they got home, and Zoe had felt sexy and aroused for the first time in months. Sex would be good, it would be great, with her standing and him standing behind her.

Zoe sighed, and tears dropped down her cheeks. "As we were rushing to the platform to make our train, he collapsed. Now, your father was a big man. When he fell, a few other people around us nearly got knocked over. I screamed. Hobson was clawing at his chest. He was having a heart attack. The police were with us in seconds, and then the paramedics. They put Hobson on a stretcher, but it took three of them to carry him out to the ambulance. I followed the ambulance in the back of a police cruiser. There was a policewoman with me, trying to write down your dad's information. I think she was worried that I was going to go into labor. I'm surprised I didn't. I don't know how to explain this, but I was very calm. It was as if I knew — somewhere deep inside me, I just knew." Zoe stopped. Tears fell. She had never vocalized these thoughts to anyone, she realized, not even Jordan — but it seemed right that she should now be telling all of this to her unconscious son. "Your father and I had something so amazing and perfect that I had always feared it wouldn't last. I had always thought he was too good for me, that his star was too bright. And I guess it was too bright, because it burned out. When I got to the hospital, they told me he was already gone."

Zoe got up and went over to the side of Hobby's bed. She touched his cheek. It was smooth; the nurses had taught Zoe how to shave him. It was one of the few things she could do for him. "But I kept you and your sister safe," she said. "I did manage to do that."

It was not at that exact moment but some minutes later — five minutes, ten minutes, twelve minutes — that Hobby opened his eyes. It looked as if he were squinting at first, and Zoe thought it was a figment of her imagination. She became alert without letting herself feel too hopeful.

And then, just like that, his eyes opened all the way — they were meadow-green — and he was looking at her. He saw her, he recognized her.

And just as Zoe had once known, deep down, that she was going to lose Hobson, so did she realize now that she had known all along that Hobby would come back to her.

"Hi," she said.

DEMETER

In the days following the accident, there had been room for only one thought: she wished it had been her who died.

She was a criminal. A thief and a murderer.

Demeter vacillated between telling the hideous truth and keeping the truth sheltered and secret inside of her, the coin at the bottom of the well that no one could retrieve.

The latter, she thought. For as long as she could, she would be a sphinx. She had the answer, but nobody knew the question.

From behind the locked door of her bedroom, Demeter heard her mother on the telephone, every second practically, talking to Mrs. Loom or Mr. Potts or Rasha Buckley. Or talking to Demeter's father, who was at Mass General, where Hobby lay in a coma.

How did Demeter feel about Hobby's being in a coma? She felt sick about it, just sick. She had been in love with Hobby when she was younger, and those years had been exquisitely painful. Demeter was overweight, doughy, and cumbersome. The boys in her class had called her a dog, a cow, an elephant, and—in sixth grade, when they were studying pre-historic times—a mammoth. They told her she stank. To add insult to injury, she had braces on her teeth, and bits of food would get stuck in them, and her breath did stink. She was unwilling to get undressed to take a shower after gym class, and so on Tuesdays and Thursdays she reeked of body odor.

Demeter had looked upon Hobby, that classic

Greek god of a human being, his muscles perfectly formed and tanned to gold, and wanted to *be* him. Her parents were such close friends with Zoe Alistair that Demeter had spent pretty much every weekend of her life in Hobby's presence when they were growing up. In the spring they would picnic together at the Daffodil Festival in Sconset. Hobby and Jake Randolph would lob a lacrosse ball to each other on the lawn in front of the old water company, and Penny would inevitably have been asked to ride in someone's antique car for the parade. How many times had Demeter stood on the side of the road, watching as Penny sat in the rumble seat of a Model A Ford, waving at the crowd like Miss America? Demeter had meanwhile stuffed her face with Zoe Alistair's ribbon sandwiches and deviled eggs and curried chicken salad and double fudge brownies. That was all she was good at: eating.

In the summer the Castles, the Alistairs, and the Randolphs all went to the beach together. When they were younger, they would play flashlight tag, light a bonfire, and sing Beatles songs, with Mr. Randolph playing the guitar and Penny's voice floating above everyone else's. But at some point Demeter had stopped feeling comfortable in a bathing suit. She wore shorts and oversized T-shirts to the beach, and she wouldn't go in the water, wouldn't walk with Penny to look for shells, wouldn't throw the Frisbee with Hobby and Jake. The other three kids always tried to include Demeter, which was more humiliating, somehow, than if they'd just ignored her. They were earnest in their pursuit of her attention, but Demeter suspected this was their parents' doing. Mr. Randolph might have offered Jake a twenty-dollar bribe to be nice to Demeter because Al Castle was an old friend. Hobby and Penny were nice to her because they felt sorry for her. Or maybe Hobby and Penny and Jake all had a bet going about who would be the one to break through Demeter's Teflon shield. She was a game to them.

In the fall there were football parties at the Alistairs' house, during which the adults and Hobby and Jake watched the Patriots, Penny listened to music on her headphones, and Demeter dug into Zoe Alistair's white chicken chili and topped it with a double spoonful of sour cream.

In the winter there were weekends at Stowe. Al and Lynne Castle owned a condo near the mountain, and Demeter had learned to ski as a child. According to her parents, she used to careen down the black-diamond trails without a moment's hesitation. But by the time they went to Vermont with the Alistairs and the Randolphs, Demeter refused to get on skis at all. She sat in the lodge and drank hot chocolate until the rest of the gang came clomping in after their runs, rosy-cheeked and winded.

And then the ski weekends, at least, had stopped happening, because Hobby had basketball and Penny and Jake were in the school musical, which meant rehearsals night and day.

Demeter thought back to all those springs, summers, falls, and winters with Hobby and Penny and Jake, and she wondered how her parents could have put her through such exquisite torture. Hobby and Penny and Jake were all exceptional children, while Demeter was seventy pounds overweight, which sank her self-esteem, which led to her getting mediocre grades when she was smart enough for A's and killed her chances of landing the part of Rizzo in *Grease,* even though she was a gifted actress.

Hobby was in a coma. Her mother was on the phone. She kept saying, "Zoe won't talk to me. I don't know why."

Demeter wanted a drink, but there was no alcohol in the house. She thought her parents must know about the bottle of Jim Beam because on one of the rare occasions during the past week when she had left her room — to get a sleeve of Ritz crackers and a jar of peanut butter from the pantry — she'd seen her mother standing at the sink with the bottles of vodka and gin and vermouth, sniffing their contents before pouring them down the drain. The jig was up: Demeter had been found out.

Demeter looked at her mother, and Lynne Castle looked back at her and smiled. She said, "Hi, honey. Are you feeling hungry for a snack?"

Demeter stared at the crackers and peanut butter in her hands as if astonished to find them there. A knife for the peanut butter would have been nice, but Demeter wasn't willing to take one step closer to her mother or the bottles she was emptying. The cabinet above the refrigerator was hanging open. Her mother must realize that Demeter had drunk the vodka and replaced it with water, and drunk the Dewar's and replaced it with iced tea. Lynne Castle *did* get it, right? Somehow Demeter didn't think she did. Her mother was living in outright denial about what was going on. Ignore the obvious signs that your daughter is an alcoholic, but please make sure she has a snack if she feels hungry.

This depressed Demeter all the more. And made her angrier. She retreated to her room.

Jake called. The first time was Sunday night at seven o'clock. Demeter was asleep, but Lynne Castle slipped a note under her bedroom door: *Jake called. He wants to speak to you.*

Okay, wait. This deserved some thought. How long and how desperately had Demeter waited for a boy to call her? How many times had she fantasized that someone like Hobby or Jake would discover something in her that no one else could see, not even

Demeter herself? Some latent, hidden beauty, some spark, some capacity for happiness, for joy?

Demeter didn't harbor fantasies anymore. Fantasies were all distinctly in the past. Jake wasn't calling Demeter so they could commiserate, so they could cry together or hold on to each other, say "Oh my God, what the fuck?" or celebrate how fortunate they were to be alive, present some kind of united front or wallow together in their survivors' remorse.

He was calling for one reason, and one reason only.

Demeter refused to take his calls. Her mother couldn't really insist, though she did try reasoning ("You might feel better if you talked to someone else who went through this with you") and pleading ("Demeter, honey, please call him back, he sounded perfectly *awful*") and begging ("Darling, please, he's called half a dozen times today alone"). But Demeter kept refusing; she said she was too upset to talk about it at all. When Jake rode over on his bicycle and knocked on Demeter's bedroom door and called out her name, she nearly buckled and let him in. How many times had she fantasized about someone like Jake sitting with her in her room, looking at her books, sneaking sips off whatever bottle she had hidden under her pillow, growing buzzed and giggly with her, reaching out to touch her hair? She did, after all, have great hair, chestnut-brown and thick, with a streak of natural blond in the front. He might let her put her hands on his back—he was forever asking Penny to massage his back, and Penny always refused, but Demeter would be glad to do it, wouldn't she?

But no, sorry, no, she said nothing, she stayed as still as a corpse until Jake gave up and she heard her mother say, "I guess she's just not ready."

He wanted the coin from the bottom of the well. He was the only one who might suspect there even *was* a coin, or a well.

She wanted a drink, she *needed* a drink. On Saturday night, the one-week anniversary of the accident, Demeter was freshly struck by the reality of what had happened. It was as if she had been wrapped in cotton batting in the interim—that was certainly probably the shock—and now, all of a sudden, she was exposed and vulnerable.

Penny Alistair was *dead.*

Hobby Alistair, ninety miles away at Mass General, was lying in a coma.

Demeter couldn't handle it. She yanked on her long, straight, thick hair and considered cutting it all off with a pair of her mother's garden shears. That was something a crazy person would do, and Demeter was, now, rapidly approaching crazy. But no, not her hair, she didn't have anything else to be vain about aside from her hair, and she was keeping it.

Try another tack, Demeter. She had a criminal mind, she should use it. Use it! She needed a drink, so she would get a drink. But where? And then, of course, she knew.

That night she waited until her parents were asleep. She had thought her parents' routines and rituals might change after the accident, but once her father came home from Boston, he and Lynne slid back into their usual ways. If they weren't out (and they wouldn't go out under the circumstances, no way, they might not go out once all summer), they turned the TV off at ten and climbed the stairs together to their bedroom. Lynne Castle always paused by Demeter's door—to check if her light was on, to see if she could hear any noises coming from her room—then sighed and moved on, announcing their retirement for the night with the click of their door.

Demeter had shut off her light intentionally. She sat in the dark, counting her breaths. Ten minutes, fifteen minutes, thirty minutes. Her plan was so twisted, so truly evil, that she couldn't believe she was really going to execute it.

But, yes, she was. She had to.

Out the window, down the sloping roof, and boom! onto the front lawn. The lawn had just been cut that day, Demeter had heard her father out on the mower, and this reminded her that she had a job set up with Frog and Toad Landscaping for the summer. She had spent the previous two summers working at Island Day Care, looking after the infants. She had spooned pears and sweet potatoes into their mouths and changed their diapers; she had held and rocked the babies, sterilized their pacifiers and mixed up formula for them. Demeter had a way with babies, or so she liked to think. Babies didn't threaten her; babies didn't know she was fat. Babies just needed love, and believe it or not, Demeter had plenty of love in her heart to give. But the day care was an indoor job, the air at the day care center was stuffy and overly warm and redolent of souring milk.

Her father had offered her an office job at the car dealership, but that held even less appeal. And so, during a moment of belief that self-improvement was possible, Demeter had decided to pursue an active summer job that would permit her to be outside in the sun, but not a job lifeguarding or camp counseling, for which she would have to wear a bathing suit. And certainly nothing in food service. Demeter eventually set her sights on landscaping. She would wear cargo shorts and work boots, she would push a mower in the sun all day, which required no actual athletic ability but would enable her to lose weight and get a tan. She would work with El Salvadoran men and improve her Spanish. The man who owned Frog and Toad, Kerry Trevor, was a friend of her father's. Kerry bought and serviced his fleet of trucks at Al Castle's dealership, so securing Demeter a spot on one of his crews had been a piece of cake.

She was supposed to start on Monday, but that wouldn't happen now. The gung-ho girl who had allowed herself to get excited about a possible personal transformation via a summer of yardwork had died in that Jeep along with Penny.

Demeter inhaled the scent of fresh-cut grass under her feet and bemoaned the loss of her summer.

Alcohol, she thought.

She couldn't risk driving. Her parents might hear the car start, and if they woke up and found that the car was gone with her in it, they would put out an all-points bulletin. So Demeter could ride her bike, or she could walk.

It was eleven-fifteen and pitch black; there were a zillion stars but no moon. It was too dark to ride, she thought. She would walk. It was far, a mile and a half, maybe two. But the exercise would be good for her.

She used her cell phone as a flashlight. She hadn't turned on her phone since the police gave back her fake Louis Vuitton bag, minus the bottle of Jim

Beam. Even having a cell phone was a sensitive issue for Demeter. So few people ever called her, what was the point? But now, when she turned it on, it started dinging and vibrating like a slot machine in Vegas. She thought it must be malfunctioning. She checked the display: seventeen text messages, nine voice-mails. From whom? Well, five of the text messages and three of the voicemails were from Jake. The text messages said: Need 2 talk 2 u, Can I come see u?, Pls call me, Need 2 talk 2 u, Coming over now.

Right.

The other text messages were mostly from other people in Demeter's class—Claire Buckley and Annabel Wright and Winnie Potts and Tracy Loom, Patrick's younger sister—and then there were two texts apiece from Demeter's two brothers, Mark, who was doing an internship with Deutsche Bank in New York City, and Billy, who was in England studying at the London School of Economics. Demeter scrolled through the texts: Claire and Annabel and Winnie had wanted her to come to the vigil that was held the day before, they had wanted her to *speak* at the vigil—and the others wanted to see if Demeter was okay, which was a euphemism for asking, *What the hell happened?* The voicemails, she supposed, were more of the same—people asking how she was, offering thoughts and prayers, people wanting to get close to her *now*, to claim a connection with her *now,* because she was, well, a *celebrity* of sorts. She had been in the car when Penny died and Hobby sank into a coma. It was likely that everyone knew that Demeter had been in possession of a bottle of Jim Beam that was found by the police—and what would they all make of that? Demeter had wondered if she would be blamed for the accident, but people knew that Penny had been driving, and Penny had, of course, been sober. So the fact that Demeter and the boys had been drinking alcohol that Demeter provided was just a sidebar. It was a given. After all, it was *graduation night,* and every single person who was out that night had been drinking, except Penny.

So there remained the mystery: *What happened?*

Demeter's phone buzzed in her hand. She was confused until she realized that a text was coming in at that very moment. She checked: it was from Jake. It said, R u awake?

Demeter was spooked. It was as if he could see her, but of course he couldn't see her, she was walking down a deserted dirt road toward the ocean.

It occurred to her to ask him to meet her there.

Bad idea. She didn't trust him. She didn't trust anyone.

The Alistair house wasn't a real house. It was a summer cottage that Zoe had done a middling job of winterizing. It sat on the bluff overlooking Mia-comet Beach, which made it a great place to live in the summer. It had a wide deck and a huge outdoor shower and a staircase down to the beach. There were sliding glass doors off the great room, and the whole place would be filled with light and the smell of Zoe's cooking. But in the winter, the doors rat-tled in the wind. Demeter's father sent someone over every year to help Zoe shrink-wrap them in plastic. Zoe kept the woodstove burning, but the house was always cold. The cottage consisted of two parts. The great room was the public part, living room, dining room, and kitchen, with a powder room. The private part was the three bedrooms—Hobby's, Penny's, and Zoe's—and a full bath that the three of them shared. Demeter had slept over at the cottage numerous times as a child and had felt uncomfort-able sharing a bathroom with an adult. At her house, her parents had a suite, she had a suite, and her brothers had the whole third floor to themselves. She couldn't imagine using the same toilet as her mother—and yet that was what Penny did, every single day. In later years Penny had talked about sharing makeup and tampons and toothpaste with her mother, and she'd talked about how Hobby stank up the bathroom in the mornings, and Demeter had shuddered, while at the same time experienc-ing awe and wonder at how closely the three of them coexisted. It seemed indecent somehow. Demeter had once asked her mother if the Alistairs were poor, and Lynne had laughed and said, "Heavens, no! Beachfront property? Any idea how much Zoe paid for that place? A fortune. She could sell it for double that now and buy a mansion on Main Street. But she won't. Zoe adores her ocean view. It makes her feel free. And God knows, Zoe likes to feel free."

The Alistair cottage was dark. Thank God: Demeter had imagined it surrounded by cruisers, crisscrossed in yellow police tape, and encircled by Claire Buckley and company, all holding candles and singing "Kumbaya." Demeter held out her phone to illuminate the sandy path that led through the eelgrass to the Alistairs' front door.

Just like Demeter's own house, the Alistair cottage was never locked, and so Demeter walked right in. It smelled like fresh basil and, under that, onions and garlic. Zoe was always cooking something delicious. Demeter debated turning on a light, then decided against it. She used her phone to negotiate her way into the kitchen. She saw the herb garden Zoe kept on the slate countertop, and a bowl of shrunken peaches covered with fruit flies. There were books and papers all over the counter, there was a wine glass in the sink, and Demeter imagined Zoe sitting out on her back deck the week before, enjoying the warm night air and the stars and the sound of the waves hitting the beach. She would have been thinking about the twins' becoming seniors; she would have been remembering how beautifully Penny had sung the National Anthem during graduation.

Demeter opened the fridge. There was three quarters of a bottle of chardonnay. Demeter lifted the bottle, her hands shaking—not in fear but in anticipation.

She drank.

She was in the Alistairs' house, drinking Zoe's wine. What is wrong with you, Demeter Castle? she asked herself. But she knew the answer:

Everything.

JAKE

The Chief had asked, "Can you tell me what happened?"

She was dead. Penny. His girlfriend. "Girlfriend" was insufficient; he was a wordsmith, he could do better. His lover. No, his beloved. His Juliet, his Beatrice, his Natasha, his Daisy Buchanan. What did it matter *what had happened* when Penny—the Penelope to his Ulysses—was dead?

Dead. He let out something between a cackle and a scream, and as he watched the features of the Chief's face soften, then harden, he could see the Chief wishing that he would act like a man, and he wanted to grab the front of the Chief's sweat-shirt and say, "I am seventeen years old, and the girl I've loved for fourteen of those seventeen years—since I was old enough to think and feel—is dead. She died right next to me."

The Chief cleared his throat and started again. "Had Penelope been drinking?"

"No."

"You're sure?"

"Yes."

"You were . . . *where* tonight? Where did you start out?"

Jake glared at the Chief. "Why are you *interrogating* me?" This was brutality, wasn't it, a barrage of questions like this? This was the Chief abusing his power. Jake's father had talked about the police overstepping their bounds because it was a small island and they could occasionally get away with it. The Chief and Jordan Randolph had had their differences; there was bad blood over some political thing or another.

The Chief said, "Listen to me, young man, I

know you're hurting. And I've been there myself. I lost my best friends, three years ago now, *lifelong friends,* and now I'm raising their children. I *know* this is difficult. It may be the most difficult thing you ever do, let's pray that it is, but I have to try and piece together what happened tonight." He pressed his lips together until they turned white. "It's my job to figure out what caused this accident."

Jake lowered his eyes to his jeans. Penny had written on his jeans in ballpoint pen — a heart containing their initials. She had written on every pair of jeans he owned, and she had written on his T-shirts with Sharpies and on the white rubber of his sneakers, and she had written on his palms. *I love you, Jake Randolph. You are mine, I am yours. Forever.* It was old-fashioned, better than a text message, she said, more visible: he couldn't just delete it. If he wanted the markings gone, he would have to scrub. But he didn't want them gone, and especially not now. It was all he had left: the memory of the pen in Penny's hand, drawing the heart, tickling his thigh.

"We started at Patrick Loom's house," Jake said. The Chief wrote that down, which was silly, because the Chief himself had been at Patrick Loom's house and had seen Jake there. "Then we went to Steps Beach."

"Who drove?"

"Me."

"Why did you drive?"

"It was my Jeep."

"But you'd been drinking."

"At Patrick's?" Jake made what Penny referred to as his "face." Had the Chief *seen* him drinking, or was he just assuming? "Yes, sir, I had one beer at Patrick's. But I was okay to drive."

The Chief paused. Jake knew he could take issue with the beer he had drunk at the Looms' house, but that wasn't important now, was it? Or maybe it was. Jake couldn't tell.

"Who threw the party at Steps?"

"I have no idea."

"Please, Jake."

"I have no clue."

"Did you know anyone there?"

"I knew everyone there. It was a graduation party. The seniors were there. Probably they all kicked in money and found somebody to buy the keg."

"Someone like who? David Marcy? Luke Browning?"

"You want to blame them, go ahead," Jake said. David and Luke were trouble; Luke had an older brother named Larry who was doing time at Walpole for selling cocaine. "They were both there, but neither one of them was bragging about buying the keg. I don't know who bought the keg."

The Chief said, "Fair enough."

Jake said, "I forgot. On the way to Steps we stopped to pick up Demeter Castle."

"Where did you pick her up?" the Chief asked.

"At the end of her street."

"At the end of her street? Not at her house?"

"Correct." Did Jake need to state the obvious here?

"So she was sneaking out, then. Her parents didn't know she was going out?"

"I didn't ask her about that," Jake said.

"And she had alcohol with her?" the Chief asked.

Jake felt relieved. He wasn't ratting her out if the Chief already knew. "A bottle of Jim Beam."

"Why did you pick up Demeter? Was it pre-arranged?"

"No, it was last-minute. She sent Penny a text message."

"A text message."

"Saying she had a bottle and she wanted to go out."

"And for that reason, you went to pick her up. Because she had a bottle."

"Well," Jake said, "yeah, sort of."

"So if she hadn't texted saying she had a bottle, you wouldn't have picked her up?"

"She texted saying, 'Come pick me up,' and we picked her up."

"So you're friends with her?"

"Sort of," Jake said. "I mean, yes. I've known her my entire life. Our parents are friends. You know they're friends. Why are you making me explain something you already know?"

"Who drank from the bottle?"

"Well, when we picked her up, it was already half gone. So it's probably safe to say that Demeter had been drinking from the bottle. And then Hobby and I had some."

"How much?"

"I don't know," Jake said. "A couple of swigs?"

"Did Penelope drink from the bottle?"

"No," Jake said. "Penny didn't drink. She didn't like it. It made her sick." Did he have to tell the Chief about the game of strip poker in tenth grade at Anders Peashway's house, where they were drinking vodka and grape Kool-Aid and Penny puked into the Peashways' clawfoot tub? "She had an incident a couple years ago and never drank again."

"So what happened at Steps Beach?" the Chief asked.

Jake put his head in his hands. What *had* happened at Steps Beach? He wasn't sure. He remembered swigging from Demeter's bottle before they got out of the Jeep, he remembered taking off his shoes, he remembered trudging up over the dunes and seeing the orange blaze of the fire and hearing a Neon Trees song playing on somebody's iPod, he remembered Penny in the sand next to him, she was drinking Evian water, always Evian water, it was soothing to her vocal cords, she said. She had to stay out of the path of the smoke from the fire, the smoke could harm her vocal cords, one cigarette or toke of marijuana could alter them forever.

At the party Penny had been in a fragile mood. She had been feeling fragile a lot lately, crying over things like graduation and how sad it was that the seniors were graduating and how scary it was that they themselves were now seniors and that this time next year it would be *them* graduating and leaving everyone behind. Penny was especially worried about leaving her mother. She and Zoe were best friends. After Penny lost her virginity to Jake, she had gone right home and climbed into bed with Zoe and told her everything.

Except lately, there had been things that Penny was telling only Ava.

"Like what?" Jake had asked her.

Penny had ignored this question, which infuriated Jake, though he realized that if there were things that she was telling only to his mother, then she wouldn't be inclined to turn around and tell him what they were.

Penny had said, "I'll be sad to leave Ava."

And then — then! — Jake remembered another thing Penny had said:

"I just want to stay in this moment forever. Like in a bubble, you know? You and me and the fire, staring at the edge of adulthood but never quite reaching it."

Jake repeated these words to the Chief, and the Chief wrote them down carefully, then cleared his throat. He opened his mouth to speak, and Jake thought, Don't say it.

"What else do you remember about the party?" the Chief asked.

What else? Kids drinking, smoking cigarettes, smoking weed, pairing off and heading down the beach to make out, kids talking to Jake and Penny, asking them what they were going to do over the summer—Jake was working at the newspaper, Penny had a job hostessing at the Brotherhood, and the last three weeks before school started, she was going to music camp in Interlochen, Michigan. Jake and Penny had repeated these plans to half a dozen people. What Jake didn't say was that he was planning on taking Penny away to Boston, where they were going to spend the night at the Hotel Marlowe, which would cost a fortune, but Jake had been saving his money for something spectacularly romantic, something that Penny would never forget, and that was what he'd come up with.

"We hung out," Jake said. "And then we left."

"Okay," the Chief said, scooting his chair forward. This was what he'd been waiting for, of course, the details of their leaving. "So whose idea was it to leave?"

Jake couldn't remember, even though it had been less than two hours earlier. The party was breaking up, and Demeter materialized, her hair hanging in her face and her mouth slack, the way it got when she was smashed. Demeter was a nice girl deep down; she'd been a part of Jake's life forever and ever, but something had changed in her, she had developed a sharp, shining edge that seemed dangerous. Jake knew enough about girls to know that it had to do with her weight and the fact that she didn't have close friends and didn't do as well as she ought to in school. The edge was her defense. She could be mean, sarcastic, snide—even with Penny, and Penny was the only person who was always nice to her. When Demeter had texted earlier that night, above Jake and Hobby's unspoken protests, Penny had said, "Let's go pick her up. She's just sitting home drinking, poor thing." Demeter had taken up drinking with a vengeance, which Jake found ironic since her parents were teetotalers and pillars of the community.

On the beach Demeter had said, "I have to pee. Come with me, Penny."

Penny had stood up, wiped the sand off her butt, and dutifully followed Demeter into the dunes.

Now Jake wondered if Penny had had to pee as well or if she'd just gone along because Demeter asked her to. What he remembered now was that once the girls had vanished, he had gone looking for Hobby and found him drinking a beer, talking to Patrick Loom. Hobby had a way with people that Jake envied. Hobby was such a phenomenal athlete that people expected him to be as dumb as a bag of hammers, annoyingly self-congratulatory, or at the very least overly interested in the topic of sports. But Hobby socialized like an adult at a cocktail party. He held his drink a certain way, he tilted his head so that you knew he was listening, he asked perceptive questions. He shone so brightly that he made other people shine too. Jake had a lot going for him, everyone told him so, but he was envious of Hobby.

He'd nudged Hobby's elbow. "Hey, man, we're going."

Hobby grinned. "Cool." He scanned the dispersing crowd. "Have you seen Claire?"

"Not in a while," Jake said. "Did you text her?"

"I did, but I got nothing back. She must have left." Hobby looked wistful. He could have had any girl at Nantucket High School, he could have plucked them out one by one and used them like Kleenexes, but that had never been his style. He liked girls, respected them, treated them like human beings. Claire Buckley was his current favorite, but she and Hobby were casual. Nothing like Jake and Penny: Jake would never have let Penny out of his sight at a party like this, even for a second. Except for right now—he realized that she and Demeter were taking a long time. Jake eyed the dunes; he could see people moving up there, but it was too dark to tell exactly who they were.

He said to Hobby, "I'll meet you at the car."

Hobby dumped his beer. "I'm coming."

The next thing Jake had a distinct memory of was leaning up against the driver's side of the Jeep, inhaling big gulps of night air. He was drunk enough that Penny would have to drive. He couldn't afford to get pulled over. His father was the publisher of the paper, and if Jake got caught, his name would appear in the police blotter, a blanket of shame would shroud the Randolph name, and Jake's prospects for Princeton or Dartmouth would be dashed, just like that.

Penny would drive. They would drop Demeter off first.

Then he realized something was wrong. Penny grabbed the keys out of his hand. She was crying. When Jake said, "Jesus Christ, Pen, what's wrong?" Penny screamed. When he tried to pry the keys out of her hand, she swung at him. He had never seen her act like that before; it was as if she were possessed. He got a sick feeling that she had heard about what had happened between him and Winnie Potts in Winnie's basement after the cast party for *Grease*. But what had she heard, and who had told her? Jake remembered looking at Demeter to see if she could shed any light on the situation, but Demeter's face was closed up tight. Her eyes were blank, her motions robotic; she was shitfaced drunk. Maybe *that* was the problem, maybe Demeter had said something mean to Penny while they were in the dunes. Oh God, Jake hoped that was the case.

Demeter climbed into the back and fastened her seat belt, and Jake tried not to notice how the belt cut into her belly. She had that shining edge, she kept it hidden most of the time, but then she unsheathed it. That must be it, then, and it had nothing to do with Winnie Potts, oh please.

Penny flung open the door. She was having a hard time catching her breath. The sobs kept coming, one more strangled than the next.

Hobby said, "Jeez, Pen, pull yourself together."

Jake said, "Penny, what is it? What *is* it?"

Penny slammed the door and started the engine, and even though Jake had been drinking, he was coherent enough to realize that she was in no condition to drive. He tried to pull the keys from the ignition, but Penny batted at him with open palms and Hobby snickered in the back and Penny screamed again, and the scream reminded Jake of another time, another place: his mother when she found Ernie dead in his crib. Jake got goosebumps, his head started to spin, he feared for a second that he was going to puke. Penny shifted into drive, and they screeched around Lincoln Circle, and the motion made Jake feel even sicker and he thought, Please stop, Penny, please stop the car. But he was too nauseated to speak. He breathed in and out through his nose, he tasted the Jim Beam in the back of his throat.

To the Chief, Jake said, "I had been drinking, so Penny drove my car. Demeter was drunk, and Hobby doesn't have his license. Penny was sober, but she was upset about something."

"About what?" the Chief asked.

"I honestly don't know," Jake said. He had been hoping it was something Demeter had said in the dunes, or maybe it was something Penny and Demeter had seen — maybe Claire Buckley had been up there having sex with Luke Browning, and Penny was upset on her brother's behalf. Maybe someone they knew had been shooting heroin or doing something even more heinous that Jake couldn't conceive of. He had a ghastly feeling, though, that this was about him and Winnie Potts and that night in her basement. Jake had been monitoring the situation for weeks, and he'd heard nothing. Winnie had been reserved but cool, but who knew what she'd said to her close friends, and who knew what those friends had said to others? If it was going to come out, it would be on a night like graduation night, when everyone was drinking. When secrets washed up like dead bodies on the beach. Jake needed to get Penny alone, they had to drop off Demeter and then Hobby. Maybe they could go for a walk on the beach so he could figure out what the problem was. He couldn't do it with other people in the car, he couldn't do it while she was driving. His more immediate problem was getting Penny to slow down, or they were going to get pulled over for sure. She was going fifty on New Lane and then nearly sixty on Quaker. She took the turn onto Hummock Pond Road so fast that Jake was sure the Jeep was going to flip. It wasn't built to go that fast. His stomach lurched, he could feel the beer sloshing around inside him, and he imagined the Jim Beam lying on top of the beer, like an oil slick on water. He felt all hot and queasy. Penny rocketed up the hill by the Maria Mitchell Observatory, and Jake said, "Penny, slow down!" It was June, and the observatory sometimes had open nights when there would be all kinds of people crossing the street. Plus, the police liked to hide in a spot just below the crest of the hill to catch speeders.

But Penny didn't slow down. She sped up and put all four windows down so that air whipped through the car in a way that was almost violent. Jake managed to glance at the backseat, where he saw Hobby pitched forward, his widening eyes on the speedometer, and Demeter with her hair blowing, a dreamy look on her face.

The wind made Jake's eyes dry. His stomach had stopped churning and was now clenched in cold fear. He could see Penny's leg tensed with the strain of pushing the pedal to the floor. He imagined the doors flying off the Jeep and the roof and the tires popping off and the whole thing lifting up into the night sky like Chitty Chitty Bang Bang. Penny was biting her lower lip; her eyes were bright and brimming with tears.

She's not right, Jake thought. He knew when a woman wasn't right from watching his mother, and Penny wasn't right. He thought of all the time Penny spent lounging across the bottom of his mother's bed, worshipping at the throne of the manic-depressive queen. His mother had become some kind of role model for Penny—but why? Why?

"Penny!" he shouted. "You have to slow down! Please!"

She screamed. Jake saw something glittering in front of them. It was the ocean. This was the end of the road.

"Penny!" he said.

"Pull the brake!" Hobby shouted.

Jake thought briefly of the ruined transmission, thousands of dollars of repair work, but then he realized Hobby was right and so he yanked on the emergency brake, but he was too late, they were launching off the lip of the embankment.

They were flying.

JORDAN

The day after the accident, he didn't know what to do, and so he worked. He was back in the office Sunday night at seven o'clock. He was the only one in, that was what he'd wanted, he needed a place to be alone, to think, to sort everything out. The phone rang off the hook—of course, people were hearing the news secondhand or thirdhand and wanted more information. In situations like these he usually leaned on the Web site, but at that moment the Web site featured a big picture of Patrick Loom in his cap and gown, pumping his fist in the air. The headline read: "Nantucket Graduates 77 Seniors. More than 70% Headed for Four-Year Colleges." On a deeper page, there was a picture of

Penny singing the National Anthem, the hem of her blue flowered sundress lifted a little by the wind. The first thing Jordan did was delete that picture.

But that was all he could do.

He had never come across a story he couldn't report. It was a commandment in the newspaper world: you printed the news, no matter what. You printed the story about the governor's sleeping with prostitutes or the senator's love child, even when the senator had been your college roommate or the governor was your wife's uncle. Jordan's grandfather's brother-in-law had stolen a car and driven it into Gibbs Pond—a relative misdemeanor that was nevertheless the leading news story that week in 1930—and Jordan's grandfather had put it on the front page, complete with his brother-in-law's mug shot.

Jordan took a deep breath. He reminded himself that he didn't have any actual information other than that Penelope Alistair, age seventeen, was dead, and Hobson Alistair, also age seventeen, was at Mass General in a coma. There had been a car accident; Penny had been driving a Jeep registered to Jordan himself. It was the Jeep that Jordan had given to Jake on his seventeenth birthday—because Jake had turned out to be a great kid, despite some pretty punishing circumstances.

Here were the other things that Jordan knew:

—Zoe had slapped him across the face in
  public, in the hospital waiting room.
—Zoe was not taking his calls.
—Jake Randolph had a bruised right knee
  and a cut across the top of his left cheek
  but was otherwise fine.
—Demeter Castle didn't have a scratch on
  her but was suffering from shock.
—A nearly empty bottle of Jim Beam had
  been found in Demeter Castle's handbag.
—Jake Randolph and Demeter Castle had
  been wearing seat belts. Penelope Alistair
  and Hobson Alistair had not been
  wearing seat belts.
—The airbags had deployed.
—Penelope Alistair had died of a broken
  neck. Nurses at the hospital had taken a
  blood sample for the tox screen, but the
  results had not yet been released.
—Nantucket Auto Body had hauled the
  Jeep up off the beach in the early hours of
  Sunday morning, and it was being kept,
  for now, in the back lot at the police
  station.

There were many more things that Jordan didn't
know. What had happened? Why had Penny been
driving so fast? Jake claimed to have no idea, but

Jordan sensed that his son was lying, or partially lying. He worried that Jake and Penny had had a fight, or that Jake had perhaps even broken up with her. But Jake was as enamored with Penny as Jordan could imagine any seventeen-year-old kid's being. Had Jordan been flirting with another girl? Had he had five or six beers and done something stupid? He said no, he told Jordan that everything had been fine one minute, and then the next minute, not.

Jordan had been forced to wake Ava up out of a deep sleep to tell her that there'd been an accident and he was going to the hospital. Ava had opted to let him go alone, once she knew that Jake was okay. He said he'd call her with any news, but he was pretty certain she'd succumb to the Ambien in her bloodstream and fall back to sleep. And so he didn't call. When he got back to the house at five-thirty, his cheek burning from Zoe's slap, Ava was still asleep, and Jake was in his room bawling like a baby. Jordan was torn between going to console his son and telling his wife about the awful thing that had happened.

He had studied Ava at that moment—her eyequilt covering the upper half of her face and mussing her hair, her mouth gaping open in delirious sleep—and hated her. And he hated himself. He knew, somehow, that this was all his fault.

He shook Ava's shoulder gently until she woke
and sat up and removed her eye-quilt. She was dis-
oriented and no doubt more than a little scared.
Jordan hadn't set foot in that room in years until
earlier that night.

She said, "What is it?"

He said, "Penny's dead, and Hobby is in a coma.
They flew him to Boston."

Ava's face remained as still and calm as a mask.
Jordan wanted to throttle her. Could she not hear
her son wailing?

She pulled off her eye-quilt, then stared at it in
her hands. Tears streamed down her face, and a sob
escaped her. Jordan knew he should reach out and
comfort his wife, but she hadn't voluntarily accepted
a touch from him in a very long time, so instead he
handed her a tissue. She blotted it against each eye,
as if cleaning a spill off the counter. Her hoarse sobs
continued. "Oh God," she said. "Poor Zoe." Jordan
took an indecent amount of interest in watching Ava
cry. Maybe he was in shock. But then he realized he
was simply amazed: for the first time in years, Ava
was crying for someone other than herself.

Three days later, the deadline for the paper loomed.
Jordan sat in his office with the door closed, which
was highly unusual. Normally he sat at his desk out
on the floor, where he could see and hear every-

thing that was going on. He had given his staff, and especially his assistant, Emily, strict orders not to say anything about the accident beyond confirming that there had been one fatality and the matter was still under investigation.

Hobby was in a coma, his condition unchanged. Lynne Castle called Jordan's cell phone every day with an update. Every day Jordan asked, "How's Zoe?" And Lynne said, "About how you'd expect. She really only talks to Al." It had, perversely, made Jordan feel better to know that Lynne Castle was in exile from Zoe's confidences, too.

Lynne addressed the unspoken question by saying, "I'm sure she feels like she hates us right now, because our children are safe."

"Is that why?" Jordan said.

He had to write a story; he couldn't just pretend the accident had never happened. He thought about handing off the assignment to Lorna Dobbs, who was his best news writer, and just doing the final edit on it. He wanted to write the article himself, but how could he? Better to give it one degree of separation. He called Lorna into his office.

Lorna Dobbs wasn't an attractive woman—she had thinning hair and a pale, pinched face—but she was smart and, more important, perceptive. She could have had a second career as a detective or a psychotherapist.

Jordan said, "I want you to write a story about the accident. Call the Chief and get what you can."

She nodded slowly. "Okay."

"It's sensitive," he said. "Obviously."

"Obviously," Lorna repeated. "Am I only covering the accident, or are we doing a tribute to the life of the girl?"

A tribute to Penny: there would be dozens of people who would want to be quoted, and a list of her accomplishments would have to be compiled, and they would need photos. They had some pictures on file, he knew, including the brand-new one of her singing the National Anthem at graduation. Hours before her death. But could he reasonably print a piece of this nature without Zoe's input?

"Just the accident," Jordan said. "Let's hold off on the tribute until..."

"Until we know about the boy?"

"Yes."

"Should I call Mass General to ask if they can give me any more details about his status?" Lorna asked.

"Yes," Jordan said. "But tread lightly, please."

"Of course," Lorna said.

Lorna emailed the story to him two hours later. Jordan saw it hit his inbox and immediately got a headache. There had been other grisly news moments in his career—certain Town Meetings, the cocaine bust of '97, the murder of a girl by her lover—but this was by far the worst.

He clicked on the article.

Car Crash on Cisco Beach Claims Life of Nantucket Student

At approximately 12:50 a.m. on Sunday, June 17, a fatal car accident occurred at the end of Hummock Pond Road. The car, a 2009 four-door Jeep Sahara driven by Nantucket High School junior Penelope Alistair, 17, crashed onto the sand at Cisco Beach after traveling at speeds in excess of 80 m.p.h. The car is registered to *Nantucket Standard* Editor-in-Chief Jordan Randolph and was primarily used by Mr. Randolph's son, Jacob Randolph, 17, who was in the passenger seat at the time of the accident but who was unhurt. Also in the car were Miss Alistair's twin brother, Hobson Alistair, 17, and Demeter Castle, 17. Miss Castle was unhurt, police officials said, but Hobson Alistair was flown in a Medflight helicopter to Mass General for the treatment of multiple broken bones and severe head trauma that has left the Nantucket High School student in a coma.

Police Chief Edward Kapenash said the cause of the accident was excessive speed. "I don't have to tell you how this kind of accident stuns and saddens a community. Here at the NPD, our thoughts and prayers are with the Alistair family."

The Chief said that no mechanical problems had been found with the Jeep. He said the four youths were driving home from an informal graduation party on Steps Beach and that the exact reason for Miss Alistair's excessive speed was still under investigation. The Chief said that both front airbags deployed but that Miss Alistair, who was not wearing her seat belt, died of a broken neck. Hobson Alistair was also unbelted, the Chief said.

A spokesperson at Mass General said that Hobson Alistair was in intensive care and that there had been no change in his condition since Sunday morning.

Jordan read the article, reread it, and read it again. It was spare and factual; Lorna had done as he'd asked. The quote from the Chief was good. There was no mention of alcohol; that was a gift from the Chief, Jordan supposed. No mention of a tox report, pending or otherwise.

Okay, he would run it.

It was just as Marnie and Jojo were pulling together the final layout that Jordan received a call from Al Castle.

Al said, "Zoe asked me to give you a message."

Jordan's heart leapt. This was all he'd been waiting for: a message from Zoe.

Jordan said, "What?"

"She doesn't want anything in the paper," Al said. "Not one word."

"Excuse me?"

"She doesn't want a single thing about this in the paper. That's what she said: 'Not one word.'"

"Not one word."

"That's what she said."

"I can't not say anything, Al."

"You own the paper," Al said. "You don't have to answer to anyone."

"So what are you suggesting?" Jordan asked. "You think I should drop the story? Pretend it didn't happen? Ignore it?"

"That's what Zoe told me to tell you: 'Not one word.'"

"But the piece I'm planning to run is benign. Just the facts about the accident. It barely says anything."

"Jordan," Al Castle said. Here it came: the elder-statesman speech. Al had just six years on Jordan, but he might as well have had sixty. He occasionally used a tone of voice that was meant to remind Jordan that he had been a selectman for twelve years and chairman for the last nine of those, which somehow made him a repository of wisdom. "Zoe is barely hanging on to her sanity. She has only said about two sentences to me in the four days that I've been here, and she's asked for nothing but this. She doesn't want you to report on the accident at all. Now..." Al paused. "Zoe is your friend too, and so all I can do is ask you to please heed her request. She's lost her daughter, Jordan."

"I'm aware of that, Al." Jordan didn't like to get shitty with Al, it had only ever happened once or twice that he remembered, but now he began to wonder whether this gag order had actually come from Zoe or if it was coming from Al himself. Al wouldn't want the accident written up in the paper because his daughter had been in the car. His daughter had been the one with the bottle of Jim Beam. "I can't not print *anything*," he said.

"Sure you can," Al said. "It's your paper." And with that he hung up.

Half an hour until deadline, and Marnie and Jojo kept knocking to see if Jordan had made a decision yet about the front page. He'd told them he was on the fence about the layout. He hadn't said anything about the content, or about killing the piece altogether.

He didn't know what to do. Believe Al Castle? Al Castle wouldn't have lied about Zoe's words or made them up. He could be a pompous ass at times, but he didn't lie. So Zoe really must have asked him to tell Jordan not to print a word. *Not one word.* She was the mother of the victims. She was his lover. He had to separate the two. If she were any other woman, would he concede?

He was a newspaperman like his father, grandfather, and great-grandfather. Zoe was basically asking him to wage war on his genetic makeup. She was asking him to change the code in his chromosomes.

He deleted the file. He called Lorna in and told her he was killing the story. She nodded calmly. Jordan opened his mouth to explain, but Lorna pivoted and left his office. He didn't know if she was angry or if she was merely saving him the indignity of trying to explain. He then told Marnie and Jojo he was killing the lead story and replacing it with a general graduation piece. They both stared at him baldly for a moment, and then Marnie excused herself, which meant she was going out back to have a cigarette. Maybe all three of them would quit. Marnie and Jojo didn't have children, but Lorna had two boys — did it matter either way? Jordan decided not to issue an explanation. He owned the paper, as Al had pointed out; he made the decisions, and this was his decision.

Back in his office with the door closed, he quieted his revolting instincts by saying to himself, This is the one thing I can do for her now.

Fifteen days after the accident, a week after Hobby regained consciousness, Zoe held a funeral service for Penny. Zoe wasn't a religious person, she didn't belong to any church, but she had asked Al Castle to arrange for the service to be held at St. Mary's. She asked Jake to be a pallbearer, along with Patrick Loom, Colin Farrow, Anders Peashway, and some of Hobby's other teammates. Eight strapping, handsome, and very young men carried Penny's coffin out of the hearse and lifted it onto the carriage that rolled down the aisle. Hobby attended the funeral on a hospital gurney that orderlies placed between the front pew and the altar. Hobby was half boy, half mummy, but he had his mind back, and he cried openly in a ruined voice. Jordan had heard a rumor that Hobby had asked to speak but Zoe had said no. She couldn't handle it. Jake had also asked to speak, as had Annabel Wright and Mrs. Yurick the music teacher, but Zoe had said no to them all. The priest said a few words about Christ and forgiveness and the glory of the hereafter, but Jordan—who was sitting with Ava, halfway back on the left—felt that it was all wrong. It was too stiff, too formal, too religious and scripted. It had nothing to do with Penny. Couldn't Zoe see that? Zoe was sitting in the front pew alone, wearing a black suit that Jordan had never seen before, a suit befitting a corporate boardroom, and that was wrong too, he felt. It was a disguise; this funeral was a masquerade. Zoe was hiding. Where was she, really? Because that woman up there wasn't anyone he recognized.

Well, yes, of course, he thought. Losing a child changed a person. Look at what it had done to Ava.

The church was packed. There was an apron of mourners gathered around the outside of the building, spilling across the street and down the block.

Why not let Jake speak? He had spent days writing something. Jordan asked to read it, but Jake wanted him to wait and hear it at the service along with everyone else. Then when Zoe said no, Jake was crushed. Jordan had almost intervened on his son's behalf and spoken to Zoe directly for the first time since the accident—but then he thought, She's punishing Jake because he survived. But why not let Hobby speak? Jordan realized that if this service contained too much of Penny, Zoe wouldn't be able to bear it.

At the end of the service, nine girls gathered before the altar: the madrigal group from the high school. The girls wore the same black skirts and white blouses that they performed in. They lined up, leaving a gap in the left front, where Penny usually stood. Jordan had never seen anything so powerful. The girls launched into "Ave Maria," and everyone in the church stood, but Jordan's eyes never strayed from Zoe. Her hands were clasped to her chest, her eyes were closed, her lips were moving.

Jordan thought, You did it, Zoe. He thought, Bravo.

ZOE

On the day that Jordan Randolph and his wife and son left for Perth, Australia, Zoe stood on her deck, which faced the mighty ocean, and she screamed at every plane that crossed the horizon, though she had no idea which one was theirs.

At some planes she screamed, "Fuck you, Jordan Randolph!"

At other planes she screamed, "I love you, Jordan Randolph!"

JORDAN

He never printed a word about the accident. People criticized him for this. A few advertisers pulled ads, but his paper was the only game in town, so in trying to hurt him, they hurt only themselves. He asked his assistant, Emily, what was being said around town. Emily was candid, Emily was no-bullshit, Emily knew everyone on the island. She was the right person to ask.

She said, "They say you're covering it up because the brakes on the Jeep were faulty. They say you're sweeping it under the rug because your son was involved. They say you're trying to protect Al Castle's daughter, who had a bottle of Jack Daniel's in her bag and pressured Penny into drinking with her in the dunes. They say Ted Field is withholding the tox report." Emily swallowed. "They say it was the mother's fault, for never making those kids buckle their seat belts. They say her car, the orange one, doesn't even *have* seat belts. They say the girl was mentally unstable. They say it was a suicide. They say it was a two-way suicide pact between Penny and your son, only your son fastened his seat belt at the last minute. They say it was a four-way suicide pact. They say the four kids were on acid, and that's why Ted Field is withholding the tox report. They say the Castle girl practices witchcraft. They say Penny was smoking Oxycontin that she got from your wife, and *that's* why Ted Field is withholding the tox report."

"Jesus," Jordan said. They said all of this, but not...? Was Emily holding out on him to spare his feelings? Would Emily do that? Certainly not. "Do they say anything else?"

"Anything *else?*" Emily asked.

People would say what they said, and what they said was that Jordan Randolph decided to take a leave of absence from the newspaper and move his wife and son to Perth, Australia, because he wanted to escape the scandal and the shame brought on his family and his family's newspaper by the death of Penelope Alistair.

And that would be partially right.

He hadn't reported the story, and this mere fact had changed the way he felt about the newspaper. All his life he'd believed the newspaper to be an absolute. It was his job as editor to print all the facts and only the facts—except for the editorials. A newspaper was pure; it was holy. And by not print-ing a word about the accident, Jordan had, in a way, disproved this. What was pure and holy in this case was honoring the wishes of a woman who had lost one child and was in danger of losing another. That woman was his lover. But that didn't matter. Jordan convinced himself that he would have done the same for anyone.

Not printing the story made him realize that the newspaper wasn't the most important thing in his life. It could be left behind. Someone else could run it for a year, or indefinitely, and he wouldn't have to worry about its integrity's being compromised, because he'd already accomplished that.

Ava had been asking him to go back to Australia for nearly twenty years. Jordan had never indulged her in this request after his first disastrous trip. It was her nation and her family, not his nation and his family. Ava had traveled back herself a handful of times, both alone and with Jake. But she hadn't been back in four years now. Not since Ernie died.

Jake didn't want to live in Australia. But if they left the island, Jordan knew, things would be better for him.

Ultimately, though, Jordan's decision had nothing to do with Jake or Ava or the newspaper or public opinion about how he'd handled coverage of the accident.

It had to do with Zoe.

For the nine days that Hobby lay in a coma in Mass General, Jordan did not hear from her. This was nine days of lying on razor blades, of picking up his phone and checking for text messages or missed calls — there were dozens of each but none from her — of debating should he or shouldn't he hop on a plane and go up there and see her. But Al Castle was in Boston, acting as a watchdog over the situation, and what would Al think if Jordan just showed up? Al might have his suspicions already. But then again, what did Al Castle matter in comparison to Zoe, who had lost her *daughter?* Zoe had slapped Jordan across the face at the hospital and nearly sent his glasses flying. Jordan had never been struck like that by anyone in his life, and the curious thing was that the slap had excited him. It had been filled with passion as well as a lot of other deep and complicated feelings, none of which she'd been able to voice, something that had been a problem for as long as they'd been together. When she left messages on his cell phone in the middle of the night, she always said, "I have no one to talk to about you other than you."

Jordan had composed text messages and then deleted them, he had sat up nights thinking, Should I call? There had been times in their relationship when Zoe said she wanted "space," but what she really meant was that she wanted Jordan closer. It was her own confusing calculus. Jordan convinced himself that the slap and the silence meant that she wanted him there to take care of her. He called her at ten o'clock on the night of the candlelight vigil —

he hadn't attended because Jake didn't want to go—but when his call went to voicemail, he hung up. Then at midnight he called back, and the call went to voicemail again, and this time he managed to croak out one word—*Zoe*—but nothing else. He tried a third time because three was a magic number, three wishes, the third time a charm, so at three in the morning he called—imagining the dim, hushed corridors of the hospital, Zoe asleep across four molded plastic chairs as Al had so vividly described, with the pancake-flat pillow and the pilled blanket that some benevolent nurse had brought her—and he thought, Goddammit, Zoe, pick up. I have no one to talk to about you other than you. But once again his call went to voicemail, and he hung up.

His head and heart were scrambled. He had never imagined this kind of emotional duress—his son heartbroken, his lover destroyed, his wife strangely neutralized, the whole island breathing down his neck, either blaming him or looking for an explanation. Penelope—a girl Jordan had adored—dead. He had to grieve too. He had to worry about Hobby and pray too. Zoe's children were, in so many ways, like his own children, but they *weren't* his own children—under these terrible circumstances, that fact had become resoundingly clear. *His* child was fine.

Zoe didn't return his calls.

Go to Boston, he thought. If she turns you away, she turns you away.

The last time he had been with Zoe was the Thursday before graduation. Tuesday and Thursday mornings were their times—Jordan drove to Zoe's house after the kids had left for school. In the summer they sat on the deck and in the winter they settled in front of the woodstove. Occasionally they walked on the beach. They talked about everything, though their favorite topic was their three kids. They also did a fair amount of talking about Ava, and lately Jordan had sensed that Zoe was growing restless and impatient with his decision to stay married to her. Zoe pretended that she wanted Jordan to leave Ava for his own good. How could he continue to live with her mood swings? Since Ernie died Ava had had only two settings: she was either angry and combative or morose and withdrawn. She held Jordan responsible for Ernie's death, and Jordan had carried this impossible burden without a word of complaint. But why? Zoe wanted to know. Why not reclaim his own life?

Here was the spot for a big, huge sigh. It was far more complicated than Zoe knew. Zoe had never had to share her kids with anyone else; she had always been their only parent. She had been married for only six months, and that was a long time ago.

Hence, Jordan suspected, there were things about marriage that Zoe had either forgotten or never learned in the first place. Such as the fact that even the worst marriages were stronger than anyone might expect. Jordan couldn't just get up and walk out the door. He and Ava had two children, one living and one dead; they had a home and a way of life. Over the past four years that way of life had deteriorated, but it couldn't be discounted. If Jordan moved out, Jake would choose to move out with him, he knew, and without their son Ava would perish. The best thing would be for Ava to go back to Australia and regain her happiness, but she wouldn't go for any length of time without Jake. Surely Zoe could see how impossible the situation was. And what did Zoe want, anyway, that she didn't already have? Sometimes she made it sound as if she wanted Jordan to move in with her, live with her, marry her. But this was ridiculous. Zoe, more than anyone Jordan had ever met, relished her freedom. She had been married, for those six months, to the man who was Penny's and Hobby's father, but Jordan had a hard time even imagining that. Zoe wearing a ring on her left hand, Zoe plunking down breakfast, lunch, and dinner for someone, Zoe relinquishing authority over the remote control or the temperature of the water in the shower, Zoe sharing her bed? She answered to no one except her kids.

On the Thursday morning when Jordan had last seen Zoe, they had lain together on the chaise on her deck. Zoe was feeling melancholy about graduation. In the fall the kids would be seniors, and this time next year *they* would be graduating. And then they'd be going away to college. And Jordan thought, She's afraid of being alone. But on that morning Zoe was excited, too, about Penny's singing the National Anthem, and about Jake's and Hobby's becoming the leaders they were born to be. Zoe and Jordan were both going to Patrick Loom's graduation party. They liked seeing each other in public; it still held a secret deliciousness for both of them. Zoe always wore something sexy and gorgeous, she put on a perfume that drove Jordan crazy, and she applied sheer lip gloss that made her mouth shine like glass.

They had made love on the chaise outside in the sun and then showered together outdoors, and then Jordan had sat at the kitchen table, his lower half wrapped in a white Turkish cotton towel, while Zoe made him a cheddar and tomato omelet with bacon, fried shredded potatoes, wheat toast with butter and homemade jam, fresh-squeezed orange juice, and hot coffee. He ate gratefully. Zoe was the only person who cooked for him, and it felt like love. He wanted her to join him, but she never did; instead she worked in the kitchen, packing him a lunch: turkey and Swiss and baby mache and honey mustard on whole grain bread, watermelon chunks, pasta salad with asparagus and toasted pine nuts, and a slice of chocolate and peanut-butter tart wrapped in wax paper. She packed all of this in a brown paper bag. Sometimes she slipped notes in with his lunch, but not often enough that he expected it. The notes were a treat.

There had been a note that Thursday, on one of the index cards that she used for recipes, folded in half. It said *I heart you.*

That was Thursday. On Friday Jordan called her on his way home from work, but she was busy prepping platters for Garrick Murray's graduation party and could talk for only a second. On Saturday Jordan saw her at graduation; they sat three seats away from each other, and his gaze meandered to her firm calf muscles — amazing, as she avoided exercise at all costs — and her toenails, filed square and painted dark purple, framed by the vamp of her kitten heels. They chatted privately for a second at the Looms' party and then, right after the kids left, Jordan offered to walk her to her car — he was heading home — but Zoe said she was going to stay a little longer. She flashed him a wicked grin. Zoe had, or pretended to have, a crush on Patrick's father, Stuart Loom, which Jordan in turn pretended made him jealous, only Jordan wasn't pretending. It *did* make him jealous, but Stuart Loom was married, and Zoe and Alicia Loom were friends, and so there was really nothing for Jordan to worry about. He left Zoe at the Looms' party. Everything was fine.

The next time he saw her, they were in the hospital waiting room, and she slapped him. And now she wouldn't talk to him. Was Lynne Castle's theory true? Was she unable to speak to them because Jake and Demeter were unhurt? Jordan had obeyed Zoe's one wish — he had kept the accident out of the newspaper — and so she couldn't fault him. He had done nothing wrong.

But before Jordan could decide how to approach Zoe, news arrived: Hobby had regained consciousness. He was cogent; there was no brain damage.

Jordan was at home when the call came. It was around ten-thirty at night; Ava was asleep, and Jake was upstairs with his door closed. The caller was Lynne Castle, who had heard from Rasha Buckley, who was at Mass General with Zoe. Jordan felt himself tearing up. He said, "Thank the Lord, Lynne."

And she said, "Oh, yes."

He wanted to call Zoe right that instant, but he couldn't bring himself to do it. She wouldn't be answering her phone anyway. She would be with

Hobby; she would want to talk only to Hobby. Not another soul would matter—not for weeks, maybe not ever.

A week later Zoe called Jake's cell phone to ask him to be a pallbearer at Penny's funeral and to tell him that she didn't want him to speak during the service.

Jordan took this news silently. He wanted to say, "Did she ask about me?"

Ava piped up and said, "She's the mother, Jake. You have to respect her wishes."

Jordan rarely found himself in the same place with both Ava and Zoe. The last time had been at the final performance of *Grease*. And now at the funeral. Ava and Zoe had been good friends once upon a time. After Ernie died, Zoe had brought over food every day for a month. She had taken Jake to the beach; she had let him sleep over whenever he liked.

Ava had let all her friendships fade away—including her friendship with Zoe—and then the romance had developed between Jordan and Zoe, and from that point on Zoe was the one who was keen to avoid seeing Ava. When the two women saw each other, they were civil, saying hello, how are you, good-bye. Jordan wasn't at all sure Zoe would want Ava at the funeral, but how could Jordan get her to stay at home? Ava was kinder than she had been in months. Before the service she walked up to Zoe and took both her hands and kissed her as Jordan watched, waiting for Zoe's inevitable questioning gaze. But Zoe didn't look his way once, not before, during, or after the funeral.

He went to see her three days later. Hobby had been moved to Nantucket Cottage Hospital, where he would have to stay until his bones healed a little more—which might take as long as three weeks. Every day Zoe went to sit with him for two hours in the early morning, then again after lunch, then again from six to eight in the evening. Jordan had ascertained this schedule from Lynne Castle, and armed with this timetable, he waited down the dirt road from her cottage until she pulled in at 8:15 p.m. He gave her a few minutes inside by herself— enough time, he figured, for her to light some citronella candles, pour herself a glass of wine, take off her sandals, and settle into the chaise.

Then he wondered, did she do the same things now that Penny was dead, or did she sink into a pile on the floor and cry?

He pulled in behind her Karmann Ghia in the driveway so she couldn't just get into it and drive off. He approached the house quietly, like a criminal. It wasn't safe for her to live alone out here at the beach, in a house that didn't lock up properly. He'd been telling her that for years, but she never listened to him. She wasn't afraid of anything, she said. Or anyone.

Normally he knocked—two long raps followed by two short ones, Morse code for the letter Z. But this time he slipped in the screen door without announcing himself. The sun was low, but it hadn't set yet. Jordan could see her, as he'd expected, out on the deck—the citronella candles, the glass of wine. Her house, he noted, was a mess. The counter was lined with fruit baskets and decaying flower arrangements and little altars to Penny that her girlfriends from school must have made, complete with photographs and framed poems and stuffed animals. There were empty wine bottles spilling out of the recycling bin. The fridge was probably filled with covered dishes, and somehow this struck Jordan as funny—the idea of other people's bringing Zoe food, inedible offerings that she would eventually toss down the stairs to the beach for the seagulls to eat.

He stepped out onto the deck. "Zoe?" he said.

She looked up, unsurprised. "Hey," she said.

"Hey"? He didn't know what to do with *Hey.* He'd been expecting a *Get out!* He'd been expecting a full glass of sauvignon blanc aimed at his head. But part of him had also held out hope that she'd jump into his arms.

He said, "I came to talk to you."

She said, "Well, yeah, I expected that. Sooner or later."

He didn't dare sit on the chaise with her, though he could see the ghost of them making love there—both of them naked, Zoe riding him, her breasts swinging, him thrusting until she cried out. June 14. Twenty days earlier. A lifetime ago.

He pulled up one of the upright chairs that matched the chaise and rested his elbows on his knees. She was wearing white denim shorts and a navy halter top and the hideous blue rhinestone earrings that Hobby had bought for her the Christmas he was ten, which had become a family joke but which Jordan suspected were a joke no longer. Now she wore them in earnest; now they were likely her favorite earrings. Zoe's hair was naturally dark, and she usually had it cut in an artful shag with the ends colored, but now the red had faded, and Jordan noticed some gray in her part. She looked pale and wore no makeup—she who liked always to be tan, even in the middle of January, and who favored electric-green eyeliner on a conservative day.

Jordan couldn't take his eyes off her. This, he supposed, must be closer to what she'd looked like as a child. He could see Penny in her today, when he had never really seen her there before. Was that tragic or poetic, he wondered—the mother's starting to look more like the daughter only now that the daughter was dead?

"I don't know what to say," he said. He had thought of things in the middle of the night, that was his job as a journalist, getting to the heart of the matter, but all that he'd so carefully scripted escaped him now.

"Nothing to say," she said. "It's not your fault. There was nothing wrong with the car. Penny was just driving too fast. She was upset about something, Hobby said."

"Upset about what?" Jordan said. "Did something happen?"

"She was a seventeen-year-old girl," Zoe said. "Things were happening with her every second of every day. I go back and forth between wanting to know exactly what it was and being afraid to know. Does it matter? I ask myself. She was driving recklessly, and she knew better. She could have killed all four of them, Jordan, and that would have made this conversation a very different one." Zoe looked at the ocean. "Can you imagine?"

If Jake had died in the accident? No, he couldn't imagine.

"What do you feel like?" he asked.

"I can't explain it."

"Try."

"I don't want to try." She slugged back some wine.

"Have you seen the tox report?"

"I have. She was clean," she said.

"She was?"

Zoe flashed her eyes at him. "You didn't doubt that, did you?"

"I didn't know. The other kids were drinking. . . ."

"Well, Penny hadn't had a drink since that horrible night at the Peashways' house."

"But she was the one driving because the other kids had been drinking. Do you feel angry about that?"

"Hobby said Jake offered to drive, but Penny insisted." Zoe rubbed her knees. "You didn't need to come here, Jordan. I don't blame you, and I don't blame your son."

"I did need to come here," Jordan said. "I needed to come here because I love you."

She laughed, a tired bleat. "Ah," she said. "That."

"Yes," he said. "That. Our relationship. My love for you. Do you know how hard it's been not being able to talk to you, Zoe? Not being able to hold you and mourn with you? You shut me out."

"Why is it always all about you?" Zoe asked.

"I'm not talking about me," he said. "I'm talking about us."

"There is no us," Zoe said. "You want to know why I slapped you? Because for nearly two years I believed there *was* an us. But when they told me that Penny was dead and Hobby was in a coma, I realized there was only a me. A me who had lost one child and nearly lost another. And there you were across the room. You were going to go back to your house with your son and your wife. I slapped you because I was angry and hurting, but also because you allowed me to believe that there was an us when there was no us. There was never an us, and there's never going to be an us."

"So what are you saying?" Jordan asked. "You want me to leave Ava? Yes, Zoe, yes: I will leave Ava."

"Now?" Zoe said. She finished her wine and poured herself some more. "Now that I've lost a child, now because you feel sorry for me...."

"That's not why."

"Why, then? Why now and not before?"

"Because I've learned about the power of my feelings. This thing, this crisis, has brought them into focus."

"Do you know how ridiculous you sound?"

Yes, actually, he did know he sounded ridiculous. Yes, he did know he was a day late and a dollar short; he should have left Ava a long time ago. He had thought he was staying with Ava out of honor, but really he'd been staying out of cowardice.

"I want to be with you," he said.

"I can't be with you," Zoe said. "It's over."

"Zoe..."

"For so many reasons," she said.

"You've been through hell," he said.

"Try not to explain my condition to me," Zoe said. "Try to let me process this on my own terms. Let me make my own decisions."

It was dark now. Jordan heard a popping noise, and he saw a flash of light in the sky. He stood up and moved to the edge of the deck. Down the beach, someone was setting off fireworks. He had either forgotten or simply not realized: it was the Fourth of July.

"And the decision you're making is that our relationship is over?" he said.

"Over."

"I don't accept that."

"You're going to have to," she said.

"I don't."

She stood up. She raised her hand, and he flinched, thinking she might slap him again. But instead she removed his glasses and wiped their lenses off on the hem of her blue cotton halter top, and the gesture was so familiar and so tender that Jordan nearly wept. When she placed the glasses back on his face, her hand grazed his cheek, and he feared this might be the last time she would ever touch him.

"Jordan," she said. She paused. Down on the

beach there was the keening of a bottle rocket, followed by a series of explosions. "Jordan, I'm sorry."

That night Jordan drove around the island for hours. It was his home, he had lived here his whole life save for the four years he had spent in Bennington, Vermont, but on this night he drove on roads he hadn't traveled in decades, and all the while fireworks were going off over his head, casting an eerie pink glow over the evening. He drove out the Polpis Road, taking an inland detour at Almanack Pond, winding back in among the acres of horse pasture and secret stands of trees. He drove around to the Sankaty lighthouse, then through Sconset with its ancient, rose-covered cottages, then down to Low Beach Road, where the houses were ten times the size of those cottages, and all built within the last decade. He wound around through Tom Nevers and Madequecham; he had never been quite clear on how the dirt roads connected in Madequecham, and he ended up lost in a scrub-pine forest. He battled through, the brush on either side of the road pinstriping his car. He popped out on a deserted dirt road that eventually led him back to Milestone.

"There is no us," Zoe had said.

He drove all the way out to the farthest edge of the Madaket coast, a trip that took him thirty minutes from the rotary. He and Ava had gone to a party out here years earlier, but he hadn't been back since. From there he traveled to Eel Point and Dionis and out the Cliff and back around until he reached the turn for the place he knew he'd been headed all along: the end of Hummock Pond Road.

Someone had pounded a white cross into the sand. Taller than Jordan, it was decorated with streaming pink ribbons and had bouquets of flowers—some of them fresh—leaning against its base. Jordan wondered if Zoe had seen it.

He couldn't believe that Zoe wanted to face the months and years of pain that were to come without him. But she had made up her mind, and he knew that she meant what she said and not the opposite: she was done. It was over, *for so many reasons.* He hadn't asked her to give him a single one of those reasons, because the reasons didn't matter. All that mattered was that he loved her and now he was alone with his love. He would leave Nantucket because he was weak, and because staying on this island without her wasn't possible. The journey he'd taken that night, the drive down unfamiliar roads, was Jordan's way of saying good-bye.

He started the car and headed back into town, toward home, thinking that he would drop by the hospital to peek in on Hobby, or stop at the cemetery and gaze at Penny's grave or the grave of tiny Ernie Randolph, who had died at eight weeks old.

He suddenly saw the appeal of a wide-open foreign land where every building and curve in the road was benign and bland, where nothing had memories attached, where nothing could pierce him.

At the turnoff for Bartlett's Farm, Jordan's engine began to sputter. He made it a few yards farther and pulled the car over to the side of the road. He had run out of gas.

"There is no us," Zoe had said.

"For so many reasons," Zoe had said.

Jordan climbed out of the car, tucked his keys in his pocket, and began walking toward home.

NANTUCKET

It was big news: the Randolphs were moving to Australia for at least a year, maybe longer. Jordan Randolph was taking a leave of absence from the newspaper, and Marnie Fellowes would run it in his stead. People questioned the logic of pulling Jake Randolph out of school in his senior year. Was it kind or cruel? Was it *wise* from a college-admissions perspective? Some people said Jake didn't want to go. Others said he couldn't wait to get away from Nantucket. Even people who knew next to nothing about the Randolphs' marriage knew that Ava Randolph was dying to move back to her homeland. If it hadn't been for the accident, people would have seen this move as a valiant attempt to fix the marriage. But everyone knew the Randolphs were leaving because of the accident.

The accident was still lurking around the edges of our minds, but it was no longer front and center. It had been, after all, an *accident:* there was no one to blame. Penelope Alistair had been driving too fast, plain and simple. Dr. Ted Field released the tox report, but it turned up nothing. Penny hadn't been drinking or on drugs. She had been upset. People hazarded guesses about the reason for that, but most of those guesses were so absurd that we disregarded them immediately. That the other kids had been drinking was whispered about, of course. If it had been during the school year, some of the parents might have rallied for an alcohol and drug awareness forum, but it was high summer. The mild June weeks turned into scorching July weeks. The summer people arrived in their Suburbans and Hummers, taking all the available parking spots, clogging up the aisles at the Stop & Shop, bringing vacation frivolity and a river of money to the island. Whole days passed during which we didn't think about Penelope Alistair at all. Don't think us callous; life was just moving on. It was summer. We had our own lives to live.

There were reminders, of course. The seven-foot white cross at Cisco Beach was the most visible of these. A few of the girls from the madrigal group started gathering at the cross every evening at sunset to sing. They sang the classical tunes they had practiced so hard, but as their audience grew (one night there were fifteen people, the next night twenty-three), they branched out to cover the Beatles and Elton John. As with anything else, there were detractors. It was in poor taste, someone said, singing each night at the spot where their friend had died. Others felt it was a fitting tribute. The cross itself put some people off. Cisco had been a popular surfing beach, but now a stretch of sand on either side of the cross remained unoccupied during the day.

One summer resident, the mother of two girls, said, "The cross scares my children. I wish they would take it down."

DEMETER

Her parents assumed she was a lost cause, and Demeter took great joy in surprising them. She told her father she intended to go to work for Frog and Toad Landscaping, just as she had said she would.

Monday, July 2, was the day of Penny's funeral—
Demeter attended with her parents and left immediately after the service, surrounded by the mysterious
aura of one who was intimately affected, though how
profoundly, people could only guess—and so Demeter started work the next day, July 3.

Her parents had tried to talk her out of it.

"Are you *sure?*" her mother said. "I don't think
you're ready."

Her father had actually had the temerity to enter
Demeter's room, sit in her papasan chair with his
hands tented like a preacher's, and tell her that she
was very courageous to want to move forward like
this. Then he went on, "But your mother fears, as
do I, that your starting a new job *tomorrow* might
be taking on a little too much a little too soon. If
you're worried about money…"

Here Demeter giggled. She was drunk when her
father came in. She had taken four bottles of wine
and a full icy bottle of vodka—its contents no less
precious to Demeter than liquid gold—from Zoe's
house. But now there was only half a bottle of
wine left, and two fingers of vodka. Demeter knew
one thing: there was no alcohol in this house. She
had considered calling Mrs. Kingsley to let her
know that she was available to babysit, but she was
afraid that Mrs. Kingsley might have heard rumors
about the bottle of Jim Beam found in her posses-

sion and connected it with the bottle of Jim Beam missing from the Kingsleys' liquor cabinet. The Kingsleys were no longer an option. Demeter had to get out into the world, pronto.

"Something funny?" Al Castle asked.

Funny? Well, only if by "funny" he meant sad and pathetic. Demeter's parents were experts in the field of doing her a disservice. They coddled her, they spoiled her, and they refused to hold her accountable for her actions. Every time Lynne Castle knocked on the bedroom door, Demeter was sure the beatings were about to begin—but it was only ever Lynne "checking in" to see if Demeter "needed anything." Lynne Castle delivered snacks and meals on a tray, she carried away the dirty dishes and collected armfuls of Demeter's laundry. She smoothed her daughter's hair and let her know that she was loved and appreciated. Lynne said she thanked God every day that Demeter was safe.

What was wrong with her parents? Didn't they see that they needed to stop bringing her food and make her exercise instead? Didn't they see that she had to get out of her foul-smelling hole of a room and into the sunshine? Didn't they see that she needed to earn money rather than have it handed to her? Didn't they see that the make-believe world they lived in was so paralyzing that their daughter couldn't bear to live in it sober?

I'm fat, she thought. I'm unpopular. I'm a drunk. I said something inexcusable to Penny, which ended up being worse than I ever could have imagined, because now Penny is dead.

Demeter composed her face. Her father was a bit more worldly than her mother; if anyone was going to catch on that she was inebriated, it was Al.

"I want to work, Dad. We told Kerry that I'd work for him, and I plan to stand by that. It has nothing to do with money. It has to do with proving my character."

"It's just so soon," Al Castle said. "Kerry understands what you've been through."

That was doubtful. Demeter suspected that what was really happening here was that Al and Lynne thought it would look bad if she started working too soon. They subconsciously wanted her to stay in her room all summer, growing fatter and stinkier and more bored and slothful and useless—because that way Lynne could continue to tell the women she bumped into at the grocery store that her daughter "wasn't doing too well." This would be preferable, according to the fucked-up social politics of year-round Nantucket, to admitting that just weeks after the tragic accident that had claimed her friend's life, Demeter was productive and happy and loving her new job.

*　　*　　*

She won, as she knew she would. Her parents couldn't keep her from doing anything. On her first day of work Demeter wore cargo shorts, a gray T-shirt, a flannel shirt, socks and sneakers, a bandanna in her hair, and a pair of Ray-Ban Aviators. She looked in the mirror. The outfit wasn't too awful. The flannel shirt was long enough to cover her backside; the shorts came to her knees. She liked the way she looked in her sunglasses, and the bandanna was cool, she thought.

She took a backpack, empty except for two bottles of water and a banana.

"You'll starve," her mother said.

"I'll be fine," Demeter said.

She hadn't driven since the accident, but she drove now; the thought of Al Castle's dropping her off was mortifying. She had a two-year-old Ford Escape, one benefit of her father's owning the car dealership. She drove to the headquarters of Frog and Toad Landscaping, which was out near the airport. She'd polished off the last two fingers of vodka that morning, then brushed her teeth. The vodka so early in the morning on an empty stomach gave her a little sparkle, a secret glow; it took the edge off things and even made her mother seem bearable.

Frog and Toad was the largest landscaping concern on the island. Kerry Trevor employed sixty-five people and ran seventeen teams a day. When Demeter pulled down the dirt driveway, she saw people gathered in the gravel yard in front of the greenhouses. Hispanic men, college kids—everyone was older than Demeter. There was no one from Nantucket High School. It was possible that no one here knew what had happened, other than Kerry himself.

One of the Hispanic men—Demeter was unfortunately reminded of the man who had mopped up her 80-proof puke at the hospital—directed her into a parking spot. She grabbed her backpack and stepped out of the car. The other workers turned and stared at her. She knew what they were thinking: Fat girl. They wouldn't be thinking this meanly; they would be thinking it only as a matter of course. There wasn't enough vodka in the world to take away the daily sting of Demeter's reality.

Kerry Trevor—blond, wiry, bouncing with energy—was giving out assignments. Team 1 to 85 Main Street, Team 2 to 14 Orange Street, Team 3 to Nonantum. Demeter was pretty sure Kerry had seen her walk over, but he hadn't made eye contact with her. The sun was hot, and she was roasting in her flannel shirt. She felt herself break out into a light vodka sweat. This wasn't exactly how she'd imagined her first day. She knew her father had called to prep Kerry for her arrival. She had thought he would take her aside, make sure she was at ease. Team 4 was headed to Tom Nevers. Team 5 . . .

Demeter didn't have a team. Kerry knew this, right? The group was getting smaller. Teams were hopping into the signature green Frog and Toad pickups and pulling out. The typical makeup of the teams seemed to be one older Hispanic man with one or two college kids. Demeter had known she'd be working on a team, but she'd been imagining all girls, girls who didn't shave their armpits and didn't pass judgment. Girls who played Phish in the truck and ate brown-bag lunches of hummus and sprout sandwiches on whole grain bread. Girls who would let Demeter be Demeter, who wouldn't notice her five trips to the bathroom, who wouldn't ask her too many personal questions.

Suddenly Demeter heard her name. She snapped to attention. Kerry was looking right at her, but she hadn't heard what he'd said. She felt as if she were in school, where this exact same thing was always happening.

She hoped her facial expression conveyed her need for clarification without making her appear to be too much of an idiot.

"You're with Jesus, Nell, and Coop," Kerry said.

"Team Nine. Out to Two Seventy-seven Hummock Pond Road."

Demeter stared at the googly-eyed bullfrog on the front of Kerry's T-shirt. The vodka was making her dizzy. Or it was the heat and her absurd choice of flannel? She didn't care what she looked like; she took the flannel shirt off and tied it around her waist. Better, cooler. Jesus, Nell, and Coop. And had Kerry said Hummock Pond Road? Really?

Tap on the shoulder. Tall boy, or perhaps Demeter should classify him as a man. He was about twenty or twenty-one, with dark, shaggy hair and a pronounced Adam's apple. Not too attractive, thank God, but kind-looking.

"I'm Coop," he said. "We're over here."

A green truck, just like all the other trucks. It had two rows of seating, but the backseat was tight, and Demeter immediately became conscious of her size.

"I'm Nell." Nell was a girl with fiery red hair and freckles, wearing an Ithaca T-shirt; nothing threatening about her either. Okay, Demeter thought, this is okay. Do we get to keep our teams?

"I'm Demeter."

"Cool name," Nell said. "Goddess of something."

"The harvest," Demeter said. Another chance to despise her parents. They had named her brothers Mark and William, then gone all Bulfinch's with her.

"The fertility of the earth," Coop chimed in.

"I guess."

"And I'm Jesus," said the Hispanic man. He was about forty and had a musical voice. "Everyone calls me Zeus."

"So we have Zeus and Demeter," Nell said.

Camaraderie. Demeter smiled. This was the real world, out of high school. People were nice. They tried to make you feel included.

"I don't know what I'm doing," Demeter admitted. "I guess Kerry told my dad I might mow?"

No one answered her. Maybe they hadn't heard. Coop tossed Zeus a set of keys, and Demeter had to worry again about how she was going to squeeze into the back of the truck.

Nell said, "Coop, you sit in the back with me?"

"I've been demoted," Coop said.

Demeter blushed. Coop was too tall to sit in the back, he'd be chewing on his knees, but there was no way Demeter would fit. She took the front passenger seat and moved her seat as far forward as it would go.

"Gods and goddesses in the front," Nell said.

That was nice.

They drove out Hummock Pond Road. Demeter thought it might cause her to have some kind of flashback. But the road was sunny and green and leafy, and there were families on bicycles headed to the beach. This road had little in common with the nightmare Demeter remembered. When she closed her eyes, she saw only black.

Zeus pulled in to the driveway for number 277 and they meandered through the woods to a clearing on the pond. The house was stunning, new construction, the shingles still sweet-smelling and yellow. There were no cars in the driveway. Demeter's pulse quickened. Her mouth was cottony from the vodka, and her stomach was starting to complain. She reached into her bag and pulled out a bottle of water.

"Let's go," Coop said.

They climbed out of the truck. The house had a dozen hydrangea bushes in full periwinkle bloom, with beds of impatiens surrounding them. There was green lawn up to the woods. There were window boxes on the first-floor windows and geraniums hanging from the porch. The whole place seemed amazing to Demeter. She lived on the island year-round, she had been born here, she went to school here, and all of that gave her a sense of ownership. But there were houses like this one — hundreds of them, or possibly thousands — that were happy, isolated pockets of Nantucket, and which Demeter hadn't even known existed.

There was a trailer attached to the back of the pickup, and in the trailer was the lawn mower.

Coop pulled it out. It was an unwieldy contraption that looked nothing like either the riding mower or the push mower in Al Castle's garage. Demeter grew anxious. Kerry had told Al that Demeter would be mowing lawns, but the truth was, she didn't even mow the lawn at home. She had grown up with two brothers who did that chore, and then once Mark and Billy were gone, Al Castle had taken great joy in spending Saturday afternoons on his riding mower. Demeter had only once been allowed to mow just the perimeter of the yard.

She gazed at the machine. "I don't know how to use that kind," she confessed.

"No worries," Coop said. "You won't mow for weeks, if ever. It's a privilege you have to earn."

"It *is?*" Demeter said. "Kerry told my dad he was hiring me to mow."

"Ha!" Nell said, though not meanly. "I only got to mow once last summer, and that was because I stuck around after all the kids from Colby went back to school."

"Oh," Demeter said. She felt like an idiot. She had actually thought a summer of mowing would be beneath her, but now she'd discovered she wasn't even good enough to mow.

"I'm mowing," Coop said. "Zeus will check the window boxes and work on the containers in the back. And you two are going to —"

"Weed," Nell said.

"Weed," Demeter repeated. Weed? When she and Al and then Al and Kerry were discussing this job, the word *weed* had never come up. But what had she thought landscapers did? Mowed the grass, ate their lunches in the sun, put their hands in the dirt.

Demeter trailed Nell to the front beds. Nell handed her a pair of gloves, a five-gallon bucket, and a tool that looked like a larger version of what her dentist used to get plaque off her teeth.

"I'm going to do the back beds, and you do these front beds," Nell instructed. "Just dig up all the weeds."

"I don't see any weeds."

"You're kidding, right?" Nell asked.

"No," Demeter said. The impatiens and zinnias were embedded in rich, dark soil.

"Well, this is a weed here," Nell said. She pulled on a green stalk that Demeter had thought was a legitimate plant. "And you have to use your trowel to get it out at the roots, okay? Without traumatizing the root systems of the other plants."

Traumatizing.

"Okay," Demeter said.

"And then when you're done with the front beds, you'll weed the brick walk. You see the green creeping up between the bricks? All of that has to come out."

Demeter eyed the walkway. Weeds were squeezing through the bricks like the mildew that grew on the grout in the high school locker room showers. How would she ever, *ever* get all of those tiny weeds out?

"Okay," Demeter said. She already felt like crying, and she hadn't even started yet.

"Did you bring music?" Nell asked. She pulled an iPod and headphones out of her back pocket.

"No," Demeter said.

"Tomorrow, bring music," Nell said. "It will help." She smiled at Demeter. "I know it's a shitty job, and you're low man on the totem pole. But you'll grow to like it. I did. If you have any questions, come find me, okay?"

"Okay," Demeter said.

Nell vanished around the side of the house. Demeter heard the motor of the mower start, and she watched Coop climb up onto the back of the mower and ride it across the yard standing up, like an Eskimo on a dog sled or a person on water skis. Demeter was glad she wasn't mowing. She was so heavy, she might have broken the mower, or else she might not have been coordinated enough to stay upright as it rocketed forward.

She knelt in the grass and put on her gloves. Her hair felt like a heavy scarf down her back; her neck was sweating. She reached for what looked like a weed and yanked on it, but it offered resistance, so she was obliged to dig at it with her trowel. She tried to get under it the way Nell had done — Nell had made it look effortless — but it was harder than it looked. The top of the weed ripped off in Demeter's left hand, the root system still lurking underground, where it would simply regenerate so that at this same time next week she would be pulling the very same weed. Like Sisyphus with his goddamned boulder. But that was the story of her life, wasn't it, and her constant struggle with her weight? She could go for a day or two days or even five days eating only grapes and rice crackers and almonds, but then her hunger would build, it would roll over her, and she would tear open a bag of Fritos and eat them with an entire container of bacon-and-horseradish dip, and then she would eat dinner with her parents: fried chicken, mashed potatoes with gravy, two slices of peach pie with ice cream, and then an extra scoop of ice cream. And she would be right back at the bottom of the mountain with the boulder.

She threw the leaves into her bucket. Her first weed of the summer, her first of thousands, certainly, if she worked forty hours a week for the next eight weeks, three hundred and twenty hours, a hundred weeds an hour, thirty-two thousand weeds. And this was only the first one.

It hurt to kneel like this. The same was true at church; she couldn't make it through the liturgy on her knees. She had to sit. She sat now with her legs splayed to the side, and she leaned forward to hunt down her next weed. She could hear Coop buzzing around behind her, but she didn't turn to watch him because she most definitely did not want *him* watching *her*.

A half hour passed, then an hour. She had half a bucket of weeds, but she was only now getting the hang of it, how to dig down and extract the hook of the root. It was sort of like pulling her long hairs out of the shower drain. The weeding left divots in the perfect dirt, which Demeter then smoothed over as though she were icing a cake. This image made her hungry. Her banana was in the truck, growing warm and soft.

Demeter scrutinized the front of the house as she crept along the edge of the flower bed. It didn't seem like anyone was home. But was the house open? And if it was, would she be able to pop inside to, say, use the bathroom? She kind of doubted it. Zeus and Coop most certainly relieved themselves outside, but what about Nell?

She weeded, she weeded. She had to kneel; it was the only effective position. Demeter's mother had a foam pad that she placed under her knees when she weeded. Tomorrow Demeter would bring it to work with her. And her music—music would make things better. Anything would be better than kneeling in the heat with nothing to occupy her mind but the weeds and their tenacious grip on the earth.

Penny was buried in the earth, in her coffin. The coffin was made of glossy wood and had brass handles. Jake Randolph and Patrick Loom and Anders Peashway and some of Hobby's other teammates had gripped the brass handles when they lifted Penny's coffin off of the trestle and loaded it in the back of the hearse. Demeter had swooned at the sight of those handsome young men carrying Penny's coffin. It might be worth it to die if she could be sure those same boys would carry her to her final resting place. They had all cried for Penny. None of them would cry for Demeter.

Demeter hadn't focused on it at the time, but Penny was *in* that coffin. Her D.O.A. body, her corpse. Demeter had taken Penny into the dunes. Demeter had been drunk, but she hadn't lied or embellished her story. She had told only the truth, and the truth wasn't her fault.

Demeter had been one of the last people to see Penny alive. Driving down Hummock Pond Road, Penny had pressed the gas pedal to the floorboard. Penny had wanted to die, Demeter understood then. Probably she had been wanting to die for a long time, since long before Demeter took her into the dunes. Penny had carried around a burden as heavy as Demeter's extra weight, only Penny's weight was inside of her. Who knew where it came from? Possibly she had been born with it, the way Demeter herself had been born with the predilection to overeat. Penny had driven that car with the intent to kill — it wasn't a game or a dare, she wasn't just trying to scare them or thrill them, she was for real, she meant it. She didn't care if she killed herself. She didn't care if she killed them all.

Coop had finished mowing and was now edging the yard with a weed whacker.

Demeter needed a drink.

She was nearly done with the beds. She was pleased with herself because even she could see that they looked neater. She could tell the difference between where she had weeded and where she hadn't.

She stood up and dusted off her knees, which held the imprints of the grass.

She walked around the house. Zeus was watering the containers that surrounded the flagstone patio, and at the edge of the property, closest to the wild grasses that preceded the pond, Nell was still weeding the back beds. She was doing the same work as Demeter, but with a water view.

"Hey," Nell said, looking up. "You're not done, are you?"

"I'm almost done with the beds," Demeter said. Her head was spinning. It hadn't occurred to her before that Penny had been trying to kill *her.* "I have to pee." She paused and widened her eyes. "Badly."

"Oh," Nell said.

"Is there protocol?"

"Yeah," Nell said. "Squat behind a tree. Or hold it."

"We can't go in the house?" Demeter asked.

"God, no," Nell said.

Demeter felt her heart drop an inch. "Not ever?"

"Well," Nell said. Her voice was a whisper. She glanced at Zeus. "Some houses, yes. Some houses have pool houses or guesthouses or staff houses where we can use the bathroom. Some owners invite us in or have an open-door policy. But in general, no."

"No one's home here," Demeter said. "Can't I just check to see if the door is open?"

Nell bit her lower lip. She was being nice when she could have been a total bitch. "You can check. But be quick and take your shoes off, okay? And be clean, you know."

"Of course," Demeter said. She ran to the side door, which was out of Nell's view. She should grab her backpack. But there wasn't time, and Coop might see her. She tried the knob: the door was open. Amazing but not *that* amazing—Demeter didn't know a single islander who locked his or her door. However, an open door indicated that the people who owned the house were on the island but just not home at the moment, which meant they might come back any second.

Demeter moved through the house. Where to look? In the fridge? There was a bottle of wine in the fridge, an unopened bottle of chardonnay whose absence would most decidedly be noticed. The freezer? There was half a bottle of Finlandia vodka in there. Oh, how Demeter yearned to take it! But no, not the whole thing. She opened the bottle and took a healthy swig. The vodka stung her throat and burned all the way down until it settled with a flut-ter in her chest. She threw back another shot, then another. She heard the ticking of a clock somewhere in the kitchen, and outside the buzzing sound of the weed whacker. Demeter put the vodka back where she'd found it and tightly closed the freezer door. The kitchen was bright and sunny and had a lot of expensive-looking polished surfaces. Where did they keep the bar? The vodka was starting to warm her; for a second she felt *totally great*. Out the win-dow she saw Nell weeding and Zeus watering, and she could hear Coop. She opened cabinet doors until she hit paydirt: bottles and bottles and bottles in neat, sparkling rows. She gasped as someone else might do upon discovering a hidden altar. She reached for a bottle of Jim Beam, but who was she kidding? She would never be able to drink that stuff again. She took a full bottle of Finlandia and slid it into the pocket of her cargo shorts, where it was hidden by the folds of her tied flannel shirt. She closed up the cabinet and slipped out the same door she'd come in through, then she hurried for the truck. She swaddled the bottle inside her flannel shirt and tucked the whole bundle into her backpack.

She felt winded but lightheaded. It had been so easy.

She strode back out to the front beds and put on her gloves. She still had weeding to do.

JAKE

Jake could see why his mother loved Fremantle. It was perfect, in the same way that he imagined San Diego in 1955 must have been perfect. Each day was sunny and beautiful, the gardens were in full bloom, the houses were occupied by smiling blond people who always seemed to be out front washing their cars or returning home with their reusable shopping bags filled to bursting with fresh produce—lettuces and strawberries and mangoes and pineapples—from the Fremantle Markets. But these things didn't keep Jake from hating the place.

He wanted to go home. He thought about locking himself in the shed and refusing to come out. He thought about staging a hunger strike. How many days would he have to go without food before his parents would agree to take him home?

When he was younger, his mother had often read him a book called *Alexander and the Terrible, Horrible, No Good, Very Bad Day*, in which, in fact, one very bad thing after another happened to Alexander, and all Alexander dreamed about was moving to Australia. This book had been a favorite, not of Jake's but of Ava's. It was as though Ava were Alexander and her life on Nantucket were one endless loop of no good, very bad days that could be fixed only by her moving back to Australia.

The sad thing was how desperately Jake now longed for this hypothesis to fail. He wished with all his heart that his mother would not find happiness in Australia, that she would be disappointed and disenchanted and they would all be allowed to go home to Nantucket.

But in just the way that water was supposed to swirl down the drain in the opposite direction in the Southern Hemisphere (clockwise instead of counterclockwise), and just as the seasons were opposite to those back home, a reversal seemed to Jake to be taking hold of his parents.

His mother was slowly coming back to life, like a person who had been frozen and was now thawing. She moved easily around their new house; she cut flowers from the backyard and put them in a vase. She put music on in the kitchen — sometimes classical, sometimes acoustic coffeehouse stuff, sometimes the Beatles or U2. Once Jake even caught her humming. She now had places to go and people to meet. She took a picnic to the green acres of Kings Park with her sister, she spent afternoons shopping in Subiaco, she went with her nieces on an outing to the Perth Zoo. She spent one Sunday sunbathing on Cottesloe Beach, and the next sailing on the Swan River with her brother Noah. She was up early, chipper and smiling; she had literally become a *new person,* a person Jake had never met. He tried to recall what his mother had been like before Ernie died, but all that lingered in his memory was an Ava who, while not wracked with grief, had been preoccupied with having another baby and was overprotective of Jake himself, alternately distracted and annoying.

Now she was — well, she was better. She had stopped watching that moronic TV show, a total irony because here in Australia, *Home and Away* aired every night at seven-thirty. Jake had expected Ava to be glued to the set as she had been at home.

But being in Australia had eradicated her need to watch a show set in Australia. Plus, she was too busy for TV. She didn't mope around the house the way she used to do on her sad days, or stalk like a hungry tigress on her angry days. Now she hit an evenhanded balance. She offered Jake a host of potential activities: sailing lessons at the Fremantle Yacht Club, an internship at the Science Museum (set up by his Uncle Marco), a visit with his cousin Xavier, who was not quite a year older than Jake.

"You used to love playing with Xavier," his mother said. "Don't you remember?"

What Jake remembered was that Xavier had given him an Indian rope burn and cheated at thumb wrestling.

"I'm too old for a play date, Mom," Jake said.

Ava insisted that he needed something to do. The American International School kept to the same schedule as schools back home, so classes wouldn't begin until September. He couldn't just sit and rot for the next two months.

He turned down all of his mother's overtures. He seethed at how happy she seemed. All it had taken was Penny's death.

His parents still fought all the time — Jake overheard them from the private distance of the shed — but now it was for different reasons. Now his father was the one who didn't want to go anywhere or do anything. Jordan refused to see anyone from Ava's family: "They all blame me, Ava," he said. "You poisoned them against me." Now his father was the one who paced the floor, impatient and restless, as if waiting for someone to rescue him.

Their first family outing was to the Harborfront for fish and chips, his mother's idea. There were half a dozen huge establishments with picnic tables over-looking the water, and they all sold the same thing: fried haddock or whiting with pale, limp "chips," which were french fries, or sort of. The restaurants also specialized in fried shrimp, fried clams, and something revolting called fried whitebait, a little fish that looked like a minnow; you were meant to eat the eyes and tail and everything.

Ava had waited tables at Cicarella's as a young woman, and so they selected an outdoor table there. Ava said, "I'm going classic: fried whiting and chips. Gentlemen, what would you like?"

Jordan said, "Nothing for me, thanks."

"What do you mean, 'nothing'?" Ava demanded.

"I mean I'm not eating."

"But you agreed to come."

Jordan sighed. "Yes, Ava, I agreed to come."

"So if you agreed to come, you have to eat. Eating is part of the deal."

"Is it?" Jordan asked.

They were going to fight again, and out in public this time. Jake agreed with his father, he didn't want to eat here either. This place was seedy; in America it would be considered almost honky-tonk, with its stench of frying oil and its scores of cawing seagulls. But his father's refusal to eat came across as being juvenile and mean, and Jake felt a stab of sympathy for his mother, who obviously had dreamed of eating here at least forty-two thousand times over the past two decades.

Jake said, "I'll have the fried shrimp."

"Prawns," Ava said.

"Whatever."

"Or you could have yabbies," Ava said. "Which are a bigger bug, sort of like crawfish."

"Please don't call them bugs," Jake said. "I'll have the shrimp."

Ava stood to order the food, and Jake was too embarrassed to look at his father, whom he felt he'd betrayed somehow. Jake was used to the usual teams—himself and his father on one side, his mother (and in some weird way, Ernie) on the other—and totally unprepared for the way their roles had switched. Jordan was, quite clearly, the bad guy now, the spoiler, while Ava was the good guy. His mother was just trying to have a pleasant evening out with her family, to show them a bit of the culture she'd grown up in.

Ava brought the fish and chips to the table wrapped in white paper, and when she unfolded the paper, they were all enveloped by steam and the smell of fried fish. Ava closed her eyes and inhaled. Then she wielded a squirt bottle of vinegar and doused her food with it, giving the whole mess a new smell.

Jake said, "Ketchup? Because I'm American?"

His mother laughed, the short, high-pitched yelp of a Yorkie.

His father said, "I'll get it."

Ava dug into her meal with a voraciousness Jake couldn't remember seeing in her before. This, to her, was the best food on Earth.

Jake's father was taking a long time getting the ketchup, and Jake's shrimp were rapidly cooling; in another few minutes, he knew, the fries would be stiff and inedible.

Ava said, "I bet he went home."

Home? thought Jake. Would his father *do* that? Pretend to be getting ketchup and just leave?

"He's miserable," Ava said.

Jake stared down into the golden grease of his dinner basket. He feared he might cry. Everything was wrong; it had been wrong back on Nantucket, and it was still wrong here. But then a handful of ketchup packets hit the table, and Jake looked up to see his father holding an icy mug of beer.

"Sorry, mate," he said.

*   *   *

On the way home, Ava wanted to stop and see the statue of Bon Scott, the lead singer for AC/DC. At first Jake thought she was joking—but no, there it was, a statue of the musician right there on the promenade. Bon Scott had grown up in Fremantle.

Ava chattered about how she and the other waitresses used to listen to AC/DC on their breaks and how Bon Scott's death had wracked the city with grief. He was buried in East Fremantle; Ava and her girlfriends had whiled away many an afternoon drinking jug wine on his grave.

"You do know he drank himself to death, right?" Jordan said. "The man was a degenerate. And they've put up a *statue* of him, like he's George Washington."

Ava smiled dreamily. "I like to remember the music."

"For God's sake," Jordan said, frowning at the statue. "An actual tribute to the man who brought the world 'Highway to Hell'?"

"You can try to ruin my evening," Ava said. "But it won't work."

"And 'Hells Bells,' " Jordan added.

"Dad," Jake said.

Jordan clammed up and kicked an imaginary pebble on the path.

Jake thought, I have to get out of here. But how?

*   *   *

A few days later, on a Friday morning, Jake and his father were sitting together in the kitchen, and his father was trying to figure out how to use the French press. Jake's father had wanted to buy an electric coffee maker, but Ava had said no, there was no need, the French press would suffice; the coffee would be better, in fact. And so every morning Ava woke up before either Jake or Jordan and made the coffee using the French press, and though Jordan now complained about nearly everything, Jake hadn't heard him complain about the coffee.

Jordan fumbled with the plunger of the French press and squinted at the small print on the package of coffee beans. He made some frustrated huffing noises.

Jake asked, "How come Mom isn't up yet?"

Jordan said, "I'll tell you how come."

Then Jake remembered that his mother had gone out the night before with some "old friends" to hear jazz in Northbridge. Jake's father had been unhappy about this, and Ava had said, "You're more than welcome to come with us, Jordan. It's not what you think."

"Here's what I think," Jordan had begun, his voice getting the hairy texture that meant he was about to attack. Jake took that opportunity to leave the room and head back out to the shed. Then he heard his father say, "I think you should go alone, is what I think."

Jake watched his father now. "You have to fill the kettle, Dad," he said. "And then pour the hot water into the carafe."

"Yeah, but how much coffee?" Jordan said. "And where does your mother keep the grinder?"

Jordan shrugged.

"Ava!" Jordan shouted.

I have to get out of here, Jordan thought once again. Here the kitchen, and here Australia.

Ava shuffled into the room a few seconds later. Her hair was knotted up in a disheveled bun, her complexion was grayish, and she walked with one hand held in front of her, like a blind person who was afraid of running into something. She squinted in the bright sunlight.

"What's up?" she said. Her voice had a raspy edge. She put a hand on Jake's head and said, "Good morning, sweetheart," and Jake smelled cigarettes. His mother, he realized, had been out *drinking*. And *smoking*. His mother was *hung over*.

"I can't figure out how to work this goddamned thing."

"Here," Ava said. "Give it to me, I'll do it."

Jordan threw the coffee beans against the counter, and the bag split open, beans scattering everywhere. He said, "Nice of you to finally make an appearance. I could have walked downtown, waited in the ridiculous line at the Dome, and walked back, and I still would have had my coffee sooner."

"I'm sorry," Ava said.

Jake found himself drawn into his parents' argument. He found himself thinking, You don't have to apologize to him, Mom. He's being a jerk.

"How was Roger?" Jordan asked.

Ava patiently gathered the spilled beans into a pile and slid them into her cupped hand. She didn't answer, and Jake found himself saying out loud, "Who's Roger?"

"Your mother's old boyfriend," Jordan said. "Who took her out to a club last night until three in the morning."

Jake found himself thinking, Really? He told himself, Get up this instant and go out to the shed. Everything was inside out and backward. His mother had gone out drinking, she had come home at three in the morning. But he couldn't move. He wanted to hear if the part about the old boyfriend was true or not.

"Mom?" he said.

She filled the electric kettle from the spigot. "I'm sorry," she said, without turning around.

But she didn't sound sorry.

His parents had turned the house into such a passive-aggressive war zone that suddenly the shed wasn't far enough away from the crossfire. Jake had to get out of the house, and so he ventured down to South Beach. South Beach consisted of three crescents of pure white sand backed by stone walls. Between the walls and the access road was a wide swath of park with a grass lawn and Norfolk pines, picnic tables, barbecue grills, a playground.

Jake grudgingly admitted to himself that he did not hate South Beach. The water was turquoise and clear to the white, sandy bottom. The café served avocado and sprout sandwiches and burgers topped with fried eggs, and short blacks (espresso) and flat whites (cappuccino). The place had an easy, liberal vibe. But what Jake liked best was the transients who lived in their camper vans in the parking lot. These people showered in the public bathhouses, they ate cereal while sitting on their front bumpers. They weren't much older than Jake; they had dreadlocks and tattoos and piercings and were deeply, unabashedly tanned. The women wore bikini tops and cutoff shorts and silver rings on their toes. Jake's mother referred to these people as "ferals." Like stray cats or dogs. For Jake, this only enhanced their appeal. Every afternoon he would take his assigned vacation reading, *The Grapes of Wrath*, by Steinbeck, and lie under a Norfolk pine or sit at a table at the café, where he would read, drink a short black, and observe the ferals.

What he liked most about them was that they were free.

On one of Jake's forays into central Fremantle — he was on his way to Elizabeth's Secondhand Bookshop to pick up the next book on his list, *The Sun Also Rises,* by Hemingway — he spied his father sitting at one of the café tables outside of the Dome. Jordan was by himself, drinking a short black. Jake thought about just walking by, not stopping at all, but that somehow seemed like it would be a great opportunity missed. He took a seat at his father's table. His father looked up, surprised.

"Hey there," Jordan said.

"Hey," Jake said.

His father had the *West* in front of him; he was doing the crossword puzzle.

"I'm having no luck," Jordan said. "The clues are all unapologetically Antipodean."

Jake nodded. It felt strange to happen across his father like this. For the first time — maybe because they were out of the house, maybe because they were away from Ava, maybe because Jordan had let his guard down — Jake noticed that his father looked...what? Different. Sad. Lonely, maybe.

"Are you okay?" Jake asked.

Jordan laughed. "Shouldn't I be asking you that?"

"Oh," Jake said. He shook his head, and stupidly, tears came to his eyes. "I'm never going to be okay again."

He expected his father to refute this, but instead Jordan cast his eyes down and took a sip of coffee. "Can I order you something?"

"Short black," Jake said.

His father flagged the waiter and ordered a coffee for Jake and another for himself.

"Dad, why are we here?"

"I thought that was obvious."

"For Mom?"

"For Mom, for you." He paused. "For me."

"You're not happy here," Jake said. "That much is clear."

"I'm doing okay," Jordan said.

"You have a strange way of showing it," Jake said. "How can you stand being away from the paper? How can you stand not working?"

"Those are tricky questions."

"Let's call this what it is. We came here for Mom. Please don't say we came here for me. We came here for Mom."

"We came here for Ava," Jordan said.

"Because she's the only one who matters."

"No," Jordan said. "She's not the only one who matters. But she's been wanting to move back to Australia for a long time, and I felt like I owed it to her to give it a try."

"She makes you feel like you owe her something," Jake said. "But you don't owe her anything."

"You're saying that because you're unhappy, and you think our coming here was the wrong decision."

"*You're* unhappy," Jake countered. "You and Mom are unhappy together. I hear you, you know."

"Hey now," Jordan said.

Jake felt immediately ashamed. He had never commented on his parents' marriage before.

"Just let your mother and me worry about what's going on between us. It has nothing to do with you."

"Except that I have to live with you."

"True," Jordan said, and his voice was softer now. "That's true."

"It's hard," Jake said. "Processing this on my own."

"I'm processing it too," Jordan said.

"Not like me," Jake said.

"You'd be surprised," Jordan replied.

"In my mind, you know, she's still alive," Jake confided. This was painfully true. When Jake was alone in the shed, he thought about Penny all the time — her long hair, her sapphire eyes, her lips, the warmth of her next to him, her voice. He had a recording of her singing "Lean on Me" on his iPod that he listened to way too often. Once he'd even masturbated to the song, and after ejaculating, he'd started to cry harder than he ever had before. He missed her, and truthfully, sex was the least of it.

The worst part was not having his friend, his love, his champion, the person he'd told everything to.

"Have you been in touch with anyone from home?" Jordan asked.

"No," Jake said. He had his computer set up; he could email Hobby, he supposed, but what could he say in an email? "Are you?"

"No," Jordan said.

"Really? Not Al Castle? Not Zoe? Not anyone from the paper?"

"No," Jordan said. "It's kind of a deal I made with myself. If I called Al or called the paper, a part of me would still be back on Nantucket. And I want to try being here for a while. That's what I was hoping for for you, too — that you'd be able to be yourself here, without having to cope with the pressures at home."

"I thought we'd left because of what people were saying."

"What were people saying?"

Jake's short black arrived, steaming. He blew across the top, then braced himself for the first sip. It was as bitter as gasoline. It was the kind of liquid that would take the enamel off his teeth; it would have corroded Penny's vocal cords on contact. But there was something comforting in how awful the coffee tasted. It went with the Steinbeck and Hemingway, and it suited his burned and broken heart, his charred hopes, his exile. The coffee tasted like adulthood, like manhood.

"That the accident was our fault because it was our car. That you didn't print anything about it in the newspaper because you were trying to cover something up. That Penny was drunk or high."

Jordan nodded slowly. His hair was a lot grayer now, Jake noticed. He looked old now, whereas at home he had just looked harried and busy. "There was nothing wrong with the car," Jordan said. "The tox report from the hospital showed no alcohol or other substances in Penny's system. And I didn't print anything in the paper because Zoe asked me not to, and as she was Penny's mother, I decided to honor that request. I don't think anyone blames us for the accident. I think people have come to terms with the fact that Penny was driving too fast."

"Demeter," Jake said.

"What?" Jordan said.

"Demeter said something that upset her."

"You think?"

"Yes. In the dunes. They went to pee in the dunes, right before we left. And when Penny came back, she was freaking out."

"About what?"

Jake shrugged. He'd been trying not to think about it. Did it matter, ultimately? Demeter had been shitfaced, and she was so clingy and pathetic and greedy for Penny's attention that she might easily have said something about Jake; she might have exaggerated the truth. There was one potential source of gossip that stuck out in Jake's mind: the incident at the cast party after the final performance of *Grease*.

The party was at Winnie Potts's house. Winnie Potts had played Rizzo, and like Rizzo, Winnie was wild. Mr. and Mrs. Potts were "cool" parents who left their kids alone in their tricked-out basement with the pool table and the movie screen and the second fridge filled with beer. Everyone in the cast started out drinking Coke and Fanta and eating the pigs in blankets and Swedish meatballs laid out by Mrs. Potts, who then very loudly and definitively announced that she was going upstairs to bed and would not be back down. At that point, Winnie discreetly began opening her father's beers and pouring them into Solo cups and passing them around. When the music got turned up and it became clear that it had become a drinking party, Penny decided to leave. She could be righteous that way; the other kids called her a goody-goody behind her back. Jake had begged her to stay as they stood together at the bottom of the basement stairs. He kissed her, and she complained that he tasted like beer, and then she pointed out that Winnie was now smoking, which meant that she, Penny, had to leave right that instant.

"That's right," Jake said. "Go home and take care of your vocal cords."

He had intended this as a playful poke — though sure, maybe he was a little angry that she was leaving, maybe he was a little jealous that even though he'd played the male lead, Danny, the only performer whom anyone had cared about hearing was Penny. She had received rousing standing ovations all four nights. Maybe he was a little annoyed that she treated her vocal cords like the Hope Diamond. Penny hissed at him, then stormed up the stairs. Jake looked after her and thought, Should I follow her? But his beer was cold and his favorite song was playing and Winnie Potts called out, "Jake Randolph, get over here!" And so he watched Penny go.

One o'clock in the morning found him still there, the last party guest. He was too drunk to drive home, which was okay because he had twenty bucks for cab fare; all he had to do was call for a ride. He took his cell phone out of his pocket and called Coach's Cab, but Coach said it would be twenty minutes.

"Twenty minutes," Jake told Winnie.

"'Kay," Winnie said. She was lying across the sofa, wearing a pair of cutoff shorts and a white tank top that barely contained her enormous breasts. Winnie Potts's breasts were a legend at Nantucket High School and probably accounted in no small part for her being cast as Rizzo. Jake knew she hadn't been dressed in that outfit earlier, but when exactly had she changed? And where had everyone else gone? They'd left, but had they driven, or had some of their parents come down to the Pottses' basement? Jake lived in fear of his class-mates' parents seeing him drunk. He had a sterling reputation among the faculty and the administra-tors at school and in the community as a whole, and he wanted to keep it that way.

Winnie said, "Come here."

"I am here," Jake said. He was lounging sideways in a club chair.

"To the sofa," Winnie said. She scooted over a fraction of an inch as if to make room for him, and her breasts bounced a little. Penny's breasts were like a child's, almost nonexistent. She complained about this sometimes, but Jake reassured her that he liked her just the way she was. Now, though, he was finding something arousing about the sight of Winnie's breasts under the skimpy tank top. He could see the outline of her nipples, dark and as big as quarters. Winnie wasn't as pretty as Penny, nor half as talented, but she had something—a grav-elly voice, a sense of humor, a sense of lawlessness— that Jake had always been attracted to. He was attracted to it now. Should he go over to the sofa? If he went to the sofa, he knew what would happen.

"I can't," he said. "I'm too drunk to move."

The next thing he knew, Winnie was rising. She was kneeling down in front of his chair. Her breasts were right there in front of him, they were buoyant. She kissed him on the mouth, then there was tongue, then his hands found her breasts. They were soft. He wasn't sure what to do with them. He felt Winnie's hand on his fly, and he was instantly hard, harder than he could remember ever having been before, which he attributed to how wrong this was, how derelict. He pushed Winnie away, he got to his feet and adjusted himself—his dick was throbbing—and he stumbled to the basement stairs. Up and out into the night air, just as the cab pulled in to the driveway. Thank God.

He told no one about this. He played it cool with Winnie, he thought, acting completely normal. She was distant and pissy; he pretended not to notice. Every time he saw her, he was with Penny. At Patrick Loom's graduation party, she came up to them and said, "So how's the perfect couple?" in a way that was utterly mocking, but Penny treated this as a compliment and said sweetly, "We're fine." Winnie was also at the party at Steps Beach. She was hanging on to Anders Peashway; she was always hanging on to one guy or another, and probably always would be. Jake could hardly have been the first guy to blow her off, yet at Steps Beach she kept giving him a look—which was meant to say *what?* he wondered. He wanted to know if she'd told anybody about what had happened between them. He was desperately praying that she'd written it off, as he had, as a drunken fiasco best forgotten. But he suspected that Winnie Potts wasn't the kind of girl who could keep her mouth shut.

Now, sitting across from his father, Jake took a deep breath. "I don't know what Demeter said."

"Well, did you ask her?"

Yes, he had asked her. It had taken him eleven attempts to get her to talk to him—she'd ignored his calls to her cell phone and his texts, and pretended to be asleep when he showed up at her house. It was only two nights before he and his parents were to leave that his cell phone finally lit up with Demeter's number.

"Hey," he said, as kindly as he could. Demeter was touchy, but he knew she could be won over. "How are you doing? I've been worried about you."

"Me?" Demeter said.

"Yeah. Are you okay?"

"Not really," she said. She either laughed or hiccupped, and Jake realized she was drunk. He didn't like to be judgmental about people, and especially not about Demeter, because he knew her life was difficult, but he did think that she was probably an alcoholic. Already, at seventeen.

"Me either," he said. "I keep thinking about the accident."

"I've blocked it out," Demeter said. "They tell me I was in shock."

"But you remember stuff from before the accident, right?" Jake said. "You remember being at the party?"

"I remember working the tap," Demeter said. "After that it all gets blurry."

"Really?" Jake said. "Because..."

"Really," Demeter said.

"Do you remember going into the dunes with Penny? I think you guys were going to pee?"

"That's where I sort of blank out," Demeter said.

Convenient, Jake thought. "You didn't say anything to Penny in the dunes?"

"We must have talked a little bit," Demeter said. "But I don't remember what about."

"Really?" Jake said. "Because she was pretty upset when she got back to the car."

"Was she?" Demeter said. "I don't remember."

"You don't remember Penny being *upset?*" he asked. "You don't remember Penny ripping the keys out of my hand, you don't remember her screaming, you don't remember her leaving burnt rubber on Cliff Road?"

"No," Demeter said. "I mean, I remember the speed. I remember going fast and being excited about it at first. I remember being scared. She could have killed us, you know."

Jake swallowed. He said, "By any chance, was Winnie Potts in the dunes with you guys? Do you remember?"

There was a long pause. Then Demeter said, "Yes, actually I think she was."

"I asked her," Jake said to his father now. He threw back his short black all at once, like John Wayne with a shot of whiskey. "But she couldn't help me."

ZOE

It was embarrassing for her now to think about how *blessed* her life had been before. The things she had taken for granted mocked her. She had known hardship, certainly—Hobson senior had dropped dead, she had been left to raise the twins alone—but for the most part Zoe considered herself lucky.

She had grown up the only child of older parents. Zoe had been an accident, born after her mother believed herself to be beyond conceiving.

Her parents were professional, urbane, and erudite: her father had worked on Wall Street for years before opening his own brokerage firm in Stamford, Connecticut, and her mother was a vice president at Mount Sinai Hospital, a job she was unwilling to give up after her daughter was born.

Zoe had been raised by a string of beautiful blond au pairs who lived on the third floor of their stone mansion in Old Greenwich and who accompanied the family on vacations so that Zoe's parents could dance the night away in the ballrooms of cruise ships. Their names remained with Zoe—Elsa, Pleune, Dagmar—though the girls themselves were interchangeable. Zoe had learned about nearly everything from these girls, including how to ride a two-wheeler, how to swim the backstroke, how to play "Chopsticks" on the piano, how to apply mascara to her lower lashes, and, later, how to roll her own cigarettes and tie the stem of a maraschino cherry into a knot with her tongue.

At fourteen Zoe had been sent out into the world—to Miss Porter's, where her natural abilities got her decent grades but where she couldn't summon the ambition to battle it out for the top ranks. She was happier being known as mellow and laid-back, a bohemian, a connoisseur of the Grateful Dead and CSNY and the Band. She wore long silk broomstick skirts or the batik sarong that her parents had sent back to her from their holiday in Bali. Zoe let her hairstyle get dangerously close to dreadlocks, inviting a firm talking-to by school administrators. She had her left ear pierced three times and got a tattoo of a dancing bear on her hip bone. While her mother never learned about the tattoo, the words of Zoe's roommate Julia Lavelle, a strait-laced girl who wouldn't even deign to watch *Life of Brian* in the commons room on a Saturday night, would later come back to haunt her: "That tattoo is going to be with you for the rest of your life, you know, and it might not seem so cool in thirty years." Julia Lavelle had been correct: the rainbow-colored bear still graced her hip, and though the men she had been with — Jordan being the most vocal among them — claimed to find it cute, to Zoe herself it now seemed sorely ridiculous.

The summer between her junior and senior years of high school, Zoe's parents took her to Italy for a month. Zoe had thought about declining this invitation, asking for the money instead, and following the Dead through the American Southwest and California. But the idea of actually spending time with her parents was novel enough to be intriguing.

And sure enough, that month in Italy had changed Zoe's life. Her parents treated her like an adult. Her mother, using the lightest touch, suggested a haircut in Rome, and the result was a layered style that, unlike the tattoo, had weathered the test of time. Zoe selected an Italian perfume to replace her patchouli; she bought suede Fratelli Rosetti boots and retired her Birkenstocks. Her new look got immediate results. One night at a trattoria in Trastevere, Zoe met an American graduate student in art history named Alex, who invited her to share a bottle of wine and a plate of fried artichokes with him. Zoe lied and told him she was a sophomore at Vassar. She lost her virginity to Alex (last name unknown, a source of minor embarrassment now) in a studio apartment in the shadow of the Vatican. She walked past Saint Peter's Square and back to her hotel at two o'clock in the morning, feeling as if she had just conquered the free world. Alex's body had been as smooth as the surface of a Bernini sculpture.

The only thing that would have made it better, she thought, was if Alex had been Italian.

Next time.

But for Zoe, the most important aspect of Italy was this: it was there that she discovered food. This happened in a tiny restaurant in Ravenna, where she and her parents had traveled to see the Basilica of San Francesco, the site of Dante's funeral. One of Zoe's father's impossibly sophisticated friends had recommended a restaurant to them, a place with just fourteen seats, where the wife cooked and the husband waited on tables. Zoe ate squid ink ravioli stuffed with fresh ricotta in a truffled cream sauce, grilled langostini, and crema calda with wild strawberries. Her parents poured her wine on the implicit understanding that she was to drink it not to get drunk but to enhance the pleasure of the food.

God, yes! Zoe thought with each mouthful. Ecstasy! Better than the sex she had so recently been introduced to by Alex Last-name-unknown. The meal was transcendent. Her parents enjoyed it, but it wasn't the epiphany for them that it was for their daughter. They had tasted food like this before. For Zoe, it was like the sun's coming up. Before they left the restaurant, Zoe peered into the kitchen at the wife/chef. Her hair was in a tight bun like a ballerina's; her eyes were narrowed in concentration as she flipped mushrooms in a sauté pan. Zoe could hear opera playing in the kitchen, and she saw that the woman's lips were moving. Yes! Zoe thought. Yes!

Zoe's parents had no qualms about sending her to the Culinary Institute. True, it wasn't Vassar (where her mother had gone) or Penn (where Julia Lavelle was headed); around Miss Porter's, it had the whiff of a vocational school. But her parents recognized Zoe's passion for food, and to their minds, her becoming a chef was preferable to her joining a nudist colony or moving to Haight-Ashbury to volunteer for some left-wing cause they'd never even heard of.

The CIA had led Zoe not only to her career as a chef but also, of course, to Hobson senior, who had in short order made her a mother. She had endured some dark, dark times: Hobson's death, the deaths of both her parents, the harrowing challenge of raising two children by herself. But at some point — when the kids were seven or eight — Zoe began to feel as if she had emerged from a tunnel. She thought, The hard stuff is behind me now. She thought, I have a good job, a house on the beach, a group of close friends to do fun things with, and two exceptional kids. She didn't have love, but that seemed okay, maybe even preferable. The kids were her love life. And she maintained her freedom.

And so, how how *how* could she explain Jordan?

They had been friends for years and years, and yet now Zoe found it hard to recall a time when they were just friends.

She had spent her first years on Nantucket living in a bubble. She had taken the job with the Allencast family and enrolled the kids at Island Day Care. Zoe met a few other working parents while picking up and dropping off Penny and Hobby, but they were all of them so busy that their interactions remained superficial. Zoe frequently worked weekends, when she hired a babysitter. She always had Mondays off, but on Mondays the rest of the world worked; it wasn't easy to forge a social life on Mondays alone. Zoe tried to get out. Her first year on-island, she attended Town Meeting and marveled at how everyone in the high school auditorium knew everyone else, friendships that clearly spanned centuries. This was one of those times when Zoe wished she'd moved to a less insular community, maybe a city, someplace with single mothers in abundance. But it was at this very Town Meeting that Zoe first laid eyes on Jordan Randolph. He was presenting an article, wearing suit pants and a crisp striped shirt and an elegant leather-banded watch—all of which screamed *lawyer* to Zoe, though she liked his curly black hair that grew past his collar, and also his rimless glasses. She asked the woman sitting next to her, "Who is that?" Zoe could still remember the look of wariness that came over the woman's face. Zoe had revealed herself as an interloper, from Martha's Vineyard, perhaps, or beyond.

"That's Jordan Randolph," the woman said. "The publisher of the newspaper."

Ahhhh, Zoe thought. *That's* Jordan Randolph. She had heard his name, of course. Mr. Allencast liked to complain about Jordan Randolph's liberal politics, which had endeared Zoe to the mysterious

Mr. Randolph before she ever saw him. She had been intrigued, even back then.

She didn't actually meet Jordan until she enrolled the twins in preschool. The Children's House was the only Montessori on the island, and it was difficult to get into. Rumor had it that people called the school from the delivery room of Nantucket Cottage Hospital and asked to have their newborns put on the waiting list. At first the twins weren't admitted. Zoe was certain this was because she was a transplant and a single working mother, and because placing *two* children in the school was five times as hard as placing one. She was secretly crushed, but she resigned herself to keeping the twins in day care. They would survive. However, when Mrs. Allencast discovered that the twins hadn't been admitted, she made a call—she and Mr. Allencast donated to the school annually—and sure enough, an invitation to enroll them soon followed.

At the Children's House, the level of parent involvement was high. There were meetings and fund raisers and potluck dinners and slide shows and student presentations. There were five precious minutes every weekday morning when Zoe stood in the cramped coatroom while Penny and Hobby changed out of their street shoes and into slippers, then solemnly kissed her good-bye and disappeared down the stairs for songs and story time.

Zoe first saw Lynne Castle in that coatroom. Lynne was instantly friendly, offering her hand, introducing herself. She was the mother of Demeter, who was the same age as the twins, though Lynne was quick to add that she also had two older boys who had gone through the school a few years earlier, making her something of a fixture there. In fact, she was president of the Board of Directors, but she said she was always thrilled to meet young, new parents who might, somewhere down the line, take over leadership roles, because really, she confided, she was getting too old for this.

Zoe had laughed. Lynne was charming. She was a little older than Zoe herself, maybe as many as ten years older, with a stolid, matronly look about her. She had graying hair that she wore pushed behind her ears, carried about thirty unneeded pounds, and boasted a wardrobe straight out of the Orvis catalog, circa 1978. Zoe wondered what *she* had looked like to Lynne, with her zippy haircut, the ends newly dyed red, and her dramatic makeup and her houndstooth pants and her chef's clogs. In hindsight, she supposed that she must have resembled a cross between Cyndi Lauper and Julia Child. But Lynne Castle seemed to like her anyway.

Zoe met Al Castle and Jordan Randolph the following February, when the school held what was known as Fathers' Night. The twins had been talking about this occasion for weeks, and it bound Zoe's stomach up in knots. She had hoped to give it a miss altogether, but the twins told her about the pictures they had drawn and the preparations they had made, and Zoe thought, All right, fine, I'll go. She wasn't sure the teachers would even let her through the door, though they knew her situation. There wasn't one suitable man in Zoe's life who could fill in. She thought briefly of asking Mr. Allencast to go, but the twins were terrified of him, and Zoe wasn't all that sure that her employer, at age sixty-eight, would want to accompany her three-year-olds to this lofty event.

And so Zoe attended Fathers' Night on her own. Her presence was alternately ignored and lauded. It made certain fathers uncomfortable, and to those men she wanted to say, "Listen, my husband is dead." One father, a man Zoe now knew to be Lars Peashway, Anders's father, had clapped her on the shoulder and said, "You're very brave." And Zoe thought, Brave? I'm not brave, mister. I'm just doing what has to be done.

The only fathers who didn't treat Zoe like an oddity or a martyr were Al Castle and Jordan Randolph. Right off the bat, they included her. They told her that their kids, Demeter and Jake, talked incessantly about her twins.

"I think Jake is especially fond of Penny," Jordan said.

"I think Demeter is especially fond of Hobby," Al said.

The two men gave each other the wink-wink, and all three of them laughed. Zoe knew that Jordan was Jordan because she had attended Town Meeting, but she let him introduce himself.

"I'm Jordan Randolph." He was wearing a sapphire-blue sweater and jeans and sneakers. The beautiful watch with the leather band. The rimless glasses. There was no reason, now, for Zoe to be anything but truthful about it: she had fallen in love with him way back then.

"You may know my wife?" he said. "Ava? She has the long braid? She's Australian?"

"Yes, yes," Zoe said. Of course, the most beautiful and best-dressed mother in the coatroom, the one with the cool accent whom Zoe had overheard talking about going to the U2 concert at Boston Garden—that was Jordan Randolph's wife.

"Jake is our only child," Jordan said. "But we're hoping for another."

"Well," Zoe said, thinking, Dammit! "Good luck with that."

Willing herself not to moon any further over Jordan, Zoe then turned her attention to Al Castle, who introduced himself and said, "You must know my wife, Lynne?"

"Ah, yes," Zoe said. Al and Lynne were a perfect match in their upstanding, verging-on-middle-aged ordinariness. "I like Lynne very much." This was true. Lynne was the only mother who consistently said hello to her and stopped to chat with her in the parking lot. Lynne knew that Zoe was a private chef for the Allencasts, and Zoe knew that Lynne was starting up a permitting business at home now that Demeter was in school all day.

"She says you drive a Karmann Ghia," Al said. "Is that true?"

"Guilty as charged," Zoe said.

"What year?" Al asked.

"Nineteen sixty-nine."

"The best," Al said. "I own the car dealership on Polpis Road. If you ever decide to trade that baby in, I'll give you an unbeatable price."

"I can't believe you're talking business to the woman," Jordan said. He stared at Zoe for a second, enough time for her to register: blue sweater, blue eyes. Then he smiled. "I'm off to do puzzles," he said. "Wanna come?"

What had followed was no less profound than an adoption. Gradually, over the years, Zoe had been taken in by the Randolphs and the Castles. They became family. Lynne Castle was officially Zoe's closest friend, though the person Zoe spent the most time courting was Ava Randolph. She wanted Ava to like her. Ava reminded her of a smoothly polished stone, with her long, honey-blond hair, her perfect skin, green eyes, and rarely seen dimples. But like a stone, she was cool, and not just with Zoe but with everyone. She disliked Nantucket and fancied herself a sort of captive there; she was always talking about how she was about to go off to, or had just come back from, Australia. Her own sun-drenched country, that place where she'd rather be. It was Ava's aloofness that captured Zoe's imagination. She played hard-to-get, and Zoe wanted to win her over. She wanted to win!

For years Zoe tried. For years she beat herself up over it, thinking, Ava doesn't like me. She thinks I'm loud and obvious and American. She thinks I'm a terrible mother because I work. Ava didn't have a job outside of her home; she devoted all her time and energy to parenting Jake. She didn't have to find a babysitter or, like Zoe, occasionally leave the children at home by themselves because she had to cater a dinner party on a Saturday night. She didn't leave permission slips unsigned or forget sneakers for the kids' phys. ed. days, or space out on getting cards for the class on Valentine's Day. These misdemeanors were Zoe's and Zoe's alone, and she couldn't help feeling that Ava Randolph might just be writing them all down on a list somewhere, a list that she secretly showed to Jordan every night before dinner.

Had it always ultimately been about Jordan? Zoe wondered. She'd been trying to woo the wife, but was it really the husband she wanted? Even back when Zoe first knew them, Ava and Jordan had openly bickered and argued. Zoe had always taken Ava's side, even when she thought Jordan was right. Eventually Zoe became the person Ava complained to about her husband: Jordan's breath stank in the morning; he had never once emptied the dishwasher; he refused to travel back with her to Australia no matter how she begged and pleaded, so that she and Jake always had to go alone; he was *obsessed* with the newspaper. Ava had never known a man who was so absorbed in his work; in Australia, she said, even bank presidents stopped to have a coffee in the afternoon. Even the mining magnates and the real estate moguls took Sundays off and pushed their children in their prams and sat down to leisurely lunches. But on Sundays Jordan wouldn't leave his house until he had devoured every inch of the Sunday *New York Times;* Ava wasn't allowed to speak to him if he had a section of the newspaper in his hands. "He doesn't get it," Ava said. "He doesn't get *me!* We want two different things!" All Jordan wanted was to work; all Ava wanted was another baby. Zoe would listen to her alternately yearning and complaining. She prayed every night for another baby, a brother or a sister for Jake. Ava told Zoe that a baby was the only thing that would make her life bearable if she had to stay in this country. This left Zoe feeling embarrassed about her own matched set of children. She assured Ava, "It's going to happen for you, I can feel it. You will get your baby."

There had been nights when Zoe truly believed that all she wanted was for Ava to become pregnant, even when the dinner party was over and the Castles and the Randolphs all walked out the door together, arm in arm and laughing, on their way to their cars, leaving Zoe standing in the doorway all alone.

She had been hiding among them. She was the lonely, swaying sapling amid the tall, rooted redwoods that were those other couples, her friends.

When Jake and the twins were in sixth grade, Ava finally did get pregnant. Zoe had to admit she'd been shocked by the news. Ava had been trying to conceive for so long that Zoe had given up hope on her behalf. She had become, in Zoe's mind, a tragic figure, a woman who was never going to get the one thing she most wanted.

But then it seemed that she *was*.

And after all those years of hoping and wishing for her friend, Zoe was even more taken aback to find herself overcome by jealousy. It was as undeniable as a stain across her face and neck. Could anyone else see it?

But with the pregnancy, Zoe and Ava grew even closer. Ava literally let her hair down—took it out of its tight braid, let it flow down her back. She was exhausted and nauseated, but she had moments of playfulness. She made fun of herself—her flatulence, her constant need to pee. She leaned on Zoe, asking if Jake could spend the night at Zoe's house so that she, Ava, could sleep in. Jake had never been allowed to sleep over before, presumably because Zoe let the twins watch R-rated movies and gave them Laurie Colwin's slumped brownies within an hour of bedtime. Ava started confiding in Zoe about how much she missed her mother and sisters back home in Australia. She couldn't believe she was going to give birth to *another American,* she said.

And then the baby was born, and there was a celebration!

Lynne called Zoe at work to tell her that Ava's water had broken and she was in labor, seven centimeters dilated. There would quite possibly be a baby by lunchtime. Zoe got off work at two o'clock and raced home to pick up the wrapped box containing a tiny pink layette (Ava was convinced the baby was a girl). She then waited for the twins to be disgorged from the door of Cyrus Peirce Middle School. They were as excited as Zoe was; Jake had been plucked out of the middle of social studies by his father.

Zoe's first instinct was to drive right to the hospital to wait for the baby to be born. But once the twins were ensconced in the Karmann Ghia, she had second thoughts. They had not technically been *invited* to wait at the hospital. They were close friends of the Randolphs', but they weren't family. But then again, Ava had no other family on the island, and Jordan was an only child. Should Zoe drive to the hospital? She was paralyzed by indecision, feeling suddenly insecure about her status in the Randolphs' life. She decided to just drive home and wait for the call.

At that moment her cell phone rang. It was Jordan.

"It's a boy!" he said. "Eight pounds four ounces, ten fingers, ten toes. Mother and child are both doing fine."

"A boy!" Zoe cried out.

"A boy!" Penny and Hobby shouted.

"Ernest Price Randolph," Jordan said. "Baby Ernie."

"Oh," Zoe said. "Congratulations!"

"Come!" Jordan said. "Come see him!"

Zoe had to admit, it was one of the most joyful moments she had ever experienced on Nantucket. Ava lay in bed, looking as if she had been through a war: she was pale, and there were bruised circles under her eyes, and her hair was matted to her head like a wet mop. But she was triumphant, she was almost forty years old and she had fucking done it, delivered a baby whole and healthy. The baby was asleep in Jake's arms, and Penny and Hobby started arguing about who would hold him next. Zoe kissed Ava's clammy forehead, and tears filled her eyes. She didn't have words; the moment was simply too big. She handed Ava her present, and Ava unwrapped the sweet pink outfit and they both burst out laughing, and the tears found their release. Then Jordan walked in carrying a bottle of champagne. A moment later Al, Lynne, and Demeter Castle arrived, and Ava showed them the pink outfit, and there was more laughter. Penny scooted down the hall with a handful of dollar bills to get sodas from the vending machine, and Jordan popped the champagne, and Zoe snapped pictures of Hobby, who at age thirteen was already six foot one, holding tiny baby Ernie. Lynne Castle hugged Ava, and Al handed Jordan a Cuban cigar that he'd gotten on his last business trip to Quebec. Ted Field poked his head in to shake hands with Jordan, then Al, and to make sure Ava was feeling okay. Jordan handed Zoe a paper cup of champagne, and Zoe toasted him and looked into his blue eyes, and she felt a moment of pure happiness for these people who had gotten their heart's desire.

Then Zoe accepted the sweet package that was Ernest Price Randolph, and she quietly introduced herself to him. "I'm Zoe," she said. "I'm your friend." Then she named the other people in the room: "Your mommy, your daddy, your big brother, Jake. Dr. Field, who delivered you. And over there are my babies, Penny and Hobby. And that's Al Castle and Lynne Castle and Demeter. Look how lucky you are, baby Ernie," she whispered. She raised him up and kissed his impossibly soft cheek. "Look at all the people who love you already."

Two months later, at six o'clock in the morning on Monday, March 31, Zoe got a dramatically different call from Lynne Castle. She could barely make sense of what Lynne was trying to tell her: Ava had gone into the nursery to check on the baby, and . . .

"What?" Zoe whispered. She had heard what Lynne was saying — "stopped breathing," "SIDS," "died in his crib" — but her mind wouldn't allow it. She had seen Ava and Ernie only a few days

before, at the post office. Ava had been standing in line, waiting to pick up yet more baby gifts sent from Australia, and Zoe had offered to hold Ernie while she carried the presents out to her car. Ernie was more alert than the last time Zoe had seen him. He could focus his eyes, which were the deep, concentrated color that Zoe could think of only as Jordan blue. She had bounced him a little; the warm, curved weight of his head fit in her hand like a ball. She had kissed him repeatedly, and he had gurgled, then smiled. Zoe was in love with her twins, she positively adored them, but they were hitting the hard, bumpy road of adolescence. Penny had just gotten her first period and was prone to unpredictable mood swings; Hobby's feet stank up the whole house. Zoe held Ernie and thought, I want another little one just like this.

Ernie, baby Ernie, had stopped breathing. Ava had gone into the nursery and picked him up and he had been as cold and inert as a doll. He was dead.

Poor Ava, oh poor Ava!

At the graveside funeral, Ava wore a black dress. Beneath the dress, her breasts had been bound with Ace bandages to keep her milk from coming in. The other children — Jake and Hobby and Penny and Demeter — released white balloons into the sky, a gesture that Lynne had dreamed up as a way to help them grapple with this unexpected death: little Ernie's soul had been released from his body and carried off by the wind, she told them.

Zoe thought this was a gross oversimplification with a little bit of mystical nonsense thrown in, but she sobbed along with everyone else when the balloons were released. She, along with everyone else, waved good-bye.

Lynne Castle took charge of organizing a meal dropoff for the Randolph family, but Zoe disregarded the schedule and took something of her own over every single day: white chicken chili for Jordan, a delicate vegetable terrine for Ava, pizza pot pie for Jake. She made blueberry muffins and squeezed pitchers of fresh orange juice. She baked loaves of sourdough bread. She made pan after pan of slumped brownies. Sometimes she handed these dishes to Jordan, who always thanked her with a depleted smile. At other times Jordan's car was gone, which meant Ava was alone inside, but Zoe never mustered the courage to knock; she just left the dishes on the front porch.

If she wants to talk, Zoe told herself, she'll call me.

But Ava never called, and what at first passed for a respectful silence turned into a gully, then a canyon.

Months passed, summer arrived. The Randolph family didn't make it to the beach even once. Zoe called Jordan at the newspaper and begged him to let her take Jake to the beach with the twins. Just one Sunday? Just for a few hours?

Jordan breathed heavily into the phone. "My hands are tied," he said. "Ava wants to keep him home."

"For how long?" Zoe asked. "Jesus Christ, Jordan, the kid is thirteen years old. He needs to be *outside*, with his *friends*."

"Zoe," Jordan said. "Please."

Zoe put a handwritten note in the mail to Ava: *I realize how badly you must be hurting. Please know I'm here anytime you want to talk.*

Zoe heard nothing back. It began to feel as if they'd never been friends at all. Zoe attended all the usual summer parties alone, or with the Castles, and she fielded inquiries about how Ava was doing. At first she wasn't sure what to say. Then she came up with a few lines and repeated them: "She and Jordan are circling the wagons, trying to get through this. Thanks for asking." What she might just as well have said was, "Why are you asking *me?* I have no idea."

Zoe broached the topic with Lynne Castle.

"Ava has gone completely silent," Zoe said. "She's shut me out."

Lynne said, "I make overtures, but I don't get very far."

Zoe wanted to know what that *meant,* exactly. Did Ava *talk* to Lynne? Did she answer the phone when Lynne called?

"Jordan and Jake have been over for dinner a few times," Lynne said.

Zoe's thoughts fluttered like a flock of startled birds. "They've been over for dinner?" she repeated.

Lynne pursed her lips, as though tasting something sour. "I think Ava is being especially hard on Jordan. Because of, you know..."

"Because of what?" Zoe asked.

Lynne sighed. "It's just so *sad,*" she said.

As the holidays approached, Zoe took on more private catering jobs. She spent time with the twins, cheering at Hobby's football games, delivering Penny to singing lessons.

She thought, Of course Lynne has had Jordan and Jake to dinner, she *can* ask them to dinner because she's married to Al; they're a respectable family. But if *I* asked Jordan and Jake to dinner, it would look like...well, it would look like something else.

Christmas Stroll weekend arrived. The Stroll was Zoe's favorite event of the year. Downtown was a

holiday wonderland. Christmas trees, lit and decorated, lined Main Street; the shop windows were
filled with elves and candy canes and glittering glass
balls. On the Saturday of Stroll weekend, Main
Street was closed to traffic so the crowds could walk
up and down the cobblestones, listening to the Vic-
torian carolers, sipping hot chocolate, and waiting
for Santa to arrive on the ferry.

That year was especially busy for Zoe. She was
catering a large party Saturday night at a home on
India Street. The woman throwing the party, Ella
Mangini, was one of Zoe's favorite new clients. She
had silver hair that she wore in a swinging bob and
an irrepressible sense of fun. She drank a glass of
champagne with Zoe in the kitchen before the
guests arrived, wearing just her slip and fuzzy slippers. Ella was unmarried, though she intimated
that she'd had many, many lovers. She was aghast
when Zoe said that she hadn't dated anyone seriously since the children were small.

"The kids are enough to fill my emotional life,"
Zoe said. "The kids are, most of the time, too
much."

"But you're so young!" Ella said. "What about
your needs?"

Zoe upended the contents of her champagne
flute into her mouth. *Her* needs? There had been
the occasional one-night stand; there had been the

front-desk clerk at the hotel in Cabo five nights in a row, which for Zoe had constituted a long-term relationship.

"What *about* them?" Zoe said.

After the party was over, Ella returned to the kitchen alone, though Zoe saw a man in a tuxedo standing just outside the door. Ella poured Zoe another glass of champagne, pressed two hundred and fifty dollars into her hand, and said, "The food was outstanding—you're a genius, and I adore you. Now go out and enjoy. The night is but a pup!"

Zoe had walked down the friendship stairs of Ella Mangini's house just as it started to snow. All around her Christmas lights were twinkling, and snowflakes were drifting from the sky. The champagne had created a fizzy bubble of possibility in her chest. *The night is but a pup!* Penny was sleeping at Annabel Wright's house, and Hobby was at a basketball tournament in West Bridgewater. Zoe could go home to her deserted, freezing-cold cottage, or she could proceed downtown and join the celebration.

Once at her car, she removed her chef's jacket. Underneath she wore a sparkly red T-shirt, a concession to the season. She fluffed her hair in the rearview mirror, put on red lipstick, and thought, Okay, here I go.

She wandered down Main Street and stopped in at the Club Car, because she heard the strains of the piano and she knew that the owner, Joe, was sure to buy her a drink.

Once she had wedged herself into the packed bar, though, she felt self-conscious. She had been single basically her entire adult life; she was no stranger to walking into a bar alone. But in recent years she had grown used to the comfortable presence of the Castles and the Randolphs; without them she felt stripped, vulnerable. The piano player was banging out "Hotel California," and people were throwing back their heads and singing along. Zoe felt a pang of regret, because how wonderful would it be if she could just get a drink and join in? If she were anywhere else, she would do it, but this island was a fishbowl, and if the eyes and ears of Nantucket saw and heard her here alone on the Saturday of Christmas Stroll, drinking and singing, people would either feel sorry for her or suspect that she was up to no good.

Someone grabbed her arm, roughly, and she spun around and landed in an empty bar stool.

"Zoe."

Zoe looked up, suspecting that the grabber was Joe, the owner, but as it turned out, it wasn't Joe at all.

It was Jordan.

Jordan had her by the arm. Jordan was sitting on the stool next to hers. Jordan had a beer in front of him and a glass of water. He always drank the two things side by side so he wouldn't get "carried away," a habit that Zoe found absurd.

"Jordan?" she said. The last person she'd ever expected to see *out* at the *Club Car* on the *Saturday* of *Stroll weekend* was Jordan Randolph. He hadn't set foot out of the house other than to go to work (and, she supposed, to dinner at the Castles') in eight months.

Zoe scanned the seats next to Jordan, looking for Al Castle or Marnie Fellowes, his managing editor, or someone else who would help make sense of his presence here—but on Jordan's other side was an attractive older woman wearing Botox, a fur coat, and a New Jersey accent, the unofficial uniform of Christmas Stroll.

Zoe squinted at him. The evening had been surreal enough thus far that she believed this might be a vision or a dream, like something out of *A Christmas Carol,* Jordan appearing next to her like the Ghost of Best Friends Past.

"I'm sorry," Zoe said. "What are you doing here?"

He raised his hand and ordered her a glass of champagne. She waited for the drink to arrive, and then she raised the glass to him and said, "Happy Stroll."

He didn't respond. He raised his water glass and touched it to hers.

She said, "I'm curious enough to ask again: what are you doing here?"

He spun his glass of water, then drank it down until the ice rattled. "I thought getting out would make me feel better," he said. "But I feel worse."

Zoe nodded. She could see how this might be the case. She said, "Want to go for a walk?"

He pulled out his wallet and put a twenty on the bar, and Zoe took another pull off her flute of champagne, then followed him out. The piano player was just launching into "Daydream Believer," which was an old favorite of Zoe's, and she felt another pang of regret at leaving, but if the point of "going out" was to commune with other people and make a meaningful connection, then she could leave the song behind and walk up Main Street in the falling snow with her broken friend.

It was after that very short walk—less than two hundred yards to where Jordan had parked his new Land Rover (new since Ernie's death, a kind of consolation prize for Ava, who had been asking for a new car for years, though now she drove the thing only to the cemetery to place flowers on Ernie's grave)—that Jordan told Zoe the thing that had shocked her but that somehow explained everything.

He leaned against the driver's side of the car, snow falling on the shoulders of his shearling jacket, snow falling in his dark curls, snow falling on the lenses of his glasses. She was tempted to take his glasses off and clean them on the hem of her shirt, but she was afraid that any sudden movement on her part might break the spell. Something was happening here, but she didn't know what.

Jordan wiped his glasses himself, then he said, "I was at work."

"Ah," Zoe said. She thought he meant earlier that night, but his tone indicated that he was making some sort of confession. "You were at work? And then you decided to come out?" she prompted.

"No," he said. "The night Ernie died. I wasn't home." His eyes locked on Zoe's face. She saw the culpability; some of that, no doubt, he felt himself, but some of it must have been pressed on him. "I was at work."

Zoe nodded slowly. He opened his mouth to speak, but she raised her hand. "You don't have to explain," she said. "I get it." Zoe understood everything in that instant. She knew why Ava couldn't talk to anyone, she knew why Jake was in lockdown, she knew it all, suddenly, with that one sentence: "I was at work." She knew why the Randolph family was so lost.

Zoe reached out for him. It was the only thing

she could think of to do. Jordan gathered her up in his arms and held her against him. They hugged fiercely, she breathed in the smell of him, she absorbed the shuddering of his sobs, she shushed him as she would have done with one of her kids. She was aware of his body, a man's body up against hers after so much time. She felt the heat and the chemistry. "What about *your* needs?" Ella Mangini had asked. How easy it would be to get drawn in here, how easy to raise her face and kiss him! But Zoe was not that woman. She wasn't going to capitalize on Jordan's sadness. And she didn't give him the words he so desperately needed to hear — though she did indeed believe them to be true — until ten or twelve minutes later, when she was back on India Street and safely tucked into her Karmann Ghia. It was only then that she texted those words to him:

Jordan, it's not your fault.

But during that brief interval when she was in his arms she seized the full rush of feeling for just a second, just long enough to admit to herself that the real reason she hadn't dated anyone in nearly ten years wasn't the twins but rather the fact that for all that time she had been in love with one person: this man. He was the only thing she wanted in world. But she wouldn't get it. She pulled away. n reached for her, he actually yanked at the sleeve of her coat, but Zoe stepped up onto the sidewalk and said, "I'm going home."

"No," he said.

She knew him well enough not to engage in an argument with him. To argue with Jordan Randolph was to lose.

Zoe headed down Centre Street toward her car, enjoying the small pleasure of her footprints in the fresh snow.

NANTUCKET

It was Beatrice McKenzie, the librarian at the Atheneum, who told everyone: Hobby Alistair and his mother had come in to the library at three o'clock on a Tuesday afternoon in the third week of July. Hobby was in a wheelchair, and his mother was pushing. The bandages had been removed from Hobby's head, revealing that half his scalp had been shaved and that he had a five-inch run of spidery black stitches over his left ear. The wound was gruesome to look at, Beatrice said, plus the boy's arm and leg were in casts, and his arm was in a sling. She couldn't believe he was anywhere other than in the hospital or at home, though she was relieved to see him alive. Beatrice's husband, Paul, now retired, was one of those old-timers who had made a point of watching Hobby play ball every chance he got. Beatrice and Paul had attended the candlelight vigil. On that night, Beatrice had closed her eyes and squeezed Paul's hand and prayed. And now here was the young man, banged up but alive, asking her for a book about colleges.

"And what about Zoe?" we asked. "How did she seem?"

"She was quiet," Beatrice said.

A few days after that, a piece was finally published in the *Nantucket Standard* celebrating the life of Penelope Alistair. This article came as a shock to the summer residents who had arrived after the Fourth of July and missed the news about the accident. Most of us felt that the tribute was long overdue (it ran in the paper, we noted, *after* the departure of Jordan Randolph), and despite the fact that the horror of the accident had started to fade by then, we were glad that the article about Penny had bumped aside yet another account of a summer cocktail party or fund raiser or a report of Mark Wahlberg's having dinner at the Pearl. It was important to us that the summer residents and the two-week renters and even the day-trippers realized that Nantucket was a community, with families and kids growing up. It wasn't a magical kingdom; it wasn't an amusement park for billionaires. It was a real place, home to real people, with all our messes, our disgraces, our steadfast beliefs, our triumphant hearts.

The tribute spoke of the Alistair family's arrival on the island, when Penelope and her brother, Hobson, were two years old. The article chronicled Penny's years at Island Day Care and the Children's House. It recounted the "discovery" of her singing voice in third grade by Helen Yurick, the elementary school music teacher. Mrs. Yurick was quoted as saying, "Never in my life had I heard such a voice come out of so young a child. I knew at once that she was gifted." The article went on to mention Penny's travels to Boston to study with a renowned singing instructor, and then it listed her many accomplishments. She had played Lola in *Damn Yankees,* Sarah in *Guys and Dolls,* and Sandy in *Grease.* She had sung the National Anthem with the Boston Pops in 2010 and, at Keith Lockhart's special request, again in 2011. In the tenth grade she had been selected to join a national chorus—composed of one singer from every state—that traveled to Orlando, Florida, Los Angeles, California, and finally Washington, D.C., where it performed for the President and First Lady. Penny was the lead soloist in Nantucket Madrigals, and Saint Mary's had made a tradition of asking her to sing

"Ave Maria" at Christmas Eve Mass. The article noted that earlier on the day of her death, Penelope Alistair had sung the National Anthem at Nantucket High School's graduation.

Penny was acknowledged to be a good student who was also well liked by her peers. Annabel Wright, cheerleading captain, said: "Penny was a warm and kind person. She was always worried about others. I can't believe she's gone. I can't believe school is going to start in September and she's not going to be in the front row of French class with her hand in the air, answering Madame Cusumano's questions with perfect pronunciation."

The high school principal, Dr. Major: "A light has gone out. It is, of course, a tragedy to lose any young person, but losing a young person like Penelope Alistair is particularly difficult. She was one of the students who lifted up our school community. She was a shining example of the pursuit of excellence, and I know I am not exaggerating when I say that she served as an inspiration to the entire student body."

Winnie Potts, close friend and castmate in *Grease:* "Penny was a paragon of goodness. I'm not going to lie: I was jealous of Penny. We all were, a little bit. It wasn't just that she was so talented. She was just so good. She loved her mother and her brother. I used to wonder what Penny would do once she graduated, but I knew that whatever she did, she would make the rest of us really darn proud."

Penny's twin brother, Hobson, was described in the article as "recovering from injuries sustained during the accident that claimed Miss Alistair's life." He said: "My sister was my hero. When we started kindergarten, I was too shy to order my own lunch in the cafeteria, so she used to do it for me." Here, the writer noted, Hobby laughed with tears shining in his eyes. "Embarrassing, I know, but true. I needed her, I leaned on her. She was my other half. I'm not sure what I'm supposed to do now. Keep going, I guess. Learn how to walk again. And figure out how to take care of my mother, who is hurting so badly."

We all nodded at this. We thought Zoe Alistair might also be quoted, but she wasn't. She must have been consulted for the article, however, because there was a double-page spread of photographs of Penny growing up: Penny at three or four years old, her face painted red, white, and blue for the Fourth of July parade; Penny doing a cartwheel on the lawn at Children's Beach; Penny asleep in the sand with scallop shells placed over her eyes; Penny kneading what looked like bread dough with flour dusting the end of her nose; Penny on stage at the Boston Pops with Keith Lockhart and Carly Simon; Penny dressed as Sandy in the musical *Grease,* wearing a pink sweater and pink poodle skirt; Penny waving from the window of a Model A Ford in the Daffodil Parade; Penny and Hobby and Zoe posing together at a party. Those in the know identified this final picture as having been taken at Patrick Loom's house, only hours before the accident.

Only hours before the accident. To some of us it seemed ghoulish for this picture to be included, and yet this was the one we were most interested in; it was the one we studied the longest. There was no denying it was a wonderful shot of the three of them. Hobby was on the left, grinning, his golden hair catching the last of the day's sunlight. He looked handsome and mature in his white dress shirt and his robin's-egg-blue tie. He was a head and shoulders taller than his mother and sister; in the photo he was leaning in, his arm long enough to reach around both of them. Zoe was on the right, and what could we say but that she looked just like herself? That wavy, layered hair with the hennaed tips, the green eyeliner and hot-pink lipstick, the gauzy top in stripes of green, blue, and purple that faded into one another like swaths of watercolor paint.

And in the center was Penny, her long, dark hair pulled back from her face by a headband, the blue of her sundress echoed in the blue of her round eyes. In this photo her mouth was partially open, as though she'd been caught laughing.

Laughing in the picture taken hours before her death. We could barely wrap our minds around it.

Overall, opinion on the article was good. Princess Diana had been no better remembered, we said. We took pride in that. Nantucket nurtured its own.

It did seem strange to us that there was no mention at all—none whatsoever—of Jake Randolph. Jake had been Penny's boyfriend since freshman year, and the two of them were rarely out of each other's sight. They had shared the kind of absorbing true love that only the luckiest among us found in high school. And yet the article hadn't mentioned Jake, and none of Penny's friends had mentioned Jake. We checked the byline: Lorna Dobbs. We wondered if maybe Lorna Dobbs hadn't known about the salt-and-pepper, peanut-butter-and-jelly matched set of Penny and Jake. But how could she not have known? Then we wondered if the long arm of Jordan Randolph could be exerting its influence from half a world away. Maybe Jordan had instructed his staff not to pair the names of Penelope Alistair and Jordan Randolph. We noted that in this article there had been only passing reference to the accident that had caused Penny's death. We initially thought that this was as it should have been. After all, the piece was meant to celebrate Penny's life, not explain the circumstances of her death. But then we began to wonder if this might not be by design also.

These questions nagged, but eventually we let them go. We saved the article, folded it carefully, and tucked it away in a drawer or scrapbook where we would find it years or decades later, only to be struck yet again by the sad mystery of it all.

JORDAN

July was winter: he had to keep reminding himself of that. But winter weather in Fremantle was humid and balmy, much like a really good day in late May at home. It was 73 degrees Fahrenheit, without a cloud in the sky; it had been raining every night, and everyone's garden was going gangbusters. The grass was so green it hurt Jordan's eyes to look at it.

On the last Sunday in July, Ava took Jake to Heathcote Park for a family barbecue. Ava had brought her son back to Australia with her four times, but not since grade school, and neither Jake nor Jordan had seen anyone from Ava's family since they'd been here this time. This had been at Jordan's specific request. He wanted to give Jake a chance to settle in. And the last thing Jordan wanted was for their rental house to be inundated by Ava's relatives. Things were bad enough as it was.

The person Jordan dreaded seeing most was Ava's mother, Dearie. Dearie had been a perfect bitch toward him when he journeyed halfway across the globe to ask for her daughter's hand in marriage, but she'd been even worse on the one occasion when she'd come to the States. On that visit, she had told Jordan that he was no better than a criminal in her eyes. He had abducted her daughter; he had broken up the freakishly close-knit Price clan. "As if losing Father wasn't bad enough!" Dearie screamed at Jordan on the penultimate evening of her visit, when she had drunk an entire bottle of Riesling by herself.

Jordan tried to point out that he hadn't *stolen* Ava. He had asked her to marry him, she had said no, and he had retreated to the States with his tail tucked, a perfect gentleman. Ava's return to Nantucket the following summer had come as a complete surprise to him; he'd had nothing to do with it. "She came back to me of her own volition," he told Dearie. The reason for Ava's return had never been clear to him — just one of many mysteries about the woman. But he refused to take the blame.

Because of his abhorrence of Dearie, Jordan had flat-out refused to go to the barbecue with his wife and son. This was very bad behavior on his part, and it led to a near-rebellion by Jake.

"I don't get it," Jake said. "Why do I have to go, but you don't?"

"They want to see you, not me," Jordan said. He thought back to the family dinner he'd suffered through on the evening he'd arrived in Perth so many years ago. All he'd wanted was five minutes alone with Ava so he could properly kiss her, but the house was so crammed with people that it verged on the comical. It was like dozens of clowns' climbing out of a Volkswagen: just when Jordan thought there couldn't possibly be any more relatives, another one would descend the stairs or pop out of the bathroom. Dearie had cooked three legs of lamb to feed everybody, and all Jordan remembered was that he was served the burnt ends. Ava, for some reason, had been seated at the opposite end of a very long table, and Jordan got the impression that though he had traveled ten million miles to see her, he hadn't gotten any closer. "You're their blood," he told Jake now. "But I'm not."

"God," Jake said.

Jordan felt sorry for his son. Jordan had met the Price family twenty years ago, and since then everyone had married and reproduced. Ava's siblings had a passel of kids among them. Ava's oldest sister, Greta, had a daughter named Amanda who was pregnant at eighteen. She was only a year older than Jake, and she was having a baby. Greta was going to be a grandmother at forty-seven. And the worst part was, nobody in the Price family saw the shame in this. Ava reported that Dearie was positively over the moon about it; she glowed as though she were the one who was pregnant. She was sixty-seven years old and about to be a great-grandmother.

The population of Western Australia was 2.3 million, and half of those people had to be Prices. In that family, progeny was more important than career or religion or net worth. This explained why Ava, when they first got married, had said she wanted "at least five" children. Jordan had laughed. *Five* children? Who, in this day and age, wanted *five* children? It was irresponsible. When Ava had trouble conceiving again after Jake was born, Jordan was inwardly relieved. Unfortunately, he'd made the grave error of letting his relief show. He'd said, "I was an only child, and I turned out just fine," to which Ava had angrily responded, "I am *not* having an ONLY CHILD!" She was a Price, after all. Her sister Greta had six; her brother Noah had three boys already, and his wife was pregnant again with twin boys, which meant they would undoubtedly try for a sixth.

Ava had pursued a second pregnancy the same way she used to play volleyball on the beach: ruthlessly. She did all the things that the desperate-to-conceive do: she bought a kit that tracked her ovulation, she took her basal temperature, she hunted down Jordan night after night so they could try out new positions that she'd heard might help: her on top, him behind her, her hanging upside down. For a while he'd loved it—what man wouldn't? But as the years passed, she grew frantic. It was bad enough that Ava was the only member of her family who had married an American, now she was also the only one who was having problems conceiving! (Dearie, it was well known, had gotten pregnant with Ava's youngest brother, Damon, at the age of forty-two *while she had an IUD in place!*) Ava began to suspect that she was unable to conceive precisely *because* Jordan was American. And an only child. She accused him of having lazy sperm; she suggested one night that perhaps he'd secretly had a vasectomy. Jordan was then subjected to a hospital visit during which he had to jerk off into a plastic cup just so the lab technician— Charlotte Volmer, whom he'd gone to high school with—could reassure him that all was well. He had millions of healthy swimmers.

The chase for baby number two grew tiresome. Ava used to appear at the newspaper on the night of a deadline and demand that Jordan lock the door to his office and have sex with her right then. The first time it happened, their subsequent emergence garnered a round of enthusiastic applause from his staff. The tenth time, hardly anyone looked up.

In ways too numerous to count, the Prices' obsession with progeny had ruined Jordan's life.

When it began to seem clear that a second baby was never going to happen, when Jordan had given up hope and he believed Ava had as well, Ava returned to Australia alone. She had planned to stay for two weeks, but she ended up staying for six. During their phone calls, Jordan gently inquired as to when she might be coming home. He missed her. He missed her as his wife, and he missed her as Jake's mother; she had left him as a single parent, and he also had a newspaper to run. Jake was only twelve years old at the time, and Jordan had to feed him, help him with his homework, and chauffeur him all over the island. Jordan was careful not to press too hard, however: Ava's trips to Australia were a touchy subject because for all the times that she had gone back, Jordan had never accompanied her. He told her it was because he couldn't leave the newspaper, which was true enough, but more than that, it was because he didn't *want* to go. In this particular instance, Jordan understood that her extended trip to Australia was something of a consolation prize: it was what he was giving Ava because he hadn't given her a baby.

When Ava had been gone for four weeks and three days—a detail that Jordan couldn't forget—she mentioned in a phone call that she had been spending time with Roger Polly, the man fifteen years her senior with whom she had once been in love. The man who had broken her heart.

"'Spending time'?" Jordan said. He was incensed by this news, and completely panicked. "What does that mean, 'spending time'?"

"We've been out," Ava said. She then let it slip that Roger's wife had drowned the year before at Kuta Beach in Bali while on vacation with some friends, adding that when she heard this news, she had called him to offer her condolences. This had led to a second phone conversation, then a meet-up for coffee, then dinner at Fraser's in Kings Park. When Jordan looked up Fraser's on line, he learned that it was one of the nicest restaurants in Perth.

He thought, She's not coming home.

He decided that though he'd refused every chance to go with Ava to Australia in the past, he would go after her right that second. He didn't care if he had to walk and swim.

As it turned out, though, Ava returned of her own volition ten days later. Jordan arranged for Jake to sleep over at the Alistair house that night. Then he brought Ava home and made love to her in a way that he hoped would exorcise all traces of old, distraught widower Roger Polly, as well as establish the national superiority of the United States.

And six weeks later, they discovered that Ava was pregnant.

Now Ava was livid that Jordan wouldn't come to the barbecue. "I suppose they'll think we're divorced, then," she fumed.

"Why would they think we're divorced when I just uprooted my whole life and left the newspaper for an entire year so I could bring you here?" Jordan asked.

That hushed her up. He had made the ultimate sacrifice. He didn't have to shake hands, drink beer, eat kangaroo sausages, or talk about footy with a bunch of Prices. But Jake did.

"Please kiss your grandmother," Jordan told him, feeling like the ultimate hypocrite.

"I can barely remember what she looks like," Jake said.

"She'll be the one on the throne," Jordan said. "Wearing the tiara and velvet robes."

"Honestly, Dad," Jake said. "Can't you please come?"

"No," Jordan said.

"I could refuse to go too, you know," Jake said.

"It would break your mother's heart," Jordan said. "Showing you off to her family has always

been her favorite thing. So be impressive, okay?"
He clapped Jake's shoulder, then lowered his voice
and added, "Nobody knows about the accident,
nobody knows about Penny. You won't have to talk
about it. You won't have anyone feeling sorry for
you. You can just be yourself."

Jake looked at his father. "I don't know who that
is anymore."

Jordan swallowed. What he couldn't tell his son
was that he felt the same way. He was a newspaperman without a newspaper. He was a citizen without
a country. He was a man without the woman he
loved.

"You'll be fine," Jordan said. "You'll be great."

Because he wasn't working, Jordan had every day
free, but today, with Ava and Jake off at Heathcote
Park for an all-day affair, he was *really* free. He sat
on the bench in the back garden and read the *Sunday Australian* while listening to the gurgling of the
fountain. It was a pleasant hour in the sun; the *Sunday Australian* was a nice little newspaper. It featured a weekly column on wine whose author seemed
very well informed—Jordan usually wrote down
his suggestions—and it made him wonder if perhaps he should add a wine column to the *Nantucket
Standard.* Maybe in summer. Maybe in winter.
Whenever he thought about the newspaper, he got

an itchy feeling. He was just biding time here in Australia; he was treading water for Ava's sake, for Jake's sake. Ava had undergone an immediate and complete metamorphosis upon their arrival in Fremantle. She was drinking, smoking, and partying like a teenager; she was sailing and going to the beach and once again singing along to Crowded House in the shower. She was living. Looking at the remarkable bloom of the flowers surrounding the fountain, Jordan thought that Ava was like a native plant that he'd uprooted and transplanted in a hostile climate. Now here she was, back on home soil. Flourishing again.

But he, most certainly, was not.

He went inside. He found himself tiptoeing like a burglar to his desk in the den. He hadn't used his computer once in the three weeks they'd been here. He had been keen to set it up, eager to establish a connection with his home ten thousand miles away, but then as soon as he'd gotten it up and running, he'd felt afraid. He wasn't sure he could handle news from home. After all, back on Nantucket, summer was in full swing. There would be things happening every day and every night: talks at the Atheneum, concerts, plays, benefits, dinner auctions, cocktail parties, golf tournaments, fishing tournaments, book signings, art openings. There would be bands playing at the Cisco Brewery in the afternoons and at the Chicken Box at night. Jordan had never been able to make it to every event in a typical summer week, but he liked to get to as many as he could. In recent years he and Zoe had attended functions separately but together. He loved nothing more than seeing her dressed up and chatting away, sipping her wine, throwing him meaningful looks, whispering funny things as they brushed past each other in the crowd. Sometimes Zoe would be catering one of these events, and Jordan would find her in the kitchen. She would be wearing her white chef's jacket with the words *Hot Mama* stitched over the breast pocket, her hair held back by a turquoise bandanna. Her Jamaican waiters would all break out in knowing smiles when they saw him: "Coming to kiss the boss lady's hand," they'd tease. They thought he came back to the kitchen for the food—a special ramekin of the truffled mac and cheese, his own plate of mini lobster rolls. And while it was true that Zoe plied him with special treats, really he came just to lay his eyes on her, to hear the jingle of her long, dangly earrings, to listen to the sound of her voice.

He had been in love with her. Besotted by her. He still was.

He wondered what Zoe's life was like this summer. He figured she had turned down all catering jobs. Possibly she'd even taken a leave of absence from her job with the Allencasts. She had a small trust fund, enough money to live on for a little while, anyway. Although maybe not: the Allencasts paid her health insurance, which she would need now as she never had before, given Hobby's condition.

Jordan envisioned her working for the Allencasts for a few hours in the morning and a few hours in the evening, then spending the rest of her time at home with Hobby. She wouldn't go out at night. She was just as definitively exiled from their previous life as Jordan was, even though she was right there.

He pictured her on her back deck, drinking wine. He pictured her screaming at the ocean. He pictured her in bed, lying among the dozen pillows that she required, crying for Penny. Her little girl.

He tapped the keyboard, and the screen sprang to life. He would email her, he decided. She might not respond, she might delete the message, but even if they were no longer lovers — *for so many reasons* — they were still connected, they were still simpatico. He knew she thought about him, they had a shared view of the world, they spoke the same language, they held common opinions. They were friends, goddammit, above and beyond and before every-thing else, they were *friends,* and he was going to email her. The house was empty, Ava and Jake would be gone for hours, and how often was he going to get a chance like this?

To: Z
From: J
Subject:

But what should he say? "I love you"? "I miss you"? "I'm thinking about you"? "I never *stop* thinking about you"? "I feel as if my heart had been ripped out and fed to a koala bear, and koala bears are surprisingly nasty little creatures"?

Zoe was right: it was always all about him.

Maybe "How are you?" Or "How are you doing?" "What are you thinking about?" "How is Hobby?" "Is there any moment of your day that is even a little bit easier than the rest of your day?" "Are you working?" "Do you need anything? Do you want anything? Aside from the obvious..."

Jordan deleted the unwritten email.

He succumbed to his nagging curiosity and pulled up the on-line version of the *Nantucket Standard*. When he saw the lead story, he coughed.

Island Remembers Nantucket High School Student

It was an article about Penny.

Jordan read every word, then he read it again, thinking he must have missed something. He read the quotes from Annabel Wright and Winnie Potts

(Winnie's should have been edited, possibly even cut, he thought; it was too honest for this kind of piece). He read Hobby's quote and felt tears coming to his eyes: "I guess I'll have to find a way to take care of my mother..." Jordan's sadness, and his shame and regret—he should have published this article, or one better than this, before he left—were cut only by the fact that there wasn't a single mention, anywhere, of Jake. Very little about the crash itself—only a brief acknowledgment at the lead-in that Penny had died in a one-car accident—and nothing, not a word, about her boyfriend, his son.

It was beastly. If Jake saw this, he'd...well, he'd feel empty and bewildered and hurt. New, fresh hurt on top of all of the other hurt.

Jordan shut down his computer. He dropped his head into his hands and yanked at his hair. Then he raised his face; he could see himself now in the dark screen of the monitor. He adjusted his glasses and sniffed.

He and Jake and Ava were gone from Nantucket, yes, they had gone away, but the surprising thing was that they had also, apparently, been forgotten.

He still had hours before the others would get home. Nothing good could come of his sitting in the house alone, he knew, and so he went out and wandered the streets of Fremantle. It was, he had to admit, a charming city. He headed up Charles Street and across Attfield, admiring the bungalows, many of which were better kept up than the one they had rented. He liked the classic limestone with redbrick quoins around the windows, the tin roofs, the bullnosed terraces that curved over the deep front porches. There were variations on the theme: on one house the trim had been painted lavender, another had stained glass in its front windows, and in yet another someone was practicing scales on the piano. Jordan stopped for a second to listen. If he were a different kind of person, he would be able to take enjoyment from the place where he found himself, rather than longing to be somewhere else.

But he wasn't that kind of person.

He stepped into a pub called Moondyne Joe's. He could have gone to the Sail & Anchor, which was a little nicer (or more "toff," as Ava would have said) and which had chili mussels on the menu and artisanal beer and a scrubbed-clean clientele. Or he could have gone to the Norfolk Hotel, which had an outdoor courtyard and two guys strumming Midnight Oil songs on the guitar. But Jordan was in the mood for someplace dark and gritty. He had discovered Moondyne Joe's on one of his aimless walks through the city. It was the kind of place where men drank up their dole money; it attracted a tough, tattooed crowd. It smelled like cigarette smoke, beer, and old beer. The concrete floors were sticky, and there was no "food" to speak of other than a warming case that held a selection of Mrs. Mac's meat pies. A TV hung in the corner of the bar, a huge, boxy thing that seemed as outdated as a cassette deck (the Ute that Jordan had bought from the car-rental agency had one of those). When Jordan was here before, it was midafternoon on a Tuesday, and there were only four or five men at the bar keeping the bartender—a stout, matronly woman who looked as if she ought to be running a home for wayward boys—company. But today the place was packed, and Jordan found himself elbow to elbow with fifty or sixty sweating blokes. (That seemed such an appropriate word for this breed of Australian men; Jordan reminded himself to look up its etymology when he got home.) He wanted to step back out onto the street, but once he was in the pub, he felt committed. Stepping back outside because he didn't like the looks of the other patrons would have been a cowardly move.

Everyone's focus was on the TV. A game was on: rugby. And then Jordan remembered what he had read in the sports section of the *Sunday Australian:*

the Australian national team was playing New Zealand. The All-Blacks. The All-Blacks were world-famous; they did a version of the traditional Maori Haka dance before each game. They were documented badasses.

Jordan moved toward the bar. He fought off the mental image of himself as an effete, intellectual newspaper editor hailing from a country that wasn't even tough enough to field a national rugby team. He was so far out of his element here that it was almost comical, but a beer might help.

The bartender—the same middle-aged woman as before—gave him a Carlton Mid-Draught, and while he had her attention he ordered a shot of whisky as well, and then, in order to gain a few more inches of bar space, he bought the muscled behemoth to his right—a man wearing a fluorescent green vest over his bare chest, who smelled like the lion cage at the zoo—a shot of whisky too. This man—he was a decade younger than Jordan—eyed the shot warily.

"What's tha?" he said.

Jordan nodded at the TV. He didn't want to speak and thereby reveal himself as an American just yet. "Game," he said.

The man needed no further explanation. He threw back the shot. "Thanks, mate."

"No worries," Jordan said.

The man did edge off a bit, giving Jordan room enough to move his arm so he could get his beer to his mouth. There was a sudden outburst of raucous booing — the All-Blacks had scored — and the man to Jordan's left stood up in disgust, leaving his bar stool empty.

Jordan waited a split second to see if anyone else was going to take the stool, someone with more of a national right to it than him, but no one stepped forward. So Jordan sat, moved his beer in front of him, and silently congratulated himself on acquiring this real estate. The whisky affected him in a way that made his situation seem wonderfully humorous. He was in a pub watching Australia battle the All-Blacks; he had a seat and a cold beer. If Ava could see him, she would think...what? That he'd done an admirable job of assimilating? Or that he was making a fool of himself or, even worse, sneering at the other men at the bar, condescending American snob that he was?

And what would Zoe think? He raised his face to the TV. Well, the old Zoe would have been happy beside him at this bar with a cold beer. She would have thought that the players for the All-Black team were hot.

Jordan had another beer, another shot of whisky, a third beer. He was getting drunk; he should ask for a glass of water. He never let himself get carried away like this, or rarely did: there was that one night on Martha's Vineyard, his first night with Zoe.

Oh, Zoe. Zoe.

Another beer, his fourth. He had to take a leak, but he was afraid of losing his seat. His eyes were glued to the TV, but the game was inscrutable to him. He yelled when the rest of the patrons in the bar yelled; he cheered when they cheered. He elbowed the man next to him and said, "Watch my seat, mate?"

The man nodded. "Sure, mate."

Mate, mate, mate. Jordan stumbled to the bathroom, which smelled like piss and beer and smoke, and as he used the urinal, he puzzled over the word *mate*. Odd term for a friend, and especially so because Australians seemed to apply it most often to complete strangers. Jordan tried to wash his hands—one of the stained sinks gave him a trickle of water—and regarded himself in the clouded mirror. He was plowed. *Plowed* was, of course, Zoe's word. She had endless synonyms for *drunk*, including *plastered, shitfaced, shattered, fucked up, schnockered, destroyed, toasted, wrecked, obliterated, blitzed, pissed, whipped, smashed, crushed,* and *labeled*. Jordan pushed his glasses up his nose. He was drunk at a pub while his poor son suffered through a barbecue with several hundred Price relatives at Heathcote Park.

No mention of Jake at all in that article. If Jake found out, he would be so hurt. Jordan didn't think Jake had been using his computer. God, he hoped not.

The barbecue would be fine. Jake would be treated like a prince; the adults would swarm him. The other kids would ask him questions just so they could hear his accent. They would think he was cool; he came from the same country as the iPhone and Kanye West and LeBron James and Stephen King and the Academy Awards. He would be a celebrity; it would boost his ego.

Jordan fought his way back to his seat. His mate at the bar said, "Had to rough a few up, but I kept it empty for you."

"Appreciate that," Jordan said. He ordered another beer.

There was no way he could ever have gone to that barbecue. He didn't like the Prices, this had always been true. But he couldn't face them now because he knew that some of them — Dearie certainly, Greta certainly, maybe all of them — blamed him for Ernie's death.

He hadn't talked to anyone about this, except Zoe.

That March 30 four years earlier was a Sunday, two weeks before Town Meeting, and Jordan had fallen woefully behind at work. His copyeditor at the time, Diana Hugo, a twenty-two-year-old Yale graduate who was taking a gap year before attending the Columbia School of Journalism, had come down with mono. This was an unfortunate development because Diana was a whiz—she would work at the *New York Times* one day, Jordan was sure—and she had been single-handedly responsible for covering Jordan's ass in the weeks after Ernie was born. He had taken entire days off so he could be at home to help Ava with Ernie; he took the baby for walks, he fed him bottles, he burped him and changed his diaper. He did the 9:00 p.m. feeding and the midnight feeding, after which he was in charge of putting him down for his longest stretch of sleep, from midnight to 4:00 a.m. Ava and Jordan were both showing signs of sleep deprivation; they were a dozen years older than they had been when Jake was a newborn, and Jordan, at least, felt it. Ava normally handled the 4:00 a.m. feeding, and then Jordan would get up with Jake at 6:30, make him breakfast, pack his lunch, and drive him to school. There were days when Jordan was too tired to go straight to the office. He would drop Jake off, drive home again, take a nap, and get to the office around 10:00. Such a late start was unheard-of for him at the paper, but there were extenuating circumstances, his staff understood, and Diana was around to assign stories, edit and proofread stories, answer Jordan's phone, and put out the small fires.

Town Meeting was two weeks away. He hadn't read a single one of the articles.

Diana Hugo had been diagnosed with mono and would be out for three, or possibly four, weeks.

Those were just excuses, however.

March 30 was a typical Sunday, technically spring but really still winter. Gray skies, 45 degrees, winds out of the northeast at 20 to 25 miles per hour. Jordan lit a fire in the morning, then started in on the Sunday *New York Times*. Ava handed off Ernie to him, saying that she was going to exercise class. She had to get the baby weight off. Jordan poked his glasses up his nose with one finger, an involuntary gesture that Ava, over the years, had come to find hostile.

There was a minor exchange between the two of them. She, in a snippy voice, said that she was sorry to inconvenience him during his sacred reading of the paper. Inconvenience him with his own son, she added.

"Not an inconvenience," Jordan said, accepting the squirming bundle that was Ernie. Although it was, sort of. The finest hour of Jordan's week was the hour he took on Sunday morning to read the *Times*. Over the years he had encouraged—okay, maybe strongly encouraged, maybe enforced—a period of quiet during his paper-reading. That Ava was now invading that quiet wasn't exactly ideal, but he understood. The exercise class was at ten, that couldn't be changed; she wanted to get her body back, which was important, even though to Jordan's eyes she looked fine.

The poking of the glasses was not really a veiled complaint, or at least he would never admit that it was. His glasses were merely slipping.

After Ava left, in something of an officious huff, Jordan placed baby Ernie in the electric swing, where he fussed for a few minutes before falling asleep.

When Ava returned an hour and fifteen minutes later, Ernie was still in the swing. He had slipped down a little; his head was cocked at an uncomfortable-looking angle, but everybody knew that babies' necks were made of rubber.

Ava squawked, "Has he been in there the whole time?"

Jordan looked up from the crossword puzzle, which he always saved for last. "No."

Jake, who was sitting at the kitchen counter eating a bowl of Golden Grahams, said, "Yes."

"It's a swing, Jordan," Ava said, snapping off the power and unbuckling Ernie. "Not a babysitter." She picked Ernie up. "And he's soaked right through his outfit. Jesus Christ."

Jordan raised his head and offered a half-hearted smile of apology, but really his mind was occupied with trying to summon up the French word for "winter." Five letters.

Ava left the room.

Jake slurped his milk. "You blew it," he said.

"Hiver!" Jordan remembered.

Later, to make amends, Jordan offered to take care of the baby while he watched a March Madness game with Jake: BYU vs. Florida. Then he volunteered to run out to the Stop & Shop for a few things that Ava needed, and he said he would take the baby with him.

"It's too cold for the baby to go out," Ava said.

"Nonsense," Jordan said. "We are a hearty, seafaring people." He bundled the baby up, packed him into his bucket car seat, and set out for the store. He was more than making amends now; he was stockpiling chits. The shadows of Town Meeting and Diana Hugo at home with mono loomed. Jordan was tempted to stop by the office — just for an hour or two — with Ernie. But no, that was a bad idea; Ava would need to breastfeed the baby. He would work later, he told himself. He would head in to the paper after Ernie was asleep.

Was there anything unusual about the nine o'clock feeding? About the midnight feeding? Later

Jordan would rack his brain and come up with nothing. He gave Ernie a bottle at each feeding, and both times Ernie sucked it dry. Jordan burped him perhaps a little more thoroughly with the first feeding. At midnight, instead of feeling the leaden exhaustion that normally weighed him down at that hour, Jordan was agitated by his need to get to the office. He set Ernie down in his crib on his back. Ernie was asleep; he fussed for a minute, just long enough for Jordan to worry that he would wake himself up, which would mean that the process of putting him to sleep would have to be restarted. But then he quieted, and Jordan tiptoed from the room, closing the door halfway behind him, as Ava liked it, so she could hear the baby if he cried.

Jordan then, feeling like a cat burglar, or like a teenager sneaking out to meet his girlfriend, left the house. He went to work.

Ernie's death was not Jordan's fault. Intellectually, he knew this. He and Ava, just like most people, were educated about SIDS, or Sudden Infant Death Syndrome. But the possibility of its affecting them seemed remote. Neither of them knew anyone, or even knew anyone who knew anyone, who had lost a baby to SIDS. It was a tragedy that resided elsewhere — maybe in a trailer park somewhere on the outskirts of Detroit, where both parents smoked and the mother worked the third shift at the Ford factory and the father, who was only nineteen himself, put the baby to sleep facedown in smothering, too-soft covers. SIDS didn't happen in a relatively affluent household with intelligent, doting parents.

Except it did.

Ernie's death was not Jordan's fault.

But Ernie's head had been cocked at that funny angle in the swing for...forty-five minutes? an hour? Why couldn't Jordan have just held him? Was that too much to ask?

And Jordan had taken Ernie outside in cold, wet, windy weather. Who knew how that had affected his lungs?

And when Ava was awakened by the hot, uncomfortable throbbing of her breasts (her milk was starting to leak); when she walked down the hall to the nursery, feeling astonished that Ernie had slept until five and ambivalent about waking him up to feed him; when she looked at Ernie and knew that something wasn't right, that he was sick or something; when she picked him up and he didn't yield and meld into her arms, he wasn't warm, he wasn't *breathing*; when Ava screamed (like a woman in a horror film, Jake would remember later, as if she were getting butchered by a chainsaw) — when all of that happened, Jordan wasn't home. Ava was calling his name, she ran into the bedroom crying, jiggling the baby, slapping his tiny cheeks, trying to revive him.

"Jordan!" she shrieked. *"JORDAN!"*

At the moment when Ava called out for him, he was probably locking up the office, exhausted but satisfied with all that he'd accomplished. He was finally getting caught up.

"JORDAN!"

Ava had raced through the house, clutching life-less baby Ernie to her chest; milk was flowing all over the front of her nightshirt. Her breasts were on fire, they hurt like hell. Ava sat at the kitchen stool and tried to nurse the baby, thinking that once he smelled the breast, he would wake up. But at the same time, she knew. Her engorged nipple dripped over an unresponsive mouth. She started bawling. Then there were hands on her. Jake.

Jake said, "Mom?"

She said, "Where's your father?"

Jake said, "Um, I don't know?"

Ava said, "Call nine-one-one."

He said, "Why?"

Ernie's death was not Jordan's fault. But he could not bear to imagine those moments in the house — the moment when Ava discovered that Ernie wasn't breathing, the moment when she tried to breastfeed him, the moment when Jake realized that his brother was dead—because the guilt leveled him each time.

He was not there.

He was at work.

When Jordan finally stumbled out of the bar at four o'clock, it was nearly dark. Nearly dark at four o'clock? He panicked. Would Ava and Jake be back? Jordan was drunk now. He needed a short black and a nap. Why was it so dark at four o'clock?

And then he remembered. It was July. Winter.

"How was it?" he asked Jake later. Jake and Ava had walked in the door at quarter to seven, which had given Jordan enough time to drink three cups of coffee and four glasses of water, take a nap, take a shower, and make himself a sandwich.

"Mmmmm," Jake said.

"And that means?"

"It was lovely," Ava interjected. She kissed Jake on the cheek, and Jake made a face, but she didn't notice. She was breezy and happy, she was humming. Of course spending the day with her family would make her feel that way. Jordan was surprised she wasn't bubbling over with bits of news and gossip; probably she knew how little he wanted to hear any of it.

Ava disappeared into the front part of the house, and Jordan tried again with his son. "Can I make you a sandwich?"

"Yes, please."

"Did you eat at the park?"

"Sort of," Jake said. "I had a sausage, but that was a while ago."

"Did you kiss your grandmother?"

"Yes."

"And you met Greta and Noah and..."

"Yes, everybody. There are a million more cousins now. All with names like Doobie and Spooner and Pats. Xavier was the only one I remembered. I couldn't keep the rest of them straight."

"I'm sure no one expected you to."

"One of Mom's sisters married an Aboriginal guy? Those kids were the only ones I really liked. You could tell they felt as much out of place as I did."

"May, your Aunt May. Married to...what's the guy's name?"

"I can't remember."

"Doug, I think. He works at a bank. So those kids were nice?"

"I guess," Jake said. "They were all way younger than me. I mostly threw the ball with them and stuff."

"I'm sure your aunt appreciated that."

"Mom acted weird. She kept kissing me and

touching my hair and asking everyone, didn't they think I was handsome, and she told them all how I was going to be a senior, only she called it Year Thirteen, which bugged me, and then she said I was going to 'uni,' which bugged me, and then one of the uncles...the big guy with the mustache?"

"Damon," Jordan said, proud of himself for remembering.

"He told me I should go to uni in Australia, and Mom sounded like she thought this was the best idea she'd ever heard. But just so you know, I'm *not* going to uni or college or whatever in Australia. I'm going at home."

"Of course," Jordan said. He pulled out some bread for Jake's sandwich. "Did anyone ask about me?"

"Everyone did. Mom said you were at home resting."

"Did she?" Jordan said. "Well, that's an interesting reversal."

Jake snorted. "To you, maybe."

That night, after they got into bed and shut off the light, Ava rolled toward Jordan and slid her hand between his legs.

Jordan's arm shot out and nearly hit her in the face. She continued on, undeterred. Her hand stroked the front of his boxer shorts.

Jordan didn't know what to do. He was paralyzed with confusion. He and Ava hadn't made love in four years. *Four years.* Since before Ernie. After Ernie, Ava hadn't wanted to. She was too sad at first, and too angry, too bitter and resentful. After a few months Jordan had tried to reason with her: they could try again for another baby. They could make this a story with a happy ending. Surely that was what she wanted?

"If we have another baby, it won't be Ernie," Ava said. *"It won't be Ernie!"*

He knew what she meant. He saw that his own desire to have another child was nothing more than a selfish way of exonerating himself. He didn't really want another child.

There was no sex at all that first year. During the second year Jordan tried again. He tried romance: on nights when Jake was sleeping over at the Alistair house, he lit candles and poured champagne. But he got nowhere with Ava. By then her anger and sadness had hardened into an enamel shell of indifference. She read *Moby-Dick,* she watched *Home and Away,* she didn't care about anything. She asked him just to please leave her alone. Not even touch her.

Jordan came to terms with the fact that his intimate life with his wife was over. He threw himself into his work and raising Jake; he made sure he was so tired every night that all he wanted to do was sleep. Eventually Ava moved into Ernie's nursery. He never entered; she never invited him in.

Then everything happened with Zoe. Did he need to explain how it felt to have a woman to love again? Someone to hold hands with, someone to kiss, someone to caress? He had been starving for affection, for physicality, for touch — and Zoe fed him.

Did he feel guilty about his affair with Zoe?

Yes.

He had striven his whole life to differentiate himself from his father, but he was cheating on Ava just as Rory Randolph had cheated on his mother. But, Jordan noted, there were differences. Ava had shut him out; Ava didn't want him, and for years he had lived like a monk. He never thought that Ava might return to him in this way.

Now here she was, stroking him. She was making a purring noise. If he made love to her now, it would be like having sex with a total stranger. But it was a moot point, because his body wasn't responding anyway. He was headachy and hung over from his afternoon at the pub, and Ava smelled like a dirty ashtray. She'd been smoking again — probably with her sister May and her brother Marco, but maybe with her ex-flame Roger Polly; maybe Roger Polly had showed up at Heathcote

Park to play surrogate husband. Jordan couldn't summon the energy to care. He was exhausted. But those were just excuses. He was a different man now than he had been then. Ava had come back to him, but it was too late.

"Ava," he whispered.

She shushed him. Her hand, insistent, slid under his boxers. She wanted this to work. And didn't he want it to work too? Wasn't that why he'd brought her here? So she would be happy again? So they could try to reconcile?

She gave up after a few minutes and rolled over.

"You don't want me," she said.

He closed his eyes and tried to remember the woman he had fallen in love with: the volleyball player in the string bikini with the ruthless serve and the bright smile. He tried to remember the young woman at the far end of her mother's table, safely surrounded by her tribe. All he had wanted back then was to be able to touch her leg under the table, but she was too far away. Unattainable. It had driven him mad.

But that Ava was gone. And that Jordan was gone. Now they were just two older, sadder people who had done years and years' worth of damage to each other.

Jordan opened his mouth to speak. But what to say? She would recognize an excuse. This was a big moment. It was, Jordan realized, the moment the whole trip had been about. He wished he were better prepared. All he was armed with was the stark truth.

"I can't," he said.

She kicked him, hard, under the covers. His shin hurt, but he didn't make a sound. He could hear Ava next to him, breathing.

"They all asked about you, you know."

"I know," Jordan said. "Jake told me."

"And what was I supposed to say? 'Jordan didn't come because he hates you. He fucking hates your guts, Mum, because you threw away his *beachplum jam.*'" Ava's voice was nasty, but curiously, Jordan relaxed. The Ava who had tried to arouse him was a stranger, but this Ava he recognized.

He sat up. He could barely see anything of her in the dark, but he sensed her sliding out of bed. He saw the ghostly white of her tank top, the shadow of her legs. "I don't hate anyone's guts," he said calmly.

"You didn't come because you *never come. You're never around.* You never once came back with me here to visit. Never once in twenty years, Jordan. You were always *working.* Always at the *newspaper.* God, how I despise that newspaper!" Ava said. "You know I never read a single page of it after Ernie died. Not a word."

Jordan felt stunned by this. He hadn't realized that Ava refused to read the newspaper. His newspaper.

"I offered to come back here with you after Ernie died," Jordan said. "Remember, I mentioned it to you..."

"I didn't *want* to come after Ernie died, Jordan," Ava said. "How would that have felt? All of my sisters and brothers with their broods of beautiful, perfect children, and me showing up just after burying the baby I had waited *twelve years* for."

"Okay, Ava, yes. Fine, I get it."

"The only reason you offered to bring me back here," Ava said, "was that you felt guilty."

There was that word. Jordan had chewed on it all afternoon at the pub.

"Yes," he said. "You're right. I felt guilty."

"Because you *weren't home!*" she screamed. "Because at the one moment in my life when I needed you most—*the very most,* Jordan, *a life-and-death situation*—you weren't there!"

"Ava," he said. She was pacing the room now, shaking her hands. Probably she wanted a cigarette. "Ava, it would have made no difference if I'd been home. Ernie still would have died, Ava."

"He was in distress. You might have heard him if you'd been home! You might have been able to save him!"

"No," Jordan said. He couldn't accept that he might have had the power to save Ernie and had failed. "No, Ava, things wouldn't have been different."

"But they might have," she said. She was crying now. "We'll never know."

"*No!*" Jordan roared.

"We'll never know!" Ava said. "But I will always wonder. *I! Will! Always! Wonder!*"

"I'm sorry!" Jordan said. "Is that what you want? I am *sorry,* Ava. I've never been sorrier about anything in my life! I was at work! Trying to do my job, to run the paper that has provided my family with a livelihood for eight generations! I didn't know anything was going to happen to Ernie! I loved him too! I've been hurting too! But since then, you have been so focused on your own pain and your own grief that nothing else has mattered to you. You let your whole life fall away! You let me fall away! Because deep down, *you blame me!*"

"*There is no one else to blame!*" Ava shrieked.

Jordan sank his head back into his pillow. She was right about that, he thought. There was no one else to blame.

JAKE

In his shed, even with the door closed and a feather pillow over his head, he could still hear them: "You're never around. . . . Always at the newspaper. God, how I despise that newspaper!"

"I'm sorry! Is that what you want? . . . You let me fall away!"

Jake sat up in bed. There was a momentary quiet; he could hear the gurgle of the fountain. He felt a little dizzy, which was probably due to the fact that he'd drunk three beers at the barbecue, grabbed from the eskie by his cousin Xavier, who had been nicer and cooler than the bratty kid Jake remembered. Somewhere in the middle of the third beer, sitting at the foot of an enormous Norfolk pine, overlooking the Swan River and the Perth city skyline across the river, Jake had confided to Xavier that he hated Australia.

As soon as the words were out of his mouth, he worried that Xavier would be offended. Xavier had lived in Western Australia his whole life. All of the Price family had.

"It's not the place, exactly," Jake said. "It's my parents. They fight all the time. And I miss home."

Xavier bobbed his head. "Man," he said. "You should just head back to the States, then. You should just bolt."

He *should* just bolt. Jake had seventy Australian dollars, three hundred American dollars, and a Visa card that his father had given him in case of emergencies, but if he used the Visa card, it would take Jordan and Ava only about five minutes to figure out where he was. They would find him and come get him. He was still a minor.

Or at least those had been Jake's thoughts earlier, at Heathcote Park. Now, having just heard his parents fighting *again,* he climbed out of bed and got dressed. He wasn't going to stay here. He packed a duffel bag with clothes, his running shoes, the Hemingway novel, his camera, and one picture of Penny. He stuffed all of his money and his credit card into his jeans pocket. He jammed his earphones into his ears and walked out the door of the shed and through the garden, quietly, quietly, until he was out the side gate and on the street. It was 11:00 p.m.

He had nowhere to go. Most of Fremantle was closed up by this time of night, except the pubs, which he was too young to enter. He walked toward South Beach because that was the direction his feet seemed to want to take him. A crescent moon hung out over the Indian Ocean. Jake was chilly; he hunted through his duffel bag for his navy blue Nantucket Whalers sweatshirt.

His parents had been fighting about Ernie. If Ernie were alive, he would be four and a half years old now, a little kid who could ride a tricycle and ask Jake for piggyback rides.

Jake stuck to sidewalks and then moved over to the bike path that meandered through the park leading to the beach. He wondered if he should be worried about getting mugged. He wished he had another beer. He looked at his iPod, and despite the fact that he knew it would make him feel even worse than he already felt, he played the track of Penny singing "Lean on Me." *Lean on me, when you're not strong:* her voice sounded real, close, nearly three-dimensional. It was like a silken rope that he could climb up, maybe, until he reached her. *Lean on me. When you're not strong.* He was not strong. He wanted to lean on her. More than anything, he wanted to hold her, tell her he was sorry, he would take the blame, it was his fault for what he'd done with Winnie, the kissing, the touching, the way his body had betrayed him. What he wanted to make clear was that he hadn't stopped loving Penny, not at all, not for a second. He had run from the Pottses' basement. He hadn't followed his lustful seventeen-year-old desires; he had understood, even while he was captive to them, that they were wrong. He should have told Penny about it himself and not let Demeter, or possibly even Winnie, tell her in the dunes.

He should never have given her the keys to the

car. He should have yanked the emergency brake. He had been worried about his transmission, for crying out loud. He'd never in a million years thought Penny would keep going, faster and faster.

He had thought she would hit the brake. Of course she would hit the brake.

At South Beach there was a group of people gathered around a bonfire. Jake stared at them from a distance. Another beach, another bonfire, the other side of the world. He didn't recognize anyone there, of course; they were all strangers. Ferals. They were kids his age or a little older with dreadlocks and tattoos, they were drinking, and Jake smelled weed. This was most certainly not the place for him. But he was freezing now despite his sweatshirt, and the idea of being next to the fire was too tempting to resist. He would go check it out.

"Hey, man."

One of the ferals stood. He was bare-chested, wore brown swim trunks, and had a bush of bronze-colored hair. He was so tan that the overall effect was of a continuous column of color—hair, skin, trunks. He stuck out his hand. "I'm Hawk," he said. "Welcome."

"Hey," Jake said. This was a cult or something for sure. Regular people weren't this friendly.

"What's your name?" Hawk asked.

"Um, Jake," he said.

"You American?" This was asked by a girl sitting a few people away from where Hawk had been sitting. She had long tangled hair and wore a white bikini top and a white eyelet skirt. How were these people not freezing their asses off?

"Yeah," Jake said.

"Come sit," Hawk said. "Join us. Warm yourself by the fire. You want a beer?"

Now would be a good time to excuse myself, Jake thought. Someone else, across the fire, asked, "You want a toke?" And everyone else laughed.

There was some tribal drumming music in the background, which gave the whole scene the feeling that someone was going to be sacrificed here tonight. Probably him, the newbie whose sweatshirt announced him as a punky American high school student.

"No, man, I gotta go," Jake said.

"Go where, man?" Hawk asked.

"Sit," the white-bikini girl said. "Have a beer. I'll get it." She ran through the sand to a big blue eskie. She pulled out an ice-cold Emu and handed it to him.

"Thanks," Jake said. He had been craving a beer. He would stay for just this one. "Who do I pay?"

" 'Pay'?" Hawk said. "We all chipped in, man, you want to throw some in the pot, go right ahead."

Jake pulled ten Australian dollars out of his jeans pocket and handed it to Hawk.

"Thank you!" Hawk said, holding the money out for everyone to see. "Have a seat, my friend. Have a seat."

One hour, three beers, and two hits of marijuana later, Jake had handed over his remaining sixty Australian dollars, as well as two hundred of his three hundred American dollars, to Hawk, securing himself a place in Hawk's van first thing in the morning. They were traveling across the Nullarbor Plain toward Adelaide, where some people would get out and some different people would get in, and then they were continuing east to Sydney. From Sydney Jake would use the credit card to book a flight back to the States, or he would jump on a container ship and cross the Pacific that way. His parents could chase after him, let them do that, or maybe they would realize how serious he was about returning home and they would do the wise thing and let him live with Zoe and Hobby for his senior year. Or he could live with the Castles. Once he reached Nantucket, it would be harder for his parents to make him return to Australia. Possession was nine tenths of ownership, after all, or something like that.

Two hours later Jake had had six or seven beers and another toke of marijuana, which had been a lot stronger than the first two hits. In one of his remaining cogent moments he wondered if it actually *was* just marijuana, or if it was something else. He remembered stumbling toward the ocean to take a piss, and when he returned to the circle, the fire was dwindling, and so was the group of people around it. The girl in the white bikini top was still there; he asked her what her name was, and she said...but he didn't hear what she said, he was too busy noticing that her feet had a sort of black rind on the bottom of them, as thick as the sole on a pair of shoes. The next thing he knew he was falling, he tried to grab for the silken rope of Penny's voice, but he missed it, and his head hit the sand with a thud that sounded like it hurt, but he barely felt it.

The other people around the fire were moving in a strange way. It looked like they were dancing. Jake had last danced with Penny on stage. *Grease. Chang chang chang chang doo wop. We go together.* Winnie Potts, he didn't love Winnie Potts, he didn't even *like* Winnie Potts, but she had put herself in front of him like a dish to taste, and he had momentarily forgotten Penny, just say it, he'd been *glad* she'd left the party so he could let loose for a minute and experience the freedom that was due every seventeen-year-old boy. I'm sorry, Penny, he thought. It could have just as easily happened to you with Anders Peashway or Patrick Loom or any other one of Hobby's friends who were always flexing their muscles for you. And if you'd told me about it, I would have understood eventually. I wouldn't have thought the world was over. The world wasn't over, Penny. I should have told you myself. I should have told you myself!

Jake woke up at dawn, convulsing with the cold. His mouth was filled with damp sand, and he could barely lift his head.

Willow, he thought. The girl in the white bikini top. Her name was Willow.

But when Jake sat up and looked around, neither Willow nor Hawk nor anyone else was around. The beach was deserted, the fire pit cold ash. When he managed to get to his feet, his head felt as heavy and dense as a stone. He turned to look at the parking lot behind him: there was one silver Cutlass in the lot, dark and unoccupied, and nothing else. No van, no Utes, no ferals.

Jake's duffel bag lay gaping open a few yards away. His stomach heaved, and he gagged and spit in the sand. He checked his pockets: no money, no credit card. He searched through the bag. They'd taken his camera and his running shoes. And the Hemingway. So they were literate thieves, he thought. He felt so stupid, so ashamed; he felt like a young, vulnerable idiot. *Lean on me. When you're not strong.*

They had left him the picture of Penny. He picked it out of the bag. It was a picture of her at the Tom Nevers Carnival, the summer between their sophomore and junior years. She was eating pink cotton candy, her bluebell eyes round with anticipation: *This is going to be sweet!* she mimed. He kissed the picture and felt a surge of gratitude. They had at least left him that.

It was still pretty early, though he had no idea what time it was because his iPod was gone too. The sun was a pink smudge in the sky. He hefted his bag, now nearly empty, and trudged through the sand toward home.

He had thought he might make it back before his mother woke up. That would be best, though he was going to have to tell his father about the credit card anyway. He might be able to claim that he'd lost it somewhere. But really, he had been drugged, and then robbed. He had been a human sacrifice after all.

Jake opened the side gate to the house silently and tiptoed into the garden. He winced as his feet crunched on the gravel. He needed a big glass of water and seventeen aspirin, eight hours of sleep, and then a big breakfast. Just the thought of his warm, soft bed was so enticing that it nearly made up for the ugly realization that he was never going to make it back to Nantucket.

He smelled smoke and turned around. It still wasn't fully light, but he could see the glowing orange ember at the end of his mother's cigarette. She was sitting on the back steps alone, in her pajamas and a long sweater. As she exhaled, he saw her taking in the sight of him—what must he look like?—and his duffel bag.

"Jake?" she said.

"I need my bed," he said. He resisted the urge to run to her, he resisted the urge to cry. He resisted the urge to say to Ava—for only Ava would appreciate it—"It has been a terrible, horrible, no good, very bad day."

DEMETER

She no longer dreaded waking up in the morning. Her alarm went off at six-thirty, and in a flash she was out of bed, brushing her teeth, taking three ibuprofen, drinking an extra glass of cold water.

She was putting on cargo shorts and a T-shirt, socks and work boots. She was taking a few shots off one of the bottles that she kept in her closet. Her collection was growing. On Tuesdays and Thursdays, when Al was at work and Lynne Castle was at spin class at the health club, Demeter would make herself a cocktail, either a cup of coffee with cream and sugar and a shot each of Bailey's and Kahlua or a screwdriver using the orange juice that Lynne squeezed fresh twice a week.

She took two water bottles to work with her every day, one filled with actual water and the other containing vodka, tonic, and lime juice, which she chilled secretly in the garage fridge.

She was, she had to admit, nearly always drunk. That sounded bad; it sounded like she was on her way to becoming the subject of an intervention reality show. But the thing was, she was happy. Finally *happy*. She loved going to work buzzed, she loved weeding and watering while she had a glow. She loved the strategy involved in hiding her condition from everyone around her: Nell, Cooper, and Zeus on the team, Kerry at the start and the end of the workday, and her mother and father at home. Her life was a game now, a game that balanced the scary thrill and fear of getting caught with the comfort of knowing that she was too smart to let that happen.

She had enough alcohol hidden in her closet now to last her the rest of the summer. She had been stealing a bottle nearly every day.

The stealing was bad, there was no denying that, but the stealing was also good because the stealing was what made the days pass so quickly. After Zeus pulled up to a job and Coop started mowing and she and Nell went off in their separate directions to weed or mulch or deadhead or water, Demeter would immediately apply herself to the task of figuring out how to get into the house. If the owners were home, forget about it, she didn't steal, except in the case of Mr. Pinckney on Hulbert Avenue, who lived at home by himself even though he was a hundred years old and couldn't hear or see a thing, or Mrs. Dekalb out in Quidnet, who had broken her leg while ice skating at the rink with Dorothy Hamill and who sat in front of the TV all day with her leg elevated, watching reality shows and drinking tequila sunrises. When Demeter first happened upon Mrs. Dekalb—poking her head in to see if she could "use the bathroom"—Mrs. Dekalb had been so bored and wanting for company that she'd actually invited her to stay and join her for a cocktail.

Demeter had said, "You're very kind to ask, ma'am, but I'm on the clock." She offered to fetch a refill for Mrs. Dekalb, however, and while she was doing so, she snatched a bottle of Mount Gay. Then she wrapped the bottle in the flannel shirt that it was too hot ever to wear, and carried it out to the truck, and stowed it in her bag.

At houses where no one was home, Demeter used one of two ploys: either the bathroom ploy—she had perfected a facial expression of *extreme urgency,* though she used it no more than once a week with Nell—or the complete sneak, where she entered the house, grabbed something from the liquor cabinet, and got out of the house (all of which took her less than two minutes) without anyone's seeing her.

Zeus had once come looking for her when she was exiting a house, but she saw him through the window and made it back to the truck in time to deposit the bottle safely and pull a bottle of Visine out of her backpack. When Zeus found her, she claimed to be battling an allergy.

"It's the roses, I think," she told him.

The stealing was bad, but it was also good. She was taking stuff that didn't belong to her, yes, but the people she was stealing from had *so much* that they would never even notice.

Demeter was nearly always drunk at work, but because Nell and Coop and Zeus had nothing to compare her behavior to, she seemed completely normal to them. The alcohol made Demeter work faster and with a smile. She put on her iPod and danced as she clipped back roses in Sconset; every day was a party. If she and Nell were working in close proximity, they would banter back and forth, and it didn't take long for this banter to develop into real conversation. Soon Demeter was hearing about Nell's problems. Nell was in love with her boyfriend's roommate. The obvious answer to this conundrum was for Nell to break up with the boyfriend, but she was afraid that if she did, she would never see the boyfriend's roommate again. Demeter took Nell's quandary very seriously and, after a few swigs from her special water bottle, came up with some reasonable-sounding advice: Nell should break up with the boyfriend as soon as possible, otherwise the roommate would get the idea that the two of them were in a committed relationship. Get out first, Demeter said, and worry about arranging a meet-up with the roommate second. Time should pass, Demeter said. A week or two. And then Nell should plan to "bump into" the roommate on neutral turf.

"Yes!" Nell said. "That's perfect! You're a genius, Demi!"

So many things about these exchanges pleased Demeter. She felt like a bona fide *relationship guru,* even though she had never been on a proper date herself. She liked how Nell had started calling her Demi, as in Demi Moore, which in itself was a much sexier name than Demeter Castle. Plus, Demeter had never had a nickname other than "Meter," which was what kids had called her in pre-school. Now she was "Demi." Coop and Zeus and Kerry all started calling her Demi too. And finally, Nell was the first friend that Demeter had ever made on her own rather than through connections of her parents.

Nell told Demeter things about the guys on their crew. Coop was a stoner, she said: he and a few guys from other landscaping teams got high before each workday, then again at lunch, and then *again* at the end of the workday. Zeus had a wife and five daughters back in El Salvador, but he regularly went to the Muse on weekend nights to hit on women. Demeter promised to keep these tidbits of informa-tion "in the vault"—a phrase always accompanied by a gesture of locking her lips. Demeter had no one to tell, but just knowing these things gave her a certain comfort. Everyone had secrets. She was hardly alone, and her sins were hardly the worst.

The other benefit to Demeter's drinking all day was that she had effectively lost her appetite. She packed a banana for breakfast but never ate it. She sat with Nell during their lunch break, and while Nell ate her tofu and raisins out of a Tupper-ware container (a lunch that Demeter found revolt-ing), Demeter drank her special water, and when

Nell asked her why she wasn't eating, she just said she'd had a "huge breakfast." Coop and Zeus usually ran down to the strip to get a burger and fries or tacos and pizza, and though they sometimes returned with a paper sleeve of waffle fries or a slice of pizza that they couldn't finish, Demeter wasn't the least bit tempted. She was flying high, reaching for her sugarless spearmint gum.

If anything, Demeter hated it when the workday was over. They knocked off at three-thirty, at which point Nell and Coop generally headed to the beach for a swim. They started asking Demeter to join them, but there was still the bathing suit issue, so she always said no thanks, maybe another time.

On good days, her mother wasn't home, and Demeter was able to walk into the house and tuck whatever bottle she'd stolen that day into her closet. She was able to safely fill her special water bottle with vodka, tonic, and a squeeze of lime juice. Occasionally she nibbled on rice cakes or saltines, but more often the sun and the fresh air and the alcohol conspired against her, and once she saw the soft pillows and duvet of her bed, all she wanted to do was nap; sometimes she even slept straight through until morning. There had been three days when she had actually gone all day without eating a single thing—and for the first time in her life, she could tell she was losing weight. She refused to get on a scale to prove this, but the waist of her cargo shorts became loose. And from being outside all day she had gotten quite a tan on her face and her arms and her legs, and the blond streak in her hair was growing lighter, and she felt about fifty times more attractive than she had in recent memory.

Of course, there were afternoons when Demeter got home from work and her mother was home— in the kitchen mixing up a potato salad or marinating steaks—and Demeter knew that there was no way she would be able to get out of sitting down to dinner. On these evenings she swigged heavily from the whiskey bottle in her stash, and then she brushed her teeth and gargled and chewed wintergreen gum until her mother called her to the table. Acting sober was far more difficult with her parents because, unlike her new friends from work, Lynne and Al Castle knew their daughter and would detect aberrant behavior. Demeter had to watch herself. She had to focus on what her parents were saying, she had to formulate reasonable answers to their seven hundred questions, she had to keep from laughing at how pathetically clueless they were.

Then came the conversation of July 25.

Lynne: "What did you do at work today, honey?"

Demeter: "Um, I don't know. Let me think." The days tended to blend together, and sometimes they visited as many as six properties in a day. Often it was just easier to make things up to tell her mother. "We were on Lily Street. And West Chester. I did window boxes."

Lynne: "Window boxes! That sounds much better than weeding!"

Demeter (nodding): "*Much* better!" Of course, in reality, Demeter would never be allowed to touch anyone's window boxes. Zeus did all of the containers, including window boxes, and he was very territorial about his work. But Lynne would never know this, and look how happy it had made her to think that her daughter, who only three weeks before had been dangerously close to being sent to some sort of juvenile prison, was now responsible for the beautiful window boxes that everyone admired so much when driving down Lily Street!

Demeter ate four bites of steak and half a plate of green salad. No potato salad, though her mother tried to force it on her three times. Demeter loved her mother's potato salad, but she didn't want food to interfere with her lovely state of intoxication. Everything was hazy and dreamlike, a colorful collage that she could take her time pondering. Her father stared at her a little too long at one point, and Demeter cleared her throat and took a long sip of her water. Did he suspect she'd been drinking? Maybe, but even if he did, he would never say anything. To say something would be to open a can of worms, one that would break her mother's heart and disrupt the domestic bliss that the Castle household was famous for.

Lynne: "Oh, I forgot to tell you! Mrs. Kingsley called. She wants to know if you can babysit on Saturday night."

Demeter chewed her steak into mush. She hadn't yet reached the point where she excused herself to go to the bathroom and then did a shot of vodka *in the middle of dinner,* but she was tempted to do that now. Her father's gaze was relentless; Demeter couldn't bring herself to meet his eyes. He for certain *knew* that she had been in possession of a bottle of Jim Beam on the night of the accident, but did he know that she had lifted it from the Kingsleys' house? Did *anyone* know that? If Mrs. Kingsley had called to ask Demeter to babysit, then she must not have heard any rumors, or else not cross-checked any rumors she *had* heard with a survey of her liquor cabinet.

Demeter: "Really?"

Lynne: "She sounded desperate. But I told her you were working for Frog and Toad now and might be too tired to work at night...."

So her mother had provided her with an out. Demeter could say no. But if she said no, would it seem as if she were avoiding the Kingsleys? She had never turned Mrs. Kingsley down before. And her old logic still reigned: babysitting on a Saturday night was far superior to staying home alone on a Saturday night.

Demeter left two bites of steak untouched and turned down the offer of blackberry pie with home-made whipped cream. Instead she went to the phone and called Mrs. Kingsley back and said that yes, certainly she could babysit on Saturday night. Mrs. Kingsley sounded like her grateful, happy self, utterly relieved that despite the tragic events of graduation night, she hadn't lost her most reliable babysitter.

"Seven o'clock?" Mrs. Kingsley said.

"See you then," Demeter said. She hung up the phone, thanked her mother for dinner, got herself a tall glass of ice, and retreated to her bedroom.

At six forty-five on Saturday night, Demeter was driving her Escape on Miacomet Road toward Pond View, which was where the Kingsleys lived, when she saw something moving up ahead. At first she wasn't sure if it was one person or two—the sun was descending, shining right into her eyes—and then she saw that it was two: a low, squat figure with a taller figure behind. It was Zoe Alistair push-ing Hobby in his wheelchair, heading in her direction.

Demeter hit the brakes so hard she bucked in

her seat. What to do? She knew the three *F*s of threatened animal behavior: Freeze, Flee, or Fight. Freezing, which was her first instinct, wouldn't be effective; she couldn't just sit in her car in the middle of the road. So she would flee, turn the car around and hide out on Otokomi Road until Zoe and Hobby rolled past. But that could take a while; they weren't going very fast, and Demeter didn't want to be late for Mrs. Kingsley.

Demeter pulled down the eye shade and adjusted her Ray-Bans. She would simply drive past them. She knew they would recognize her car: Zoe, Penny, and Hobby had all been at her sixteenth-birthday "party," when Al Castle had presented it to her, tied up with a big red bow. Demeter had given Penny and Hobby a ride around the neighborhood in it, and Hobby had played with the sunroof and asked questions about the gas mileage. Penny had said, "Hobby wants his own car *so* bad." So bad, and yet he had never made a move toward getting his license.

Demeter stepped lightly on the gas, and the car inched forward, closing in on the two approaching figures. Demeter tried to decide what to do. She hadn't heard from Hobby since his return from the hospital, and she counted this as a good thing. He didn't have probing questions to ask her about what had happened in the dunes, as Jake did. The shameful thing was that Demeter hadn't called either Hobby or Zoe to offer her condolences. She just couldn't. Did they understand why she couldn't? She had been right there, an integral part of it all, and their families had so much history together, and for both of those reasons, she couldn't just *call* and say she was *sorry,* the way the rest of the island had done.

Should she wave and breeze on by? That was a hideous notion; to wave would be to acknowledge their presence, while at the same time letting them know that they weren't important enough for her to stop and talk to. She should stop. She should... say something. This was a sign from above, this random encounter with no one else around, and for the first time in days, Demeter was sober. She hadn't had a drink since the night before—well, that wasn't true, she had done a shot of vodka at ten o'clock that morning to stop the uncontrollable shaking of her hands, but that was all. She wanted to be sober and alert for Mrs. Kingsley and the three Kingsley children.

Demeter got closer, close enough to see that Hobby had his arm in a sling and his leg in a cast and that half his head was shaved. Zoe was pale, and her hair was flat. Zoe was saying something to Hobby, and Hobby was craning his neck to look at her. Demeter, coward that she was, took this opportunity to step on the gas and cruise right past them, her mouth set tight, without giving them a wave or a glance or anything.

She wondered if they were turning around in disbelief, asking each other, "Was that Demeter who just drove by?" She didn't check her rearview mirror; she just kept driving with a mounting sense of relief. She had escaped a painful and difficult situation. This relief was quickly followed by man-eating guilt. It was all her fault. She could tell herself that it was Penny who had flipped out, Penny who had been driving the car, Penny who had put their safety in peril. But it didn't take away her certainty that she, Demeter, was to blame.

She had had the best intentions for the evening, but the sight of Zoe and Hobby toppled her like a house of cards. Demeter hurried the night along: she put the three Kingsley children in the bathtub, then handed them towels and clean pajamas. She offered them each a bribe of two Oreo cookies and half a glass of milk in exchange for an earlier bedtime. She supervised teeth brushing and read them a chapter from *Harry Potter and the Order of the Phoenix* in such a way that she heard herself saying the words aloud even though her mind was elsewhere. She was back on Miacomet Road, watching Zoe push her son in his wheelchair along the edge of the pond, pointing out wild irises or red-winged blackbirds or this house or that house where she had catered a fancy party. Or perhaps they were talking about Penny—how she had been crazy about chocolate-chip cookie dough but not about chocolate-chip cookies, or how she had prayed for snow so she could go sledding in Dead Horse Valley, flat on her back on the ancient Radio Flyer that Zoe had bought at a yard sale. If she didn't become a professional singer, Penny used to say, she wanted to be an Olympic luger.

Demeter's leg was twitching as she lay between Lyle and Barrett Kingsley. She had to get downstairs. Before she left (Mr. Kingsley had not been around, and his absence had not been addressed), Mrs. Kingsley had said those fateful words that Demeter both longed and dreaded to hear: "Help yourself to anything you want." Demeter checked to see how many pages were left in the chapter. Three.

Demeter thought about Zoe. She thought, I am to blame, but no one is innocent in this. She thought, It's worse to be the mother of the hurt person than the hurt person herself.

She kissed the Kingsley children good night (she had missed them), and then she hurried downstairs. The sun had set, the house was darkening, and despite the late-hour injection of chocolate into the children's bloodstreams, they were quiet upstairs.

Stillness.

"Help yourself to anything you want." The pantry, as usual, was filled with bags of barbecue-flavor Fritos and Funyuns and pretzels and cheese curls; there were boxes of crackers and cookies and cherry hand pies. The fridge held dips and cheeses and salamis and containers of broccoli slaw and lobster salad from Bartlett's Farm.

But food no longer appealed to Demeter. "Help yourself to anything you want." She couldn't possibly pour herself a drink, she thought, not after what had happened. But she found herself powerless. She opened the Kingsleys' bar and discovered a brand-new bottle of Jim Beam sitting in the exact same place where the other one had been. This spooked Demeter; she shut the liquor cabinet. She went to the freezer and pulled out a frosty bottle of Ketel One. The shaking had returned to her hands, but this might be due to anticipation, she realized. She brought the bottle to her lips and drank until her eyes watered and the vodka burned the lining of her throat. She gasped for breath.

Zoe Alistair had looked...well, she had looked ruined. The strange thing was that Demeter's mother hadn't said a word about Zoe in weeks. To Demeter's knowledge, Lynne Castle hadn't seen or spoken to Zoe since that night at the hospital, though she still maintained tight control over the dropoff dinner schedule.

Demeter took another pull off the vodka bottle. The reassuring feeling returned: everything was going to be okay. She poured three fingers of vodka into a juice glass and added ice. It looked just like water. She would drink just this much, and then she would be done.

Just as she brought the drink to her lips, she heard the mudroom door slam, and she nearly dropped the glass on the floor. She set it down on the counter and whipped around in time to see Mr. Kingsley breeze in. He was sweaty, wearing white shorts and a white polo shirt and carrying a tennis racquet. He seemed as stunned to see Demeter as she was to see him.

"Hey!" he said. He squinted at her and smiled, and she thought, I've babysat for these people for five years, and he's forgotten my name.

"Hey, Mr. Kingsley," she said. Her head was spinning from the vodka. If he discovered what was in her glass, her life was over. But Demeter felt strangely calm. There was something about Mr. Kingsley that she recognized immediately, something in his demeanor, in the way he was swaying while standing still: he was drunk. He threw his tennis racquet to the floor with a clatter, and Demeter instinctively looked up the stairs, to where the children were sleeping.

"Demeter," Mr. Kingsley said, as if her name

were a tricky crossword-puzzle clue that he had just figured out. "You poor thing, you." He took a step forward, then stopped. "Is Mrs. Kingsley home?"

"No," Demeter said. "She left at seven for a... cocktail party in Sconset, I think?"

"Right," Mr. Kingsley said with an exaggerated nod. "I'm supposed to meet her there. I just got held up at the club."

"Okay," Demeter said. It sounded like he was offering her an explanation, but she didn't need one. She just wanted him to retreat—to shower or change or whatever—so she could pour out her drink. But instead of vanishing into the nether regions of the house, he moved toward her with his arms open. "Demeter," he said. "You poor thing."

Demeter allowed herself to be enveloped in an embrace from Mr. Kingsley. Thank God for the vodka; it had lent her a certain remove. She had never before given Mr. Kingsley a second thought; he had always been just the benign presence standing next to his wife. Mrs. Kingsley's first name was Elizabeth. Demeter didn't know what Mr. Kingsley's first name was.

After two or three seconds of hugging—during which Mr. Kingsley was literally patting her back—Demeter tried to pull away. But Mr. Kingsley held on to her. He had his arms wrapped around her—no small feat—and his hips suddenly locked against her hips, and she felt something else there. Was she imagining it? She was at once intrigued and grossed out. Mr. Kingsley was an attractive man, she supposed. He had blond hair styled shaggier than most men wore theirs, though this might be because he was balding on top. He had pale blue eyes and a perpetually sunburned face. He was good-looking enough, but he was old, he was the children's father, he was Mrs. Kingsley's husband, and yet here he was in his own kitchen, drunkenly mauling the babysitter. It was stereotypical enough to make Demeter laugh, except it wasn't stereotypical because it was happening to *her*.

"You poor thing," Mr. Kingsley said yet again. He looked at Demeter, and then he kissed her. The kiss was sloppy, and it took her by surprise, but by far her most prominent emotion was fear that he was going to taste the vodka on her lips. However, Mr. Kingsley noticed nothing of the sort. He moved in for another kiss, longer and deeper this time. Demeter felt as if she were standing on the other side of the kitchen and watching herself kiss Mr. Kingsley, but at the same time she was right there, allowing the man to stick his tongue in her mouth.

This, Demeter thought sadly, was her first kiss. The first one, that was, except for the dry peck on the lips that she'd received in sixth grade from

Anders Peashway, at a birthday party held in Annabel Wright's backyard. But that kiss from Anders had been a dare, a joke; he had lured her behind the potting shed, and when they emerged a second later, everyone was laughing, and David Marcy gave Anders a high five, and Anders made some kind of animal noise that Demeter pretended not to hear. And yet she had clung to the memory of that humiliating kiss ever since, because she had nothing else.

Well, now she had this. Mr. Kingsley's hand found her breast and squeezed it with strong fingers. Demeter realized that if she indulged this behavior for very much longer, he would try to have sex with her. And so Demeter, for once in her life determined to do the right thing, put a hand in the V of Mr. Kingsley's white tennis shirt and pushed him gently backward.

Mr. Kingsley said, "Yes, that's right. I have to go." He turned so abruptly that the rubber soles of his tennis shoes squeaked against the tile floor, and then he vanished down the hallway. The second he was out of sight, Demeter grabbed her drink off the counter and swallowed the whole thing down.

Adults, she thought.

ZOE

It was Dorenda Allencast who told Zoe about the seven-foot-high white cross embedded in the sand at Cisco Beach.

Dorenda was waiting for Zoe with a pot of peppermint tea and a plate of store-bought shortbread on the day she reported back to work. Zoe had never before seen Dorenda do so much as fold a napkin in her own kitchen, and so the event of the tea and the cookies was noteworthy and touching. The Allencasts had, naturally, been as devastated as anyone about Penny's death; they had known her since she was a toddler. They had seen her every Easter and Halloween and Christmas, the holidays on which Zoe felt the Allencast house would benefit from the presence of children. Dorenda had always given the children elaborately wrapped baskets of candy purchased at Sweet Inspirations, and Mr. Allencast had slipped them five-dollar bills.

Dorenda carried the tea and shortbread to the formal living room — furnished with portraits of Allencast ancestors and a grandfather clock — where Zoe had never known *anyone* to sit. She nearly recused herself. She didn't want to be subjected to this expression of tea and sympathy from Dorenda, no matter how well meaning it was. But there were some people Zoe couldn't refuse, and the Allencasts were two of them. When they'd asked, after the accident, what they could do to help, Zoe had begged them just to please not give away her job. She would be out for weeks, certainly, and she realized it was summer, but if she lost her job, her salary, and her health insurance, things would become very difficult for her and Hobby. Mr. Allencast had assured her that her position was safe, that she could take as long as she needed. He had been as good as his word: her checks had continued to arrive, and her health insurance had covered all but five hundred dollars of Hobby's medical expenses, even though they had run well into six figures. Zoe knew that the Allencasts must have been living on takeout sushi from Lola; they must have been regular fixtures at the early seating at the Sea Grille.

And so Zoe accepted this sit-down with Dorenda Allencast as a necessary part of her return to work. She wanted to get into the kitchen and start making a beef Wellington, or maybe the shrimp remoulade that the Allencasts liked in the summer. But.

Dorenda Allencast poured two cups of tea and handed one to Zoe.

"So," she said, and her eyes filled with tears.

Zoe took a sip of her tea and burned her tongue. "Dorenda," she said. "You didn't have to go to all this trouble."

"'Trouble'?" Dorenda said. "I want to know how you're doing."

Yes, right: everyone wanted to know how she was doing. The phone rang all the time, but Zoe never answered it; her voicemail was so full that it was no longer accepting messages. Hobby picked up the land line at home if he was awake and mobile, fielding calls from this concerned person or that one. He explained that his mother was asleep, or down on the beach taking a walk, or unable to come to the phone just then. After he hung up, he would turn to Zoe and say, "Mrs. Peashway called to see how you're doing."

Zoe understood what people wanted: they wanted to hear that she was all right. It was something particularly American, or perhaps it was just human nature to ask, "How are you doing? Are you doing all right?"

"Well, I lost a child," Zoe thought she might say. "And not only my child, but my best friend. So, no, I am not doing all right. And if that's not the answer you're looking for, then please don't ask me."

But Zoe had been raised well by her parents, she had spent four years at Miss Porter's; she didn't have it in her to be rude.

"I'm okay," she said now, to Dorenda. "I guess. Considering the circumstances."

Dorenda seemed satisfied with this answer, and

Zoe wondered just how much of a lie she was telling. *Was* she okay? In her opinion, she had managed to do only the bare minimum. She had buried Penny properly. She had examined and then dismantled the dozens of altars that had been dropped off at the house, tributes of flowers and candles and photographs and stuffed animals and poems. She had put the photographs in a shoebox and thrown everything else away. She had opened all of the condolence cards and letters she received. She had cleaned her kitchen and gotten rid of the trash and the recycling. She had visited Hobby at the hospital, followed his progress through physical therapy, and focused only on his homecoming. Once he was home again, things had become both better and worse. Zoe wanted him where she could see him and take care of him, but she bristled at *his* efforts to take care of *her*. He wanted to talk about Penny all the time. Accepting her death had seemed to come easily to him—how was that possible? He talked about her casually, as though she were away at the music camp in Interlochen, as though they would both see her again in a matter of weeks. He was either a lot better adjusted than Zoe or a lot worse off.

"She's not coming back," Zoe wanted to tell her son. "You do know that, right?"

Zoe had believed she knew all she needed to know about dealing with death. She had lost Hobson senior; she had lost both her parents. She understood death's grim permanence. But when it was your own child, that took on a new dimension. She would never see Penny again. Penny—the little girl she had pushed from her womb, nursed at her breast, held in her arms, kissed, cuddled, spanked, taught, fed, talked to, laughed with, cried with, loved.

On the night Penny lost her virginity to Jake, she had climbed into bed with Zoe. She had thrown an arm across her mother's barely conscious body, laid her head on her shoulder, and said, "We did it, Mommy."

Zoe had opened her eyes and inhaled the scent of her daughter's hair and felt tears burn her eyes. She was crying not because of the news itself—if anything, Penny and Jake had waited longer than Zoe had expected they would—but because Penny was sharing it with her. In some important way, Zoe realized, she had succeeded as a mother. "You can tell me anything," she had told Penny, and Penny had taken her at her word.

"Are you okay?" Zoe asked.

"Yes," Penny whispered. "I love him."

And Zoe said, "I know you do."

Over the weeks and months that followed, Penny had climbed into bed with Zoe often, and Zoe had marveled that the little-girl-becoming-a-woman had wanted so much love and comfort from her mother. All of Zoe's other friends were complaining of the opposite. But Penny and Zoe had always had that kind of relationship.

"I love you twice as much as any other mother loves her child," she'd sworn to her once.

Penny's body had been as familiar to Zoe as her own. How was it possible that she would never hold that body again? The answer was, it wasn't possible. In which case Hobby was right: they could live only in some sort of suspended state of delusion, certain that Penny would someday be returned to them.

Dorenda said, "That was a lovely piece in the paper."

"It was," Zoe agreed, though she hadn't actually read it. She had, at Hobby's insistence, sent some photographs to the newspaper, but she hadn't been able—forgive her—to face reading the article about her dead daughter. She had folded the piece and saved it in a drawer. Down the road, maybe, when she was better equipped for it emotionally than she was now, she would take it out and read it.

"And how about the white cross?" Dorenda said. "I had Philip drive me down so I could see it for myself."

"Cross?" Zoe said. Her automatic response to anything even vaguely religious was one of severe allergy, falling just short of anaphylactic shock. "What cross?"

"The big one at the end of the road," Dorenda said. "Where the girls have been singing."

Zoe tilted her head.

Dorenda said, "You haven't seen the cross?"

"I don't know what you're talking about."

"Oh," Dorenda said. For a second she seemed embarrassed. "Well, it's hardly a secret. There's a seven-foot cross at the end of Hummock Pond Road. And the girls from the madrigal group gather there to sing each night at sunset. It's a tribute to Penny."

Zoe asked, "Who built the cross?"

"I don't know," Dorenda said. "One of the girls' fathers must have. It's just two boards nailed together. But there are bouquets of flowers at the base and ribbons fluttering around it, things like that."

Zoe bent her head. Dorenda Allencast laid a feather-light hand on her back. Dorenda probably thought she was overcome with emotion at the beauty of the gesture. But what Zoe felt like shouting was that there shouldn't be a tribute unless she *said* there should be a tribute. A seven-foot cross? Bouquets? Girls from the Nantucket Madrigals singing every night at sunset? What Zoe thought was, She was my daughter! How can anyone's grief matter but mine? This was a horrible, awful, ungenerous thought. Penny's death was turning her into a small, mean person.

*　　*　　*

That night, on her way home from work, Zoe drove out to the end of Hummock Pond Road to look at the cross. It was visible from two hundred yards away, even in the dark. Its white arms reached up from the sand like a ghost's. Zoe parked her car and got out. The night was warm enough, finally, that she didn't need a jacket, but her hands were ice-cold. Here she was, in the spot where it had happened. The cross must mark the point of impact.

The cross was as white as bone. As Dorenda promised, there were bouquets of flowers at the base, and satin ribbons wound around it that reminded Zoe of a maypole without, however, doing much to ameliorate the stark religious significance of the cross itself. The cross meant what? she wondered. That a soul had departed from this spot? A girl was driving too fast, and then she crashed the car and died.

Part of Zoe wanted to pinpoint exactly who was responsible for constructing the cross, who had painted it, which father had loaded it into the back of his pickup truck and driven it down here. Who had erected it? Whose idea had the singing been? But Zoe guessed that it had been a collective effort by the girls, Penny's friends and acquaintances, who wanted to make a statement dramatic enough to match their overwhelming emotions. A girl they had grown up with, had known and loved, had admired and looked up to, had *died*.

She existed for more than just me, Zoe thought. For more than me and Hobby.

Penny had been part of a class, a school, a community. Other people wanted to pound a cross into the ground for her, sing for her, publish a valediction in the newspaper for her. Who was Zoe to tell them they couldn't? She didn't like it because it made her feel as if there were less of Penny to claim. She needed Penny all to herself. She was *mine*, she thought. *Mine*.

Selfish, horrible thoughts, but there you had it. They were real.

She was too spooked by the cross to stick around for very long. She thought maybe she should *do* something, throw a rock at it or kiss it or kick it or cry in front of it, but none of those things felt right.

She climbed into her car and turned the key. It was nearly nine o'clock. She needed to get home to Hobby. But she sat for a second, staring at the ocean. Over the course of a single day she had gone back to work and then had come to look at the cross. These things seemed noteworthy. She wished there were someone she could tell.

But there was only one answer to that: Jordan.

Jordan, Jordan, Jordan. Zoe didn't have the strength to think about Jordan. But she couldn't stop thinking about him, either.

There was that night during Christmas Stroll, the two of them embracing up against Jordan's car, which they later referred to as "the moment." The moment when they knew.

Nothing happened after that. The next time they saw each other was in early January. They were in a crowded gym, at a middle school basketball game in which Hobby scored 28 points. Jordan walked in with his notepad. Sitting down next to Zoe, he told her that he'd come to report on the game.

She asked, "You've been demoted?"

He said, "My sportswriter quit."

She said, "You spell our last name A-L-I-S-T-A-I-R."

He said, "Yes, I know how to spell your name."

And in this way everything returned to normal. The night in the new December snow was tucked away somewhere deep inside Zoe. She was sure that Jordan treasured that night also, but she was equally sure they would never speak of it again.

Fast forward: June 29, not of that year but of the following one. The twins were fifteen years old. Zoe traveled to Martha's Vineyard to watch Hobby play baseball in the Cape and Islands All-Star Tournament. She had reserved a room at the Charlotte Inn as a treat for herself and Penny. She knew that booking such lavish accommodations made her seem snooty (the rest of the parents were staying up the street at the Clarion), but she had been doing this All-Star thing since Hobby was nine years old, and she was tired of weekends away that included overly chlorinated indoor pools and communal "dinners" consisting of bad pizza and margaritas from a can. She still had some of the money left to her by her parents, though she didn't broadcast that fact; she constantly had to reassure herself that it was nothing to be *ashamed* of. She was going to get a nice room for her and her daughter, and they were going to have a nice dinner. Let the other parents talk.

But then Penny didn't come with her. Annabel Wright was having a birthday, and her parents had gotten tickets to see *Mamma Mia* in Boston and invited Penny to go.

Even better, Zoe thought guiltily. She would luxuriate in the room at the Charlotte Inn all by herself. She would light candles and read in the clawfoot tub. She would order room service from L'Etoile. She would sleep naked between the luscious 1000-thread-count sheets.

She thoroughly enjoyed step one: she soaked in the peony-scented water and read the final chapters of John O'Hara's *Appointment in Samarra* by the light of three beeswax tapers that she'd asked the front desk to place in her room. She washed the dust and the sweat of the ball field off her skin and took breaks between pages to remember Hobby on the mound, the lean, graceful form of him throwing fire at the alternately eager and fearful batters from Harwich, South Plymouth, and the Vineyard. Nantucket had won all three games for the first time in its forty-year history of playing in the Little League. Hobby had pitched a no-hitter, and over the course of the three games he had gone nine for twelve as a batter, including two home runs. After each game Zoe had watched her son accept handshakes from the coaches of the other teams. She studied Hobby closely: he was grinning but not gloating. He was a good kid. Zoe imagined him at that very minute devouring spare ribs and potato salad at a barbecue with the other teams. He was spending the night with the family of the Vineyard's first baseman, in Oak Bluffs.

As Zoe climbed out of the tub and reached for her waffled robe, her cell phone rang. Penny, she thought, calling to tell her about the musical. But when she looked at the display, she saw it was Jordan.

"Hey," she said. "I'm on the Vineyard."

"I know," he said. "I am too."

"You are?" she said.

He told her he had come over that afternoon for

a fund raiser for a Democratic congressional candidate—Kirby Callahan, Zoe knew of him—and that afterward he'd met Joe Bend, the publisher of the *Vineyard Gazette,* at the Navigator for drinks, which had turned into a sail on Joe's sloop. Jordan had then headed to the airport to catch the six-thirty plane, but he'd missed it. So now he was stuck.

"You're at the airport?" Zoe asked. She checked the clock in her room. It was five minutes past seven.

"Turns out that was the last plane," he said. "So I'm at the Wharf Pub."

"In Edgartown?" Zoe said. It was right down the street.

"Come meet me," he said. He sounded drunk, which was novel. He always drank beer and water side by side so as not to get "carried away," and he always limited himself to two beers. On special occasions he might have a third beer, but by "special occasion" he meant Christmas, or the Super Bowl. At dinner parties he had one glass of wine.

"Um," she said. The menu for L'Etoile was spread open on the bed. Zoe had already decided on a bottle of the Cakebread chardonnay, the prosciutto-wrapped watermelon and haloumi cheese appetizer, the softshell crab entree, and the grilled pineapple with macadamia crunch ice cream for dessert. Was she supposed to give all that up?

*   *   *

She met him at the bar of the Wharf Pub. He was drinking something amber-hued in a highball glass.

"What is that?" she said.

"Glenmorangie."

"Scotch?" she said. "You?" She gave him the once-over. He was in a navy blazer and tie, a snappy blue-and-white-striped shirt, crisp white pants, his Gucci loafers worn without socks. She rarely got to see him this dressed up, and she had never seen him drinking scotch. She gamely took the bar stool next to him and ordered a glass of Sancerre; her regret over the missed softshell crab faded away. She ordered a lobster roll with french fries and an extra side of coleslaw.

"Have you eaten anything?" Zoe asked.

He bobbed his head. "I had a cracker on the boat."

She ordered a lobster roll for Jordan as well. "Where are you staying tonight?" she asked.

"Campground."

"Seriously?" she said.

"Seriously," he said. "I checked with the Chamber of Commerce. Every hotel room on the island is booked."

She studied him. "How did you know I was here?"

He snorted. "I run a newspaper. I know everything. Cape and Islands Babe Ruth All-Star tournament this weekend, where else would you be? Plus, Penny told me."

Of course. Penny would spew forth all of Zoe's business without giving it a second's thought. "Did she tell you where I was staying?"

"The Charlotte Inn," he said. "Fancy."

"Lap of luxury," she said. "I'm not sure why I'm sitting here, eating with you."

"Because you love me," he said. Something about the way he said this made Zoe turn. His voice was tender instead of teasing. There was only a quarter inch of scotch left in his glass. Zoe didn't think it was the alcohol talking, though certainly two or three or six Glenmorangies had eased the way for those words. Zoe saw that she had a choice: she could either laugh the words off or affirm them.

"Yes," she said. "I do."

He pushed his glass away. "Let's get out of here."

"Where are we going?"

"Where do you think?" He stood up and threw a hundred-dollar bill on the bar.

She remained planted on her stool. So many years, and now, out of the blue, he was...what?

He stared at her. "Zoe," he said.

"Okay," she said, and she followed him out.

She remembered the kissing that night, and she was certain that half a world away, wherever Jordan was now and whatever he was doing, if he was asked about that night on Martha's Vineyard, what he would remember was also the kissing. It might have been the influence of their younger counterparts, Penny and Jake, at work. Zoe and Jordan had been witness to the sweet urgency of their lips and tongues, their desire to taste each other, to consume each other. It was a powerful narcotic, kissing. Zoe and Jordan were lying on top of the field of white cotton that was her sumptuous hotel bed; they were hidden from the eyes and ears of Nantucket, from their children and from their friends. It was just the two of them and the history of their friendship that night.

Later, after Jordan fell asleep—no campground for him—Zoe picked up the phone and ordered the softshell crabs.

And later still—at two or three in the morning, when Jordan awoke and croaked that he needed a glass of water, and Zoe, unused to slaving over anyone except her children and uninclined to begin now, lay silent and still until Jordan fended for himself by sucking from the bathroom spigot—they talked.

Zoe said, "Question."

Jordan returned to bed with her wine glass, which he had filled with water. He said, "I took six Advil. Shoot."

She said, "Did you miss that plane on purpose?"

He said, "I missed the plane legitimately. But I

lied about calling the Chamber of Commerce. I didn't even look for a room. I knew you were here, and I wanted to be with you."

"Oh," Zoe said.

"Even if you made me sleep on the floor," he said. He rolled over so he was facing her. "I have been lonely for you for so long."

"You mean just lonely," Zoe said.

"No," he said. "I mean lonely for you."

In the morning, sunshine streamed through the windows, and Zoe heard birds in the garden outside, and there was a knock at the door: the coffee she'd ordered from room service, before knowing about Jordan, for seven o'clock. She opened the door wide enough only to get the tray through. Jordan was an unidentifiable lump in the bed.

She poured coffee — real, percolated coffee, with real cream. The other baseball parents would be drinking the drip stuff if they were lucky, and instant with creamer if they were not. For some reason this thought threw Zoe into a panic.

What had she done? She had slept with Jordan Randolph, another woman's husband. Not only had she betrayed Ava, she had also betrayed her kids, she had betrayed the community, the island. How could she sit at Hobby's game today and cheer with the other parents? What if one of them had been at the

Wharf Pub last night and seen her and Jordan there together? That would be far worse than their being spotted together anywhere on Nantucket, especially when paired with the knowledge of Zoe's fancy hotel room at the Charlotte Inn. What if someone had seen them hurrying up Main Street?

"Jordan," Zoe said sharply.

Jordan sat bolt upright in bed, a glazed look in his eyes. He had no idea where he was, Zoe could tell. Oh God, this had been such a mistake. He reached for his glasses, and when he could see her, he smiled.

She said, "You have to get out of here."

He frowned. "Okay."

"And this can never, ever happen again."

His frown grew deeper. "Okay," he said.

She sat next to him, on the edge of the bed. She reached out and pushed his hair out of his face. She loved him, and she knew he loved her, but come on—if everyone slept with the person he or she had secretly fallen in love with, the world would be chaos.

"You have to promise me—" She stopped. She wouldn't put the onus on him. She started again. "We have to promise each other that we won't let this happen again, okay?"

"Okay," Jordan said.

But of course, they didn't keep that promise.

* * *

There had been good days with Jordan and there had been bad days. They developed a routine of keeping Tuesday and Thursday mornings just for themselves, and those mornings became anticipated and sacred. When they had to skip a day for one reason or another—Jordan had a meeting he couldn't miss, or one of the kids was home sick from school—Zoe felt her world tip off kilter. They saw each other in public too, sometimes in the company of Al and Lynne Castle, and every once in a while Ava would emerge from the house to attend a school function or other event, and Zoe would be treated to the sight of the incredibly beautiful, broken woman she was betraying.

It was usually after seeing Ava and Jordan together that Zoe would try to end the relationship. She would call Jordan's cell phone and say the predictable things to his recording: "I can't do this anymore, it's not fair to Ava, it's not fair to me or to you or to the kids. If you're going to stay married, then stay married. But you can't have us both, Jordan." She would pause dramatically, then shout, *"You can't have us both!"*

She had broken up with him at least a dozen times in this way.

It was nearly nine o'clock in the morning in Perth. What would Jordan be doing now? She had no idea.

*   *   *

Their longest breakup had lasted eighteen hours. It happened on September 30, which was Jordan and Ava's wedding anniversary. Zoe had respectfully kept her silence that day—no texts to Jordan, no phone calls. She was the one who had, in the preceding days, encouraged Jordan to mark the occasion with a card or flowers or dinner out at Le Languedoc, which had once been Ava's favorite restaurant. Jordan had protested: Ava didn't want to mark the occasion, he said. All she wanted was to be in Australia. All she wanted was Ernie back. Zoe acknowledged that this was probably true, but still she prodded him to do something special. She was talking out of guilt; she wanted him to celebrate the marriage in order to mask the fact that he was betraying it. But then, when the day itself arrived, Zoe experienced a gripping jealousy. Jordan would bring Ava breakfast in Ernie's nursery, she imagined. They would make love. Zoe actually retched into the toilet at the thought, then wanted to slap herself for being so hypocritical. When, at four o'clock, Jordan texted and asked her to meet him at the now-closed snack shack at Dionis Beach, she couldn't get there fast enough.

They made love in frantic haste, standing up against the side of the snack shack. Zoe felt like a desperate teenager. She wanted to ask Jordan what he had done to honor the day, but she was afraid to ask. She wanted him to offer it up on his own, but she knew he would never risk hurting her feelings. She was elated and relieved that he had wanted to meet her today, on this holiest of married days, but it sickened her as well.

She straightened her skirt. In front of them were the starkly beautiful sand dunes of Dionis. September 30: the wind held a chill. It would be fall soon. She and Jordan had been seeing each other for three months.

She said, "We have to stop."

"Zoe."

"It's your wedding anniversary," she said. "How long have you been married?"

He cleared his throat. "Eighteen years."

"We have to stop."

"Zoe, no."

"If you don't want to stop, then leave her."

" 'Leave her'?"

"Leave Ava."

"I can't leave her, Zoe. You know what she's like."

Zoe stared at him. Blue eyes, glasses, shaggy dark hair. She knew him, she understood him; they were the same person. Yes, Zoe knew what Ava was like. Yes, Zoe knew that Jordan wouldn't leave her. He would stay with her forever, and Zoe would always, always come second. She would remain in the shadows, hidden, concealed, lied about.

Zoe walked to her car, climbed in, slammed the door, started the engine. Was she going to drive away? Jordan was approaching with long strides, his hands out, his face beseeching.

Zoe backed out. Drove away.

She spent a sleepless night wondering how she had gotten herself into this mess. It had been years and years in the making, she knew; she had loved the man ever since he asked her if she wanted to do puzzles, on Fathers' Night at the Children's House. He poured her wine, he lit her woodstove, he washed her hair, he kissed the back of her neck. She loved him.

She felt ill when she woke up in the morning, then worse when there were no calls or texts from him. So he had gone home and taken Ava out to dinner and presented her with a bouquet of dahlias and a card. Goddamn him! Zoe wanted to scream. She wanted to throw something. But she had two kids to care for. Penny had madrigal rehearsal at ten, and Hobby had a football game at one, so Zoe found herself standing at the stove making her famous fried egg sandwiches on grilled English muffins with Swiss cheese and strawberry jam. Penny woke up in a Beatles mood, so they played "Good Day Sunshine" and "Drive My Car" and "Let It Be" as they ate, and Penny's voice was so sweet, and Hobby's shoulders were so broad and strong in his

practice jersey, and the egg sandwiches were so delicious, that for one second Zoe thought, as she had
for so many years before, Who cares about love? I
have all the love I need right here in this room.
Breaking up with Jordan had been the right thing
to do. It had been the *only* thing to do. If the twins
somehow found out what was going on in her head
and her heart, if they knew how she spent her Tuesday and Thursday mornings while they were sitting
in French class or American History, they would be
destroyed. Zoe had always said they could tell her
anything, but that didn't go both ways. She had
never been one to shelter her kids from the harsh
realities of life, but this reality, yes. It was too private
and awful to share. It would remain private, but it
was no longer awful because it was over. She and
Jordan had broken up. She was clean and righteous.

That feeling lasted until ten o'clock, when Zoe
pulled in to the high school parking lot to drop
Penny off. Penny kissed her and got out of the car
and ran for the doors of the school—Mr. Nelson
had told her if she was late one more time, she
would lose her solo—and Zoe watched her daughter disappear into the building, and though she still
had things to do (she had to go home, pick up
Hobby, deliver him to pregame practice, and then
help set up the concession stand), she felt an empti-
ness encroaching on her.

At that moment her cell phone rang.

Jordan.

"Hello?" she said.

"Will you stay with me?" he said. "Please?"

"Yes," she said.

Now, in the car, at Cisco Beach, in the looming presence of the white cross, Zoe cried out, "I miss you!" Her voice was hoarse. "I love you!" She was a certifiable crazy person, yelling these things out to the dark interior of her car. But she had a freedom here that she lacked at home, where she had Hobby to think of.

"I love you!"

So there, she was admitting it to herself. Her anger at Jordan had been a carapace over her real feelings, but now it was cracking and falling off in pieces. It wasn't Jordan's fault that Penny was dead and Jake was alive, it wasn't his fault that he couldn't step inside her grief and discover just how unbearable it was. She had sent him away, and now he was gone and she missed him and she loved him and she missed Penny and she loved Penny.

She was alone, profoundly alone.

No, she was not doing all right. She would never be all right again.

PART TWO

August

NANTUCKET

It was August, and the hottest, brightest, busiest days of the summer were upon us. The most important thing for the summer residents and renters and visitors seemed to be that everything was as hot and bright and busy as they remembered it from the year before, and the year before that. Sameness was the island's currency. The families that had been summering on the island since 1965 or 1989 or 2002 had created traditions that had to be upheld. On their first night on-island they had to eat at the Brotherhood of Thieves, where they would order medium-rare bleu cheeseburgers with curly fries. They had to wait forty-five minutes in line for ice cream at the Juice Bar because nothing tasted better than a hot fudge sundae in a waffle cup when you ate it on Steamship Wharf as you watched the stream of cars unload from the ferry. They had to bike to Sconset and get turkey salad sandwiches from Claudette's; they had to take their annual picture in front of the peppermint stick of the Sankaty lighthouse, where someone had to remark that erosion was most definitely eating away the bluff, and that if someone didn't do something about it soon, the lighthouse would certainly topple into the ocean. They had to take the launch up the harbor to the Wauwinet for lunch, and someone had to recall the time Margie's Peter Beaton hat flew into the sea and the captain of the launch fished it out—soggy but not much worse for wear—with an elderly gentleman's cane. They had to drive onto the beach at Great Point with a case of cold Heineken and meatball subs from Henry Jr.'s. They had to meet Anne and Mimi at the Nantucket Yacht Club for doubles tennis followed by lunch, during which they would talk over the piano player, the same beautiful raven-haired woman every year, who never grew older and was always willing to play "As Time Goes By." They had to "forget" to bring sunscreen to the beach at least one day—yes, they knew it was as bad for them as smoking a pack of unfiltered cigarettes— and go home feeling the warm, tight stretch of tanned skin. They had to attend the same parties every year—the Leeders' party on Cliff Road, the Czewinskis' in Monomoy, the fete for the Nan-

tucket Preservation Trust, the Summer Groove for
the Nantucket Boys & Girls Club.

More than one summer resident noticed that
things weren't quite the same this year at the
O'Dooleys' annual cocktail party on Hulbert Avenue. Everyone loved this party. The O'Dooleys
sprang for a good dance band from New York, and
a celebrity or two could always be counted on to
attend — Martha Stewart, Samuel L. Jackson, Bill
Frist. But this year the party wasn't catered by Zoe
Alistair, as it had been for so many years in the past;
instead, Doris O'Dooley had brought her regular
caterer up from New York, and the food wasn't half
as good. Guests missed Zoe's crab cakes with lime
zest and ginger aioli, as well as her hot corn fritters
with maple syrup. Mr. Controne, of Squam Road
and Louisburg Square, Boston, was overheard saying, "I've been dreaming about those corn fritters
all year, dammit."

That was the thing we realized: for visitors,
Nantucket wasn't just a place; it was also a fantasy
of American summertime that kept people warm
and happy all year long.

No one had the heart to tell Mr. Controne that
the reason there were no corn fritters with maple
syrup was that it was Zoe Alistair's daughter, Penny,
who'd been killed in the one-car accident out at

Cisco Beach on graduation night, and that Zoe was consequently taking a break from catering.

It was at the O'Dooleys' cocktail party, too, that two homeowners talked about the petty thefts from their houses. Mrs. Hillier had discovered an unopened bottle of Mount Gay rum missing from her liquor cabinet, a bottle she had planned on using to prepare her husband's welcome-to-the-weekend cocktail. Where had the bottle gone? She had just purchased it from Hatch's a few days before. The cleaners, she thought. It must have been the cleaners, because what burglar would come into the Hillier home and take *only one bottle of rum?* Standing next to Alice Hillier, Virginia Benedict nodded vigorously. "The strangest thing," she said. She had noticed that two bottles of Chateau Margaux were missing from her wine cellar. There had been twenty bottles on Tuesday, but only eighteen on Friday. Virginia Benedict had a son, Blake, who was a sophomore at Dartmouth, and initially she had assumed that he was the culprit — though what a nineteen-year-old boy would want with some dusty old bottles of wine, Virginia had no idea. Now, talking to Alice Hillier, Virginia Benedict began to wonder if something else might not be going on. She wondered if she should report the missing bottles of wine to the police. Would that sound silly? They were worth several hundred dollars apiece.

"Well, *I'm* reporting it to the police," Alice Hillier said. "A full bottle of Mount Gay, gone."

We, the year-round residents of Nantucket, who bumped into one another constantly in the winter — at the gas station, at lunch at A. K. Diamond's, at the community pool, at five o'clock Mass on Saturdays, among the shelves of Nantucket Bookworks, at the paint counter in Marine Home Center, and in the aisles of the Stop & Shop (we always saw at least half a dozen people we knew every time we set foot in the Stop & Shop) — rarely had any contact in the summer. In the summer we were busy working, or we went away to our houses in New Hampshire while renting out our Nantucket homes for ten thousand dollars a week. Or we took trips to the Grand Canyon, or had houseguests — our brother from Chicago with his wife and two kids — and found ourselves doing things like driving up to Great Point with meatball subs from Henry's, waving to all the strangers on the beach. And then, of course, when we did randomly see one another — say, while waiting to use the ladies' room upstairs at Le Languedoc — we were happy. Another Nantucketer! A member of our tribe! We talked quickly, eager to catch up but reluctant to stay away from the dinner table for too long.

It was during one such chance meeting — Sara

Boule and Annika DeWan were both waiting for prescriptions from Dan's Pharmacy, Sara for her Ativan, Annika for Augmentin to cure her son's tenth ear infection of the summer—that the topic of Claire Buckley arose. Annika asked Sara, who was a great good friend of Rasha Buckley's, if Claire was "okay."

"Because I've called her to babysit no less than four mornings this summer, and all four times—maybe five, come to think of it—she turned me down. And then last week, when I took the kids to the Juice Bar for frappes, I saw that she wasn't working there, either. Doesn't that seem strange?"

Sara met this question with what struck Annika as a loaded silence. "Yes," she finally said. "That does seem strange. I think perhaps there *is* something going on with Claire."

And in this way, as only something as insidious as gossip could manage, the following was discovered:

Claire Buckley had been fired from her job at the Juice Bar, not because she had called in sick three times in a row with the stomach flu, but because when she finally *did* come in to work a shift, she left her post briefly to vomit in the back alley.

"This is ice cream," the manager purportedly said upon finding Claire a retching, weepy mess. "There's a line out the door, and every third one of those people is going to walk out of here with your germs because you weren't considerate enough to think of our *customers* and call in sick."

"I didn't want to get fired," Claire supposedly said.

"You're fired," said the manager.

Claire wasn't going to field hockey camp at Amherst College this year, as she had done for the past two summers. In fact, she wasn't planning on playing field hockey in the fall at all, even though she was slated to be the team captain. Kate Horner, the coach, was on a biking vacation in France and couldn't be called upon to verify these claims, but surely she must have been crying into her Cabernet. To lose her best senior! We couldn't believe it. We could hardly remember a time when we had seen Claire without her mouthguard.

Claire Buckley had been seen twice out in public over the summer. Once was on the fast ferry with her mother, Rasha. The girl, usually so peppy and outgoing, had on this occasion seemed pale and quiet and reserved. She was reading *The Secret Life of Bees* and barely looked up when Elizabeth Kingsley came over to say hello. It was Elizabeth Kingsley who made allowances for the fact that perhaps Claire wasn't herself because of all that had happened with the accident. After all, hadn't she been the one to sit at Hobby Alistair's bedside when he was in his coma? "I think that accident affected our teenagers"—Elizabeth used the royal "our" here; her own kids were only eight, five, and three— "more deeply than we realize," she said. "My baby-sitter, Demeter Castle, is totally changed. I can't really say how; she's just...*different* now."

The other place where Claire Buckley was spotted was in the waiting room of Dr. Field's office, again in the company of her mother, Rasha. More precisely, Claire and Rasha were holding hands, and Claire was visibly upset. This was reported by Mindy Marr, who conceded that the girl *might* still be shaken up by the accident—but while Ted Field was many things, he was *not* a shrink.

"No," Mindy said. "I think Claire was there for another reason."

"*What* reason?" we asked, as though Mindy Marr held the answer, as though she were something more than just a random person who happened to walk through the waiting room at the right time.

"She looked heavy," Mindy said. "Heavi*er*."

Could be depression, we thought. But Mindy's voice was coy; it contained unspoken possibilities. Something else? Another reason?

And then, instead of being disproved, as we were certain it would be, the suspicion was confirmed:

Rasha Buckley confided in Sara Boule, and Sara Boule, constitutionally unable to keep a secret, told one of the rest of us: Claire Buckley was ten weeks pregnant.

"Pregnant!" We gasped. "Ten weeks pregnant!"

We were unable to say another word. But in this shared silence, it became clear that we were all thinking the same thing.

HOBBY

He had watched her go. They had been connected since before birth, so it seemed only right that he should be the one she'd choose. They were squeezed together in an unfamiliar place—not life, not death, but somewhere in between. It was as dark and moist as a womb, and he and Penny were face to face, and Penny was saying to him, clear as a bell, "Listen, I'm going."

Casually, as though she were telling him she was walking home from the library:

"Listen, I'm going."

He hadn't had an answer ready; he had been unable to speak. He had a vague understanding that they'd been in an accident, and he figured he must be much worse off than Penny because she told him she was leaving while he couldn't seem to get a message from his brain to his tongue. What would he have said? "I'm coming with you" was his first instinct. But then he realized that if he went with Penny his mother would be left alone, and he understood that he could not leave his mother alone. He wanted to say, "Don't go. Stay. Please don't leave." But Penny was willful, stubborn, she did what she wanted, she would never listen to him, he couldn't make her stay.

He remembered seeing her blue eyes get bigger and bigger until they were like oceans he could swim in. Then she evaporated before his eyes. She was gone, and he knew she wasn't coming back.

His mother asked him if he remembered anything about being in the coma. Had he had any dreams? Had he felt any pain? The answer to both of those questions was no. He'd been in a coma for nine days, they told him, but to him it had felt like only a few seconds. He remembered being in the car and Penny's flooring it. Hobby had watched the speedometer out of sheer awe and stupid drunkenness. How fast could the car go? His thoughts were those of a child. He'd never believed they'd get hurt. Even when they approached the end of Hummock Pond Road and Penny sped up instead of slowing down, Hobby had thought only, Oh, shit, we're going to crash. But he didn't think of getting hurt, and he certainly didn't think of dying. They were all seventeen years old, and seventeen-year-olds didn't die. Their bodies were made out of things that bounced back: rubber and fishing line.

Then there were the moments with Penny, the two of them suspended like water vapor in some strange atmosphere. Then Penny said, "Listen, I'm going," and Hobby decided to stay, and everything went black.

As he was regaining consciousness, he'd had some thoughts. He'd been aware that the world he was returning to didn't have Penny in it. And he was aware of another shadowy presence that he wanted to grasp, hold on to.

Claire's baby. *His* baby.

The nine days in a coma scared Hobby only now, in retrospect. He'd asked a couple of the doctors at Mass General if a person in a coma was technically dead or technically alive.

"Neither, really," the doctor said. "You're in a third state. The state that we call a coma."

Another doctor said, "A coma is when your body is alive, but your brain is unresponsive."

"So your brain is dead," Hobby said.

"I didn't say 'dead,' " the second doctor corrected him. "I said 'unresponsive.' "

What Hobby believed was that he had been partially dead for nine days. And then magically, miraculously, blessedly, he had returned to life. His mother had been sitting there. He remembered her face upon seeing him open his eyes — man, her face alone had made coming back to life worthwhile. He saw that he had made the right decision in letting Penny go by herself. His mother needed him more.

Claire had been at the hospital that day too, though it had taken a while for anyone to tell Hobby that. When he first returned (this was Hobby's term; his mother preferred to say "woke up"), he saw his mother first, and then a whole slew of doctors and nurses came in to grin and gawk at him and announce that they had seen a miracle that day and praise the Lord, the boy was okay, they were just going to do some tests and did he know his name and did he know who this woman was and could he name the President of the United States?

When he croaked out "Barack Obama," the whole room practically burst into the Hallelujah chorus.

They took his temperature and his blood pressure, and it was only then that Hobby realized he was in a shitload of pain. Pretty much all over his body. It felt like he'd been sacked forty times by that monster lineman from Blue Hills. He said, "Mom? I hurt."

There was talk of upping his morphine, and seconds later the pain subsided, that was fine, his mother was still crying, that was fine, but Hobby sensed that he had a lot of other business to deal with, he felt jammed up, like he had a paper to write and a chemistry test to study for and nine innings of baseball to pitch before nightfall.

He said, "Mom?"

Suddenly the room cleared of nurses and doctors. Only his mother was left, and she was laying ice chips on his lips. The cold wet was like heaven. He was so thirsty.

His mother said, "You have some broken bones."

He wanted to ask if he was paralyzed, but he couldn't form the word; it had too many syllables. He tried moving his right hand, his throwing hand, and his right foot, and both of those worked, so he figured he wasn't paralyzed. Nothing on his left side moved, but people didn't get paralyzed *that* way, did they? Side-to-side?

His mother said, "Your clavicle, three ribs, your left radius, your left femur..."

Oh Jesus, his femur. His eyes fluttered closed, and he felt his mother's icy fingertips on his forehead, brushing back his hair. She said, "Do you remember what happened, Hob?"

"Accident."

There was a long pause. He opened his eyes to

see if he was correct about the accident, though of course he was correct, he hadn't broken all those bones in his sleep. His mother's face was blurry. She was crying, that was the problem. She had her lips pressed together, and tears were streaming down her face.

She said, "I have something to tell you."

He didn't want her to say it. He wanted to stay in this not-knowing-for-sure state for a little while longer. He wanted to stay in the jubilant condition of newly-arrived-back-on-Planet-Earth-from-who-knew-where-the-fuck-he'd-been. But Zoe had shored herself up to say it, so she was going to say it: "Penny is dead."

He nodded. It hurt to nod. His head hurt. It felt like a cracked egg. "I know," he said.

"You know?" Zoe said. "How could you possibly *know?*"

"I saw her," Hobby said.

"You saw her?" Zoe said. She was looming over him, the cup of ice chips rattling in her hand like dice. "You saw... what? Her neck snap? She broke her neck."

Hobby shook his head, but gingerly, gingerly. How the hell could he explain this to his mother? "I saw her. She said, 'Listen, I'm going.'"

"Going where? Leaving the party, you mean?"

Hobby shook his head again. He'd have to tell

her later. But her mention of "the party" had brought something else to mind. "Claire," he said.

"Claire," Zoe said. "Sweet Jesus, I nearly forgot! Claire is here! She's here at the hospital! I can send her in. Do you want me to send her in? Are you up for it?"

"Yes," he said.

When he saw Claire, he knew she hadn't done it. He knew this not from how her body looked—it was still too soon for that—but from the expression on her face. The unadulterated joy. And something else: a collusion. They had a secret, they still had it, thank God, thank God! If Hobby had had the energy, he would have burst into his own Hallelujah chorus.

"Hi," she said.

"Hi," he said back.

He reached for her with his right hand, and without saying a word, she pressed it to her belly.

Life, he thought. Thank God.

The hospital, his return, his homecoming to Nantucket, so many well-wishers, enough to fill a stadium—all of those were fine. But there were many other things that followed that were not fine.

Penny's funeral. Hobby went off his pain medication for a few hours because it was the funeral of his twin sister, and he wanted to be cogent for it; he wanted to remember every detail so he could tell her about it later. Hobby wasn't a particularly spiritual person—his mother had never been big on church, and he certainly wasn't mystical—but he felt very strongly that he would see Penny again, in the whatever-came-after. Their conversation wasn't over. It couldn't be over. She was his sister. She was his *twin*. When he died, and he hoped that would not be until seventy or eighty years in the future, she would be on the other side waiting for him. And he would tell her about everything. All that she had missed.

The funeral was sad, and Hobby was in pain, and he cried along with the rest of the people in the packed and stifling church. He cried for his mother. He had done the right thing, absolutely, in staying alive, because his mother couldn't have sustained the loss of both of them. She was strong for the funeral, or sort of strong, but she was weird. She wouldn't let Hobby speak, she wouldn't let Jake speak. She couldn't bear it, she said. Hobby protested, and she said, "Maybe I'm not being clear, Hobson. If I have to listen to you speak about your sister, I will break. The same goes for Jake Randolph. I'm keeping this service simple."

Hobby saw his coaches at the funeral, and his teammates and the fathers of his teammates. They had all come for his sake, he knew, and not because they felt any deep connection to Penny. (Although she had diligently kept the stats on his basketball games at the Boys & Girls Club—had he ever thanked her for that? Probably not, dammit. He would have to do that later too.) Hobby accepted rushed, manly hugs from these men, but he saw the look in their eyes. His body was broken: he had sixteen fractures in all. His future career as a quarterback or a shooting guard or a pitcher was over. He would walk again, he would run, he would throw, but the 24-karat-gold caliber of his playing was gone forever.

Hobby listened to the madrigal group—all those pretty girls—sing "Ave Maria," and he was filled with gratitude. It was music, and he could hear it. He cried just for that reason: he was alive. And elsewhere in this church, a tiny knot of a being the size of his thumb was alive inside of Claire. Penny was dead, but he would see her again, and he would tell her how beautiful her funeral had been. He would tell her about the music.

There were weeks of rehab at Nantucket Cottage Hospital. Time to allow his bones to heal. The start down the long road of physical therapy. That was all predictable. What wasn't predictable was the stuff going on in Hobby's mind. He became terrified of going to sleep, certain that if he did, he would never wake up again. He had a private room, thank God, and he asked for the lights to be left on at all times, along with the TV. The nurses reported this to Dr. Field; Dr. Field came in to see Hobby. It was like getting a visit from the school principal, except that the real principal, Dr. Major, was a lot less intimidating.

Dr. Field said, "They tell me you don't want to sleep."

Hobby said, "Can you blame me?"

Dr. Field laughed his dry laugh. Then his expression went back to being serious. "Your body needs sleep in order to heal, Hobson."

"I take naps," Hobby said. This was true. He was so exhausted during the day from not sleeping at night that he drifted off all the time, in brief catnaps where he was just beneath the surface of consciousness but always able to see some light. He had to be aware that life was continuing on around him.

"You need real sleep," Dr. Field said. "I'll have the nurses give you something."

"I don't want them to give me anything!" Hobby shouted. He never shouted except on the playing field, and certainly never at an adult. But he was scared. He was shouting now in the name of self-preservation. "What if they give me something and I don't wake up?"

"Okay," Dr. Field said. "Okay, fine. We'll take it slow."

Jake came to visit. Jake looked awful—of course he looked awful, he and Penny had been in love, really in love, not just saying they were. If Penny said her throat hurt, Jake would be up off the couch making her a mug of hot water with lemon before she finished her sentence. They read the same books, they practiced their lines for the musical together, they watched movies and laughed at the same things, they spoke to each other in French and Spanish and Latin. They drew pictures of the house they wanted to live in someday and made lists of names for their future children. When Penny sang, Jake closed his eyes to listen. He had taken good care of her.

Even in the relative isolation of the Cottage Hospital, Hobby had heard Jake's name being bandied about in an unflattering way because Penny had died while driving his car. But that hadn't mattered. Hobby wished he had the words to tell people what he knew: Penny was bound and determined to leave this world behind. If she hadn't done it in Jake's car, she would have found another way.

"Hey," Jake said.

"Hey," Hobby said.

They shook hands. Jake sat in the visitor's chair

that was most frequently occupied by Zoe, who was now back at work.

"How do you feel?" Jake asked.

"Like shit," Hobby said.

"Good," Jake said, and they both laughed. "Good that you can tell me the truth, I mean."

"How do *you* feel?" Hobby asked.

"Like shit," Jake said. He teared up, then wiped away the tears with the back of his hand, and Hobby felt like telling him not to bother. Hobby was sick of seeing people try to hide their feelings. What had happened was tragic, and there was no reason to pretend otherwise, no reason to stop the tears. Who cared about being a man? That had no meaning anymore. Being human was far more important than being a man, and human beings expressed their emotions. "My parents are making me move," Jake told him.

"*Move?*" Hobby said. "Are they sending you away to school?"

"No," Jake said. "We're moving, all three of us, to Perth, Australia."

"Perth, Australia?" Hobby said. He was something of a geography buff, and as such, he knew that Perth was on the western coast of Australia; it was the most isolated capital city in the world. "For how long?"

"A year."

"Your dad too?" Hobby asked.

"Yeah, my dad too."

"Your mom's *from* Perth, right?"

"Yeah. I'm not sure why she can't just go by herself."

Hobby had no answer for this. Jake's mother was a mystery. Hobby had seen her maybe once in the last four years. She was like a cicada or a lunar eclipse.

"My dad doesn't even want to go," Jake said. "But he tells me we have to."

"Because of the accident?"

"Because of something."

Hobby wondered if his mother knew about this. She came in to sit with him every morning and every evening, but she hadn't mentioned anything about the Randolph family's moving to Australia. And Jordan Randolph was his mother's best friend.

"So I wanted to tell you that," Jake said. "And there's something else I wanted to ask you."

Hobby sensed a heavier topic. "What's that?"

Jake puffed a few times into his clenched fist and Hobby thought, Oh, shit, what is it?

Jake said, "I want to know why."

"Why what?"

"Why she did it. What the hell went wrong? She was fine right up until she went into the dunes with Demeter. And then she was a basket case, right? So something happened in the dunes. Either Demeter told her something or someone else told her something. A secret or whatever."

"A secret?" Hobby said. His leg was starting to itch inside its cast, a condition brought on by stress, Dr. Field had told him, but it made Hobby want to cry out for amputation. He took a sip of the lukewarm water at his bedside.

"And I was wondering." Jake went on, "if you might know what Demeter said. If you'd heard from anyone else what Demeter said. I know you've had a lot of visitors."

"I haven't heard anything," Hobby said. "I think people are trying to shelter me from some of the difficult stuff. Have you asked Demeter?" It occurred to Hobby that Demeter hadn't been in to see him. Her parents, Al and Lynne, had come; Al had apparently been with Zoe at Mass General for the first few days, and Lynne had organized the meal dropoff at his house. Zoe had brought in some of the dishes to share with Hobby, since it was better than the hospital food. But Demeter—nope. He hadn't seen or heard from her. Was that weird?

"I asked Demeter," Jake said. "I had to call her, like, sixteen times before she even answered the phone. I asked her what she and Penny had talked about in the dunes. And she said she couldn't remember."

*   *   *

"A secret or whatever." A secret? Hobby was daft when it came to females, his mother and sister had been telling him this for years. He knew only that Penny had been determined to drive off the end of the road, and yes, obviously he knew she was upset, but he hadn't gotten around to asking himself why. *Why?* His mother had tried to broach the question with him also, he now realized: "What was Penny *like* at the party? Did anything *happen?* Anything *unusual* that you can remember?"

But during the party at Steps Beach, Hobby had been preoccupied by two things. The first was thinking about Claire and the baby. And the second was getting drunk in order to forget about Claire and the baby.

He wondered if the "secret news" Penny had heard in the dunes was that Claire was pregnant. Oh God. He felt like he was going to vomit, and his leg—*goddammit*, his leg itched! He wanted to scour it with steel wool; he wanted to dip it in a vat of lye.

"So Demeter said she couldn't remember," Hobby said. "Well, she was pretty drunk."

"That's what worries me," Jake said. He *really* looked green now, Hobby thought—as if he were about to puke. Hobby had a shallow dish next to his bed, and he nearly passed it over to Jake.

"Do you want some water or anything?" Hobby asked. "I'm sorry, if I'd known you were coming, I would have baked cookies."

Jake held up a hand. He didn't crack a smile or anything. His hair was greasy, sticking together in clumps, and he was wearing the jeans that Penny had written on. "Listen, I'm going to tell you something, but you can't repeat it. Ever, to anyone. Okay?"

Hobby nodded. He had his own secret now, so he was newly attuned to the fact that some matters had to be kept completely confidential. "Of course. What is it?"

"This thing happened between me and Winnie Potts," Jake said. "The night of the cast party. We were all in the Pottses' basement, and we all stayed up late drinking. Not your sister, she went home. But I was there, and Winnie was, and some others, you know."

"You raided Mr. Potts's beer fridge," Hobby said.

"Exactly. Anyway, everybody else left, so it was just me and Winnie. And she put the moves on me big time."

Winnie Potts. Mmmmmm. Yeah, she was dangerous. She had been the first girl in their class with boobs, and she knew how to flaunt them. She had been Hobby's lab partner in ninth-grade science, and what could he say other than that working with her had been distracting?

"I didn't sleep with her," Jake continued. "I got out of there long before that, but I did kiss her, and things got pretty heated. And I think she was pissed that things didn't go any further, or she was angry and embarrassed that I ran out of there, and you know she's always been jealous of your sister, and I'm afraid that for any or all of those reasons Winnie might have exaggerated what happened between us. I'm afraid she might've told someone about it, and somehow Demeter got hold of the information and told Penny."

"Would Demeter *do* that?" Hobby asked.

"She might," Jake said.

Hobby had to concede: she might indeed.

"But the thing is, it also might not have been Demeter at all. Penny might have run into Winnie in the dunes. Winnie might have told Penny herself."

"Oh, man," Hobby said.

Jake started to really cry now. He said, "I didn't do it to *hurt* your sister, man. It just *happened*. Winnie was all *over* me. I was drunk, I wasn't thinking. But I mean, I got my ass out of there. I *ran* out of there."

"Believe me," Hobby said, "I know how Winnie is."

"You *do*, right? Everyone knows how Winnie is. Even your sister—*especially* your sister. But that wasn't going to make things any better. If Penny heard that, she would be...well, she'd be..."

"Hysterical," Hobby said.

Jake dropped his head into his hands.

Hobby said, "Yeah, but we don't know for sure what it was that set Penny off."

"What else could it have been?" Jake asked. His voice was so loud and so filled with anguish that Hobby was afraid it was going to attract the attention of one of the nurses.

"It could have been anything, man," Hobby said. "This is my sister we're talking about. Remember how she acted after the tsunami in Japan? She cried for three days. And right after your brother died? She had to go see a therapist. She was different like that, man. Stuff affected her. We don't know what was going through her head that night, and we'll never know. But it's not going to do you any good to blame yourself. She loved you, Jake."

Jake wiped at his eyes with the pointed collar of his shirt. He stood up. "I can't deal with the fact that she's gone, man, that's tough enough, but thinking it's my fault for doing something so *fucking stupid....*"

"Jake, man," Hobby said, "you can't blame yourself."

"I do, though," Jake said. "I do. Even if Penny

didn't know about it, what I did was still wrong. And I'll never get to make it up to her." He put his hands in his hair and pulled, and his eyes popped out, and Hobby thought, He's losing it. But then Jake composed himself, or he sort of did, and said, "I just had to tell someone."

"Yep, I get it," Hobby said. "And it ends with me, I promise."

"Thanks," Jake said. He reached out to shake Hobby's good hand, and Hobby held on and said, "Hey, man, take care, be safe, okay? Stay in touch."

"I will," Jake said. "Thanks, Hob. And heal up. You're the one lying there with all those broken bones, and I'm the one crying."

"We're all broken," Hobby said. This was a heavier statement than he'd meant to make, but oh well, it was true.

Jake stared at Hobby for a second, then he backed out the door.

Hobby was certain he would see Penny again, but he wasn't so sure about Jake. Jake might travel to the other side of the world and decide never to come back. It was unfair, Hobby thought. He'd already lost Penny, and now he was losing Jake, too. Jake was one of his best friends, not a friend the way the guys on the football team were friends— all jokey, back-slapping, hanging out—but more like a cousin or a brother. More like family. And there he went, out the door, leaving Hobby to sort through everything alone.

Jake with Winnie Potts. Was *that* the reason? Until Jake brought it up, it hadn't even occurred to Hobby that there *was* a reason, but of course there was a reason. Still, the reason could just as easily have been that Penny found out that Hobby had gotten Claire pregnant and that Claire had an appointment for an abortion. It was a toss-up.

Hobby thought back to the fraught weeks before graduation. He had asked Claire Buckley to the junior prom. He had texted her between Chemistry and American History, when he knew that she had study hall and would be working out in the weight room alone. He pictured her in her team shorts and gray Whalers T-shirt, all sweaty, her blue eyes intense, her light-brown hair pulled back in that swingy ponytail she wore. He wanted her to see the text when she was alone rather than surrounded by forty girlfriends, as she so often was.

Be my date for prom?

He should have asked her in person, he wasn't too daft to have figured that much out, but what people didn't realize was that Hobby was shy with girls. This made no sense. He lived with two females, he had girls calling and texting him all the time, he had girls from other schools handing him roses and folded notes with their cell phone numbers on them: *Call me anytime!* Hobby could chat on a basic, friendly level, but as soon as the talk nudged toward romance (could it properly be called romance? he wondered), he fell behind. He didn't know how to flirt; he was slow to pick up on cues. He wasn't sure how he was supposed to kiss or feel up a girl whom he'd just met and still remain the kind of person he believed himself to be: a good guy, a gentleman.

Hobby had lost his virginity the summer before to a college girl (a freshman at Amherst, she said, but he was pretty sure she meant UMass). She worked at Henry Jr.'s making sandwiches. Hobby had a job across the street loading lumber onto trucks at Marine Home Center, and he got his lunch from Henry Jr.'s every day. This pretty brunette with a killer smile remembered his order (two roast beef and herb-cheese subs with tomatoes, cucumbers, and horseradish mayo). "Are they both for you?" she asked sweetly. "Yes," he said, "I'm a growing boy." He learned that her name was Heather, and from then on he made it a point to say hello to her personally when he picked up his lunch and always to leave a dollar in the tip jar.

Hobby bumped into Heather unexpectedly at a beach party in Dionis. He was pretty drunk, he was out with Anders Peashway and the disreputable David Marcy, and when he saw Heather, he knew only that he knew her, but not *how* he knew her. She had been drinking, too, and she toyed with him, making him guess, until finally she said, "Normally when you see me I'm wearing a white apron." And he said, "Henry! I mean, Heather!" They embraced like long-lost friends. After a few more beers, Heather was feeling *very* friendly. She led Hobby away from the party, down the beach, and they started kissing. And Heather, who was at least three years older than Hobby, took charge. Soon they were lying on Heather's cashmere hoodie, and she was straddling him, and he tried to stop her because he was ready but not prepared—he didn't have a condom!—but she told him she was on the pill, and he thought, Okay, then. And he thoroughly enjoyed himself, taking as much pleasure in being at last shed of his virginity as he did in the act itself.

But then a couple of days later, when Hobby walked into Henry Jr.'s beaming with excitement about seeing her again, Heather was short with him. Her sentences were clipped; she didn't smile. She made his sandwiches, wrapped them in white butcher paper, and slammed them down on the counter. Hobby obviously knew something was wrong, but he had no idea what it might be. He had called her cell phone and left a nice voicemail about how much fun he'd had with her. What had gone wrong? He wanted to ask her, but there was a line of construction workers behind him, so there was no way he could broach the topic. He paid her, and she handed him his change, and he hesitated, wondering if he should leave a tip. Would the tip be misconstrued? Would she think it crass? If he *didn't* leave a tip, would *that* seem crass? He'd always left a tip before, so he deposited a dollar in the tip jar, said thank you, and walked out of Henry Jr.'s into the hot parking lot, thinking, I just really don't have any talent with women.

But with Claire Buckley, things were different. Hobby had put in a lot of time with Claire. They had gone to school together since kindergarten. He'd always known that Claire was smart, a cut above the other students. And she had developed into a phenomenal athlete as well, playing field hockey, basketball, and lacrosse. She was tall and strong, more interested in her quad muscles than in her breasts—though, as Hobby happened to notice, she had very nice breasts. But what Hobby found most attractive about Claire was her drive. Claire wanted to excel at whatever she did, just like Hobby.

She responded to his text:

Of course.

Of course she would be his date for the prom. Hobby got that text just before lunch, and he grinned and thought, Excellent. He ate two meatball subs draped in gooey, melted mozzarella cheese, and he thought again, Excellent!

One reason Hobby hadn't asked Claire in person was that he feared she might say no. There had been a time—in late fall, between Thanksgiving and Christmas—when he and Claire were seeing each other every day. Basketball season had just started, and they were both in and around the gym all the time. Claire had a car, and she often offered Hobby a ride home. There had been one time when the moon was coming up over Miacomet Pond, big and round and shining a cool gold color. It looked like a giant sugar cookie, Hobby thought, but that was a stupid thing to say, so he kept it to himself. Claire pulled over on the dirt road that led to Hobby's house so they could properly ogle this moon, and the next thing he knew, they were kissing and he was really turned on and so was she and he thought they might and she thought they might— but they were two good kids, and they didn't want their first time having sex to be in Claire's car on the side of the road, and so they stopped. Caught their breath. Stared out the window at the moon and the reflection of the moon on the pond.

The kissing and getting all worked up had subsequently continued—on one occasion, Hobby's pants were around his knees, and Claire was sitting on his lap, but no, they *still* didn't. Then Claire got sick with bronchitis, then Hobby went away for the weekend for a basketball tournament, then they were both busy studying for their SATs, then the boys' team made it into the playoffs but the girls' team didn't, and Claire and Hobby lost the momentum that had been building between them.

And then Hobby heard a rumor that Claire had hooked up with Luke Browning, whose brother, Larry, was in the correctional facility in Walpole, which was exactly where Luke was destined to wind up too. Luke was known as something of a ladies' man, but Claire Buckley was too smart to fall prey to his obvious charms. Right? *Right?* Hobby saw Claire in class and around the halls, and she was nice to him, but then again she was nice to everybody. She wasn't going out of her way to start a conversation with him, and she didn't offer him any more rides home. The good thing was that when he saw her out — at the second night of the school musical, *Grease,* for example — she was always with her girlfriends. So he thought maybe the rumor about Luke Browning had been just stupid Nantucket gossip, which bit its victims like a pit bull and shook them until there was no life left.

Hobby decided to ask Claire to the prom because he didn't want to go with anyone else.

Of course, she said. As though it were a given.

*   *   *

Claire and Hobby had sex for the first time on the Wednesday morning before prom. They were supposed to be at school, but Hobby's American History teacher had called in sick and the front office couldn't find a sub, so he had a free period. He decided to work out in the gym, and he bumped into Claire by herself in the hallway in front of the locker rooms. She said she had been planning on working out, but it was such a beautiful spring day that she thought she might ditch for one period and drive to the beach. Ditch? thought Hobby. Seniors were allowed to leave school during their study halls and lunch period, but nobody else was. Still, Claire was right, it was springtime, the janitors had just cut the grass, and the scent wafted in through the windows. And they were *practically* seniors.

Hobby said, "I'll go with you."

They climbed into Claire's car, and without their exchanging a word, Claire knew to drive right to Hobby's house. He jiggled his leg; he couldn't be misreading any cues. This was it.

Claire shut off the ignition in his driveway. "Your mother's at work?"

"All day," he said. He couldn't stop his leg from doing its own dance.

"Are you nervous?" she asked him.

The cool answer would be no. Hobson Alistair

Jr., who had scored the winning touchdown in a Hail Mary against the Vineyard with thirteen seconds left in the game, nervous?

"Yes," he said. He was nervous about many things: he had never skipped school before, and he was afraid of getting into trouble. If he got caught, Coach might not let him pitch in the game against Dennis-Yarmouth, and it might go down on his school record, and what if some admissions director at Stanford or Duke noticed it? He was nervous that his mother might show up for some reason. Hobby's bedroom door didn't lock; Zoe would feel no compunction about barging right in, even if she did recognize Claire Buckley's car in the driveway. And finally, he was nervous because he wanted this to go well. He wanted her to enjoy it. Probably this was her virginity they were talking about, and if it wasn't, then Hobby wanted to be better than the other guy. That was just his competitive nature.

It went well. Very well.

Despite the fact that Hobby was openly nervous and Claire was nervous but hiding it, they took their time. They kissed without touching each other until they couldn't stand it anymore, and then they touched each other. Claire was wet to melting; the sound that escaped from her lips when Hobby touched her was so erotic that he nearly came in his underwear. He climbed on top of her.

She said, "Yes, I'm ready. I'm so ready."

She had said this at the exact moment when Hobby was reaching for a condom. He had a box of three, as yet unopened, under his bed. But when Claire said, "Yes, I'm ready, I'm so ready," Hobby construed this to mean that it was okay for him to enter her right then, without a condom. He figured she must be on the pill. What he thought was, Okay, she's on the pill, lots of girls are on the pill, it helps with acne or whatever. Heather was on the pill, even Penny is on the pill. Claire's mother, Rasha, is cool, she must have made sure he daughter was on the pill, that's what cool mothers do.

He entered her halfway—not wearing a condom—and checked with her. "You okay?"

"God, yes!" she said. "Go!"

So he went, slowly at first, gently, kissing Claire's face, and then he went faster and faster, and Claire cried out and again the sound aroused him like nothing else had in his entire life, and he came all the way up inside her.

Eight days before graduation, on June 8, she was standing by his locker in the morning, and he knew. It was written all over her face. But maybe not, he thought. Maybe she just looked like that because she'd bombed her Chemistry final.

"Hey," he said.

She dissolved. Tough Claire, cool Claire—she was a wreck. Hobby collected her in his arms. Claire was tall, but he was taller, tall enough to kiss the top of her head. To the rest of the runty adolescent population of their school, he supposed they looked like a couple of mating giraffes.

"Hey, it's okay," he said.

"It's *not* okay," she said. "I'm seventeen."

Yes, that was something he could identify with. He was seventeen also. A daft seventeen-year-old boy. He'd assumed she was on the pill. Wasn't she on the pill? he asked gently. And if she wasn't on the pill, what had she thought they were using for birth control?

She'd thought he would pull out, she said. She had been with someone over the summer—not Luke Browning, but a summer guy by the name of Wils something or other—and Wils had pulled out and everything had been fine. Then, when Hobby came inside of her, she panicked a little, secretly, but not too much because she'd just finished her period, and anyway she went immediately on the pill—immediately as in later that same day. She'd had the pill pack sitting in her underwear drawer, she had gotten it back in December when things between her and Hobby were so intense, but then after things cooled off between them, she hadn't seen any reason for birth control.

"It's my fault," she said.

"It's *my* fault," Hobby said. "I should have used a condom."

"What are we going to do?" Claire said.

They were two good kids, among the best that Nantucket High School had to offer. Hobby was going to be given a free ride to a top-tier school. Claire would either shoot for the Ivy League or opt to play lacrosse someplace like Bucknell or Williams. They were rocket ships, side by side. A baby? A baby was unthinkable.

"Let's wait a few days," Hobby said. Just at that moment Patrick Loom walked by, slapping Hobby's shoulder as he passed. Patrick Loom was headed to Georgetown in the fall. When Hobby looked at Patrick and thought about Georgetown, he saw everything he wanted for himself: brick buildings, manicured lawns, lectures and readings and film series and pretty girls in sweaters and crisp leaves underfoot and an indoor stadium packed to the rafters as Hobby jogged out onto the floor wearing a dove-gray Hoyas jersey, like Patrick Ewing.

"I heard there's a guy on the Cape," Claire said.

"On the Cape?" Hobby said. He had thought they were certainly looking at a trip to Boston, or possibly out of state. He didn't know. He was daft. So fucking daft.

"It's supposed to be quick," Claire said. "They

knock you out and you wake up and it's over and the guy gives you a prescription for Percocet."

"That's what you want to do?" Hobby said.

Claire nodded.

Yes, that was what Hobby wanted to do too. He wanted to fly to Hyannis — tomorrow wasn't soon enough — and see this guy and have it taken care of quickly and painlessly. Relief flooded his chest cavity, but it was trailed by something unexpected and unwelcome: guilt. The course of action they had taken just thirty seconds to decide upon — say it out loud, *an abortion* — seemed so selfish. They were two good kids, but this decision felt sinister. And yet to decide otherwise would be to ruin two brilliant futures.

And yet, and yet.

Hobby kissed Claire gently on the lips, and she went to class. Hobby's mother had asked him a few months earlier if he'd ever been in love, and then she'd asked about Claire specifically. Did Hobby love Claire? No. Hobby liked Claire, Hobby thought Claire was cool. He and Claire were friends, they'd been lovers, they had this situation now and they were going to deal with it together, like good business partners who wanted the same outcome.

And yet, and yet.

Hobby had learned most of what he knew about

the adult world from listening to his mother and her friends—Al and Lynne Castle, Jordan and Ava Randolph—as they sat around the dinner table after the meal had been consumed, when all that was left was to finish the wine, watch the candles burn down to nubs, and talk.

He had once heard his mother describe what it had been like for her to get pregnant, unexpectedly, at the age of twenty-two. She had been in her final semester at the Culinary Institute, she was dating Hobby's father, Hobson senior, they were in love and living together. Hobson senior was a master butcher, a professor of Meats, and Zoe was a superstar, she had accepted an externship at Alison's on Dominick, which at the time was the most sought-after job in the whole city. But then she discovered she was pregnant.

Zoe hadn't seen Hobby lurking around the corner. She thought he was in bed, fast asleep.

She told her friends, "I'm not going to lie to you. I wanted an abortion. I had a life to live. A career to pursue. I was too young to have a baby. But Hobson talked me out of it. We got married at City Hall in Manhattan. We had been married six months when he died."

There was silence around the table. Hobby could remember seeing Lynne Castle hold her face in her hands. She was staring at Zoe.

Zoe said, "Thank God I kept those babies. They are so precious to me. They are all I have, sure, but they're also all I want."

Those words weren't lost on Hobby. His mother had had a choice to make. She could have gone to some guy and had the embryos growing inside her taken care of quickly and painlessly. She could have pursued a career, made a name for herself, opened her own restaurant; she might be as famous as Mario Batali by now. But she had chosen him and Penny instead.

Claire called and made an appointment with the guy on the Cape. It was for Tuesday morning; she would have to skip school. Hobby convinced her to postpone it for a week, to wait until school was out, until after graduation. He didn't tell her that he was having second thoughts because he wasn't sure what kind of influence he would have with her. It was, after all, *her* body. It was ultimately *her* senior year that would be affected, and possibly her chances for college. Hobby wasn't prepared to *marry* Claire. God, if he asked her, she would laugh at him. But he wondered if he could convince her to have the baby, and then they could put it up for adoption.

He tried to talk with her about it on the night of graduation. She was at Patrick Loom's party, and Hobby cornered her by the food table. Her expression was that of a trapped animal. Her eyes kept darting around the party; she was looking for someone to save her.

Hobby said, "Claire, listen, I don't know about this."

She said, "Next year, this is going to be us. It's going to be *us* graduating, going away to school, all the parents thinking we hung the moon."

"You don't have any doubts?"

She looked at him. Her eyes held a wild light. "Of course I have doubts, Hobby. But I'm seventeen. My mother is a single parent, your mother is a single parent. I am not going to be a single parent, and especially not at seventeen."

He said, "Well, there's adoption. We haven't talked about adoption."

"Adoption?" she said. Her voice was incredulous, as though he'd suggested doing bong hits in the steeple of the Congregational Church. She took a big sip of whatever was in her Solo cup—Hobby hoped it was seltzer—and excused herself to go to the bathroom.

He saw her later, at Steps Beach, where she was most definitely drinking beer. Or at least holding a beer. Hobby tried to discern how much of it she was actually drinking, but he was so smashed himself from swigging off the bottle of Jim Beam that

Demeter had brought that he wasn't turning out to be much of a detective. Claire was surrounded by her entire posse, and when Hobby approached, she glared at him. He knew he was being what his mother would call relentless, he knew he should wait and call Claire the next day, when their conversation would be both private and sober. But he had the nagging feeling that their decision had to be made that night.

He said, "Claire, can I speak to you for a sec?"

Claire said, "Hobby, please go away."

"Come on, Claire. Five minutes."

Annabel Wright, who had cheered for Hobby since they were both eight years old at the Boys & Girls Club, was not cheering for him now. She said, "Hobby, leave Claire alone. You're drunk."

Annabel was right. He *was* drunk. He stayed put, his feet planted in the sand, his hand gripping the cheap plastic cup of not-quite-cold-enough beer that Demeter had poured for him from the keg. Annabel and Claire and the other girls wandered down the beach toward the dunes. At that point Hobby considered asking Demeter to let him have what was left of the Jim Beam. She would probably want to drink it with him, but that might not be too bad. Hobby liked Demeter; partly this was the result of conditioning by his mother, who believed Al and Lynne Castle to be the finest people on earth, and partly it was organic. Hobby thought Demeter was a nice person despite her self-destructive behavior. She had a weight problem, she wasn't exactly going to be voted Homecoming Queen, but her isolation and her loneliness made her seem wise to Hobby, sort of like a solitary owl. He wondered what would happen if he told Demeter that he had gotten Claire Buckley pregnant. What would she say?

Hobby never followed through on this idea. He got to talking to one person and then another, then Jake found him and Hobby thought to look for Claire one more time — this time just to be polite, to say good-bye; she was, after all, carrying his child — but Claire was nowhere around. He tried texting her, but she didn't answer, and Hobby was running out of time.

They were leaving the party.

By the beginning of August, Hobby was out of his wheelchair and on crutches. The physical therapist at the hospital, a woman named Meadow, said that he was the best patient she'd ever had. She attributed this to the fact that he'd been so healthy, so strong, and such an exceptional athlete to begin with. But a lot of times, Meadow said, it was the former athletes who were the most challenging to work with, because they were used to having things

come easily. They weren't willing to try. Their fragile psyches didn't allow for the possibility of failure.

Ha! Hobby laughed at this, while at the same
time identifying with it. He wouldn't be human if a
part of him didn't mourn, didn't *ache* for his old,
unbroken body and its talents. Coach Jaxon (football) stopped by twice to watch his physical therapy
sessions, and both times Hobby saw the gleam of
hope in his eyes. Hobby tried to eavesdrop on the
whispered conversations between Coach Jaxon and
Meadow while he did his twenty-five reps of a
simple neck roll, but all he saw was Meadow shaking her head. He wasn't going to be ready in September, nor the September after that; his body
would never again be able to absorb the kind of
trauma that football delivered. Another concus-
sion, Meadow told Hobby, if it didn't kill him,
would most likely leave him a vegetable for life. He
would never have the quickness or endurance for
basketball at the level that he wanted to play it, and
though his pitching arm was unharmed, his left
arm would always be weak. He was lopsided now,
off balance.

Hobby fought against self-pity. He had seen
movies about embittered athletes battling back
from injury (what movie was he thinking of? he
could no longer remember things the way he used
to). He wasn't going to allow himself to become

embittered. He could be like Penny, in a box in the ground. He could be brain-dead already, a vegetable that his mother would be saddled with the rest of her life. He wasn't going to stress out about battling back. He was going to put in the work so he could do the normal things: walk, carry a bag of groceries, and toss a ball, someday, to his son or daughter.

Hobby liked his crutches. They were better than the wheelchair. He had a lot more mobility. His mother didn't fret about him as much. She started working almost normal hours at the Allencasts'. Hobby thought working was good for his mother; it kept her mind occupied. He was worried about her. She spent a lot of time on the back deck at night, muttering things at the ocean. One night her muttering sounded so conversational that he thought she was on the phone.

When she came inside he asked, "Were you talking to Jordan?"

"No!" his mother screamed. "I was talking to myself!" And she burst into tears.

His mother refused to see a therapist. Meadow had asked Hobby about this, as had Dr. Field. They had apparently both suggested it to Zoe, but to no avail. They thought if Hobby encouraged her, she might agree. He brought it up one night at dinner. The dropped-off meals had ended, thank God. His mother's food was so much better. But dinnertime was tough. The two of them sat at the table out on the deck, which had three chairs. Penny's place was empty.

Hobby said, "I think you should talk to someone, Mom. I'll go with you if you want."

Zoe said, "If you want to talk to someone, by all means, do it. I'll set it up for you. But *I'm* not going."

"Why not?"

Zoe said, "Because I'm going to process my daughter's death the way I'm going to process it. I don't want anyone — not even the kindest, most perspicacious therapist on Earth — telling me how to go about it."

"I don't think they *tell* you anything," Hobby said. "I think they just listen." He paused. His mother was moving her corn salad around on her plate. "Don't you want someone to talk to, Mom?"

Zoe didn't answer. Hobby cleaned his own plate of corn and steak and greens and dug in for seconds. He asked, "Do you miss Jordan?"

Zoe eyeballed him. Her fork, with nothing on it, was suspended in midair. It felt to Hobby as if he had asked exactly the wrong question, the question that only a daft seventeen-year-old boy would ask.

"Yes," she said. "Yes I do, actually. I miss him very much."

*   *   *

That night Hobby had heard his mother crying in bed. He rubbed the heels of his palms into his eye sockets and thought, Penny, wherever you are, can you help me here? He thought of his sister as a magical force, potentially capable of performing any number of miracles now that she was dead. Can you please deliver Mom some comfort? he asked her. It occurred to Hobby that he was passing the buck to his sister yet again where his mother was concerned, and it further occurred to him that he had the power to comfort Zoe himself. He could tell her about the baby. The baby that they'd nearly aborted but that Claire had decided to keep when she found out there had been an accident and learned that Penny was dead and Hobby was in a coma. Life, Claire told him, had suddenly seemed like something else entirely, something huge and precious. And she had life inside of her, a life that was hers and his, and she wasn't questioning what they would do or how they were going to make it work. She was just keeping his baby safe. She had stood in the midst of the nearly two thousand people who gathered on the football field for the candlelight vigil, and she had felt privileged to be carrying a part of Hobby inside her.

Hobby could tell his mother about the baby; it would, at the very least, distract her. But Claire wanted to keep the news a secret until after her first ultrasound appointment, which was scheduled for the second week of September. Claire's mother, Rasha, knew about the pregnancy, and Rasha had told her best friend, Sara Boule. Hobby didn't love the fact that Rasha Buckley and Sara Boule (a woman who basically gossiped for a living, as a receptionist for Dr. Toomer, Hobby's dentist) both knew, while Zoe didn't. However, Zoe's reaction wasn't something that Hobby felt he could predict. She might be overjoyed. Or she might not.

The door to Penny's room had remained shut since Hobby's return from the hospital. He knew the window in there was open because the door rattled in its frame with the breeze off the beach. At night this rattling was spooky because who wanted to hear rattling from the bedroom door of a dead girl? Hobby suspected that his mother had done nothing about Penny's room—all her stuff was probably still in there.

One day after Zoe left for work, Hobby stood outside Penny's door, balanced on his crutches. He looked at the door—just a crappy plywood box door painted white, with a dent that Penny had kicked in it...when? Shit, Hobby couldn't remember. He tried to determine if he had the emotional fortitude required to open the door and look around. He was still mulling over what Jake Randolph had told him. He thought it was indeed possible that some real or exaggerated version of what had happened between Jake and Winnie in the Pottses' basement had reached Penny's ears, either through Demeter or through someone else, perhaps Winnie herself. And hearing that news, he knew, would have caused Penny to lose her shit, especially if it was exaggerated.

But in Hobby's mangled memory, Penny hadn't seemed angry at *Jake.* If the problem had been with Jake, wouldn't Penny have said something to indicate that? Wouldn't she have refused to drive his car home? Penny hadn't said *anything.* She had just come completely unglued; if she'd gotten some kind of news, it must have been too horrible to repeat. This caused Hobby to worry that someone (Demeter?) might have told Penny that Hobby had gotten Claire Buckley pregnant. Was this the news that had tipped Penny's fragile scales into mental illness? She would have been most upset about which part? he wondered. That Claire was planning to abort? Or that Hobby hadn't confided in her himself? Her own twin. The truth was that Hobby hadn't even considered telling Penny because he was afraid the news would make her hysterical. Penny didn't like being confronted with the harsher realities of life.

Hobby's conclusion was that Penny would have been devastated if she'd heard from a third party that Claire was pregnant. How devastated, he just couldn't say. She also would have been devastated about Jake and Winnie Potts. He wished he remembered more about how Penny had been that night, but for all intents and purposes, his coma had started when they all gathered at Jake's car. He didn't have a single clear memory after that point.

He could call Demeter. They had always had a decent relationship; he might have better success with her than Jake had. But Al and Lynne Castle had dropped off the radar, and the one time Hobby had seen Demeter since the accident, she had completely ignored him. He was still in his wheelchair then, and his mother was pushing him around Miacomet Pond. It was a beautiful, balmy night, and Hobby was concentrating on taking huge gulps of sweet summer evening air, rather than feeling like the survivor of some private war. His mother had seemed better that night; she was the one who suggested the walk. They both saw Demeter's car approaching, and Zoe said, "There's Demeter."

And Hobby said, "Yeah, you're right."

Zoe said, "Not a scratch on her."

And Hobby said, "Mom, come on."

Zoe said, "Sorry, Hob, I'm human."

Hobby wasn't 100 percent surprised when

Demeter passed them without stopping or waving or anything. She hadn't come to the hospital or to the house; she hadn't sent a note. "She's probably just not ready to deal with it all yet," Hobby said as he watched the taillights of her Escape disappear down Pond View Road.

"She's guilty," Zoe said. "She can't face us because she feels guilty."

"You mean she's got survivor's remorse?" Hobby said.

"I mean, that girl is guilty," Zoe said.

Hobby turned the knob on Penny's door, and it swung open, of course—there wasn't a door in the house that locked properly.

Penny's room.

Okay, weird, Hobby thought. Weird in that it looked the same as it had six weeks earlier, back when Penny was alive. Her four-poster bed was neatly made with the blue flowered sheets and the sky-blue duvet and the two white eyelet pillows propped up against the headboard and a collection of her favorite stuffed animals—old Bear, Gladys the sock monkey, and a scrawny-looking tiger that Jake had won for her at the Tom Nevers Carnival—nestled between the pillows. Penny had been a young Nazi about her bed. She made it perfectly every morning and constantly smoothed the wrinkles out of the duvet. She said she couldn't lie on it otherwise. The easiest way for Hobby to get Penny hysterical was to launch himself onto her bed, mess up the duvet, unprop the pillows, and start juggling the trio of sad little animals. She used to *shriek*. Hobby would have laughed remembering it if it wasn't so tragic. He thought, Well, Penny, wherever you are, you can rest easy. Your bed is perfectly made. He smoothed out an imaginary wrinkle just to be sure.

There was her dresser with the big mirror, the biggest mirror in the house. Zoe came in here all the time to check herself out, and this, also, gave Penny fits. "Use your own mirror!" she would yell at her mother.

And Zoe would say, "Jeez, Pen, chill. I'll be out in a sec."

"Why don't you use your own mirror? Seriously. We're not poor, you could buy yourself a full-length mirror."

Zoe never let Penny get her angry. She said, "Because I like your mirror better. It makes my ass look smaller."

How many times had Hobby complained to his mother about Penny? "She drives me crazy," he would say. "Why can't she just relax like a normal human being?"

"Her heart is made from the finest bone china," Zoe would answer. "Like a teacup." And then Zoe would smile, and so would Hobby.

On Penny's dresser was her paddle brush, filled with long, dark hairs. She used to keep it in the bathroom, but Hobby had protested when he found one of Penny's hairs wound through the bristles of his toothbrush. There was her fancy perfume atomizer, which had never held a drop of perfume. There was her jewelry box made from bird's-eye maple. Hobby opened it. He sorted through friendship bracelets woven out of embroidery thread, her real gold hoop earrings, her pearl on the gold chain that had been their grandmother's, her pin from the National Honor Society, and a sea-foam-green box from Posh that contained a pair of silver dangly earrings edged in chips of blue sapphire. Jake had bought her those earrings for their two-year anniversary.

Hobby opened the top drawer of Penny's dresser and found himself staring into a tangle of lacy underwear. Okay, embarrassing. He quickly shut the drawer, but as he did, he caught a glimpse of the edge of something red and shiny. A book. A journal. He nudged aside the lacy things to confirm that what he was looking at was the red leather cover of a journal. He flipped through the pages to make sure it was Penny's handwriting—loopy and girlish—then he put the journal back and shut the drawer again. Original, Pen, hiding your journal in your underwear drawer, he thought. I found it in the first place I looked.

The shade on the window was flapping in the breeze. Hobby inspected Penny's bedside table. There was a glass of water, evaporated down to an inch or so, with a film of dust across the top. A box of Kleenex. A copy of *Moby-Dick*, which Penny referred to as her independent reading. She'd been telling people this for at least nine months, but when Hobby checked now, he saw that she had read only up to page 236. She had died without even getting halfway through.

From the bedside table, Hobby could pivot and open Penny's closet. On the inside of the door was a cork board displaying a photo montage of Penny and Jake. Penny and Jake in *Guys and Dolls*, Penny and Jake in *Damn Yankees*, Penny and Jake in *Grease*. Penny and Jake in the stands at one of Hobby's football games, Jake carrying Penny down the beach on his back, Penny and Jake with marshmallows in their mouths, Penny and Jake at the prom. There was also a picture of himself and Penny on Christmas morning in front of the tree, Penny in some ridiculous high-necked flannel nightgown that made her look like Laura Ingalls Wilder, her hair in braids to heighten the effect, and him in boxers and one of his father's vintage Clash T-shirts (his mother had kept his father's concert T-shirts, and she gave Hobby one every year on his birthday). In this Christmas photo, Penny was beaming and apple-cheeked, and Hobby was bleary-eyed and scowling. It was this past Christmas. Penny had woken him up at seven-thirty. He would have been content to sleep until noon and then eat three quarters of his mother's Christmas coffee cake and *then* open his stocking. But not Penny. She had been a freaking Christmas elf.

And that's it for you and Christmas, Pen, Hobby thought. Maybe for all of them and Christmas. His mother had already talked about taking a trip to St. John at the holidays.

Penny's clothes were hanging in the closet. His mother had said something about Goodwill, when she got around to it. Hobby fingered Penny's favorite blue blouse, which had cost a fortune—two or three hundred dollars. Penny had seen it on line, she wanted to buy it with her own money, but Zoe said no, there was no reason for a teenager to spend that kind of money on one article of clothing. And then a few weeks later, Penny had been asked to sing in front of the Boston Pops for the second year in a row, personally, by Keith Lockhart, and Zoe had bought Penny the blouse for the occasion.

Hobby touched the silky material. The blouse was still here, but Penny wasn't. It was messing with his head.

He hopped over to the edge of her bed. Her poster of Robert Pattinson was still hanging, her *Twilight* books were still on the shelves. Below her books were CDs—Charlotte Church and Jessye Norman next to Puccini's operas next to *Send In the Clowns* by Judy Collins. Certainly Penelope Alistair was the only seventeen-year-old in the world to own a Judy Collins CD. That was truly the music she liked best, however: those godawful songs of the 1970s. Crystal Gayle, Anne Murray, Karen Carpenter. It was Penny's dream to become one of these women. By the time she was "grown up"—say, in 2015—she figured the world would be ready to hear these songs again. If Penny ever made it onto *American Idol,* she planned to sing Debby Boone's "You Light Up My Life." She used to sing it all the time in the shower.

"Even your voice can't save that song," Hobby said. "Pick something else."

"I'm afraid I have to agree with your brother," Zoe said. Zoe had good taste in music. She was a Deadhead. She had a cardboard box with all of her bootleg tapes stashed under her bed. And she liked modern stuff, too—Eminem, Spoon, Rihanna.

But Penny continued to sing "You Light Up My

Life." And the soundtrack to *Fame*. Hobby would have laughed if it hadn't been so tragic.

He closed the door to the closet. Penny had a drafting table instead of a desk, just as Hobby did in his room. Hobby had a drafting table because he wanted to be an architect; Penny had one because she was a copycat. She kept a sketchpad and a box of colored pencils on her drafting table because she liked to "draw," though she wasn't much of an artist. But now Hobby stared at the sketchpad, wondering if his sister had left behind some sort of note. He had gathered — though no one had said it to him directly — that certain people thought the accident had been a suicide.

Hobby crutched his way over to the drafting table. If there was a note, he would have to show his mother. If it turned out that Penny had committed suicide, he was going to boil over in anger.

But the sketchpad was blank, except for a heart drawn in black pencil. A heart she was probably planning on filling with Penny + Jake, TL4EVA. It was something of a joke around school that Penny had graffitied every pair of jeans that Jake Randolph owned.

She would have been really upset to hear about Jake and Winnie. She would have done something drastic, maybe.

No suicide note. That was good. Hobby wondered if his mother had already been in here panning for one. She must have, right? Immediately afterward? But maybe not. This place looked untouched.

Hobby was about to vacate the premises. He couldn't shake the feeling that Penny was watching him. "Matter cannot be created or destroyed"—so she existed somewhere, right? She would *not* like the idea of Hobby's hobbling around her room on his crutches, poking through her stuff. So he would go.

But who was he kidding? He wasn't leaving without the journal. He moved over to the dresser and, without looking at himself in the mirror, slipped the journal out from under Penny's underwear. Then he lumbered out into the hallway and shut the door.

Wherever she was, she would *not* want him reading her journal. But what had Zoe said? "Sorry, Hob, I'm human." Yep, Hobby got it. He thought, Sorry, Pen, I'm human. I can't pass up the chance to read it.

None of the entries were dated, so Hobby had to orient himself based on content. The journal seemed to start a few years earlier because it referenced Mrs. Jones-Crisman, who had been Penny's homeroom teacher during freshman year. In the very first entry, Mrs. J-C calls her out for kissing Jake in the hallway. In the next entry, Penny has a fight with Zoe because she kissed Jake in the back-seat of the Karmann Ghia. Zoe said, "I don't get paid enough to listen to the two of you swapping spit. Do it in private."

Like where? Penny wondered in her journal. *If I can't kiss him at school and I can't kiss him in the car, where am I going to kiss him?*

Hobby worried that the whole thing was going to be about kissing Jake. And it was, for the most part—at least at first. Penny wrote about every time she made out with Jake; she compared kissing him to "eating something really delicious and you don't want to stop. Like Mom's apple fritters with the Bavarian cream."

Hobby stopped. It was too bad Jake was in Australia. He would have appreciated that his kissing was on par with Zoe's apple fritters. Hobby would have laughed at this himself if it hadn't been so tragic.

He skipped ahead. He didn't want to read about Penny's getting felt up, or Penny's discovering Jake's erection. (He accidentally stumbled across the line *Do you feel yourself change when we do this?*) He didn't want to read about Penny's argument with her voice coach. He was looking for something bet-ter, more interesting.

He thought, Come on, Pen, give me something I can work with.

And then, two thirds of the way through the journal, the tone changed. Penny started referring to everyone by their first initials only. Jake became J. Hobby found references to himself and his mother: *H at practice, Z at work. J and I home alone but I don't want to, I can't explain it, I just don't feel like it. I'm too sad. Sad about what? J asks me. He wants me to have a reason so he can fix it. But I don't have a reason. I'm just sad, and* sad *isn't even the right word. I'm empty. Since I don't have a reason, J applies his own reason: hormones.*

A few pages later Hobby read this line: *A told me to read* Moby-Dick. *Says I'll like it.*

Hobby thought, A? A is the reason Penny spent nine months plodding through *Moby-Dick,* only to finally get bogged down on page 236?

A appeared more and more. Hobby couldn't read fast enough.

J at paper all afternoon. I skipped madrigals, I don't care if I lose my solo. I spent two hours in the bedroom with A.

Hobby's head snapped up. While Jake was working on the newspaper, Penny had spent two hours in a bedroom with someone whose name began with an *A.* Hobby racked his shell-shocked brain. The only A he could come up with was Anders Peashway.

Had his sister been fooling around with Anders behind Jake's back? Anders *was* good-looking, he was a very fine athlete, a forward on the basketball team, the catcher on the baseball team, one of Hobby's top lieutenants. But really? Penny and Anders? Anders seemed too clueless for Penny, too provincial. Anders Peashway would go to college someplace where he could play baseball — Plymouth State or, if he was lucky, Northeastern — and then he would return to Nantucket and work for his father building houses. He would buy a boat and fish, he would have children and watch them play in the same gym and on the same fields where he played. Penny could never be interested in someone like Anders, could she?

A told me to read Moby-Dick. *Says I'll like it.* There was absolutely no way Anders Peashway had told Penny to read anything, much less an eight-hundred-page classic that dealt with what Anders would have referred to as "old-fashioned shit."

Hobby kept going. *Lay down with A today. Talked. A understands me. A says that sometimes the heart pumps black blood. And that is exactly how I feel. I am poisoned with something, this evil sickness, this lethargy, the inability to care. I'm supposed to be joyous about my voice, my "natural gift." Z says I have a "responsibility to myself" to develop my talent. God gave me this voice for a reason, Z says. Everyone and their "reasons." It's like the rest of the world doesn't realize that everything that happens is random. A woman kills her two teenagers, she shoots them. She'd had it, she says. They were mouthy. Everyone sympathizes with the kids, and I sympathize with the kids. But sometimes I sympathize with the mother. Sometimes I feel like I've had it.*

Hobby shut the journal. He shouldn't have opened it. He was going to have to show his mother. Or maybe not. *The heart pumps black blood.* There was a black heart on the sketchpad. Penny had been sick, and none of them had known it. Well, one thing had changed: Hobby no longer felt guilty about invading Penny's privacy. He felt as if she'd meant for him to find her journal.

J is mad that I'm spending so much time with A. Not healthy, he says. He doesn't get that A is the only one who understands me.

So Jake knew about A, Hobby thought. The idea that A was Anders Peashway still nagged at him. Jake would certainly have said that Penny's spending so much time with Anders was not healthy. But the *Moby-Dick* thing? No. Not Anders. No way.

I ask A about her marriage.

Hobby was so surprised to read this line that he nearly ripped the journal in two, and a shooting pain traveled up his bad arm and throbbed in the spot where he'd broken his clavicle. A was a *woman,* a woman who either was or had been married. So that meant what, exactly? That his sister had been a lesbian? That she was having a relationship with a grown woman? She had been "lying in bed" and sharing her most intimate thoughts with an adult woman, and Jake knew about it and didn't think it was healthy.

Then Hobby got it. He was daft, yes he was; another person — his mother, for example — would have figured it out right away. A was Ava Randolph.

A says she's felt alone ever since Ernie died; her loneliness is a shroud and a shield. She internalized the pain she felt over losing her son, and it ate up everything inside her. A is lucky. Ernie is her Reason. It's something she can pinpoint. I feel like I'm being eaten away from the inside, but I don't have a Reason. Then I wonder if my Reason is my father, the father who died before I was born. A touches my hair and says, "That's possible."

Jesus! Hobby thought. It sounded as if Ava Randolph had been mentoring Penny in the art of insanity and depression. How could Penny feel the loss of a person she'd never known? Hobby was in the same boat, he'd lost his father before he was born too, but he had hardly given it a moment's thought. On Father's Day he sometimes felt a twinge, or when he saw other kids throwing the baseball with their dads, but it wasn't something he ever wanted to *cry* over. If anything, he was grateful to Hobson senior for giving him top-notch genes. He certainly hadn't inherited his size or his athletic ability from Zoe.

The most notable thing for Hobby was that in the last fifteen or twenty pages of Penny's journal, J was hardly mentioned at all. It was all about A.

A wants to move to Australia, but JR has work and J has school. A misses her family. I ask her why she doesn't just move back alone, and she says she's in a double bind.

Hobby knew there was no way he could show the journal to his mother. Zoe would hate the thought of Penny's communing with Ava Randolph. Hobby tried to summon his own images of Ava Randolph, but as with so many of his memories, it was as if someone had broken into the bank and stolen them all. Then he had one: Ava Randolph at the funeral for her baby. She had set the tiny coffin in the hole in the ground, and then she alone had taken up the spade and filled in the hole. The rest of them, including Jordan Randolph, including Al Castle, including the cemetery attendant, had just stood there and watched her. Hobby had been only thirteen years old, but he remembered how the muscles in Ava Randolph's forearms had tensed, he remembered the way she'd smoothed the dirt across the top, he remembered how, when she was finished, she had stabbed the earth with the blade of the spade, and then she had turned to the rest of them and started to wail.

"He's gone," she'd cried. "He's gone!"

Hobby had never felt so helpless in all his life.

A is the only one who understands me, Penny wrote. *I love A.*

AVA

It was barely dawn when Jake walked into the garden. Ava was startled, thinking maybe it was an intruder, maybe it was a drunk from the corner pub who had stumbled home to the wrong house. Then she realized that the figure sneaking into the yard was her own child, and he was carrying his duffel bag. They locked eyes for a second, and Ava saw the desperation and defeat on his face. She felt a colossal relief that he was walking toward the shed and not away from it.

"Jake?" she said.

"Mom," he said. "I need my bed."

Ava took a drag of her cigarette—a nasty habit, one she would have preferred to keep secret from him. She exhaled, then nodded. She let him go.

For four years she had been adrift. She had lost a baby. Her son Ernie. She had carried him for nine months, pushed him out of her body without any drugs, she had nursed him and cared for him for eight weeks. These weeks had been blissful. Ernie was constantly in her arms, his hungry mouth tugged on her breast, his tiny hands grabbed at her hair. How smitten she had been, how helplessly in love. Jordan got tired and occasionally grumbled when he had to get up for a feeding, but she never complained. She wasn't tired; she was bursting with purpose, dizzy with joy.

And then the inverse of that. The horror.

He had been perfectly healthy. Ava had just taken him for his two-month checkup, and Ted Field had declared him thriving. There was no discernible reason for the fact that he stopped breathing. And since there was no reason, it was impossible to comprehend. There must have been some mistake, he would wake up and be returned to her, squirming and flashing his toothless smile. For days afterward Ava had awoken each morning believing that she would find Ernie alive.

But no.

Jordan had been at the newspaper. He walked in a few steps behind the paramedics, holding his briefcase. Ava was confused by this at first. The head paramedic lifted Ernie out of her arms and laid him on a mat and tried to revive him, doing CPR with two fingers. Ava dissolved into Jordan, and he held her, both of them shaking, as they watched the fruitless efforts to save their son.

Jordan whispered, "I am so sorry, Ava. I am so, so sorry."

The apology made sense only later, once she'd pieced together the fact that Jordan hadn't been in the house that night. He had been at work.

Ava fancied herself a reasonable woman. She had grown up in a family of six children, she had lived on two continents, she had a reservoir of understanding about human beings and the things that motivated them and the ways they sometimes acted.

But Jordan's being at work, on the night Ernie stopped breathing? That was something she could not reconcile. She knew that Jordan's absence hadn't caused Ernie's death, and yet the two facts were linked in her mind. Ernie's death was a mystery. There was no one to blame. Jordan At Work was a reason Ava could cling to. It was a shard of obsidian that she polished over and over.

"He was in distress. You might have heard him if you'd been home! You might have been able to save him!"

In the grip of Ava's mind, Jordan was at fault. He hadn't caused Ernie's death, but he had made the circumstances of Ernie's death unbearable.

Ava knew about Jordan and Zoe. She had first suspected they were having an affair in May of the previous year. Since Jake and Penny started dating, Jordan and Zoe had shared the responsibility of transporting the young lovers back and forth. One day Ava looked out the window of Ernie's nursery and saw Jordan and Zoe sitting on the hood of Zoe's orange car, talking. Jordan seemed happy and animated, and Ava thought, He never looks that way when he talks to me. Then she thought, He never talks to me.

And then, a month or two later, she climbed into the Land Rover to drive to the cemetery with a bouquet of while lilies for Ernie's grave, and her senses were assaulted by a foul smell. It was a hot day, the car had been closed up overnight, and Jordan had left a crumpled brown lunch bag on the passenger seat. The bag had a dark stain spread across the bottom, and it was leaking some kind of milky liquid all over the leather. Ava carefully picked up the dripping bag and carried it to the trash can in the garage. Before she threw the bag away, she looked inside.

There was a small Tupperware container—not quite closed—of spoiled, reeking coleslaw. That was the culprit. Also in the bag were some sandwich crusts and a fudge brownie, wrapped in wax paper. Ava studied the brownie. This particular kind of brownie...in *wax paper.*

Ava thought, *Zoe.*

Huh?

Then she saw that there was a recipe card in the bag, folded in half.

It was a note. It said: *It's ridiculous how much I love you.*

Ava didn't say anything to Jake about their encounter in the backyard of the bungalow in Fremantle, and eventually her silence was rewarded: on August 14, the coldest day of the winter—the temperature was a brisk 52 degrees Fahrenheit—Jake entered the kitchen at five-thirty in the morning. Ava was at the table, drinking Lady Grey tea and doing the crossword puzzle from the previous day's newspaper. Jake was wearing a pair of jeans that Penny had scribbled on and his navy blue Nantucket Whalers sweatshirt. He entered the kitchen with an air of intent, as though he and his mother had an appointment, and Ava thought that while some warning would have been nice, she had no reason to be surprised. She had caught him at something, and Jake was the kind of kid who would want to explain himself.

Ava said, "Would you like some tea?"

"Actually, I've started drinking short blacks," he said.

"Short blacks?" Ava said. She had to suppress a smile. She didn't want him to know how much it delighted her to hear him use the Australian term. "Have you really?"

He gave a serious nod, and she brought out the French press and the espresso powder and started the kettle. This bought her some time. All she hoped was that Jordan would stay asleep. On Nantucket he was always up at the crack of dawn, but here he woke when he wanted to, sometimes as late as eight-thirty.

When the coffee was ready, Ava poured a cup for Jake and brought it to the table.

"Thanks," he said, and he took a sip as she watched him.

"As good as at the Dome?" she asked.

"Better."

He was lying, but it was sweet.

"So," she said.

He took a big, heaving breath. Then he stared at her, mute.

She was afraid to prompt him. She was afraid of scaring him away.

Finally he said, "I want to ask you about Penny."

"Penny?" she said.

"When the two of you . . . when she was with you in Ernie's nursery, what kind of stuff did you talk about? I know you were close. I know she told you things, Mom."

Ava had not confronted Jordan about Zoe. She had thought she might, especially in the first days after finding the note. *It's ridiculous how much I love you.* Ava felt betrayed. Of course she felt betrayed! Ava and Zoe had been good friends before Ernie died. The five of them—she and Jordan and Zoe and Al and Lynne—had been a group, a merry band. All those weekends together, so many shared hours with the kids. Ava thought back to how Jordan and Zoe had acted together over the years. They had been close, they had been aligned, they had had that American camaraderie, they had the same political views, they liked the same music, that kind of thing. Ava had never cared about that. And the fact of the matter was, she didn't care what Jordan and Zoe were doing behind her back now. Let them carry on like Penny and Jake, like a couple of horny teenagers! Let them leave little love notes for each other! Jordan had proved himself to be no better than his father, a common philanderer! Jordan could seek comfort in another woman's arms, even if that woman was Ava's friend. Ava didn't care. They could both go to hell. She had bigger things on her mind. She had lost her child.

Their affair alleviated her guilt. She had abandoned her marriage, and also her friendship with Zoe. Now the two of them didn't need her anymore. They had each other. Ava wanted to be left alone. They would leave her alone.

In her more generous moments she thought, Jordan tried to love me through the worst of it, he tried to pull me out of the hole. She thought, Zoe tried too. She made and delivered all that food, and I never once thanked her, I never once reached out. She sent that beautiful letter, and I threw it away. I couldn't talk to either of them, I couldn't talk to anybody. So they turned to each other. Was that really such a surprise?

When had Penny first approached Ava? When had she first knocked on the door of Ernie's nursery? When had she asked Ava what she was watching (the umpteenth rerun of *Home and Away*), when had she asked her what she was reading (Melville)? Ava didn't remember exactly. One day when Jake wasn't home, Penny had just appeared, and in that lovely, innocent way of hers, she had started talking — about Jake and school, and then about her voice, the impossible burden of it, and then about the leaden weight in her heart that she couldn't account for, which she said she couldn't tell anyone else about.

"You're the only one who gets it," Penny had said. "I can't tell Jake, and I can't tell my mother."

For months Ava had borne witness to the girl's sadness, to the lows of Penny's psyche—unfathomable, probably, to anyone *but* her. Ava had stroked her pretty head and said, "Yes, I know how you feel, darling girl."

Ava had believed that Penny was suffering from the malaise common to all teenage girls: "No one understands me. My mom and I used to be close, but now she doesn't get it. She thinks I'm the luckiest girl alive. If I told her I felt like this, she would ship me straight off to a psychiatrist. She's done that to me before."

Ava had thought, Every girl needs a woman to talk to who is *not* her mother; every girl needs a place to vent her feelings where she won't be judged. Ava was pleased that Penny had sought her out, she was gratified. She had won over Zoe's daughter. She thought, I'm taking good care of her.

Now, with Jake, Ava faced a monstrous guilt. Ava *had* seen the warning signs, she *had* seen that Penny was capable of putting herself or others in danger, and she had done nothing to prevent that possibility. She should have told Jordan, or Lynne Castle. Or Zoe. Of course, she should have told Zoe.

Ava said, "She used to talk about what was on her mind, Jake. Her concerns, her worries, her sadness. She felt safe talking to me about those things, I think, because I was so sad too, about Ernie."

Jake nodded. He sipped his coffee.

Ava said, "If I had it to do over, I would go to her mother. I would tell Zoe some of the things that Penny told me. I would try to get her some help."

"It wasn't your fault, Mom," Jake said. "It was *my* fault. It was something I did." He looked at her, and his eyes filled with tears, and then he was sobbing, and Ava went around the table and knelt in front of him and gathered him into her arms.

"Oh, honey, no," she said. "You were wonderful to Penny."

"No, I wasn't," he said. "I mean, most of the time I was pretty good, but not always."

Ava shushed him and smoothed his hair. She had spent so long mourning the child she'd lost, she thought, that she had missed out on caring for the child she had. She said, "It's impossible to do right by someone all the time, Jake. I am very much living proof of that. We hurt the people we care about, intentionally and unintentionally. But if there is one thing I'm confident about, it's that Penelope Alistair knew that you loved her."

Jake sniffed and wiped at his nose with his sweatshirt, and Ava rose to grab a box of tissues. She eyed the door to the master bedroom: still closed.

Jake sighed and seemed to collect himself. He took another sip of coffee. "This is good."

Ava refilled his mug. She wasn't sure whether to stand up or sit down. He was talking to her and she was listening, but what Jake didn't know, what he wouldn't know until he was a parent himself, was how grateful she was. She didn't deserve this.

He said, "So as you probably figured out, I tried to run away."

She decided to sit. Her throat felt as if it were going to close. *Run away.* She said, "Where did you go?"

He said, "I went to South Beach. I hung out around this bonfire with a bunch of people I didn't know. Ferals."

Ava winced. The term was awful. *Ferals.* And yet such people had been hanging around Perth and Freo since she was a young girl, and that was what they'd always been called: feral. Ava had seen them at South Beach herself thirty years ago — the dreadlocks, the tattoos and piercings, the dirty mattresses that they dragged out to the park and lounged across as they smoked marijuana and played their guitars and sketched in journals and read Orwell or Proust. They cooked on camp stoves and slept with their dirty feet hanging out of the windows of their vans.

"One of them, this guy named Hawk, said I could ride with him across the Nullarbor, to Adelaide first and then across to Sydney." Jake paused. "I gave him some money."

"Oh," Ava said. She tried not to sound alarmed. "How much?"

"Two hundred and sixty dollars," Jake said. He stared into his coffee cup. "It seemed like kind of a bargain at the time."

"So then what happened?" Ava asked.

"Well, then I had some beers, and I...smoked some marijuana, or what I thought was marijuana, and then I blacked out in the sand. And when I woke up, they had taken the rest of my money and my credit card and my shoes and my camera, and they'd left."

"Ah," Ava said. She had heard from Jordan that Jake had *lost* the credit card, and that after giving him a lecture about fiscal responsibility, Jordan had called to cancel it. "I see."

"So then I came back here," Jake said.

"And that's when I saw you sneaking in the side door with your bag," Ava said.

"You didn't tell Dad?"

"No."

"I knew you didn't tell Dad," Jake said. "He would have wanted to have a heart-to-heart about it right away."

"No doubt."

"In a way I'm kind of glad it didn't work out," Jake said. He took a deep breath. "Because I couldn't stand to think about you being worried, not knowing where I was, not knowing where I was sleeping or what I was eating or who I was with."

"Thank you," Ava said.

"I know you love me, Mom."

Ava felt tears burning her eyes. "You know I love you, but you'll never understand how much."

"You seem really happy here."

"I never thought I would feel like myself again," Ava said. "But now I do."

"Dad's not happy," Jake said.

"No," Ava said. "He's not. I know he's not."

Jake said, "I wish there was a way that we could all be happy at the same time, in the same place."

Ava had been stunned when Jordan came to her and said he thought they should move to Australia.

"We'll go to Perth, we'll rent a house, we'll try it for a year," he said. "I can take a leave of absence; Marnie can run the paper, she's more than capable."

Ava said, "Jake? School?"

"He can go to school in Australia."

"His senior year?" she said.

"Ava, we need to get him out of here."

She had flared up with anger. She had been asking Jordan to move to Perth for *how many years,* and they were leaving now because *Jake* had to get off the island?

She said, "So this is all for Jake, then?"

"And you," Jordan said. "Mostly for you. If I just wanted to get Jake off the island, if that was my only motivation, I could think of places we could go that are a hell of a lot closer than Perth, Australia."

Yes, Ava thought. Anywhere was closer.

"But you want to move home, and I am taking you home," he said.

Yes, Ava did want to move home. She was an idiot for playing devil's advocate, but something wasn't computing.

"And you're going to *leave* the paper? And Marnie's going to run it?" she asked.

"For a year, yes."

It was inconceivable. Ava was missing something. She saw conviction in Jordan's eyes. He meant it. He was going to leave the paper, leave the island; she saw that he *wanted* to. But why now, when before he had regarded even a two-week trip to Australia as a fate worse than death? Her mind raced. She thought back to the Fourth of July. Jordan had said he was driving on Hummock Pond Road when the car ran out of gas. That had seemed odd to her. Jordan wasn't the type of man who ever let his car run out of gas. Ava had asked him, "What were you doing on Hummock Pond Road?"

"Driving around," he said.

Ava had mulled it over for hours, willing her brain to make sense of it. They were moving to Australia for an entire year. Jordan wanted to go — for Jake, but also for her, he said. But no — she would offer her apologies here — she didn't think Jordan Randolph was that selfless. Why would *he* want to go? Why would *he* want to get away?

And then she understood that it had to do with Zoe.

Zoe had turned him away.

Zoe didn't want him anymore.

Since they had moved to Fremantle, Ava had been happier than she could have imagined. In the early-morning hours she drank her tea and worked her crossword puzzles. Then she made breakfast — eggs and rashers, grilled tomatoes, beans. She went to Woolies during the week for groceries, and on the weekends she shopped at the Fremantle Markets. She came home with mangoes and fresh Turkish bread and baby cos for Caesar salad. She spent time with her brothers and sisters and her mother; she saw friends from secondary school and girls she'd once waitressed with at Cicarella's. She had been out with her old boyfriend, Roger Polly, on two occasions, and both times she had laughed as she hadn't done in years. Was this how Jordan had felt when he was with Zoe—energized and young again, like a new person?

"I wish there was a way that we could all be happy at the same time, in the same place," Jake had just said.

Ava tried to imagine what would have happened if Jake had journeyed across the country in some stranger's van. What if she and Jordan had woken up that morning, and Jake's bed had been empty, his things missing? Jordan, with his reporter's instincts, would probably have headed into town first, and then maybe to South Beach, to grill everyone he saw about his son's whereabouts. He might have found someone who remembered Jake—Jake would have stuck out, as an American kid, clean, in expensive clothes, reading Hemingway. But what if they hadn't found him in time? What if those people had kicked him out of the van on the scorching hot, deserted stretch of the Nullarbor, without any food or water?

Ava checked the clock. It was still only quarter

after six. Outside the kookaburras were hooting. It had been quite a morning already.

"What is it you want?" she asked Jake. "More than anything else, what do you want?"

"I want to go home," he said.

A pink glow of possibility had been growing inside of Ava for weeks, an idea, a life change, but she had been afraid to tell anyone about it. She finally confided in her sister May over dinner at the Subiaco Hotel. They ordered glasses of the Leeuwin chardonnay and a bowl of chili mussels to share, and Ava nearly had to pinch herself. She was in *Subiaco,* having dinner with her favorite sister, exactly as she had fantasized about doing on so many bitter Nantucket nights. Ava's prevailing thought was that now that she had this life again, she couldn't let anyone take it away.

She said to May, "I've made a decision."

May said, "Boob job?"

"No," Ava said. "I'm going to adopt a baby."

May clapped her hand over her mouth to keep from screaming. Her eyes bulged. Ava laughed.

"People are staring," Ava said.

"Oh my God," May said. "So much better than a boob job. I think that's a bloody *brilliant* idea. I don't know why you didn't decide this sooner."

"Well...," Ava said. She wasn't sure how much her family knew about her emotional state of the past four years. Probably they would have said she was "going through a bit of a rough patch," or perhaps acting "not quite herself." That would have been an example of typical Australian understatement, or else a consequence of the fact that she lived ten thousand miles away. "I wasn't ready before. But I've made up my mind, and I'm ready now. I'm thinking I want a little girl. From China."

"Oh, Ava!" May said. She came around the table to give her sister a hug. Of all the Price children, May was the most like their mother, Dearie. She had the pillowy bosom and the pragmatic attitude. She had learned to knit and could make dinner for ten even if there was nothing in the fridge. She had gray hair already, but she didn't care. With six kids of her own, an average week for her entailed four cricket matches, three trips to the dentist, and ten bloody noses. Who wouldn't have gray hair? "Oh, I am so happy for you! This is a wonderful thing." She sat back down, sipped her wine, leaned forward across the table. "And Jordan, is he excited?"

"Jordan doesn't know," Ava said. "This is my decision. It's a decision I'm making for *me*."

"So does that mean you're leaving him?" May asked. Ava had expected her sister to be scandalized. There hadn't been a divorce in the Price family in three generations. But May merely seemed matter-of-fact about it.

*   *   *

Ava had debated exactly when and where to talk to Jordan. One afternoon as she was walking home from the Fremantle Markets, she spied him drinking alone at the bar at the Norfolk Hotel, and she nearly walked in and tapped him on the shoulder, but she didn't want the conversation to be an ambush. She needed a block of time and a safe, wide-open space—and so she arranged for May to take Jake overnight, and she booked the two of them a day trip to Rottnest Island.

She said to Jordan, "You and I are going to Rottnest Island tomorrow morning. The ferry's at a quarter to nine."

Jordan's head whipped around so quickly that his glasses slid to the end of his nose. "No," he said.

"No?"

"I don't feel like an excursion," he said. "I'm not up for it. And certainly Jake doesn't want to go?"

"Jake's not invited," Ava said. "Jake is going over to May and Doug's. This is for you and me."

Jordan looked even more alarmed. "We're not spending the *night?*"

"No," Ava said. "Just a day trip. We'll rent bikes. See the island. See the quokkas."

"Oh," Jordan said. His lips twisted in that disapproving way of his. "I don't know. I had some things I wanted to do tomorrow."

Ava studied her husband. She could have said, "What things are those? Drinking at the Norfolk? Watching the cricket on TV? Wallowing in your misery?" But instead she smiled. "Cancel them," she said. "Because we're going to Rottnest."

She was jangling with nerves. The drive from their house to the ferry was perhaps the tensest eight minutes she had ever spent with her husband. He sulked like a recalcitrant child. He didn't want to go on a day trip alone with Ava. The only saving grace was that she understood. If their roles had been reversed and it had been Jordan dragging *her* out—say, for a day trip to Tuckernuck Island—she would have been just as miserable. As she drove, Jordan pressed his forehead against the car window, like a dog being driven to the pound.

Once they were on the ferry, Ava stood out on the bow while Jordan sat in the cabin with a short black, rereading the very same newspaper that he'd read earlier that morning at home. It was chilly on the bow; the wind sliced through Ava's sweater. Really, Rottnest was better appreciated in the summer, but what she needed to do had to be done now. She looked out at the blue water frosted with white-caps. She couldn't believe they had stayed together so long. They had wasted so much time.

When they disembarked on Rottnest, Ava was

so overcome with nostalgia that she nearly forgot the purpose of her mission. The Price children had stayed here for a week every year over the school holidays in January. They had always rented push-bikes, and after a certain age they had been allowed to explore the island on their own. It wasn't a lush tropical paradise by any means. The landscape was stark and barren, an expanse of parched brown acres with scattered eucalyptus trees and low-lying scrub brush. Ava's father used to award a dollar coin to the first child who spotted a quokka, the strange-looking marsupial indigenous to the island. The Price family would camp in a tent just off Geordie Bay, and the best night of the trip was always the night they ate sandwiches and played billiards in the pub at the Hotel Rottnest. That was thirty years ago. Now Rottnest was posher. There was a Dome, and a Subway, and a waterfront café. People came from Perth on their sailboats or motor yachts and anchored off the beach and snorkeled.

Ava stepped onto the dock and inhaled the scent of salt water and eucalyptus. "My God," she said, "I love it here. I've always loved it here. And I never thought I'd see it again."

Jordan made a snorting noise.

They rented mountain bikes with twenty-one gears, a far cry from the bikes of Ava's youth, which hadn't even had hand brakes. Ava took a map from the young man behind the rental counter and said to Jordan, "We have to do the whole circuit, all the way down to Fish Hook Bay, and we have to go and see the lighthouse. We'll have lunch at the hotel. That's where we used to go with Mum and Dad."

Jordan shook his head. He didn't want to be here.

They climbed onto their bikes and started riding. How long since Ava had been on a bike? Her first summer on Nantucket, she had ridden a used ten-speed all over the island, sometimes in her bare, sandy feet. One time Jordan had pulled his Jeep up alongside her and tried to convince her to accept a ride, but she had turned him down. She would pedal herself.

Now she and Jordan struggled up the hill toward the Vlamingh Lookout. At the crest Ava stopped, a little winded, and pointed across the island toward the Basin and Little Parakeet Bay. The day was clear enough that she could just pick out the coastline of the mainland, five miles away.

Jordan followed Ava's finger with dull eyes. He swigged from his water bottle. "What are we doing here, Ava?" he said.

"You don't like it?" she said. "In the summer you can swim at these beaches. You can snorkel. We used to collect these purple sea urchins, and my brothers used to fish for skippies with nets."

"What are we doing here?" he asked again.

She had hoped to make it to lunchtime, to a booth in the pub of the hotel, where they could relax and have a pint. Ava closed her eyes. The pub used to have a jukebox. Ava and her siblings would play Bruce Springsteen and the Who, but her mother would always choose "Waltzing Matilda," and then her mother and father and a few of the drunk strangers sitting at surrounding tables would belt out the lyrics together.

"I'm going to adopt a baby," she said. "A little girl, from China."

This was met with silence, which Ava had predicted. She couldn't look at Jordan's face. She desperately wanted a cigarette.

"No," he said. "I am not adopting a baby. I am not raising another child. I am not."

"You weren't listening to me," Ava said. "I said *I* am going to adopt a baby."

"So what does that mean?" He drank from his water bottle, then spit the water into the grass on the side of the road. "What does that *mean*, Ava?"

"It means...I want to stay here, for good, and I want to adopt a baby. And I think you and Jake should go home."

"What?" Jordan said. "What *is* this? This is you... what? *Leaving* me? You brought me here to godfor-fuckingsaken *Rottnest Island* so that you can tell me you're leaving me and you're going to adopt a baby?" He got off his bike and threw it onto the road, where it jumped and clattered. "This is *bullshit,* Ava!"

"Jordan."

"This is *bullshit!* I gave up my life for you, I left my *entire life* back on Nantucket and brought you here because that was all you ever wanted. You never wanted to live on Nantucket with me, that was perfectly clear twenty fucking years ago when I showed up here the first time and you laughed in my face and showed me the door. But you came back to me, *you came back to me, Ava*—and yet I've spent most of this marriage feeling as if I were the one who was making you miserable. I was the reason we couldn't get pregnant again, I was the reason Ernie died, I was the one who was too absorbed with work, everything was always *my fault.* And so now I do the selfless thing, I act in the name of our *marriage,* in the name of our *family,* and you tell me that you're adopting a baby and that Jake and I should go *home?*"

Cigarette, she thought. Or a cold pint. Anything to make this easier. But she would be glad later, she supposed, that she had had no crutches. Nothing to do with her hands but let them hold her bike steady, nowhere to put her eyes but on her husband.

"I know about Zoe, Jordan," Ava said. "I've known for a while now."

This was the real ambush; Jordan was caught completely off guard. She watched half a dozen emotions cross his face, and because they had been married for so long, she recognized every single one: denial, incredulity, contrition, anger, sadness, resignation.

"Jesus, Ava," he said.

"It's okay," she said. "It wasn't okay, I don't think, for a long time, but it's okay now." She thought back to their recent awkward encounter in bed. She had known then that things were over. She had allowed her marriage to rust, like a bicycle-built-for-two left out in the rain. And then, when she finally decided she wanted to climb back on it, she'd been surprised when it didn't work. When she reached out for Jordan, he was ten thousand miles away. At first Ava had felt angry and rejected, until she realized that the passion she felt that night wasn't for Jordan, it was for something else: Australia, her mother and brothers and sisters, the nascent idea of a new family.

"I can't believe this is happening," Jordan said. He screamed at the open sky: *"I CANNOT BELIEVE THIS IS HAPPENING!"*

She couldn't believe it either. She took a deep breath of the bracing Rottnest air. She had come to this island as a child; she could never have foreseen the circumstances that she found herself in now. For years, no matter how wretched she had felt, splitting from Jordan had been unthinkable. But why? Why?

"Go back to Nantucket, Jordan," Ava said. "That's where you belong."

Jordan opened his mouth to speak.

"You can protest," Ava said. "You can deny it all you want. But I know the truth. You want this over too."

"And what about our son?" Jordan asked.

"Jake is a sorry mess," Ava said. "A couple of weeks ago he tried to run away. He met some kids down at South Beach who had a van. He gave them some money because they said they would drive him to Sydney, where he was going to hop on a plane, or a container ship, back to the States. But they drugged him or something, I guess, and then they robbed him, and so he came back to the house. I caught him coming in the side gate at five-thirty in the morning with his duffel bag."

"Jesus," Jordan said. "Why didn't you tell me? Why didn't *he* tell me?"

"And ever since he told me what happened, all I've been thinking about is what I would have done if I'd lost him. Really *lost* him, the way we lost Ernie, the way Zoe lost Penny." Ava blinked. The wind whipped her hair, and she tried to collect it into an elastic at the base of her neck. "What would I have *done?*"

"I don't have an answer for that," Jordan said. "I don't seem to have an answer for anything anymore."

"I asked Jake what he wanted more than anything in the world. And you know what he said? He wants Nantucket."

"Ava. We're not going to decide this today. You can't dissolve a *twenty-year marriage* in one day."

"Just think about it, Jordan, please. Take Jake home and keep him safe. Get him into college somewhere. Put him on a plane to see me every once in a while. Run the newspaper, serve the island, do what you were born and raised to do." She swallowed. "And get Zoe back."

"Ava."

"I am serious," she said. "And I am sincere. Go after what you want."

Jordan poked his glasses up his nose. This gesture always used to bother her, but now she saw it as his way of expressing bewilderment. "And what about you?" he asked.

"I've got what I want right here." Ava mounted her bike and coasted down the backside of the hill. A quokka bounced across the road in front of her, and she thought, I win the dollar coin!

She was home.

LYNNE

Lynne Castle's favorite line was, "I'm too old for this." Lately, though, she had felt like adding an expletive onto the end of that; now she wanted to say, "I'm too old for this shit." But Lynne wasn't one to swear. She was solid, she was responsible, she was the voice of reason, she was a model citizen, she was a loving wife, she was a good mother.

But was she, really?

Welcome to the summer of self-doubt. Lynne and Al had everything a couple could want. Al had the car dealership and local politics. Lynne had a permitting business that kept her as busy as she wanted to be. They had a lovely home, the Castle castle. They had two boys away at college who were poised to take the world by storm. And they had Demeter.

On the outside, their lives looked good. Life had always looked good for the Castles. Al was in charge of everything on this island, and what he wasn't in charge of, Lynne was in charge of. But lately something deep inside their life seemed to be emitting a foul smell.

Lynne wasn't stupid, she wasn't an idiot, she knew that the problem was Demeter. Her youngest child, her only daughter. Lynne had been thrilled when she gave birth to a girl after the two boys. It was a dream come true: all that pink, the baby dolls, dance lessons, tea parties. Demeter had been a precocious little girl, cute and tiny, with a high-pitched candy voice.

What had gone wrong? Could Lynne just look back and be honest with herself for once?

By the time Demeter was ten or eleven, she was overweight. Lynne wasn't quite sure how this had happened. It was true that Lynne and Al were not small people, and there never seemed to be enough time in the day for regular exercise, but neither one of them was what you'd call *fat,* either. And both the boys were trim and athletic.

Lynne had enrolled Demeter in spring soccer; first she sat on the bench — because she was no good at the sport, because she was too heavy to run more than a few yards downfield without getting winded — and then she quit. Al bought her a mountain bike for her birthday, but by that point Demeter had few friends, and so no one to bike with, no one to go and see on her bike. She was ostracized at school because of her weight, but at home Lynne was afraid to address her size because she didn't want to make it an *issue,* she didn't want Demeter to think that her *own mother* believed she was fat. Instead she strove to promote a positive body image by telling her daughter she was beautiful, and of course she could have another piece of cake.

Demeter got bigger. She refused to ski during their weekends in Stowe. She refused to put on a bathing suit when they went to the beach on Sundays.

Fat camp? Lynne wondered. A summer away might help, but the idea seemed cruel. And outdated. Lynne had had a friend in high school who'd gone to fat camp and returned with an eating disorder.

Al was little help. Lynne crawled into bed at night and said, "What are we going to do about her? She's so lonely. I could cry thinking about it." And Al said, "I'll do whatever you want to do, honey."

This sounded like support, but really it was Al passing the buck. He was too busy with the dealership and his civic duties to do anything about Demeter. Demeter was a girl, Lynne was her mother. Certainly Lynne would know the best course of action. Al had put in his intense parenting time with the boys. Little League coach for eight years, science projects, college visits—he'd done it all. Lynne could hardly fault him for taking a pass here.

But she did fault him. And she faulted herself. What she thought was, I'm too old for this shit.

*   *   *

Adolescence, Lynne had tried to tell Demeter, was like a bad ride on the ferry. You got tossed about in the waves, you crested to the top, you sank into the troughs, and the motion between the highs and the lows made you sick to your stomach. You thought with every passing minute that you were surely going to drown. The good news was, the ride eventually came to an end. You docked in Hyannis Harbor and disembarked from the boat. Demeter would graduate from high school, she would reach adulthood, and things would get better.

Demeter had looked upon her mother with a jaundiced eye. "A bad ride on the ferry"? *That* was what her mother had to offer?

A little before 1:30 a.m. on June 17, Ed Kapenash had called the house and told Al that there had been an accident. Demeter was at the hospital, but she was unhurt.

Al relayed this message to Lynne, who was by that point sitting bolt upright in bed. "There was an accident, Demeter's at the hospital, but she's unhurt."

Lynne said, "She's not at the hospital. She's in her bedroom."

And Al, trusting every word that came out of his

wife's mouth, said to Police Chief Ed Kapenash, "Demeter is in her bedroom."

To which Ed responded, "I'm looking right at her, Al. Can you come down here, please?"

Even *then,* Lynne didn't believe it. She threw on the skirt and blouse by her bed, the same outfit she had worn only hours before to four graduation parties, and she marched down the hallway to Demeter's bedroom. Knocked on the door. There was no answer, but that was hardly unusual. Lynne tried the knob. Locked. Again, not unusual. What teenage girl *didn't* lock her bedroom door? She knocked again, and Al came up behind her with a metal pin.

"Jesus Christ, Lynne, step aside, please."

Lynne half turned to him, shocked. He never spoke to her like that. He popped the lock and reached for the light and then they were both standing in Demeter's empty bedroom, where the window was hanging wide open. In a daze Lynne walked to the window and looked down.

"She...what?" Lynne said.

"Climbed out the window," Al said in a snarky tone of voice.

"And then what?" Lynne said. The screen for the window lay on the shingles of the roof, but from the roof line it was probably eight or nine feet to the lawn below. "She *jumped?*"

"She must have," Al said. "I'm going to the hospital. Are you coming with me?"

"Of course I'm coming with you," Lynne said. Her daughter had been in an accident, her daughter was at the hospital, her daughter had climbed out her bedroom window and jumped to the lawn below. Her daughter had fooled them. Lynne was so tired, it was the middle of the night, she had gotten only a couple hours of sleep. She was too old for this.

But once she reached the hospital, she couldn't have been more awake. Ed Kapenash met them *out in the parking lot,* and Lynne thought, This can hardly be standard protocol. Maybe he had lied about Demeter's being unhurt so they wouldn't drive off the road while trying to get here. Why else would Ed be waiting for them outside?

Ed spoke in a low voice. Lynne had never heard him sound so serious. Jake Randolph's Jeep, Penny driving, Penny D.O.A., Hobby alive but unresponsive. The helicopter was on its way. Demeter unhurt, Jake Randolph unhurt.

Lynne couldn't quite keep up. "Wait a minute," she said. "What did you say about Penny?"

Ed pressed his lips together.

Al said, "Honey, she's dead. She was dead on arrival."

Lynne felt herself falling. But no, she was upright.

But she had dropped something. Keys. Her keys had fallen from her hand onto the asphalt. She bent down to pick them up. She hiccupped, then started crying.

"I met you out here because I thought you should know," Ed said. "So you'll be prepared. Jordan's on his way. Zoe's on her way."

"Do they know?" Lynne asked. "Does Zoe know?"

"Not yet."

Jesus, this was awful. Lynne's life wasn't set up to accommodate this kind of awful.

"I also need to inform you that we found a bottle of Jim Beam in your daughter's bag," Ed said. "It had an inch or two of whiskey left in it. She probably wasn't the only one drinking it, but the paramedics said she was inebriated when she arrived. I'm going in to talk with her now. I just wanted to tell you that myself. Because we're friends."

"Thank you, Ed," Al said.

"Jim *Beam?*" Lynne said. "Where on Earth, really, *where* would Demeter have gotten a bottle of Jim *Beam?* We don't drink. You know we don't drink, Ed."

"I'm just telling you what we found."

"Someone must have put it in her bag," Lynne said. "One of the boys." But not Penny. Penny didn't drink at all; Lynne knew this from both Demeter and Zoe. Although it *was* graduation, so maybe she'd been drinking tonight. Maybe that was what had caused the accident. Maybe Penny had put the bottle in Demeter's purse. Demeter would have let her do that — anything to be accepted by those kids. "Was Penny drinking?"

"We know almost nothing else," Ed said.

Al said, "Honey, let the man do his job. He came out here to warn us as a *courtesy*."

Was Al expecting her to thank him, then? Say something like "Thank you, Ed, for telling us that our daughter was the one with the near-empty bottle of booze in her purse"? Lynne didn't like being the mother who insisted on her child's innocence — those mothers were nearly always delusional about their own children — but in this case she had no choice. There was *no way* the Jim Beam or whatever it was they'd found in Demeter's purse actually belonged to her.

Lynne couldn't believe she was even worrying about this. *Penny Alistair was dead.* And Hobby — what had the Chief said about Hobby, again?

"What did he say about Hobby?" Lynne asked Al, as the Chief's back receded toward the bright glass doors of the Emergency Room. She was shivering as if it were January instead of June.

"Let's go inside," Al said.

*   *   *

Now, two months later, Lynne had a hard time piecing together what had happened after that. Her memory was shattered like a broken mirror. She remembered seeing Zoe walk in; the two of them exchanged a look, and Lynne feared for the expression on her own face. She hated that she knew that Penny was dead while Zoe didn't; she despised Ed Kapenash for telling them first.

She remembered Zoe's slapping Jordan. Oh yes, that she remembered. She would remember that for the rest of her life. Zoe nearly knocked the glasses off of Jordan's face. And why? What had Jordan done wrong? That wasn't clear.

Al was the one who helped Zoe get to Boston, though at first she refused his help. But Al held firm: "I'm taking you, goddammit, Zoe. You can't do this alone." He got her to Mass General; he stood by her side while the doctors delivered the ghastly news. Hobby was still unresponsive. In a coma. There was nothing they could do but wait.

Meanwhile, Lynne and Jordan had sat side by side in the waiting room of Nantucket Cottage Hospital until Ed Kapenash finished interrogating their children. Had the two of them talked? Lynne couldn't remember. She did remember Demeter's coming out to the waiting room, pale, shaking, and smelling like vomit. Lynne touched her all over in a way that she hadn't touched her in years, checking to make sure she was in one piece.

"Let's go, Mom, please," Demeter whispered.

"Yes," Lynne said. She remembered that Jordan was still sitting, waiting for Jake to emerge. She remembered that his blue eyes tracked her and Demeter, and his mouth opened to say something. But did he speak? And did Lynne say good-bye?

She couldn't remember. But she must have. She would never have left without saying good-bye.

Another mother might have addressed the issue of the Jim Beam right away. Another mother might have acknowledged — even if only to herself — that the vomit fumes coming off her daughter in the passenger seat did, in fact, reek of whiskey. Another mother might have asked her daughter the simple question, "What happened?" So that at least she would have a baseline to work from.

But Lynne Castle addressed, acknowledged, and asked nothing. Things might have been different if Al had still been with them, but Al had gone with Zoe, so Lynne was left to deal with Demeter by herself, and she was at a loss. Demeter had carried a pillow, sheathed in an aqua pillowcase, out of the hospital. Every so often she would lean over, bury her face in the pillow, and emit a soundless scream.

And Lynne thought, She's in shock. That was what Dr. Field had said. He'd pressed a prescription for a sedative into Lynne's hand, but it was too late, or too early, to get that filled at the pharmacy now.

At home Lynne said, "Daddy's gone to Boston. Do you want to sleep in my bed with me?"

Demeter said, "God, no."

Lynne tried not to take offense at this, but she was tired, and for some reason these words, or perhaps the disgust with which Demeter uttered them, hurt her feelings. She reminded herself that Demeter had never been a snuggler, and that the two of them didn't have a touchy-feely relationship. Zoe and Penny have that kind of relationship, Lynne thought—or at least they *did* (God, the first use of the past tense, it was hideous!). She knew that Penny used to climb into bed with Zoe when she was scared or there was a lightning storm, and they always cuddled together on the couch during Patriots games on football Sundays, and they lay next to each other on towels at the beach. Demeter and Lynne just weren't like that, fair enough, but was it too much to ask for a little physical closeness between them *tonight,* on the very night when Penny Alistair had been killed and Demeter might have been killed herself?

Lynne and Demeter stood at the open door of Demeter's bedroom. The light was on, the window wide open. Was Lynne going to confront her daughter about her locked door, her exodus, her blatant deceit?

No, not tonight. Outside, the birds were starting to chirp. June on Nantucket: the sun rose at 4:30 a.m.

"Are you going to be okay?" Lynne asked.

Demeter eyed her mother.

Right, Lynne thought: stupid, vague question, too big a question to answer. She narrowed it down a little. "Do you want a sleeping pill?" she asked. "I can give you one of mine."

"Okay," Demeter said.

It was something concrete Lynne could do. Something she had to offer. One of her Lunestas. She had asked Ted Field for them back in April, when Al was running for selectman for the fourth time. The stress of local politics, of negative campaigning aimed at Al, of insinuations that he had Ed Kapenash, among other people, in his back pocket—all of this had kept Lynne up at night. Ha! She had worried then, when nothing was wrong. Al had won in a landslide.

Lynne placed the tiny pill in Demeter's palm, and Demeter dry-mouthed it down. Lynne grimaced. Probably not a bad idea to suggest that she take a shower and brush her teeth: she stank to high heaven. But as Lynne was searching for the words to gently convey this thought to her daughter, Demeter stepped into her bedroom and slammed the door shut, leaving her mother alone in the hallway.

"Good night, darling," Lynne said.

Now it was August, and the worst was behind them. Hobby had woken up from his coma, Penny had been properly buried, the Randolph family had moved halfway around the world. Demeter had defied all odds and honored her commitment to work at Frog and Toad Landscaping. She got up and went to work five mornings a week. She was never late. She was the color of toast and she had, most definitely, lost some weight.

But something still wasn't right. Demeter was less forthcoming than ever. She rarely spoke unless spoken to, and half the time, when Al or Lynne asked her a question, she gave a nonsensical answer and broke into giggles. And yet Lynne was afraid to dissect this behavior because Demeter did, in fact, seem happier than she had seemed in a long, long time. She was working and bringing home a weekly paycheck, she looked good. She had made some friends, she said, on her crew. A girl named Nell. A boy named Coop. A man named Zeus.

"Zeus?" Lynne said. "That's an interesting name."

"'Gods and goddesses in the front,'" Demeter said, and then she giggled.

Lynne wondered if Demeter had started a relationship with one of the men on her crew. Maybe this Coop, or this Zeus. Zeus was more likely, Lynne thought. An older Hispanic man with a wife all the way down in Central America — to him, Demeter would seem young and ripe and lush. *Too* young, though. Lynne couldn't stand to think about it.

It crossed Lynne's mind that Demeter might be doing drugs either before or after work. Because, to be honest, her whole demeanor was altered. She was a different kid. All of her angry, bitter, resentful, woe-is-me attitude seemed to have disappeared, and in its place was this vacant insipidness. Demeter used to be an avid reader. Her marks in school weren't great, they were just-getting-by, but she always read very good books, both classic and contemporary. But had she read a single book this whole summer? Lynne didn't think so. Lynne wasn't naive, she knew that landscapers were famous for smoking marijuana, and she also knew that Demeter might not have the resolve to say no. She was a perfect target for peer pressure, wanting so badly to be accepted and to fit in. Lynne had gone so far as to sniff her daughter's clothes before she stuffed them into the washing machine. They smelled like sour sweat but not smoke. Later she extended her olfactory investigation to the inside of Demeter's Escape, where her nose was overpowered by the smell of breath mints and piney air-freshener and something else that was sickly sweet but unidentifiable—until she pulled a black, rotten banana out from under the passenger seat.

Lynne didn't find any signs of marijuana. But there was something—*something*—going on.

Demeter had been through one hell of an ordeal this summer. She had lost Penny, who was as much of a friend as she had had, and she had lost Jake too. Hobby was still alive, thank God. Lynne kept tabs on him through the grapevine; it seemed she was always talking to someone who had just seen him in town or out for a quiet dinner at 56 Union with his mother. Lynne learned that he was out of the wheelchair and onto crutches and making excellent progress, but that Coach Jaxon had finally come to terms with the fact that he would never play football again. It was just too dangerous. Hobby was apparently spending lots of time with Claire Buckley, which was good, Lynne thought. Claire was a nice girl.

Lynne wished she had gotten all this news about Hobby from Zoe herself, but Zoe was incommunicado. Lynne had arranged dropoff meals at the Alistair house for six weeks after Penny's funeral but Zoe had never called or written to say thank you. Not that a thank-you was necessary; Lynne certainly hadn't scheduled the meals because she wanted gratitude. She had done it because it was one stupid, paltry thing that she and the other women in the community could do—offer food so that something healthy and delicious would be on hand whenever Zoe got her appetite back. Lynne had also left several messages on Zoe's voicemail, she had lost count of how many, four or five, but these had gone unreturned. She had tried to tread lightly, saying, "Hey, Zoe, it's me, just checking in, no need to call me back, just wanted to see how you're doing, thinking of you." So Zoe had managed to make it out to 56 Union for dinner with Hobby, but she hadn't been able to call Lynne back? Lynne was—or had been—her best friend. Lynne had to assume that status had been altered in Zoe's mind. Perhaps Zoe couldn't bring herself to talk to her for the same reason that she'd slapped Jordan in the hospital waiting room: a firewall of anger. She had lost a child, and they hadn't.

She had lost a child. Lynne couldn't pretend to know what that felt like.

They had all been through one hell of an ordeal this summer.

So whatever was going on with Demeter, Lynne told herself, would pass. There was no describing how badly she wanted to ignore it. If Demeter could just make it through the summer... things might change once she was back in school... her senior year... things were always great in senior year, so for Demeter they should at least be tolerable. She would be accepted to college somewhere, probably not a top-tier school like her brothers, but maybe Michigan State, where Al had gone. He donated money to MSU, he should be able to pull those strings if needed, and then Demeter would be away at school, and Al and Lynne would be empty-nesters. There was a way in which the two of them had been born to be empty-nesters. They both had more than enough interests and involvements to keep them busy for the next three centuries. (Although their interest in each other, at this stage of the game, was limited: they had sex only two or three times a year, on prescribed dates — their anniversary, Al's birthday, and Valentine's Day — and frankly, even that much was more than enough for Lynne.) Maybe, Lynne thought, her eager anticipation of an empty nest meant that they should never have had children at all.

Demeter's strange behavior continued. On the night she returned from babysitting for the Kingsleys, Lynne happened to be awake, standing next to the open freezer door, shoveling Chunky Monkey into her mouth. She had been indulging in this kind of late-night stress eating more and more lately, but when Demeter walked in, she hastened to fit the top back onto the carton and shove the ice cream back into the freezer, because what kind of example was she setting?

"Hey, honey," Lynne said. She positioned her body to block's Demeter's view of the sticky spoon on the countertop.

Demeter didn't respond to her greeting, didn't acknowledge her mother's presence at all. She clutched her backpack to her chest and proceeded up the stairs.

"Demeter!" Lynne snapped. Her voice was louder than it ought to have been in the middle of the night—Al was sleeping—but Jesus Christ, she was *sick* of being ignored.

"What?" Demeter said.

"How was babysitting? How were the Kingsleys?"

Demeter let out a shrill, high-pitched laugh that was unlike anything Lynne had ever heard come out of her daughter's mouth. It made Lynne worry that maybe Demeter's problem was that she was possessed by the spawn of Lucifer. "Babysitting?" Demeter said. "At the Kingsleys'? It was awful. It was goddamned fucking awful, if you must know, Mother." Then Demeter laughed again, and it gave Lynne the shivers.

*　　*　　*

Two days later Lynne stood in front of Demeter's bedroom door with the metal pin. Demeter was still at work, and Lynne had been trying to work in her home office as well, but Demeter's words kept playing through her mind: "It was goddamned fucking awful, if you must know, Mother." And that demonic laugh. Something was going on, and Lynne intended to find out what it was.

She popped the lock on Demeter's door as she'd seen Al do the night of the accident. She entered her daughter's bedroom. She was one of those mothers now, she thought. One of those mothers who nosed around her child's personal space, one of those mothers who couldn't be trusted. She had never had to do this with the boys. The boys had been easy to raise; the boys had been a breeze.

Demeter's room smelled funny. It had been a hot couple of weeks, and Lynne had kept the central air on, so Demeter's window was shut tight. Sunlight streamed in, and dust motes hung in the air. The bed was unmade. Demeter used only a fitted sheet and a duvet, anyway. Lynne sniffed the duvet. Abominable—body odor, along with whatever cheap teenage scent her daughter used to mask body odor. Lynne rarely cleaned in this room anymore; she had basically been denied access for the past three years, though she did make a point of asking for Demeter's sheets and towels occasionally. But she hadn't asked once this summer, and now the whole room smelled of dirty linen. Lynne started stripping the bed right then and there. Something was under the pillow and fell to the floor, and Lynne scrambled to pick it up. It was a paperback copy of *The Beautiful and Damned,* by F. Scott Fitzgerald. Lynne sat on the bare mattress and flipped through the book. Demeter was reading Fitzgerald. Was Lynne worrying herself sick over nothing?

Lynne set the book down on Demeter's bedside table, next to her water glass, which had a wedge of lime floating in it. Lime in her water glass? That was Zoe's influence right there. Zoe kept a pitcher of chilled water in her fridge, and it always had lemon or lime slices and sometimes fresh mint and sometimes cucumber slices floating in it, and it always tasted fresh and delicious.

God, Lynne missed Zoe. She wondered what would happen if she just turned up at Zoe's house unannounced. That was what a real friend would do—go over there and check on her. Lynne would bring her something, maybe a hanging begonia from Bartlett's Farm or a topiary from Flowers on Chestnut.

Lynne picked up the water glass and emptied it into Demeter's bathroom sink. She threw the lime wedge in the trash and carried the liner down to the kitchen trash. The bathroom trash seemed to be mostly crumpled tissues and dental floss and a bunch of wrappers from sugarless gum and breath mints. So maybe Demeter *was* having a relationship with someone at work—or, more likely, she'd developed a crush. Which could either end well or end badly.

Lynne went back up to Demeter's bathroom and collected all the towels and the bathmat. She gathered the sheets as well and carried everything down to the laundry. Demeter would be angry when she found out that her mother had been in her room, but she'd appreciate having clean sheets and towels.

Lynne had work to do—three clients needed titles cleared—but she hated to leave a job half done. She lugged the Dyson up to Demeter's room and found a yellow dust rag and fetched her bucket of cleaning supplies and the mop. The cleaners came once a week, so this kind of time-consuming effort on Lynne's part had been rendered unnecessary in the rest of the house. But the cleaners weren't allowed to go in Demeter's room, and it badly needed cleaning.

That smell, Lynne thought. How did Demeter stand it?

Lynne dusted and vacuumed. This gave her a legitimate excuse to peek under the bed—nothing there but a dusty suitcase, which made her wonder if what they really needed was a vacation, which made her think of the Randolphs in Australia. They'd gone because, Jordan said, he needed to get Jake and Ava off the island for a while. Ava had been asking to move back to Australia for years, Lynne knew, but the accident was what had prompted their departure. So it seemed — to Lynne, and probably to the rest of Nantucket — as if they had left in shame. Lynne had heard people castigating Jordan for not printing anything about the accident in the paper, and she had done her best to correct this misperception by telling anyone who brought it up within her earshot that Zoe had asked him not to print a single word. His actions had been noble, she believed.

Lynne wondered if Jake had somehow been to blame for the accident. The police report had been so vague.

Lynne was glad that she hadn't found any strange or unidentifiable objects in Demeter's room. No weird altars or vials of tiger blood or voodoo dolls. Of course, she hadn't looked through the drawers. She would look through the drawers — maybe — once she was done with the bathroom.

No one in the world enjoyed cleaning a bathroom, and this one smelled especially bad. Lynne was generous with the Windex; she tried not to gaze into the toilet bowl as she scoured it with the brush. She checked in the cabinet under the sink and saw that Demeter was down to her last roll of toilet paper and her final two tampons. Lynne replenished the supplies from the stockpile in her own bathroom. The girl was suffering from neglect.

Lynne struggled with the bathtub. She pulled Demeter's hair out of the drain, then she took down the shower curtain. That could use a run through the washing machine as well.

She checked the medicine cabinet. There was a large bottle of ibuprofen that Lynne knew she herself hadn't bought. Strange, she thought. She checked the bottle's contents to make sure it really was ibuprofen, and it was.

Okay, she was feeling paranoid now. Why would Demeter have spent her own money on ibuprofen? Why not just write it down on Lynne's shopping list?

Lynne went back into Demeter's bedroom and thought, I have to check her drawers. She didn't *want* to check the drawers, but to be thorough, she had to. Then there was the dark screen of Demeter's computer. Should she check the computer? Would she know what she was looking for? Demeter didn't have a Facebook page, or she hadn't the last time Lynne checked, which was some time before the accident. Even Lynne had a Facebook page, complete with 274 friends. Penny had been Lynne's friend on Facebook, that was the kind of dear child she was, but Lynne hadn't had the heart to go in and see if Penny's page had been taken down yet. Lynne collapsed in Demeter's desk chair and stared at the computer. There were so many places for kids to hide things. How were parents supposed to win at this game?

She would check the dresser drawers, she decided, but would leave the computer alone for now. She would ask Al about the computer, maybe. He had to pull his weight in this.

Lynne slid open Demeter's drawers. She was holding her breath as though she expected to see a nest of snakes in there. But all she found was a mess of very large clothes — overalls, jeans, T-shirts, and the hooded sweatshirts that made Demeter look like a hoodlum from Jamaica Plain instead of a nice girl from Nantucket. This was Lynne's chance to surreptitiously remove them, but she was so glad not to have found anything worrisome in the drawers that she let the sweatshirts remain, and even resisted her urge to fold and straighten them. She closed the drawers.

Her search had turned up nothing. Nothing except the Fitzgerald.

Lynne was about to leave the room when she caught sight of the closet door. It was slightly ajar, which seemed like an invitation for her to open it and check inside. Lynne noticed how blank the door was, how blank the whole room was, really. There were no pictures of friends, no pictures of her or Al, or Mark or Billy, no trophies or awards or ribbons or framed certificates of achievement, no maps of places they'd visited, no posters of actors or rock stars. (Even Lynne, yes, straight Lynne Comstock, had had a poster of Lynyrd Skynyrd taped to her wall.)

Suddenly Demeter's room seemed like the saddest place on earth.

Lynne took a step toward the closet.

"Mom?"

Lynne gasped.

"Jesus Christ," she said to Demeter. "You scared the shit out of me."

Demeter stared at her mother. Lynne wondered when the last time was that she had taken the Lord's name in vain and sworn in the same sentence. College? She hadn't always been such a straight arrow; she hadn't always been such an upstanding citizen. She had listened to Lynyrd Skynyrd in the front seat of Beck Paulsen's Mazda RX4. She had smoked Newports with Beck and drunk Miller beer from cans.

"What are you doing in here?" Demeter asked.

"Cleaning," Lynne answered honestly. "It smelled

awful. I took your sheets...." Lynne nodded at the naked bed.

"Yes, I see that."

"I cleaned your bathroom, you're welcome. I'll return your linens to you by dinnertime, freshly laundered, you're welcome."

"Wasn't this room locked?" Demeter asked.

"Yes, but..."

"How did you get in?"

"I popped the lock."

"You *popped* the *lock?*"

"With a pin," Lynne said. Apropos of nothing, she laughed. She had broken into her teenage daughter's bedroom, and she had nothing to say in her own defense. She had put so much effort into cleaning that she had lost track of time. Now she was busted, as though she were the teenager and Demeter the parent.

"Get out," Demeter said.

"Honey, really, I just needed to get in here to clean—"

"If you really need to get in here, you ask me," Demeter said. "You don't *pop* the *lock* with a *pin* while I'm at *work*. You're like a common thief."

"Thief?" Lynne said. "I didn't *take* anything."

"A spy, then," Demeter said.

"Honey, I wasn't spying. I told you, the smell—"

"I *like* the smell."

"Your sheets needed to be changed."

"What happened to my water glass?" Demeter asked.

"I emptied it. It's in the dishwasher."

"I don't know what you're *doing* in here!" Demeter's voice took on the shrill edge of hysteria. She was still in her work boots—which were, naturally, tracking dirt and sand into the newly vacuumed room. She was clutching her backpack to her chest like a shield, just as she had done the other night when she got home from babysitting.

Clutching her backpack. Okay, Lynne wasn't naive, she wasn't in the wrong here, this was her house, she was the mother and Demeter was the child and something was going on with Demeter and Lynne wanted to know what it was.

"Do you have a Facebook page?" Lynne asked.

"What?" Demeter said. "No, I don't."

"I can check, you know."

Demeter said, "Fine, check. I don't have one." Her tone of voice was both calm and bored. Facebook wasn't the culprit.

"Let me see your phone."

"What?"

"Your phone. Let me see it."

"My phone?"

"Your phone." Demeter had an iPhone 4S that Lynne had bought for her in the spring. Lynne had noticed that she kept a passcode lock on the phone. Now she wondered, Why would she keep a passcode lock unless there's something she's trying to hide?

Demeter pulled her phone out of the pocket of her cargo shorts and handed it to Lynne.

"Unlock it, please," Lynne said.

Demeter unlocked it. "You're acting like a psycho."

"No," Lynne said. "I'm acting like a parent. Finally." She looked at the face of the phone. Apps—she knew that those colorful squares were apps, but she didn't know what to do with them. She was acting like a *clueless* parent. She had a cell phone herself, but she kept it in her car and used it only when she was on the road or away from home. She didn't know how to text. Zoe knew how to text, and Jordan knew how to text—the two of them had been texting buddies for years, that was how they communicated. But not Lynne. She was a clueless parent and a fuddy-duddy who didn't text and couldn't navigate her way around an iPhone. She handed the phone back to Demeter.

"Did you find what you were looking for?" Demeter asked.

Lynne sighed. She wasn't getting anywhere. "Demeter, what's going on with you?"

"What do you mean?"

"I mean, what's going on? Something is funny. Something is wrong."

"I'm working," Demeter said. "I spend all day on my knees weeding. If I'm very, very lucky, I get to water. Or deadhead." She held up one hand and clutched at her backpack with the other. Her hand was blotched with purple stains. "Daylilies."

She clutched the bag, clutched the bag. Lynne said, "I'd like you to open your bag, please."

"What?" Demeter said. She tightened her grip on her bag, which only made Lynne more determined to see what was inside it. "You've got to be kidding me."

"Set the bag down and unzip it for me, please," Lynne said.

"I suppose the cavity search is next," Demeter said. "Do I need to call my lawyer?"

"Just do it," Lynne said.

Demeter did not release her hold on the bag. "I can't believe you're doing this. What is *wrong* with you?"

"What is wrong with *you?*" Lynne said. Her voice sounded positively lethal; she felt herself losing her grip. She rarely got like this. If Al had been home, she would have ducked out of there already. She would have made herself a cup of chamomile tea and gotten into a cool bath, played some Mozart, read some poetry. "Put the bag down, please, and unzip it."

Demeter did as she was told. The backpack gaped open. Lynne took a step forward and peered inside, as though she expected to find someone's severed head in there. But all she saw was a flannel shirt. She rummaged a little deeper. Two bottles of water, one of them with a lime floating in it—more Zoe water—and another rotting banana. That was all.

Lynne extracted the banana. "Waste of a perfectly good banana," she said.

"Call the fruit police," Demeter said.

Lynne held the black, weeping banana. She was so relieved, she thought she might cry.

Demeter collapsed against the closet door; it closed with a sound like a gunshot.

"Mom," she said.

"What?" Lynne said.

"Get out, please?"

"Yes," Lynne said. "Okay."

Lynne was so embarrassed by the incident in Demeter's bedroom that she said nothing about it to Al. She laundered Demeter's sheets and towels and left them in a neat pile outside her daughter's bedroom door. She swore to herself that she wouldn't use the pin to force entry again. Demeter was a seventeen-year-old girl. She needed her privacy.

*　　*　　*

On August 14, Lynne was working in her home office. She was listening to a Bruce Springsteen CD, drinking freshly brewed iced tea with mint. She and Al had a date to meet at Ladies Beach at four o'clock. They did this every August, right when Al realized that summer was almost over and he hadn't taken any late-afternoon swims. And this year, because of all that had happened, they hadn't gone to the beach even once. Jordan was gone, and Lynne had been afraid to call and inflict herself on Zoe.

Lynne was looking forward to the swim. Afterward she would try to convince Al to go to Dune for dinner.

Downstairs, the phone rang. Lynne ignored it. God knew, if she picked up every phone call that came in to the house, she would never get any work done. Because of all that had happened this summer, she was running behind. The answering machine picked up. The Castles had to be the last family in America that even still had an answering machine. Everyone else used automated voicemail. Lynne tried not to listen to the voice on the machine—if she was so keen to know who was calling, she told herself, then she should have just picked up the phone in the first place. But she listened anyway, just long enough to discern that the voice belonged to Zoe.

Zoe. It was Zoe, finally calling her back. Lynne sprang from her desk and rushed down the stairs to get the phone, but by the time she picked it up, she was talking to a dial tone. She was just about to call Zoe back when the phone rang in her office, and Lynne thought, Of course, Zoe would call my office phone next since she couldn't reach me on the home phone. Lynne hurried up the stairs, calling out pointlessly, "I'm coming, hold on, here I come!" When she picked up the phone, she was out of breath. She was too old for this. But it was Zoe. At last! She couldn't wait to talk to her.

"Hello?" she said.

"Lynne," Al said. "I need you to sit down."

Twenty minutes later Lynne and Al were meeting in the hot, unvented offices of Frog and Toad Landscaping with Kerry Trevor and a hysterical Demeter. It was difficult for the adults to talk about what had happened with Demeter making so much noise.

"Honey," Lynne said. "You have to calm down."

But Demeter was a volcano intent on erupting. She hadn't emoted nearly this much after the accident or after Penny's funeral, which was probably why she was such a mess now. All of that difficult stuff was surfacing.

"Actually, maybe Demeter should wait outside," Kerry said.

Was that a good idea? Lynne wondered. At this point, she knew, Demeter was a flight risk. If she was left unsupervised, she might just get into her car and drive away. She might do something stupid.

"Jeanne will keep an eye on her," Kerry said.

"Okay," Lynne said. Jeanne, Kerry's right-hand woman, had grown up in Brockton, where, she liked to tell people, she had earned her doctorate in badass.

As soon as Jeanne took Demeter by the arm and led her from the room, it was much quieter.

Lynne said, "Maybe you should start again at the beginning."

"Demeter was caught trying to steal two bottles of vodka from a client's house," Kerry said. "She had a bottle in each hand; she was hurrying for the side door. The clients weren't home, but a member of their staff caught her."

"A member of the staff?" Lynne said.

"I have to tell you this in extreme confidence," Kerry said. "The clients were the Allencasts."

Lynne thought she might vomit in her lap.

"And the person who caught Demeter was their personal chef, Zoe Alistair."

"We know Zoe," Al said. "We're close friends."

"I realize that," Kerry said. "And Zoe handled the situation sensitively. She called me right away. She said she had taken the bottles from Demeter and decided that she wasn't going to tell the Allencasts. She said she would let the three of us handle it."

Lynne thought about the phone call from Zoe. She had been calling to warn Lynne of what was coming. To let her know that *her* daughter—the girl who had survived—was a thief.

"Anybody else would probably have alerted the owners," Kerry said. "And called the police."

"Of course," Al said.

"Now," Kerry said, "I have more bad news."

"Oh God," Lynne said. The room was quiet for a second, and they could all hear Demeter sobbing on the other side of the door.

"I've had three separate complaints about missing bottles of alcohol from clients, which I dismissed because my crews never go inside the houses. However, when I spoke with Demeter's crew members, they indicated that she enters clients' homes all the time—most frequently to 'use the facilities.' My employee Nell, who worked closely with Demeter, told me that Demeter used the bathroom only when the clients weren't home. I cross-checked the names of the clients who complained against the assignments of Demeter's crew, and they all matched up."

"So now you're accusing my daughter of… what?" Lynne said.

"Honey," Al said.

"I don't think this stealing today was a onetime thing," Kerry said. "I think it's possible she's been doing it all summer."

"Stealing *alcohol?*" Lynne said. "But what *for?* I just don't get it. What for? We don't drink at home. Not a drop."

"I think you'll have to ask Demeter that," Kerry said. "And I'm going to let you do that privately, because I know you're good people and good parents. Demeter is finished working here, however, and I won't be able to give her a reference."

Kerry stood up and cleared his throat. He was wearing the standard-issue green Frog and Toad Landscaping T-shirt and a pair of khaki shorts. He was sunburned, and his hair was bleached-out blond. Lynne had always liked Kerry. She and Al sometimes saw him surfing at the South Shore after work. But what Lynne felt for Kerry now was anger and hatred, which was backward, she knew: she should be grateful that he wasn't calling Ed Kapenash. Demeter had been *stealing.* She had been entering people's homes as an employee of Frog and Toad and burgling them.

"I know Demeter has been through a lot," Kerry said. "And you two as well."

There was something that Lynne could agree with. "Yes," she said. "Thank you."

*   *   *

When they got home, all of them, at two o'clock that Tuesday afternoon, Lynne listened to the message from Zoe.

"Hi, Lynne, it's Zoe. Listen, something happened at work just now, and I have to speak with you about it as soon as possible. Call me, please. On my cell."

Lynne listened to the message again, then a third time. The first thing that struck her was that it was Zoe's voice, and that she'd missed her. The second thing she noticed was that while the voice held urgency, it didn't sound either angry or vindictive. This episode was *not* something Zoe had dreamed up to prove that Demeter was a bad person. To prove that the wrong girl had died.

Demeter was headed straight for her room, but Al stopped her. "Oh no, young lady," he said. "You are going to sit right here"—he pointed to her usual seat at the dining room table—"and tell us what the hell this is all about."

Lynne was glad for this. She needed Al's help, even though she thought his tone sounded too harsh.

Demeter sat in the chair and dropped her face into her hands and bawled. Lynne fixed her a glass of ice water and, as a little treat, added a wheel of lime.

Lynne set the glass down on the table next to

Demeter, and Al glowered at her. Demeter lifted her head and sucked the water down to the bottom, and Lynne realized that because of the lime, the drink looked like a cocktail. The roiling, nauseated feeling returned to Lynne's stomach. She went over and turned up the air-conditioning a little, then sat down next to Demeter.

"Let's start with the accident," Al said. "Did you have a bottle of Jim Beam with you that night?"

"No," Demeter said.

"Honey," Lynne said. "We know the police found a nearly empty bottle of Jim Beam in your purse."

"It was in my bag," Demeter said, "but it wasn't mine."

"Whose was it?" Lynne asked.

"I don't know," Demeter said. "Some kid at the party gave it to me. I had a sip of it, and so did Jake and Hobby, but it wasn't mine. I just ended up with it somehow. It was in my bag because I had a bag to put it in."

"So you're saying some kid at the party gave it to you," Al said. "Some kid you didn't *know?*"

"A kid from off-island," Demeter said.

"So either you're lying to us now or you lied that night to the police," Al said. "Because you told Ed Kapenash that the bottle was yours and that you had bought it off-island."

Really? Lynne thought. This was a detail that Al hadn't shared with her. Bastard bastard bastard. Al and Ed and all those other bastards were part of this men's club that discussed confidential matters and then decided how very little to pass along to their wives.

"I was lying to the police," Demeter said. "I said I'd bought it so that I wouldn't get anyone else in trouble."

"This other kid from off-island, you mean?" Al said. "The one you didn't even *know?* You lied to Ed Kapenash, Chief of the Nantucket Police, in order to protect some stranger from off-island?"

"I was in shock," Demeter said.

"That is *bullshit!*" Al roared. It seemed to Lynne that the walls of the castle were quaking; she had never seen Al this angry. "You tell us the truth *right now!*" he demanded.

"I *am* telling you the truth," Demeter said. She had shrunk, Lynne thought. She was losing weight; her face was getting back its beautiful contours. She was deeply tanned, and the blond streak in her hair was as light as Lynne had ever seen it. It seemed unfair that Demeter should appear so pretty, so genuinely pretty, on the very day that she was being revealed as a liar, and a thief, and possibly something even worse.

Al paced around the dining room table like a

wild animal waiting to be fed. Who knew he could *be* like this?

"Why did you take two bottles of vodka from the Allencasts' house?"

"I don't know."

"Tell me!"

"I don't *know!*" Demeter cried. "I went in to use the bathroom, I saw the vodka in the bar and I just... *took* it. I guess I wanted to... I don't know... act out."

" 'Act out,' " Al said. *"Act out?* Did you know that Zoe was in the house? Did you think if she saw you, she'd let you get *away* with it?"

"No!" Demeter said. "I had no idea Zoe was there, obviously, or I never would have..."

"Say it."

"Taken the vodka."

"*Stolen* the vodka," Al said. "You *stole* it, Demeter. You are a thief. A criminal."

"Al," Lynne said.

"Zoe Alistair is one of our oldest, dearest friends," Al said. "Do you have any idea how mortifying it is for us that *she* was the one who caught you? She lost a child. Penny is dead. You, my dear, are alive. You got a second chance. And what have you done with it?"

"I didn't know Zoe was there. I didn't even know it was the Allencasts' house. I'm sorry I embarrassed you." She took a gulping breath. "I'm sorry I didn't die in the accident instead of Penny."

"Demeter!" Lynne said.

"No, it's okay," Demeter said, in a voice that was all of a sudden nearly serene. "I know that's what people wish would have happened—that it was me instead of her."

"No one wishes that, sweetheart," Lynne said.

"Zoe does."

"Not even Zoe."

"Hobby and Jake do."

"Demeter."

"What were you going to do with the vodka once you took it?" Al asked. "Were you going to drink it?"

"No," Demeter said.

"But you drank the night of the graduation party?"

"That night, yes, a little bit."

" 'A little bit,' " Al repeated. "Your blood alcohol content was point one-four. That's more than 'a little bit,' my dear."

Really? Lynne thought. Another piece of secret information that Al and Ed Kapenash had kept from her!

"I drank that night because it was graduation," Demeter said. "Everyone was drinking."

"But not Penny?" Lynne said.

"No. Not Penny."

"Kerry said he had complaints from three other clients about missing alcohol. He said he discounted them because his crews don't go inside the homes. Then Nell, from your crew, informed him today that *you,* Demeter, *do* go inside, on a regular basis, when the clients aren't at home, in order to 'use the facilities.' Is this true?"

"I've had problems with my stomach," Demeter said. "What am I supposed to do? Take a shit on somebody's beautifully manicured lawn?"

"Have you done this before?" Al asked. "Have you taken bottles of alcohol from houses before today?"

"No," Demeter said. "This was the only time." She started to cry. Lynne rose to fetch a box of tissues. "And I don't know what came over me. It was like I was temporarily insane. I saw those two bottles, and I just…wanted them. I've been trying *so hard* to hold it together this summer. I mean, I could have spent all summer in my room, but I made a promise to Kerry, and I wanted to honor it. You guys have spent God knows how many thousands of dollars supporting me, and I wanted to earn some money on my own. I didn't want to do the predictable thing and fall into a depression, but the fact of the matter is, I do think about the accident just about every second of every day, and I do think everyone would have been better off if I had died instead of Penny." Demeter plucked a tissue out of the box and blotted her eyes. "I'm sorry about the vodka. I don't know what I was thinking."

"So just to be clear, you're telling me that you didn't take bottles from any other homes?"

"No."

"And you weren't going to drink the vodka you stole? What the hell, Demeter? What were you going to do with it?"

"I don't know," Demeter said. "Give it away."

" 'Give it away'?" Al said.

"Other kids drink, Dad," Demeter said. "I guess I might have given it to Anders Peashway or Luke Browning or David Marcy. And then those guys would have been...I don't know...grateful. They would have liked me a little better. Hung out with me, maybe."

Lynne and Al were silent as Demeter sniffled. Lynne thought, *She's lonely. She's so desperately lonely that she did this awful thing.*

Al said, "Go to your room."

Demeter rose.

Al said, "You've lost your job and your chance of ever procuring a reference from Kerry for another job. So starting tomorrow you're coming to the dealership with me, and you're going to do filing all day.

You've lost your car, your phone, and your computer until the start of school. Is that understood?"

Demeter nodded. Lynne wondered if it was wise to cut her off socially when it was her loneliness that was the cause of this mess. But Lynne wasn't brave enough to undermine Al's authority.

Demeter said, "Can I still babysit for the Kingsleys if they call?"

Al pursed his lips. "Fine," he said. "But your mother or I will drive you."

"Okay," Demeter said. Her eyes lit up with hope for a second, and Lynne thought, The Kingsleys? She would have guessed that Demeter would be finished with the Kingsleys after the last time. What was it she'd said? "It was goddamned fucking awful, if you must know."

Demeter ascended the stairs to her room, and Al placed his two hands on Lynne's shoulders, and Lynne felt grateful for that. The Castles were known for their solid marriage. For their united front, no matter the circumstances.

Al said, "I'm taking the rest of the day off. Let's go for that swim."

"Do you think it's safe?" Lynne said. "Shouldn't one of us stay here and keep an eye on her?" That, of course, was the problem with grounding your kids: you were essentially grounding *yourself* too.

"It'll be fine," Al said. "I have both sets of her car keys."

"What about her phone? What about her computer?"

"I'll collect them when we get back. Come on, I could really use it."

Yes, Lynne could really use it as well. She would go change into her suit. She had the nagging feeling that there was something she had to do, something unpleasant. What was it? And then she remembered: she had to call Zoe. Call now to grovel and apologize and thank her. Lynne stood up, and her joints complained. She would call Zoe back tomorrow, she decided. When her head was clearer.

That night Lynne had a dream about Beck Paulsen. Very little happened in it; it was more a dream of ambience, set in 1976 in Moorestown, New Jersey, where Lynne grew up. Lynne's father was a doctor; Lynne and her brothers and their parents lived in an enormous white center-entrance Colonial formally known as the George M. Haverstick House. The Comstocks were considered well off. The boys attended St. Joe's Prep, but Lynne was sent to public school. She had had her bitter moments about this, but ultimately she would appreciate the diversity that public school offered. Beck Paulsen was from a different social stratum altogether. He was a bad kid, a druggie, he smoked marijuana, he wore shitkicker boots, he listened to Led Zeppelin, he worked at Arthur Treacher's to make pocket money. Quite famously, he had bought a brown Mazda RX4 before he even had his license.

Lynne dated Beck the summer between her junior and senior years of high school, when she was the same age that Demeter was now. Lynne and her girlfriend Abby used to hang out at Arthur Treacher's because it was halfway between their two houses and they could both bike there. They also both loved fish and chips, even what passed for fish and chips at Arthur Treacher's. One night Beck invited them to stick around while he closed up the shop. Abby said no way and rode home; Lynne said no way but stayed. She and Beck made out that night in the Mazda, and that night led to other nights, all summer long. What could Lynne say? To her, Beck was an exotic. He wasn't preppy and assholish like her brothers and their friends. He was mellow and kind. He was nearly always stoned, and that summer Lynne was nearly always stoned too. Beck drank Miller beer out of cans, most frequently when he was driving around with Lynne, to Maple Shade or the Cherry Hill Mall. Beck's mother worked in Admitting at the same hospital where Lynne's father was a thoracic surgeon.

In Lynne's dream she and Beck were back in the Mazda again, summer air rushing through the open windows. They were driving up to Lake Nockamixon to go fishing. When Beck caught something, they were going to eat it. There was a Styrofoam cooler in the backseat that held a six-pack of Miller Genuine Draft, a package of hot-dog rolls, and a stick of butter.

Also in the back were two fishing poles. Beck had brought his father's for Lynne to use. They were going to steal a canoe—or as Beck said, "borrow" one—and paddle to the good part of the lake. Lynne knew that all of this was wrong. She should be in Avalon for the weekend with Abby and her parents; she should be at home helping her mother prepare for her annual garden club cocktail party. But she was with Beck Paulsen, who had feathery dark hair like David Cassidy's and was wearing a black Styx concert T-shirt with white sleeves and jeans and his shitkickers, even on this hot summer day. She was drinking and smoking dope and listening to Meat Loaf on WMMR. If her parents had seen her at that moment, they would have been appalled. But Lynne was happy doing what she was doing. She was happy.

Lynne snapped awake from her dream, and the good, hazy feeling evaporated, and she mourned its loss.

She was back on Nantucket, lying in bed next to her husband of twenty-three years, Al Castle, and they would have to get up the next morning and deal with the debacle that had just landed in their lap. Please, couldn't she go back to that dream? Then Lynne wondered if perhaps her seventeen-year-old self had materialized in her subconscious in order to offer her assistance.

Okay, seventeen-year-old Lynne Comstock—what should I do? she asked.

Seventeen-year-old Lynne smiled dopily. She was stoned. She had been stoned all summer, and her parents had never once suspected. It was a seventeen-year-old's job to have secrets.

Demeter's secrets had just been revealed to Al and Lynne in all their heinous splendor. Or had they?

Lynne looked at the clock next to her bed. It was ten past two. She thought back over all the things Demeter had said: "I saw the vodka in the bar and I just... *took* it." "I was in shock." "Other kids drink, Dad." "I said I'd bought it so that I wouldn't get anyone else in trouble."

Lies, Lynne thought. All of it, lies.

Seventeen-year-old Lynne nodded. She agreed.

What did Lynne *know?* Demeter's bedroom smelled, there were empty breath mint tins and sugarless gum wrappers in the bathroom trash, there had been a lime in the water next to her bed. She was reading F. Scott Fitzgerald. Maybe Lynne was reaching here, but had a more famous alcoholic ever lived? Her car smelled like breath mints. Ibuprofen that Demeter bought herself was in the medicine cabinet. Lynne had checked everywhere— in the trunk of her car, under the bed, in her dresser drawers, under the bathroom sink. But she hadn't checked the closet. The smell. Demeter had leaned against the closet door, and the door had slammed shut. She had said that babysitting for the Kingsleys were awful, then she asked if she would be able to go back to the Kingsleys'. There had been a lime in the water next to her bed. When Lynne put a lime in Demeter's water, it looked like a cocktail. There had been a lime in one of Demeter's water bottles. Good God.

Lynne slipped out of bed. Calm down, she thought. She was tempted just to take a Lunesta and drift back to sleep. Beck Paulsen: where was he now? Was he anyplace worse than where she currently found herself?

She had sworn she would never use the pin to open Demeter's door again, and yet she had put the pin right there on her nightstand. She crept down the hall to Demeter's room. She should wake up Al. If this was going to be done, it should be done by both of them together. But something about this felt personal: Lynne to Demeter, mother to daughter. Was Lynne thinking of Zoe and Penny? Of course she was.

It looked as though Demeter's bedroom light was off. Lynne put her ear to the door. Silence. She half expected to walk in and find the window open again, and Demeter's bed empty.

She popped the lock. The sound was loud to Lynne's ears, and she held her breath. Waited, waited... and then eased the door open.

Demeter was asleep on her back, snoring. Lynne tiptoed over to the bed. She was assaulted by the obvious memories of Demeter as a baby in her crib, the soft spot on her head palpitating as she worked her pacifier. There had never been a sweeter, softer baby. Then as a little girl in footy pajamas, in smocked nightgowns. A chunky early adolescent in long nightshirts, her toenails painted blue, a smear of chocolate around her mouth, swearing that yes, she had brushed her teeth, when she most certainly had not.

Childhood ended here.

Lynne lifted the water glass from Demeter's nightstand and tasted it. The liquid burned her tongue and she spit it out, and the glass shook in her hand. She tasted it again, however, just to make sure. Ugh, awful! It was straight vodka or gin; she couldn't tell which. Her eyes filled with tears. She held on to the glass and switched on the light, but Demeter didn't wake up. That was fine, though. That was preferable.

Lynne opened the closet door.

There on the floor, where another girl would have lined up her shoes, were bottles and bottles of alcohol: Mount Gay rum, Patron tequila, Kahlua, Dewar's, Finlandia vodka, and wine, sauvignon blanc and two bottles of Chateau Margaux, which even Lynne, as a teetotaler, knew was outrageously expensive. Lynne set down the glass on Demeter's desk and stumbled back into the nether regions of the closet, where she found a black Hefty bag cinched at the top. Lynne dragged it out into the room. The clinking gave the contents away: dozens of empty bottles.

Fruit flies swarmed. The smell. Lynne gagged.

Demeter rolled over. "Mom?" she said.

Ted Field suggested a facility outside of Boston called Vendever.

"For how long?" Lynne asked.

"As long as it takes," he said.

Lynne packed a bag for Demeter and dropped it off at the hospital. She reminded herself that her daughter was lucky. Many of the people who ended up at Vendever had only the clothes on their backs. Many of the people who ended up at Vendever didn't have two loving parents who would take any steps necessary to help them get better.

An alcoholic at seventeen? Lynne knew that this happened. But for it to happen to them, the Castles?

Demeter had fought her fate at first. She had jumped out of bed, grabbed the Hefty bag from Lynne's hands, and started swinging it at her. Lynne had a bruise on her ribs to prove it. Al had woken up and restrained Demeter. Then he'd called Ted Field, who had met them at the hospital.

Now, just a few hours before her departure, Demeter seemed accepting. Four weeks. She would go through detox and counseling. She would meet other kids who were dealing with dependency issues, and professionals who were trained to help such kids. Demeter lay in the white hospital bed looking so hopeless and despondent that Lynne couldn't help herself.

She said, "Is there anything I can do for you before you go?"

There was such a long silence that Lynne figured her daughter was ignoring her. Then Demeter took a breath. "Yes," she said. "I'd like to talk to Hobby."

DEMETER AND HOBBY

He was hanging out with Claire on his mother's back deck, and it was almost like regular summertime. His mother brought them cold ginger ales and a bowl of nacho chips with her homemade salsa that she'd made from the first of the Bartlett's Farm field tomatoes. The ocean unfolded before them. Hobby was dying to jump in and let the cool waves cradle him, but he still had a cast on — just the one, on his left leg — and so there would be no ocean for him for a while. His leg itched as if the Devil himself were inside the cast. Hobby swore that as soon as the thing was off, he was going to climb down those stairs and jump in the water; he didn't care if it was Christmas Day.

He thought maybe Claire would want to go down and have a swim, but she was nursing her ginger ale, holding the cold glass to her temple, and she hadn't even tasted the salsa. She was either sick or nervous. They were planning on telling Zoe about the baby that night at dinner. Claire had been lying low, but in the past few days her phone had started blowing up: Annabel Wright, Winnie Potts, Joe, her boss from the Juice Bar. They'd all left messages urging her to call them back. Claire was convinced that everyone knew. She and her mother had had a huge fight because Rasha had told Sara Boule, and Sara Boule had most likely gossiped about it to every person who had been to Dr. Toomer's office to get a cleaning over the past three weeks. Claire had wanted to wait to announce the news until after the ultrasound, once they knew the baby was healthy and whole. She had wanted to tell Zoe then, and Coach Horton of the field hockey team, who had just returned from France. Now, thanks to Rasha and Sara Boule, Zoe was in danger of finding out third-hand, and what a terrible, cruel thing *that* would be. Hobby agreed that they couldn't let that happen.

Penny, Hobby thought. Had Penny heard about Claire's pregnancy from someone else? If she had, wouldn't she have demanded an explanation from Hobby? Or would she have just flipped out and gone off the deep end?

They had to tell his mother, and pronto. He'd asked Zoe if Claire could stay for dinner, and Zoe had said yes, of course, and then she'd set about making an occasion out of it. They were having grilled lobster tails and French potato salad and corn on the cob with lime-cilantro butter, and crema calda with blackberries. Hobby knew that Zoe was excited about cooking for someone other than him and the Allencasts for a change. And she was relieved, perhaps, that Penny's chair at the table wouldn't sit empty tonight.

It was two o'clock now. Dinner was scheduled for seven. Hobby and Claire were left to marinate in their worry for five more hours. He had no idea what his mother's reaction would be. She had always assured him that he could tell her *anything*. But he wasn't sure; this was a pretty big "anything." Zoe had gotten pregnant by accident eighteen years earlier, so by rights she should understand. But what if she didn't? What if this news was the thing that finally broke her? Zoe had made no secret of the fact that despite Hobby's injuries, she still expected great things from him. She expected him to get into an elite college and get a degree in architecture. He couldn't forgo college so he could stay on Nantucket and work in construction and raise a child. He could not—*could not*—break his mother's heart.

Would she be disappointed in him? Would she do the predictable thing and blame *Claire?* God, he hoped not. Claire was so nervous that she couldn't eat at all, but Hobby reacted the opposite way. He guzzled down his ginger ale and shoveled in chip after chip loaded up with tangy salsa. His mother had added jalapeños to the salsa, which was something she used to do only when Penny was at a sleepover or away at camp. Penny didn't eat spicy food; she worried it would damage her vocal cords. And so the fact that Zoe had added jalapeños to the salsa and presumably would be adding jalapeños to the salsa every time she made it from now on — *since Penny was dead* — further depressed Hobby and made him eat even faster. His manners, which were usually pretty decent, were appalling right now; he knew this, but he couldn't help himself. Salsa dropped from his chip and stained his khaki shorts. He had crumbs down the front of his shirt. The speed with which he had polished off the ginger ale caused him to emit a loud and prolonged belch that smelled like onions. Claire shook her head at him. She was probably wondering why she had ever allowed herself to couple with such an artless boor. She was probably fearing for the way he would raise their unborn child.

"Excuse me," he said.

Claire's eyes looked weary. She was sick, or sick of him, or sick of their situation. They might have been married for forty years already.

"Let's tell her now," Claire said. "I can't just sit here and *wait*."

Hobby brushed the crumbs off the front of his shirt and sat up a little straighter. *Yes!* Tell her now and get it over with. Waiting was torture. He burped again, more quietly this time. He regretted having eaten so fast.

"Okay," he said. "I think you're right. You're definitely right. We'll tell her now."

"Just like we talked about," Claire said. "You start."

The phone in the house rang. Hobby's heart seized. There were ringing phones and there were ringing phones, but this ringing phone was so ill timed that Hobby could imagine only that the person on the other end was someone who had chosen this precise moment to spoil their news. It must be Beatrice McKenzie, the librarian at the Atheneum, or Savannah Major, the principal's wife, calling to congratulate Zoe after hearing "through the grapevine" that she was going to be a grandmother.

A grandmother. Zoe was forty years old. Hobby burped again.

Inside, Zoe answered the phone, a fact that Hobby found startling. He heard her murmuring, using her private voice. It was the same voice she used when she talked to Jordan on the phone. Hobby wondered if there was any way the phone call could be from him. God, that would be something! But it was the middle of the night in Australia now.

Zoe stepped out onto the deck. She said, "Hobby, can I speak to you for a minute, please?"

Hobby twisted in his chair. His mother's face was inscrutable, but he was no dummy, it was something bad. She *knew.* He felt his insides start to roil; he burped again and tasted jalapeños. She knew. Someone else had told her. She wanted him...

what? to come inside? She did realize that he had an eight-pound cast on his leg and that moving from one location to another was still an arduous task for him, right? He struggled to his feet. Even on his worst days he moved more gracefully than he was doing right now. Something about his mother's face and Claire's face—man, truthfully, Hobby couldn't even *look* at Claire's face, but he knew it was bad—and the hot sun and his aching, itching leg and the goddamned jalapeños in the salsa, and Penny dead, never to not eat jalapeños again or use her vocal cords again: all of these things conspired against him, and his stomach heaved, and he pivoted with the help of one crutch, and then he projectile-vomited off the deck, down into the dune grass below.

"Hobby!" his mother cried.

He vomited again. He hated to admit it, but it felt good, getting the poisonous stuff out. He could hear Claire making unpleasant noises behind him. She was probably going to sympathy-puke. This was like some godawful Monty Python movie. He closed his eyes and saw colors—swirling pink and orange—and he thought, Penny, can you help me here, please? She would probably refuse him. He could just hear her, wherever she was, saying that she was not some angel slave whom he could just summon whenever he got into a tight spot.

A glass of ice water appeared at his elbow. His mother. She said, "Are you okay?"

He wiped at his mouth with the back of his hand and accepted the water. "Yeah," he said. "I ate too fast."

She said, "I really need to talk to you inside. Privately."

Hobby checked on Claire. She was sitting ramrod straight with her eyes closed and her legs folded in a way that reminded him of a yoga position. He said, "Claire? I'm going in for a minute."

She nodded, though barely.

Hobby crutched his way inside and followed his mother into the nether regions of the house. Her bedroom. He looked around as though it were a room in a museum. It had been years and years since Hobby had done anything more than peek in here. Penny used to go into their mother's room all the time, she would spend a string of nights sleeping in Zoe's bed. Zoe and Penny had been ridiculously close, they'd had that best-friend thing going on, a girl thing, and Hobby had been more than happy to stand clear. Still, there were aspects of the room that Hobby had memorized long ago: the oval mirror with the gilt frame (true, not as big as Penny's mirror, not even close), the dressing table with the engraved silver brush with the soft white bristles that, as a child, Hobby had liked to rub across his face, the photograph of Zoe and Hobson senior on the steps of the Culinary Institute, both of them in their chef's whites and toques. A large pink conch shell that Zoe had gotten on a trip she'd taken, alone, to Cabo. The faded quilt on her spindle bed that she'd inherited from her mother's sister, who had married an Amish man and lived somewhere in Iowa. Over the door, the enamel cross that Zoe had bought in Ravenna, Italy, where she had gone on vacation a million years ago with her parents. The one time Hobby had asked her about the cross, she'd said that she viewed it as a piece of art, not a religious symbol. The cut crystal candy dish filled with beach glass on her night table, next to a stack of books. The bottom book was *The Collected Works of M. F. K. Fisher*. This was Zoe's favorite book of all time, and it had been Hobby's father's favorite book as well.

All of these things about his mother's room were as familiar to Hobby as the parts of his own body, and yet somehow he'd forgotten about them.

Why were they talking in *her* room? Wasn't the kitchen private enough? Or the hallway? This was very bad. This was what he'd been dreading, or worse.

Zoe closed the door.

Hobby collapsed on the bed. At that moment he yearned for his old body back. He wanted to run away as fast as he could. He wanted to jump fences and swim ponds. Anything to get away.

Penny, help me!

Zoe said, "Lynne Castle just called."

Hobby thought, Oh, Jesus.

Zoe said, "Demeter is in bad shape. She's going away to a hospital called Vendever to be treated for alcohol abuse."

"What?" Hobby said.

"They're holding her right now at the hospital," Zoe said. "And she's asked for one thing before she goes."

"What's that?" Hobby said.

"She wants to talk to you."

Hobby brushed his teeth and splashed cold water on his face. He thought, Demeter wants to talk to me.

In the living room he found Claire lying on the sofa with a wet washcloth over her eyes.

"She doesn't feel well," Zoe said. "Maybe she got too much sun. Or maybe the two of you caught a bug."

"Not a bug," Hobby said. He looked at Claire, his princess in repose. Her left hand was resting across her abdomen in a way that he felt stated the obvious. Should they tell Zoe now, before he went

off on this heinous mission of talking to Demeter
at the hospital?

"Mom...," he said.

"I told Claire that we needed to run an errand,"
Zoe said. "And that we'll be back in an hour or so.
That will give her a chance to rest."

Claire nodded, and Hobby thought, All right,
get this over with, then tell Mom. Tell her over dinner, like we planned.

"We'll be back in an hour," he said. "Maybe
sooner."

They used the Emergency Room entrance and found
Lynne Castle waiting for them. Lynne reached out
for Zoe, and the two women hugged for a long time.
Zoe was crying and Lynne Castle was crying and
there seemed to be a lot of apologizing going on: "I'm
sorry..." "No, *I'm* sorry..." Lynne was so sorry for
everything, Zoe was sorry for not calling Lynne back
sooner, Lynne was sorry for her daughter's behavior,
Zoe was sorry that she'd had to be the one to blow
the whistle. Hobby hung from his crutches and
thought, Can we please get this over with? I have my
own drama waiting for me at home. But Zoe and
Lynne kept speaking in whispers, wiping away tears,
squeezing each other's hands. "I was so blind," Lynne
said. "I was a blind, stupid cow."

"The important thing," Zoe said, "is that now she can get the help she needs."

Hobby let out an audible breath, a cue that his mother — being immune to his childish cries for attention — ignored but Lynne Castle picked up on.

She said, "Hobby. Thank you for agreeing to do this."

"No prob," he said. He crutched toward her, hoping to expedite the forward motion that would get this done and get him back home to Claire, then get them to the dinner table where he would tell his mother that he had fathered a child.

Lynne said, "I'll take you up. Follow me."

"I'll wait here," Zoe said. She eyed the chairs of the waiting room. The place was completely deserted; Dr. Phil was on TV. She put her hand to her mouth, and Hobby thought, This was the place where she learned that Penny was dead.

"Actually," Zoe said. "I'll wait in the car."

Hobby and Lynne walked down the corridor in silence. They waited for the elevator.

Lynne asked, "How are you feeling?"

"Better," he said. "Everything else works, just not the leg."

"How much longer with the cast?" Lynne asked.

"They're not sure," Hobby said. "Three more

weeks, maybe? I'm hoping to get it off before school starts."

"That would be nice," Lynne said.

Hobby nodded in agreement.

The elevator doors opened, they filed in, Lynne pressed the button for the third floor, the elevator doors closed. Hobby worried that he smelled like puked-up jalapeños and onions.

Lynne said, "Your mother told you what happened?"

"Not really," Hobby said. "Just that Demeter is going to Vendever to be ... treated."

"She was caught stealing vodka from the Allencasts' house while her landscaping crew was working there," Lynne said. "You mom was the one who saw her do it, actually. And so Demeter got fired. When I asked Demeter, she said she wasn't planning on *drinking* the vodka. She said she was going to give it away to friends. And I, like a fool, believed her."

Yes, Hobby thought, that was foolish. Demeter drank all the time, she drank a lot. She was ... well, other kids like Anders Peashway called her a lush. But maybe Mrs. Castle hadn't realized that Demeter drank, or maybe she'd known that Demeter drank but not how much. Parents were funny that way, always wanting to believe the best about their kids. When Hobby was a father, he was going to be the ultimate realist. He wasn't going to believe a word his child said. He was going to be a vigilante—especially if he had a girl.

Lynne went on: "Then I found, oh, maybe two dozen empty bottles in her closet and an additional eighteen bottles that were still full. Vodka, tequila, wine. I could hardly believe it."

Hobby's eyebrows jumped. *Really?* Man, that was something.

"All of the bottles were stolen," Lynne said. "She took them from the houses where she was landscaping. Oh, and she stole from the Kingsleys, the family she babysits for. That was where she got the bottle of Jim Beam you were all drinking on the night of graduation."

"Ah," Hobby said. To say anything more seemed unwise.

"She stole the bottles because she had to have the alcohol and we don't keep any around the house," Lynne Castle said. "Not a drop. And she had to have it. Because she's an alcoholic."

Hobby clenched the grips of his crutches.

"An alcoholic at seventeen," Lynne said.

The elevator doors opened—Thank you, God, thought Hobby—and he and Lynne Castle filed out. Hobby followed Lynne down the corridor. His hospital room had been on the second floor and not the third floor, that was a small blessing. As it turned out, the third floor was even bleaker and more hopeless-seeming than the second floor. Hobby broke out in a sweat despite the air-conditioning. It was hard to be back here.

Demeter was the only person in a double room. Hobby had pictured her lying in bed wearing a johnny, like a sick person, but she was in her regular clothes—cargo shorts and a T-shirt—sitting on the side of the bed, reading a book. When she saw her mother and Hobby, she set the book aside and gripped the edge of the bed as if it were a ledge she was about to leap from.

Lynne said, "Look who I found!" As though Hobby's sudden presence in the room were a happy surprise and not 100 percent by design.

Demeter stared at him. Her eyes were vacant, and Hobby thought, They've drugged her.

"Hey, Meter," Hobby said.

She gave a little smile, and Hobby had a flashback to sitting in the circle at the Children's House next to her when they were little. He remembered her dimpled knees and pigtails. He remembered the cream cheese and jelly sandwiches in her lunchbox.

"Hey," she said.

She didn't look half bad. She was tan, and she was thinner. She had brushed her hair, and it hung down long and straight and shiny. The blond streak was so pretty that Hobby wanted to reach out and touch it.

Lynne Castle said, "Well, I guess I'll leave you two alone." As though they were on a date or something. Hobby looked down at the floor and counted this as one of the most awkward moments of his life, and to make matters worse, Lynne Castle, instead of leaving as she had just promised, lingered for a few strangled moments longer, looking from her daughter, Demeter, an alcoholic at seventeen, to Hobby, who had recently lost his twin sister and spent nine days in a coma. She was no doubt thinking about the children they had once been and wondering what had gone so horribly wrong, and whether it was her fault or just bad luck visited on them from above. Probably Lynne wanted to stay and hear what Demeter had to say, and could Hobby blame her? He was both dying of curiosity and waiting in dread.

What? What was she going to say? What did she have to tell him?

His leg itched in its cast.

Lynne Castle sighed, then turned and left, closing the door firmly behind her.

DEMETER

He looked supremely uncomfortable, dangling from his crutches like a scarecrow propped up in a cornfield.

"Do you want to sit?" she said.

"No," he said. Then he changed his mind: "Actually, yes." He moved to the chair and sat down, his left leg straight out in front of him in its cast.

She didn't know how to start. She sort of felt like she should thank him for coming.

He said, "Jesus Christ, Meter, what is it? Just tell me!"

She had rehearsed it in her head. "I told Penny something in the dunes."

"About Jake?" Hobby said.

About *Jake?* she thought.

"What *about* Jake?" she said.

"About me, then?" Hobby said. His eyes were rolling, and his forehead was sweating. "Did you tell her something about me?"

"No," Demeter said. "I told her something about your mom and Jordan Randolph."

Hobby narrowed his eyes, and his nose twitched. He leaned forward in the chair, and Demeter noticed the toes on his cast-foot wiggling. "What?" he said. "What did you tell her?"

"That I saw them together."

"What the fuck does that mean?" Hobby said. "You saw them together, so what? They used to be together all the time. They were friends. You know that."

"I saw them *together* together," Demeter said.

"What? You mean, like, kissing?"

"I mean like more than kissing."

"For God's sake, Meter, *what?*"

"I saw them... well, I saw them having sex. On the deck of your house. A couple of days before graduation."

Hobby stared at her. His expression was inscrutable. This, Demeter decided, was the most frustrating thing about life: it was impossible to tell what other people were thinking.

"What do you mean, you saw them *having sex?*" Hobby said. "I don't get that."

Demeter's hands were shaking. She needed a drink. But she was never going to drink again. Never again, for the rest of her life. That was impossible of course, but that was what Dr. Field and her parents had been trying to convince her of. In less than an hour she would be picked up and transported to Vendever, where counselors and doctors and addiction experts were going to teach her how to live without drinking.

"I saw them having sex," she said. "I cut school. That Thursday."

It had been a glorious day with a scrubbed-clean feel to the air and a pure June-blue sky. That morning Demeter had drunk the dregs of a bottle of Dewar's, the last of her parents' stash, and she had also taken a few swigs off the bottle of Jim Beam that she'd swiped from the Kingsleys'. But she needed more alcohol, another bottle at least, and the idea of stealing from someone she knew had lodged in her brain. It had been so easy to lift the bottle from the Kingsleys' house. Demeter ran through a list of all the people she knew, or whom her parents knew, who drank, and Zoe was the most promising candidate. Zoe always drank wine, though Demeter also had memories of margarita parties at the Alistairs', and cosmopolitans and martinis, and hot rum toddies in winter. She knew Zoe's kitchen practically as well as her own, she knew that Zoe would be at work, and she knew that the sliding door facing the ocean would be unlocked.

So Demeter drove to the end of Miacomet Pond and parked her Escape. She told herself she was just going for a walk on the beach, no crime there. She trudged the two or three hundred yards to the Alistairs' steps. She left her sandals on the beach and was unusually light and quick up the steps in her bare feet. She was dreaming of having a cold glass of white wine, and maybe a short nap in the sun on the chaise longue, before returning to school after lunch, just in time for English, which was the only class she could stand.

Demeter was just four or five steps from the top of the stairs when she heard the breathing and whispering and moaning. She didn't quite know what to make of it; she never heard such noises in her own house. She listened. She thought, Turn around and leave, right now. Zoe had a man up there. Demeter had no reason to be surprised by this; Zoe was single and she was young, barely forty. But instead of turning around, Demeter crept upward. She had a feeling that she couldn't identify. This was obviously something private that she was about to witness, something secret. She had never been privy to any kind of secret before, other than her own hideous secret about her drinking. She knew that other kids kept secrets and told secrets, among them Annabel Wright and Winnie Potts and Anders Peashway, kids who had a lot more going on in their lives than she did.

She kept going, up one step then the next until she could see clearly: Zoe and…Jordan. Zoe naked, straddling Jordan on the very same chaise that Demeter had been planning to use for her nap.

Demeter turned and flew down the stairs and,

after grabbing her sandals, dashed across the sand toward her car. When she was safely out of view, she slowed down and tried to catch her breath and slow her galloping heart and her racing mind and her careening emotions.

Zoe and Jordan.

She was shocked, God, she felt as if she'd been electrocuted and was now vibrating and buzzing, but could she honestly say she was *surprised?* Zoe and Jordan. They were always together, always somehow *aligned;* they had seemed far more comfortable together than Jordan and Ava, even though Ava was Jordan's wife and Jake's mother. Everyone remarked about how Zoe and Jordan were such great friends. They were friends like Jerry and Elaine on *Seinfeld,* or like Beezus Quimby and Henry Huggins in the books Demeter had read growing up. Best friends: one boy and one girl. This kind of relationship was frequently portrayed in books and movies and on TV, but it never seemed to happen in real life—except in the case of Zoe and Jordan. But now that myth was dispelled. Their relationship was something else entirely.

"I was looking for booze," Demeter explained to Hobby. "I knew I could get some at your house. So I walked down the beach and up the stairs, and I saw your mom and Jordan on the deck. And they were—"

Hobby held up a hand like a traffic cop. Demeter shut her mouth.

"Why?" he said.

Demeter wasn't sure what he was asking. *Why? Why* was she looking for booze? Well, now he knew, now everyone knew: she was an alcoholic. Or did he mean, why were Zoe and Jordan together? That wasn't something Demeter could answer.

"Why what?" she said.

"Why did you tell Penny?" he whispered.

Why *did* she tell Penny? She had asked herself this question half a million times: Why did I tell Penny? She must have known that Penny would be stunned; she must have known she would be hurt. Confused, sad, angry, disgusted. Yes, Demeter had known all of that. But the answer to why she had told Penny was that she had been unable *not* to tell Penny. The news was like a gold ingot in her hand, and for someone as emotionally impoverished as Demeter, it had been impossible not to squander it. The secret was valuable only if it could get her something she wanted, and what she had wanted, more than anything in the world, was Penny Alistair's complete attention.

"I told her because I finally had something she didn't. I had social currency."

" 'Social currency,' " Hobby repeated.

"I knew she was going to be upset," Demeter

said. "But I thought I could help her work through it. That was what I wanted." The words were so brutally honest that Demeter couldn't believe she was actually uttering them. "My plan was to tell Penny the news and then be the one to help her deal with it. It was a secret that was going to bond us together." She swallowed; her throat was dry and sore. "It was supposed to make us friends. *Real* friends."

Hobby blew out a stream of air. He looked pale and sick. It occurred to Demeter that telling Hobby this news about his mother and Jordan might turn out to be a second disaster. Back in the dunes, with Penny, she had spoken with the self-righteous assurance that she was doing the correct and just thing by exposing the nefarious lies of the adults in their lives. Now, with Hobby, she was confessing only to her own transgressions. What had taken place between Zoe and Jordan was nobody's business — not Penny's, not Hobby's, and certainly not Demeter's.

"If I could take it back...," she said.

"Well, yeah," Hobby said. He was rubbing his forehead aggressively, as if willing his brain to work.

"Anyway, I wanted you to know that what happened with Penny was my fault. That was what I told her. She seemed cool with the news at first, like it was no big deal. But then, by the time we got back to the car, she was a mess."

" 'A mess,' " Hobby said.

"I killed her," Demeter said. "I might just as well have put a gun to her head and pulled the trigger."

Hobby was quiet. Demeter thought he might try to say something to make her feel better, but he did nothing of the sort. So he was going to hold her responsible. He was very possibly going to report all of this back to Zoe, and then the whole world would hold her responsible for Penny Alistair's death. But Demeter had concluded that telling Hobby was the only thing that would make her feel better. She could tell the story in group therapy at Vendever, but it wouldn't have any meaning. Telling strangers would offer no relief from the insidious pressure that had been building inside her: I told Penny a horrible thing. I got in the middle of people's personal affairs that had nothing to do with me. I am the reason Penny Alistair is dead. Me. If I had kept my mouth shut, Penny would still be alive.

Hobby struggled to his feet. Really? Demeter thought. He's just going to leave? She wasn't sure what she'd expected. Yelling, maybe. A scene. But there was a way—wasn't there?—in which this was Zoe's and Jordan's fault. They, after all, were the ones who'd been lying and cheating. They were the ones who had crossed a line. They were *adults*— really good, cool, important, responsible adults, or so Demeter, and Hobby and Penny and Jake, had always been led to believe. And yet there they were on the deck, having *sex,* making those animal noises. Demeter hadn't wandered into anyone's bedroom. They were *outside,* practically in *public.* Demeter had wondered if perhaps she'd happened across a onetime thing. Maybe Jordan had stopped by to help Zoe change out her storm windows for screens, and they'd gotten to waxing nostalgic about graduation, and to talking about Penny and Jake and how much in love they were, and then one thing had led to another, and what Demeter had witnessed was like a shooting star that burned bright once, then faded away.

But Demeter didn't think so. She'd glimpsed them only for a split second, just long enough to imprint in her mind Zoe's bare back (with the white stripe of a tan line), and Jordan's arms locked around her, and their movements and their sounds. It had seemed like they fit together perfectly in a way they might not have done if it were their first time. (Although what did Demeter know about sex? Really, what did she know?) And when she thought back on the way that Zoe and Jordan *were* together—their easy camaraderie, their inside jokes, the fact that they always sat next to each other, whether it be at a dinner table, at the beach, or in the ski lodge—she knew that this had been going on for *a while,* probably months, possibly even years. It was an industry of lies that they had produced. They had been lying not just to poor Ava Randolph but to *everybody*. Including their own children. Didn't that make it Zoe and Jordan's fault? Did Demeter have to take the blame just for repeating the awful truth?

Demeter wanted to initiate this debate with Hobby—and it would have to be here and now, while she was still around, while the topic was still hot and immediate—but she didn't know how to broach it without making it seem like she was trying to pass the buck and deny the blame.

No, she thought. There would be no passing the buck or denying the blame. She was seventeen years old. That was old enough to accept responsibility for who she was and what she'd set in motion.

"I'm sorry," she bleated.

Hobby shook his head violently, as if trying to dislodge something. "Yeah," he said. "Me too."

HOBBY

One thing at a time. Maybe before the accident he could have dealt with *both* Demeter's shell-shocking news and telling Zoe about the baby, but he couldn't do it now. His head was filled with white noise. Too much, too much.

His mother and Jordan. Whoa. He would have to think about that carefully.

If he'd had two good legs, he would have chosen to walk home, but the cast necessitated that he climb into the car with his mother, who was paging through an issue of *Bon Appétit*. She set the magazine down and looked at him.

"That go okay?" she asked.

"Not really."

She regarded him for a second. He could feel her eyes, feel the questions hanging in the hot air of the car.

"Believe me," he said, "you don't want to know."

Still she watched him. Hobby made a fist over and over again with his left hand. He wanted her to drive. He wanted the air-conditioning on full blast so he could cool down. He wanted to get back to Claire. But he couldn't tell Claire about this; he couldn't tell anyone. Demeter had just saddled him with a ridiculous burden. Did she feel better now? he wondered. He hoped so. He really fucking hoped so.

"Hobby?" Zoe said.

"Please drive," Hobby said.

"I can handle it, you know," Zoe said. "If you want to tell me something, if you want to talk this out with me, I can handle it."

"You've handled enough," Hobby said. He felt a surge of pure, vermilion anger at Demeter. She had used his mother's secret as *social currency,* to *bond* with Penny, to try and make them *real* friends, but what had it cost *her?* Penny had lost her life, Zoe had lost her daughter, Hobby had lost his twin sister and the agility and quickness and coordination that had been his natural gifts. Demeter had lost nothing. Sure, she might feel as if she were losing something because she was being carted away to Vendever, but that was destruction by her own hand. Demeter had drunk and stolen and drunk some more because she couldn't handle the truth: she had caused the accident.

But what was up with his mother and Jordan, anyway? Would his mother *do* that, sleep with Jordan while he was married to Ava, who was her friend too? Was his mother lonely and desperate enough to do that, and if she was, what did *that* say about her? Was she *in love* with Jordan? Of course she was in love with him. God, it seemed so obvious to Hobby right at that second that it was painful for him to think about. The phone calls and the texting and the way Zoe was always happier when Jordan was around, the way she made special food for him and he made such a big deal about how delicious everything was, and the way they liked the same music and had the same politics. If a certain Springsteen song came on over the car radio, Zoe would call Jordan's cell phone and play a snippet into his voicemail, no words or explanation needed. When Barack Obama was elected President, the first person to call Zoe was Jordan: before midnight on November 4, 2008, they spent more than an hour talking on the phone together, as giddy as kids. "Do you miss Jordan?" Hobby had asked his mother a few weeks ago. "Yes," she'd said. "Yes I do, actually. I miss him very much." And then he'd heard her crying that night and thought she must be crying about Penny. He wondered now what it was like for his mother to have Jordan so far away; he would have liked to ask her, but at that moment he realized he didn't want to know his mother's innermost thoughts. He didn't want to know about her sex life or her heart's secrets. He wanted her to be his *mother.* Although of course he also wanted her to be happy. Jordan Randolph certainly made her happy. So did he want Zoe to be with Jordan? He wasn't sure. His brain wasn't working correctly, goddammit. He couldn't make sense of any of this.

"Just drive," he said to his mother again. "Please."

Zoe started the car, and the air-conditioning kicked in. They backed out of the parking spot, and Hobby felt marginally better with the movement.

"Did you see Lynne on your way out?" Zoe asked.

"No," he lied. He *had* seen Lynne standing over by the vending machines, talking to Percy Simons, who served on the Board of Selectmen with Al Castle, but he'd walked right past them.

"I wonder how Demeter is getting to Vendever," Zoe said.

Hobby shrugged. He imagined just coming out with it: "Demeter told Penny that she saw you and Jordan having sex. And that was the thing that did it, I guess."

That really might have been the thing that did it, too, he thought. Penny had been so close to their mother. Penny told Zoe everything, and it would have come as a devastating shock that the river didn't flow both ways. Penny had always been happy that Zoe didn't date; she wanted her all to herself, whereas Hobby had always worried that their mother was lonely. But she had never seemed lonely when Jordan was around.

Then Hobby remembered the journal. Penny had kept nothing private from Zoe except her close relationship with Ava Randolph. So it was a double whammy: not only had Zoe betrayed Penny, she had also betrayed Ava, who was Penny's friend and confidante.

This might have been what drove Penny to do what she did. But it could just as easily have been the knowledge of Jake's kissing and touching Winnie Potts in the Pottses' basement after the cast party. Or it could have been the whispered news that Hobby had gotten Claire Buckley pregnant and they had scheduled an abortion.

The whole world had secrets, Hobby thought. Everyone was fallible. Everyone. Zoe Alistair, Jordan Randolph, Ava Randolph, Al and Lynne Castle—all fallible. Penny would have hated that answer. She'd been tethered to this world only by her belief in the people around her. If she'd somehow lost that belief, if the people she loved and trusted the most had turned out not to be who she thought they were—yes, Hobby could see how she could have just floated away.

Which was exactly what she'd done.

It had been *her* choice. Penny herself was to blame. She had caused the accident. She had killed herself.

"Listen," she'd said to him. "I'm going now."

Hobby felt tears running down his face. He wiped at them, and this immediately attracted his mother's attention.

"Honey," she said. "What's wrong?"

"Claire's pregnant," he said.

PART THREE

September

ZOE

The day before school started, Zoe took Hobby to get his final cast off. They had spent an absurd amount of time at the hospital over the past three months, and now, with Claire having the baby, there would be even more hospital time in front of them. But that would be good, happy hospital time, just as getting the cast off was good. Hobby sat on the examining table, all six foot six of him, and Ted Field got out his Sawzall and cut the plaster into pieces. Hobby's leg underneath was pale and shrunken, which only emphasized how brown and strong his other leg was. He looked like a doll that had been cobbled together out of mismatched parts.

Hobby dug at his newly exposed leg with his fingernails. "It doesn't even itch," he said, "but I've been dying to scratch it for months."

Ted Field laughed. Zoe saw the humor too, but

she felt tears rise. The final cast. She thought, Thank God you're alive.

That afternoon, at home, Hobby slowly made his way down the steps to the beach and went for a swim in the ocean. Zoe watched him from the deck. He waved. She waved back.

Claire came for dinner. She did that so often these days that Zoe saw no point in getting rid of the third chair at the round outdoor table. It would always be Penny's chair, but at least now there was someone else there to occupy it.

Claire was starting to show. There was a swell at her belly, and her breasts were full to bursting, and her skin was clear, and her hair had shine. Her fingernails were long for the first time in her life — playing field hockey and basketball and lacrosse, she'd always had to clip them — and Zoe took her to R. J. Miller for a manicure. Someone in the salon who didn't know them asked if they were mother and daughter.

Zoe froze. *Mother and daughter.* She didn't know how to answer that question.

Claire piped up, "I'm her son's girlfriend."

Both Zoe and Rasha Buckley went with Claire and Hobby to the ultrasound appointment. The four of them saw the shadowy, ghostlike image of the baby floating on the screen, and Zoe was overwhelmed with emotion, thinking back to her own ultrasound eighteen years earlier: the moment she had learned she was carrying twins. Hobson senior had whooped like a rodeo hand, as if he'd hit for a hundred grand on the penny slots. Stick a little something in, get back something priceless.

Claire and Hobby had decided not to ask the sex of the baby, but from the picture on the screen, there was no doubt.

"Oh," Claire said. "It's a boy."

"Look at that equipment!" Hobby said.

Claire was due in February The plan was for her to keep up with her schoolwork at home until the baby was six or eight weeks old, and then go back to school for the end of her senior year. She and Hobby were both going to apply to colleges—and the next fall, when the baby was seven months old, Zoe and Rasha would take over. Zoe would have the baby for three days a week, and Rasha for four. Zoe would turn Penny's room into a nursery. She would become a mother again. She couldn't lie: she had been hoping and praying that the baby was a girl. She had been thinking it might be another Penny, a Penny reborn, reincarnated, *returned to her* in the form of this baby. But that was Zoe's delusion, her false assumption, her pointless hope.

The baby was a boy.

"A boy," Rasha said with equanimity.

Zoe wasn't ready to speak yet, though she could feel the others waiting for her to chime in. She studied the image on the screen: a baby, a real, live, human baby. If the accident had never happened, if Penny were still alive and Hobby were still whole and he had told her that he'd gotten Claire pregnant, Zoe would have advised her to have an abortion. But now, looking at the screen, at the baby's tiny toes and his thumb in his mouth, she marveled that her former self could have dismissed the wonder of life so hastily.

"A baby boy," she said.

"We decided that if it was a boy, we'd name him Hobson," Hobby said. "Hobson the third. It's like the name of a king."

Zoe let out a soft cry.

The day after Hobby got his cast removed, Zoe dropped him off at school. The first day of senior year, a scant three months after the last day of his junior year, and yet now his world was completely different.

"Thanks, Mom," Hobby said. He wrestled with his backpack and the single crutch that he still needed for walking. "I promise I'll get my license soon."

"I would be just as happy if you never learned to drive at all," Zoe said.

"I know," Hobby said. He patted her knee. "But it'd be a little weird, you driving me and my baby around."

Zoe smiled and nodded. She was short on words. Today was one of those days that she had been dreading; she hadn't slept at all the night before. Zoe watched the other kids filing into the school, the girls all brushed out and made up, dressed carefully in capri pants and cute tops. They congregated in groups, shrieked, giggled, talked a million miles an hour. There was that palpable energy in the air, the buzz that surrounded something's *starting.* If things had been different, if Penny had been alive and Jake and Jordan had been here, this day would have been one to celebrate rather than one to survive. Penny had always loved the start of school, the fresh notebooks and sharpened pencils, the new pink erasers, the unopened books.

She was dead. In the ground.

Zoe watched Hobby make his way to the entrance. He was mobbed by people. Of course. Zoe didn't even recognize some of the kids, but all of them wanted to high-five Hobby, the sports hero who was a sports hero no longer, who was something bigger and more important now. He had cheated death. He had survived.

Zoe waited until Hobby had disappeared through the front doors of the school, then she drove off.

She wanted to *do* something: go home and make a soufflé, or take a spinning class, or rummage through her desk drawers for the unsmoked joint that her catering client Jonesy Vick, a graying, ponytailed record producer, had given her at the end of a particularly debauched dinner party. She hadn't smoked dope in years, but something about the thought appealed to her today—get high, put on one of her bootleg Dead tapes, stare at the ocean.

But really, Zoe, she thought.

She decided she would drive to Cisco Beach to see the white cross. She had been doing this more and more often lately. She drove to the cross and thought about Penny, and sometimes she hummed "Ave Maria." It made her feel better. It was, she supposed, a little like a prayer.

Zoe Alistair praying, she thought. And she laughed, because who would ever have believed it?

It was September 4, an absolutely perfect blue morning, warm but not hot and sticky, as the last half of August had been. Zoe drove with the car windows down, her left elbow poking out into the sun. Now that Hobby was back at school, she could start catering again, get her business up and running before the holidays. Football started next week. Zoe had notions of calling Al and Lynne and inviting them over, and she could ask Rasha and Claire, too, and she could make clam chowder. Maybe she would go up to Coatue one afternoon and harvest the clams herself.

She thought about dragging her ancient clam rake (bought at a yard sale during her first week on the island, because she had believed then that every real Nantucketer should own a clam rake) through the soft, marshy sand of the low-tide shallows on Monomoy Beach, coming up with a handful of cherrystones at a time. It never got old; it was always as exciting as panning for gold and finding nuggets in her sieve. She would take two or three dozen clams home and shuck them herself, then she'd sauté a diced Vidalia onion in half a stick of butter. She'd add the clams, some fresh Bartlett's corn, fish stock, white wine, fresh thyme, and heavy cream, and an hour later she'd have a pot of chowder. She and Hobson senior had fantasized about just this kind of sustainable cooking, about owning cows and pigs, and growing herbs and carrots and baby lettuces, and running a farm-to-table restaurant. Making clam chowder, she realized, was probably as close as she was ever going to get to that dream, but that was okay.

As she approached the end of Hummock Pond Road, she experienced the particular floaty feeling that she'd been having recently whenever she came here, as though she were levitating. She wasn't sure if it was a response to seeing the white arms of the cross or if it was her imagining what Penny had felt in the final seconds of her life. The speed, the lift, the flight.

Zoe saw the arms of the cross bisecting the brilliant blue of the sky. The visual effect was no less majestic than that inspired by the *Cristo Redentor,* overlooking Rio de Janeiro. But then something else caught Zoe's eye: a familiar car, a Land Rover, and a man leaning against it.

Zoe hit her brakes. Her legs were liquid, threatening to dissolve. She felt panic, then euphoria, then panic again. She narrowed her eyes, certain she was mistaken. She wouldn't let herself believe it.

She pulled up next to the car. The man turned.

Jordan.

Zoe had an urge to do what Penny had done on that terrible night in June: hit the gas and keep going. The car would crash, she would die, but so what? Anything was preferable to experiencing the overwhelming fact of Jordan, here. It *was* Jordan, right?

He walked toward her car. She bent her head forward and pressed her fingertips into her eyes.

She thought, My God, what do I do?

He reached in through her open window and circled his fingers around her wrist and gently pulled her hand away from her face.

"Hey," he said. "I was wondering if you ever came here."

His voice. She couldn't stand it. She was going to collapse, she was going to crumble. She loved him. She had tried to forget the love. She had tried to shrink it with the power of her mind until it was small enough to tuck away. She had tried to focus on other things—Hobby, Claire, the baby, her cooking. She had tried to tell herself that life was long and she was young and she would find someone else. She tried to convince herself that by leaving, Jordan had done them both a favor.

"Zoe," he said.

She turned her face and bravely took in the sight of him. The blue eyes that she had first noticed on Fathers' Night at the Children's House. *Did she want to come do puzzles with him?* The lips she had first kissed in the room at the Charlotte Inn on Martha's Vineyard. What they had done was wrong, there were no excuses, but Zoe could at least say she had done the wrong thing for the right reason. She had done it for love.

"Are you real?" Zoe asked. So many strange things had happened already this summer that it was not impossible that she was now hallucinating. Her mind so desperately craved Jordan that she had conjured him. She thought, Why didn't you call me or email me or text me? Why didn't you tell me you were coming home? Why didn't you warn me? But she knew Jordan, and therefore she knew that he had been too afraid to call. He would have wanted to see in her person, so he could tell her whatever he had to tell her face to face. He'd come back because there was a problem at the paper, or he'd come back because he missed her, or he'd come back because he and Ava had patched up the marriage and they were moving permanently to Australia.

"I'm real," he said. He still held her by the wrist, and with his other hand he reached out to wipe away her tears.

JORDAN

He got the words out as quickly as he could. He was a journalist to his core. Report the facts.

"I came back. Jake came back. Ava stayed behind. We're divorcing. She's adopting a baby. I love you, Zoe. I love you."

528

JAKE

He skipped the first week of school. This was surprising. All he'd wanted was to leave Australia and get home. Together his parents had jumped through all kinds of hoops to get him home in time, and yet when the morning of the first day arrived, he found himself unable to go. He worried that his father might have been right after all; maybe he should have stayed in Fremantle and finished up at the American School there. Because the thought of returning to the halls of Nantucket High School without Penny spooked him. He had been many things—an honors student, president of the Student Council, editor of the newspaper, star of the annual musical—but none of these things mattered or made sense without Penny. It was his senior year, he had to endure it, he didn't have a choice, and yet what he kept thinking was, Why bother?

What he thought was that there would be memories of Penny everywhere. Every single kid at that school would know about his loss. He would have to face people like Winnie Potts and Annabel Wright and Anders Peashway. He would have to face Hobby.

Australia, he thought, would be better. Anonymity and loneliness would be better.

To his father, he punted. "I don't know how to explain it," he said. "I'm just not ready."

"They're expecting you," Jordan said. "I brought you all the way home for this. You told your mother this was the only thing you wanted."

"I know. I'm going to do it. Just not yet."

"I'll give you a week," Jordan said. "One week. Then you go. Am I understood?"

"You are understood," Jake said.

He went to the cemetery and sat by Penny's grave. As he'd predicted, grass had grown in over the rich, dark soil. Her headstone had been erected: *Penelope Caroline Alistair*. March 8, 1995–June 17, 2012. Beloved daughter, sister, friend.

Headstones, Jake decided, were stupid and pointless. They told you nothing. When you looked at this headstone, you didn't know that Penny had bluebell eyes or that she had perfect pitch or that her favorite word in French was *parapluie*. You didn't know that her favorite color was lavender or that she wore flip-flops right up until Christmas because shoes made her feet feel trapped, or that she'd had her first orgasm on the catwalk of the auditorium their sophomore year, during a break in a rehearsal for *Guys and Dolls*.

Jake sat at Penny's grave and thought about how, in many ways, Australia had been like a dream—

Hawk and the ferals around the bonfire and the gurgling fountain in the backyard and his half-Aboriginal cousins and his mother's happily dousing her fish and chips with vinegar and ogling the statue of Bon Scott. Had any of that been *real?* Real enough, he supposed, because his mother had stayed behind. She was keeping the Ute and the rental house on Charles Street, and she was adopting a baby girl from China. She and his father were getting divorced. It was weird to think about, his parents' being *divorced;* they had been miserable together, but the thought of their splitting hadn't seemed feasible. But his parents had been cool and unified in their decision; this would be better for everyone, and Jake would go back and visit Ava at Christmas.

Jake had learned something about love just from saying good-bye to Ava at the Perth airport. He'd learned that when you loved someone purely enough, all you wanted was for that person to be happy. Jake knew that his mother was making a tremendous sacrifice in letting him go home. She wanted him to be happy.

There were things about being back on Nantucket that Jake loved: the familiar streets of downtown, the Bean (where he got a cup of American coffee), the flag snapping at Caton Circle, the peppermint stick of the Sankaty lighthouse, the offices

of the *Nantucket Standard,* which smelled familiarly
of ink and dusty paper. The Jeep was totaled, and
there wouldn't be another car for Jake, so he'd been
riding his bicycle. He'd biked past the Alistair
house the day before. Zoe's car was in the driveway
and the front door was open and Jake could hear
music playing and he remembered all the times
he'd driven up to the house and heard Penny singing inside. Sometimes she sang scales or vocal exer-
cises ("Red leather, yellow leather!"), but other
times it was "Fee" by Phish ("In the cool shade of
the banana tree..."), or Motown ("Stop! In the
Name of Love"), or something folksy, like "If I Had
a Hammer," which was the song she was singing at
age eight when Mrs. Yurick first discovered her
voice. The thing Jake always thought when he
heard Penny singing was that he could listen to her
forever, and it would always feel like a privilege.

It had been a privilege. That was painfully obvious now.

The week went by, then the weekend. Jordan had
gone back to work at the paper, and he came home
with two pieces of startling news: first, he told Jake
that Demeter Castle was spending thirty days in a
facility off-island where she was being treated for
alcoholism. Then, two days later, he came home to

say that Hobby had gotten Claire Buckley *pregnant,* and the two of them were having a *baby* in March.

Jake accepted these bulletins with close-lipped, wide-eyed wonder. He'd been away for less than two months: was it really possible that things could have changed so dramatically in his absence?

On Monday Jake had to go to school. That was the deal.

"I'll drop you off," Jordan said.

"I'll ride my bike," Jake said.

"Jake."

"I'm serious. I'll ride my bike. I'll be fine."

"Hey," Jordan said. He clapped Jake's shoulder, and Jake thought, Oh no, not the shoulder thing again. "I know you'll be fine," Jordan told him.

He wore a pair of the jeans that Penny had written on, and he wore the sneakers that Penny had written on. His father regarded the jeans and the shoes with suspicion, and Jake saw his point and thought about changing into something else, but he couldn't make himself do it. He wanted to wear Penny + Jake 4ever because his reality would, in some way known only to his heart, always be Penny + Jake 4ever, even when he was an old man, married to someone else for decades, with children and grandchildren. He decided it was better just to announce this, as if he were a walking billboard, than to hide it away.

He locked his bike at the rack in front of the school. Kids were clustered together, he could hear them talking, and as he swung his backpack over his shoulder and headed for the front door, he heard the conversations stall, then quiet down, then completely stop. He was wearing a pair of his father's sunglasses, Ray-Ban Wayfarers, so he looked like Tom Cruise or some other old-time movie star, and he figured it probably took people a few minutes to realize it was him. He didn't look at anyone directly. He just wanted to get inside, see Mrs. Hanson in the front office, get his locker assignment and his class schedule, and go to school.

He was about ten steps from the front door when he heard a shriek.

"Jake?"

He turned, despite the time he had put in at home rehearsing not reacting to this kind of thing. It was Winnie Potts. Of course. She'd straightened her brown curly hair, and it had blond highlights now. She was wearing a white top that pushed her boobs up and out. She looked older and sexier. It was her senior year, and Penny Alistair was no longer an obstacle to Winnie's goal of being the Queen Bee of Nantucket High School. Jake thought about how high school was two things. It was *school*—he would learn calculus and read *Macbeth* and *The Canterbury Tales*—but it was also a social universe with its own rules and hierarchy. How he would have loved to get a hall pass from this second aspect, how he would have relished just being able to go inside and learn and then, at the end of the day, go home, eat pizza with his dad, talk about current events, read his assignments, and go to bed!

But this just wasn't possible.

"Hey, Winnie," he said.

"Oh. My. *God!*" she said. "I thought you were never coming back. I thought you'd moved away for good. I mean, you moved to Australia, right?"

"I did, sort of," he said. "But we're back now."

She crushed him in a bear hug that she executed with her elbow and her bosom. "I. Am. So. Psyched. You're. Back." She pulled away and eyeballed him. "Are you doing okay?"

"Sort of, yeah," he said, though already he felt his eyes burning, and he was grateful for the sunglasses.

"So you're still pretty hung up, then?" Winnie said. She pulled away and sniffed. "I see you're wearing the jeans."

Still pretty hung up, Jake thought. Well, Penny hadn't been dead for even three months yet. Maybe Winnie had forgotten about her, maybe she had come to terms with the accident, maybe Winnie, like so many other teenagers, had been cursed, or blessed, with a short attention span. She had been saddened by Penny's death, but it was old news now, and she was moving on.

Jake pulled away from Winnie, but she didn't seem to notice. She whipped out her phone and began madly texting. Probably broadcasting the news of his return. In ten seconds everyone would know.

There was a song that Zoe used to play on the cassette deck of her Karmann Ghia called "Uncle John's Band," and the first line went like this: *Well the first days are the hardest days, don't you worry any more.* Jake sang this to himself as he moved through the halls, fielding amazed and inquisitive *Hey man*'s from his classmates. Some kids' names he'd completely forgotten. He tried to focus on the school part of school—the Calc, the Physics, the A.P. European History. The teachers, at least, did their best to act professional and nonchalant—or possibly they really *were* professional and nonchalant. They, after all, were adults, with mortgages and children, and aging parents, and water heaters that needed replacing. They were nice people and good citizens; they all knew that Penny had died and that Penny had been Jake's girlfriend, and maybe they even knew that Jake had spent the summer/winter in Australia, but they didn't feel inclined to take Jake's emotional temperature—they were too busy and consumed with their own worries to meddle much in others' lives—and for that, Jake was grateful.

On his way from European History to his elective, Personal Narrative, which was a sort of creative writing class (and one he was greatly looking forward to), he felt a hand on his shoulder. He feared for an instant that his father had popped into school to check on him, but when he turned, he saw the principal, Dr. Major.

"Jake," Dr. Major said. "Welcome back."

"Thanks, Dr. Major," Jake said.

Dr, Major smiled at Jake kindly. His blue eyes watered behind his glasses. Was he going to *cry?* Dr. Major was known around school as the ultimate good guy, sometimes too good a guy to do some of the more difficult tasks his job required. Kids who got suspended often got their sentences commuted by Dr. Major. He believed that kids, more than anything, needed adults to listen to them. This openhearted approach worked out for the most part; the students of Nantucket High School felt protective of Dr. Major and generally tried not to let him down.

"How was your trip?" Dr. Major asked.

"It was weird," Jake said.

Dr. Major tilted his head. The head tilt was his

signature gesture, a cue to let kids know he was listening. Jake didn't want to be the recipient of Dr. Major's head tilt. Kids were streaming past them like water around two rocks. This wasn't the time or the place for Jake to detail the oddness of his time in Australia.

"I can't explain it," Jake said. "Not right now, anyway."

"Fair enough," Dr. Major said. "Well, I have to say, this school isn't the same without Penelope."

Jake nodded once, sharply. "Right. I know."

Dr. Major clapped Jake's shoulder again. "I just wanted to tell you…" Here he trailed off, and his eyes filled, and Jake had to look away rather than see the man cry. "…If you ever need a place to take a moment away from everyone, you're welcome to sit in my office. As you know, I'm rarely there."

Yes, Jake knew this; everyone knew this. Dr. Major roamed the school, no crevice or alcove was safe or private. Dr. Major was likely to appear out of nowhere. "Going about my rounds," he called it. He stopped in to the junior Spanish class and learned how to conjugate irregular verbs, and he entered the art room and asked for a demonstration of the pottery wheel. He didn't like to sit behind his desk, he said. Four or five times a day, Mrs. Hanson's voice would come over the intercom, paging him for a phone call.

"Thank you," Jake said. It was nice of Dr. Major to offer up his office for what amounted to Jake's own personal crying room. "That's very nice."

Dr. Major smiled. His eyes were brimming, but no tears fell, thank God. "We're all rooting for you," he said. "And we're glad to have you back."

At lunchtime, Jake wasn't sure what to do. Seniors were allowed to go off-property for lunch; it was one of the things he and Penny had been looking forward to. They had talked about how they would hit the burger shack at Surfside Beach in September while it was still warm, how they would go into town to the Brotherhood on Fridays in the winter, how they would sneak back to Penny's house on days when Zoe was working. It was going to be forty-five minutes of daily bliss.

But what now?

There wouldn't be a senior in sight in the cafeteria. That might be okay, Jake would be able to eat alone, none of the underclassmen would be brave enough to approach him. But the younger kids would talk about him, and the things they said would be half true and half false, and Jake didn't feel like cutting the kind of tragic figure who sat alone and pretended to ignore the fact that everyone was discussing him. He needed to leave the building, but having only his bike left him few options. If he biked all the way home, he would have time only to drink a glass of water before he had to turn around and come right back. He could bike to the beach, he supposed, but he was fairly certain that Winnie Potts and Annabel Wright and company would all be there, and he sure as shit didn't want to run into them. Or anyone. He needed forty-five minutes of quiet, of alone time, and it did occur to him that he could take Dr. Major up on the offer of his office, but even then, he worried that Mrs. Hanson or Mrs. Coffin or one of the other secretaries might fuss over him.

He would bike to the cemetery, he decided, and sit on Penny's grave. Whoa, that was morose, that was completely Emily Dickinson of him, but the cemetery was green and quiet and relatively nearby.

He strode out of the school, put on his sunglasses, and tried to look like he was moving with purpose, like he had somewhere to be, an important meeting or a date. He had to remind himself that Penny wasn't actually *at* the cemetery. His father had effectively made that point when they left for Australia. There was just a box in the ground that held her remains, marked by a stupid headstone that told nothing about her—but whatever. It was all he had.

He saw other seniors making an exodus. He saw Winnie Potts in her red convertible Mini backing

out of a parking space, and to avoid another con-
frontation, he ducked around a tight corner — and
there, sitting on a granite bench with one leg
straight out in front of him, was Hobby.

Jake stopped in his tracks. He hadn't admitted it
outright to himself, but he had spent all day subconsciously avoiding Hobby. He had breathed a
long sigh of relief when Hobby hadn't turned up in
his Physics class. Claire Buckley was in his European History class, but old-fashioned Mr. Ernest
had sat them alphabetically, and so Claire was on
the other side of the room, and no contact was
required. He had noted that Claire's physique had
changed enormously; she was all rounded curves
now instead of sharp angles. So what Jordan had
reported must be true.

Hobby started a little. "Whoa, Jake! I heard you
were back, man, but I didn't believe it!"

"Yeah," Jake said. He wanted to run away, he
couldn't say why, but seeing Hobby was *too much.*
Hobby was Penny's twin, he was the closest relation
she had, he had been present for all of it, her freak-
out and the crash, and he had suffered in ways that
Jake couldn't even imagine. Furthermore, Jake had
told Hobby about his mistake with Winnie Potts,
which in retrospect had been a foolish thing to
admit to. After a couple of months of ruminating
on this, what must Hobby think of him? That he

was a faithless bastard, that he hadn't been committed to Penny at all, that he was an utter *hypocrite* for showing up wearing marked-up jeans?

Hobby said, "I'd stand up and hug it out with you, man, but I'm kinda slow on the uptake." He nodded at his stretched-out leg.

"Oh, right," Jake said. He stuck out his hand, and they shook, and Jake didn't sense anything but Hobby's usual good-guy-ness.

"Great to see you, man," Hobby said. "I mean, it's *really* good to see you. When you walked out of my hospital room that day, man, I thought maybe that was it. I thought you were gone for *good*."

"Yeah," Jake said. "I thought that myself." If it weren't for the grace of his mother, he would be attending the American School in Perth, wearing a blue suit and skinny tie like a Mormon, reading Yeats and Auden alongside the sons of foreign mining executives.

"Sit down," Hobby said. He scooted over on the bench and moved the brown-bag lunch that Zoe had obviously packed for him. Jake recognized the chicken salad with pine nuts and dried cherries, the container of her homemade broccoli slaw, and the slumped brownies wrapped in wax paper. His stomach complained. The funny thing was that in all his deliberation about where to spend his lunch hour, he hadn't once thought about food. But there was food — meaning pizza and takeout Thai, which Jake and his father were once again eating in order to survive — and then there was *Zoe's* food.

"Um," Jake said. Could he tell Hobby that he was on the way to the cemetery to sit on his sister's grave? No. Never. "I don't want to bother you."

"*Bother* me?" Hobby said. "Dude, I'm here by myself. I don't have my license, and I'm too gimpy to walk anywhere. Last week I ate here with Claire, but today she's tutoring some freshman in geometry." He popped a grape into his mouth. "It's a thing she's started doing. Looks good on the transcript."

"Oh," Jake said. "Well, what about Anders and Colin and those guys?"

"They've been going to Nobadeer," Hobby said. "They swim and throw the football around, and I'm just not that mobile yet." He took a bite of his sandwich, and Jake tried not to stare, though it looked delicious, with baby lettuce peeking out like lace from between the slices of nutty whole grain bread. "Plus, Claire hates Anders. She thinks he's common."

This made Jake laugh. "She's right."

"She *is* right," Hobby said. He chewed his sandwich, took a sip of iced tea out of his plastic thermos, then said, "So, I guess you've heard?"

Jake nodded, happy to have a topic to discuss that had nothing to do with him. "My dad told me. It's true, then? You're going to have a *baby?*"

"A boy," Hobby said. "Hobson the third."

A boy, Jake thought. Hobson III. Penny used to say that she wanted five kids—three boys and two girls—and the oldest child was going to be a boy and she wanted to name him Ishmael, after the protagonist of *Moby-Dick.* Jake had pretended to like the name Ishmael for her sake.

"That's great, man," Jake said. But he wondered, *was* it great? Having a *baby* in *high school?*

"Well," Hobby said. "It was unexpected. She, uh, got pregnant before the accident."

"Oh," Jake said. He hadn't thought about that. "Wow."

"And we'd pretty much decided to get rid of it," Hobby said. "We were scared shitless, you know. But then when I was in the coma, Claire changed her mind. And when I came out of it, I was so happy that she'd decided to keep it. Man, it was the only thing that mattered."

"Yeah," Jake said. "I guess I can see that."

"So now we're having a baby and we're psyched about it, and we've decided we're still going to college—separately, you know, wherever we get in—and my mom and Claire's mom are going to split time taking care of the baby." Hobby swallowed. "It's not a conventional arrangement, but Claire is bound and determined to get an education, and so am I, and we may end up together or we may not, but the baby will have four people who love him, so hopefully that will be enough."

Jake bobbed his head. He could barely keep up.

"Sit down, man," Hobby said. "You look like you're going to run for the hills. It's making me nervous."

Jake hesitated, then sat. This was the same granite bench where he and Penny used to sit and make out after school while they waited for their parents to pick them up. Mentally, Jake threw up his hands. It was impossible to escape places and objects and people that reminded him of Penny. This was their high school; it was saturated with reminders of her.

Hobby said, "You want the other half of my sandwich? My mom packed too much for me, as usual."

Well, Jake wasn't about to turn down *Zoe* food. He picked up the half sandwich and thought, This alone was worth coming home for.

Hobby said, "There's something I want to tell you, man."

Jake tried to concentrate on the perfect composition of the chicken salad sandwich: The tartness of the dried cherries, the tang of the mayonnaise, the succulent chicken. He didn't want to hear what Hobby had to say. He just didn't want to hear it.

"I talked to Demeter," Hobby said.

Jake thought he might gag. He swallowed with difficulty, then reached for Hobby's thermos of iced tea, even though Hobby hadn't offered it to him. His heart felt like clay that was oozing through the powerful fingers of Hobby's clenched hand.

"She told me what she told Penny in the dunes," Hobby said. "And it had nothing to do with you."

"What?" Jake said.

"It had nothing to do with you or what you told me before you left. Nothing at all."

Jake took a breath in, then forced it out. He did a neck roll.

He didn't believe it.

"I don't believe you," he said to Hobby.

"Well, I wouldn't lie. What she said to Penny had nothing to do with you."

"What was it, then?"

Hobby popped a handful of grapes into his mouth and stared across the street. "Here's the thing," Hobby said. "I can't tell you."

"Oh, come on."

"I promised Demeter I wouldn't," Hobby said. "And man, you don't want to know it anyway. It's... it's adult stuff, nothing to do with us, none of our fucking business."

"Well, whatever it was made Penny pretty damn upset," Jake said. "Whatever it was made her want to pile-drive the car into the sand."

"Penny was sick," Hobby said.

"What?" Jake said.

"She was sick," Hobby said. "She was depressed. Messed up in the head. Emotionally disturbed. Whatever you want to call it."

"No she wasn't," Jake said. But he knew, even as he denied it, that Hobby was right. Ava had confirmed as much. Penny was sad and fragile, she cried a lot, every hard knock floored her, she missed the father she had never known, she felt broken, damaged, confused. Even her voice weighed on her as a burden. No one had been able to make her feel any better—not Zoe, not Jake, not Ava.

"Ultimately it didn't matter what Demeter told Penny," Hobby said. "Anything could have set her off—the thing about you and Winnie, or the fact that Claire was pregnant and I hadn't confided in her. For the longest time, I worried that *that* was the reason. I thought Penny had found out about my secret with Claire and flipped out. But it was this other thing. Or maybe it *wasn't* this other thing, maybe she just *did* it, maybe she'd been planning to do it for a while, or maybe it just occurred to her in the moment. We'll never know. Blaming ourselves or each other isn't going to help. She's not coming back."

Jake nodded. Penny wasn't coming back. That was the simple, awful nut of the truth.

"We have to forgive ourselves, man," Hobby said. "I've thought a lot about it. I even wrote to Demeter and told her not to blame herself because it wasn't her fault either. It wasn't anybody's fault."

"You did?" Jake said.

"I haven't heard back from her," Hobby said. "But I hope she took what I said to heart. We're the ones who survived. We have to be grateful for that. We have to take care of ourselves."

Jake finished the half sandwich in silence, and then, wordlessly, Hobby handed him the container of broccoli slaw, and he devoured that as well.

"Do you want a brownie?" Hobby asked. He unwrapped the wax paper. Zoe had packed two.

"I'd be a fool to turn that down," Jake said.

They ate the brownies side by side, in silence. The convertible red Mini occupied by Winnie Potts and Annabel Wright pulled back into the parking lot, and when the girls got out of the car, they waved to Jake and Hobby, and Jake and Hobby waved back. A few seconds later, as Hobby was consolidating his lunch debris, Claire appeared before them.

She said, "Thanks for saving me some."

Hobby said, "Sorry, my brother is back."

Claire smiled at Jake. There was something

incandescent about her now. "Ahhhh, yes, he's back. The school is abuzz."

Jake smiled despite himself. He said, "You know, I always wanted a brother."

"You know," Hobby said, "me too."

They said this lightly, sidestepping the ghosts of Ernie and Penny, amazed that this could be done. Then the bell rang to announce the start of sixth period. Jake and Hobby stood up, and Hobby took Claire's arm, and Jake found that he was happy to follow them inside.

NANTUCKET

The first home football game of the season was contested on the third Friday night in September. The weather on Nantucket had just started to turn; the evenings had a crisp edge to them, and the sunsets were spectacular sherbet swirls of pink and orange. Bartlett's Farm had harvested its first crop of pumpkins, and on the night of the game, people wore jeans and sweaters.

It might be assumed that no one on Nantucket wanted to see the hot, luxurious days of summer end, but those of us who lived here appreciated the many charms of the fall: crisp apples, cranberries, available parking spots on Main Street, empty and windswept beaches, the leaves of the Bradford pear trees turning flame orange, the air the perfect temperature for a long bike ride or a run over the crimson-colored moors. And football, of course— we all loved our football team, the Nantucket Whalers.

Turnout for that first game was legendary. The high school parking lot overflowed, there were cars parked on the lawn of the school. Across the street, on Vesper Lane, cars were lined up as far as the eye could see.

Dr. Field's wife, Anne Marie, was walking over from the hospital with Patsy Ernst, the nurse who had been working in the Emergency Room on the night of the crash, and they marveled at the size of the crowd filing in through the gates. It seemed like far more people than usual. They knew why. We all did. The previous school year had ended on such a tragic note, we all wanted to put our eyes on the kids and reassure ourselves that they would be okay.

It was old news that Hobby Alistair was no longer able to be the team's quarterback, so the excitement of watching him in action and knowing we would win was missing. In Hobby's place, Coach Jaxon had decided to start a sophomore named

Maxx Cunningham, who was broad-shouldered like Hobby and blond like Hobby but who seemed woefully young and inexperienced compared to his predecessor.

Still, we were excited by the bright lights shining down on the green field. We could smell the burgers and hot dogs on the grill, and it was chilly enough to enjoy cups of chowder. The cheerleaders were fresh-faced and peppy. Annabel Wright, the captain, had fashioned her usual long ponytail into three braids that whipped around like ropes. The kids in the stands seemed like just that—kids—though the boys wore flat-top Red Sox hats and baggy jeans low on their hips like rap stars. And the girls looked like nascent supermodels—some in tops that showed off their midriffs and pierced belly buttons, most wearing tight jeans and makeup and perfume—and we felt a mixture of sadness and nostalgia because we remembered these same girls when they were pudgy and freckled and wearing pink sneakers whose soles lit up when they ran under the bleachers chasing their brothers and their brothers' friends.

The game had yet to begin, so the crowd was still milling around: people greeted one another, found seats in the bleachers, and bought blocks of raffle tickets for the fifty-fifty, which supported the Nantucket Boosters. The Atheneum librarian, Beatrice McKenzie, and her husband, Paul, who had played for the Whalers in 1965, sat in the front row, just off the handicap ramp.

What many of us didn't know was that Jordan Randolph and his son, Jake, were walking in the back entrance. Word had reached nearly all of us that Jordan Randolph had returned from Australia with Jake but without Ava. No one was surprised by this. We all understood that Ava came from and belonged to a city, a country, and a continent on the other side of the world. A few of us had heard that Ava was adopting a baby girl from China, which we agreed was a wonderful thing.

Jordan and Jake paid their five-dollar entrance fee and walked down the hill to the northwest corner of the playing field. We thought they might make their way over to the bleachers, but they decided to hang on the fence. We remembered that Jordan had always been a fence-hanger. He liked to watch every down of the game, reporter-at-heart that he was, but Jake used to sit in the bleachers with Penny. Penny, unlike her scantily clad counterparts in the stands tonight, always wore her brother's navy blue away jersey with *Alistair* printed in white letters across the back, above Hobby's number, which was 11. It was hard for us to think about Penny in that jersey, and it must have been even harder for Jake to think about it. We understood why he was keeping his distance.

Standing together, Jordan and Jake Randolph looked remarkably alike. We were glad to have Jordan back at the helm of our newspaper, not only because some of us felt that the standards of the newspaper had slipped (the content of lesser quality, perhaps, and the editing not as sharp, a few more corrections appearing in the following week's editions than we were used to seeing) but also because, for as long as any of us could remember, a Randolph had headed the *Standard.* We hoped we were right in assuming that Jake Randolph—despite all he'd been through in the past few months—would resume his position as editor of *Veritas,* the student newspaper, then go on to major in journalism in college, and come back and work alongside his father, and eventually take over the legacy.

But we were all of us finished with trying to predict the future.

The front center bleacher had been roped off as "reserved," and we had our suspicions about why. Sure enough, a few minutes before the team took to the field, a hush came over the crowd, and Hobby Alistair, Zoe Alistair, and a pregnant Claire Buckley walked in single file in front of the stands, up the stairs, and into those reserved seats. The three of them looked good. Hobby loped along, barely limping, Zoe held her head up; her hair was back to its artful shaggy style, the tips recently having been highlighted cherry-cola red. But it was Claire Buckley who stole the show. For the first time, possibly ever, her hair was down, flowing long over her shoulders, and the front of her sweater was filled out in a becoming way, and below her full breasts was a discreet swell.

We all wanted to comment on the three of them—how strong they looked, how luminous, and most of all, how unified. We wanted to comment on the mysterious aspects of life, those things almost beyond language, such as how it would feel to lose your seventeen-year-old daughter, or what it had been like for Hobby to spend nine days suspended in the netherworld of a coma, or how poetic and right it was that Claire had realized the sanctity inside herself and decided to keep Hobby's baby. We wanted to explore these topics and more—What happened when we died? How were we to know that death wasn't as profound an adventure as life was?—but just at that moment, the team stormed the field, and the crowd let out a great roar.

The names of the Nantucket Whalers were announced over the loudspeaker one by one, and while our eyes were on the field, they were also on Hobby. How would it feel for him to watch his former teammates being cheered, knowing that he could no longer play among them? How would it feel to hear Maxx Cunningham introduced as the team's new quarterback?

Hobby handled it not only with grace but with exuberance. Despite his still-healing leg, he alone in the crowd stood for the announcement of each player. He clapped and whooped. When his lieutenants were announced—Anders Peashway, Colin Farrow—he whistled. And he cheered perhaps the loudest when his successor, Maxx Cunningham, rushed onto the field.

At the center of the field, Coach Jaxon took the microphone.

He said, "Ladies and gentlemen, I'd like to call Hobson Alistair onto the field."

Hobby turned to his mother. The crowd quieted. We watched as Hobby scooted out past Claire and made his way down the stairs and through the gate that led onto the field. The players on the sideline parted to let him through. With what looked like painless ease, Hobby jogged out to the center of the fifty-yard line.

Coach Jaxon said, "Ladies and gentlemen, Hobson Alistair."

Instinctively we all stood, and the applause was thunderous. Hobby looked shocked by the whole thing at first, but then he grinned and waved. We watched Zoe and Claire standing right along with everyone else, clapping. Claire gave a piercing whistle, loud enough to raise the dead.

Coach Jaxon held up the white home jersey, #11 *Alistair,* that Hobby used to wear and would have been wearing right then if things had been different. He said, "Tonight we retire number eleven."

The crowd went wild.

Coach Jaxon handed Hobby a football, and with the perfect spiral we all remembered, Hobby threw the ball to Maxx Cunningham, who, though startled, managed to put out his hands and catch it.

We thought we were witnessing the resolution of the story right there on the Whalers' field, but of course there were other, connected narrative lines unfolding simultaneously elsewhere.

At seven o'clock in the morning in springtime air that smelled of a peppermint grove, Ava Price Randolph was finishing her second cup of tea and the previous day's crossword puzzle. Her hands shook a little as she washed her teacup in the sink. She was nervous. In a scant hour, her sister May was coming to drive her to her first appointment with the adoption agency. When Ava had talked to Meaghan, the adoption counselor, on the phone, she had said that the adoption process could take up to five months, and that it would require patience and fortitude.

"I'm committed," Ava said.

"Good," Meaghan said.

Meaghan already knew the salient facts about Ava's situation. The applicant was the mother of one son, age seventeen, who was currently living with his father in America, and another son who had died of SIDS at eight weeks old. She was single, but supported by the husband from whom she was now amicably separated. She had a large family with many helping hands all within a twenty-kilometer radius. She was committed to being a mother again.

Ava missed both Jake and Jordan enormously. For nearly twenty years she had been married, and for more than seventeen years, a mother. Now she was alone. She missed the sound of Jordan's snapping open the pages of a newspaper and Jake's humming along to the music on his headphones—but in the sunny bungalow in Fremantle, in contrast to the dark days she'd spent living in Ernie's nursery in the house in Nantucket, Ava didn't feel lonely. She liked the quiet, and when she closed her eyes, she saw a bright light that she knew was her future.

If Ava could have seen the action unfolding on the football field on Nantucket just then, if she could have seen Jordan and Jake and Zoe and Claire all applauding as Hobby took a bow for the crowd, raised two fingers in a V for victory, and yelled out, "Retired at age seventeen!" she would have smiled. She would have thought, They are where they're supposed to be. And so am I.

Ava's cell phone chirped. She had a text message from Roger Polly that said, Good luck today! She smiled, thinking, Such a lovely man. Although God only knew what would happen there. She texted him back, Nervous!

Then she heard a car honking outside, and she checked out the front window to see her sister May idling at the curb in her minivan. God forbid any member of her family actually take thirty seconds to stop the car and come to the door.

Ava gathered her purse, her spring coat, and her documents, which were nestled in a manila folder, and she closed the door behind her. She hurried down the steps.

"Come on!" May called through her open window. "Let's go get ourselves a baby!"

At seven o'clock in the evening on that September Friday, Al and Lynne Castle were driving to Vende-ver to pick up their daughter, Demeter, who had successfully completed thirty days of treatment for alcoholism. It still boggled Lynne's mind that this had actually transpired, that Demeter had developed this disease while living under her parents' roof, and that she and Al had had absolutely no idea. Lynne had run through the gamut of emotions herself, from denial to anger to grief. She had questioned the very core of her being. She had thought of herself as a good mother, and yet her youngest child, her only daughter, had essentially slipped through the cracks into a dark and sinister netherworld *on her watch.* Lynne had been too busy to notice, too smug, too self-absorbed, too self-congratulatory. On the night of the accident, where had she been? She had been at a series of graduation parties for Pumpkin Alexander, Patrick Loom, Garrick Murray, and Cole Lucas. She hadn't considered the fact that while she and Al were "putting in appearances" at no less than four parties, Demeter was sitting home alone. Of course the girl was drinking. In merely imagining the isolation and loneliness that her daughter must have felt that night, Lynne wanted to reach for a glass of bourbon herself. Lynne wasn't the wonderful mother she'd thought she was. She was hardly a mother at all. She was a silly woman who had put her business and her clean, orderly home and her charitable boards and her committees and her position in the community ahead of her own daughter.

As Al drove through the gathering dark, Lynne sighed.

In response, Al turned up the radio. He listened to the worst music ever made, what Lynne always thought of as A.M. Gold—Tony Orlando and Dawn, Ambrosia, Dr. Hook. Listening to the radio with Al made her feel a hundred years old. And the fact that he *turned the music up* when he heard her sigh instead of asking her what was on her mind simply infuriated her. She nearly asked Al to pull over right that second so she could get out. He would never do that, of course. She would have to demand that *he* get out, and then she would have the satisfaction of leaving *him* behind as she sped off with some decent music playing. Lynyrd Skynyrd or Bruce Springsteen, something she had listened to back in the Mazda RX4 with Beck Paulsen.

But she would never do that, either.

If Lynne Castle could have seen the scene unfurling at the football field—Jordan and Jake approaching the stands and, after an affirmative nod from Zoe, taking seats on the bleachers directly behind her and Hobby and Claire, and the five of them standing as the elementary school music teacher, Mrs. Yurick herself, sang the National Anthem in her warbling soprano, and Zoe reaching back and squeezing the heck out of Jordan's hand because every atom of her at that moment yearned for her daughter—well, Lynne would have wished only that she were among them. She would have acknowledged the new, startling circumstances of their lives—that Penny was dead, that Hobby was permanently sidelined, that Jordan and Ava had split, that Jake was heartbroken, that Demeter was an alcoholic, that Claire Buckley was pregnant, that Zoe loved Jordan but didn't know how to make that feel right, that Jordan was determined to find a way to make it feel right, that none of them were quite the people they seemed, or even the people they thought they were—and she would have said, "Okay, fine, I'll take it all. As long as we're together."

Demeter stood waiting at the exit of the facility, which was a hundred and twenty feet and a world away from the entrance she'd walked through a month earlier. She was thirty-one pounds lighter and she was 80 percent clearer in the head, but the remaining 20 percent of her that struggled would, she realized, probably always struggle. She would struggle with her desire for a drink, the slow burn down the throat, the warm ball of honeyfire in her chest, the ensuing release. She would struggle with her weight. She would struggle with what she had said to Penny Alistair on the night of the accident. She would struggle with her relationship with her parents. She would struggle with unrequited love and sought-after friendships that would never come easily.

But, as her therapist here at Vendever, Sebastian,

had said, only 20 percent of her was struggling, which was a lot better than most people. Sebastian had said, "You're a good kid, Demeter. You're going to be fine." Sebastian was handsome and funny and immeasurably kind, and Demeter was half in love with him, as were all the other girls at Vendever, and so his words made an impact on her. If Sebastian thought she was a good kid, a kid worth rescuing, if he thought she was going to be fine, then maybe, just maybe, it was true.

Demeter's mother had sent manila envelopes filled with Demeter's schoolwork and assigned reading, and with each batch she had enclosed a simple note saying, *I love you, Demeter. xo Mom.* Demeter had kept these notes in a pile by her bed. She knew they were true, she knew her mother did, in fact, love her very much. Demeter had been a difficult child, and she meant to both change her ways and apologize. Along with her mother's notes was a letter Demeter had received from Hobby that said a lot of things, and among them these most important lines: *You aren't responsible for Penny's death any more than I am responsible or Jake is responsible or my mother or Jake's mother and father or your mother and father are responsible. The only person who was responsible for Penny's death was the person who was driving the car that night, and that was Penny herself. I don't know why she did what she did, but when I see her again—oh, and I will see her again—I'm going to ask her why, and then pray for God's help in understanding.*

Demeter decided that she would keep this letter and her mother's notes for the rest of her life so that when that 20 percent of her was struggling, she could pull them out and read them.

It was dark now, fully dark at seven-thirty, and whereas a part of Demeter knew that ninety miles away on the island where she had been born and raised there were lights burning brightly on a football field, the only lights Demeter cared about now were the headlights of her parents' car. When, a few seconds later, they pulled up to the Vendever exit, which was also the entrance to the rest of her life, Demeter turned around and said to Sebastian, who was patiently manning the sign-out desk, "They're here! They're here! I'm going home."

The Nantucket Whalers lost their first home game by a score of 35 to 7. It was a whipping the likes of which we hadn't seen in over a decade, but no one, not a single one of us in the stands that night, cared about the score. We had learned some things over the past few months. We had learned that when we looked upon our children, the young heroes and goddesses of Nantucket Island, all we could do was hope. We knew they would struggle; we knew they would fall prey to the same temptations we did, they would have lonely and sad moments as we did, they would eat too much and drink too much and cheat at golf and slander their neighbors and fail to recycle assiduously and speed on the Milestone Road and do the wrong thing when the right thing was smack in front of their faces, just as we did. But what we could see as the team filed off the field— some of the kids smiling even in defeat, some of the kids hopping in their cleats because they were *so eager to play again next week*—was that they had survived with their spirits intact.

We saw Claire Buckley's hand fly to her abdomen, her mouth pursed in an astonished O, and we knew that as she walked away from the field that night, she had felt her baby kick for the first time. Hobson Alistair III.

We would all of us persevere. We would keep going. We would move in the only direction we could move, and that was forward.

ACKNOWLEDGMENTS

I must start by thanking my editor, Reagan Arthur, for consistently encouraging my very best work. She is the Smartest Person in the Universe and always manages to take the rough gems I give her and make them shine. Thank you to the rest of my devoted and brilliant team at Little, Brown, including Michelle Aielli, Michael Pietsch, Amanda Tobier, Heather Fain, Mario Pulice, Terry Adams, Sarah Murphy, Justin Levine—and at Hachette, the gracious and forever fabulous David Young.

I have two amazing agents who not only advocate on my behalf but also serve as valued readers, and who are among my most treasured friends and confidants. They are the Best Agents in the Universe: Michael Carlisle and David Forrer.

Acknowledgments

And then there are the people who keep the carousel of my life spinning. I know I sound like a broken record, but I could not live and certainly could not write without their continued presence in my every day and, more important, in the every day of my children: Rebecca Bartlett, Richard Congdon, Margie and Chuck Marino, Debbie Bennett, Elizabeth and Beau Almodobar, Wendy Rouillard and Illya Kagan, Anne and Whitney Gifford, Wendy and Randy Hudson, Shelly and Roy Weedon, John and Martha Sargent, Norman and Jennifer Frazee, Evelyn and Matthew MacEachern, Mark and Eithne Yelle, Helaina and Dewey Jones, Lorri and Brian Ryder, Scott and Logan O'Connor, Jill and Paul Surprenant, Jeanne and Richard Diamond, John Bartlett, Holly and Marty McGowan, Jamie Foster, Rocky Fox, West and Manda Riggs, Jay Riggs, Andrew Law and David Rattner, Heidi and Fred Holdgate, Kristen and Dan Holdgate, Sean and Milena Lennon, Stephanie McGrath, and always and forever the rudder on my boat, Heather Osteen Thorpe.

For time and space and love and laughter, I have to thank my own home team: my husband, Chip Cunningham, who has, over the past nineteen years, made all of my dreams come true; my all-star son Maxx Cunningham (who gets his first cameo in one of Mom's books); my son Dawson "the

Dawg" Cunningham, who is coming out on top; and my radiant daughter, Shelby Cunningham.

It may sound strange, but I'd also like to thank the places that inspired me during the writing of this book. Thank you Fremantle and Margaret River, Western Australia. Thank you Smith Court, Beacon Hill, Boston. And thank you Nantucket Island — I love you, of course, the best of all.

ABOUT THE AUTHOR

Elin Hilderbrand: novelist, mother of three, sports enthusiast, avid fan of Bruce Springsteen, Veuve Clicquot, and four-inch heels. She serves on the Board of Directors of the Nantucket Boys & Girls Club and Nantucket Little League and is a founding member of Nantucket BookFest. Her resting pulse is 65.